Sky Light Ends

Whisperers Book 3

Donna E. Lane

ISBN: 978-1-7342675-2-5

ACKNOWLEDGEMENTS

I would like to express my deep appreciation for my Book Dragon Critique Group, Tabitha Bouldin, Naomi Craig, Lisa Renee, and Sara Beth Williams, for your support, encouraging, editing, and helpful suggestions. I am grateful for your willingness to include me in your wonderful group of authors.

I would also like to thank my son, Hayden Lane, for your thoughtful critique, your search for plot holes and character problems, your theological evaluation and insights, and careful edits. As always, your suggestions were invaluable and improved the quality of the final work. I appreciate you more than you know.

Finally, I would like to thank my husband, David Lane, for your patient sitting in silence by my side while I type away, for your willingness to read and reread and read again, and for your love. I would never have written a word without you.

DEDICATION

To Hayden and Lindsey: you are the lights of my life. May the love of the Forever always fill your heart and guide your steps.

'TIL FINAL BATTLE'S FATE IS WON

FOR FAIRER SHORES AND KIND.

(Aleshanee's Travel Song)

The Map

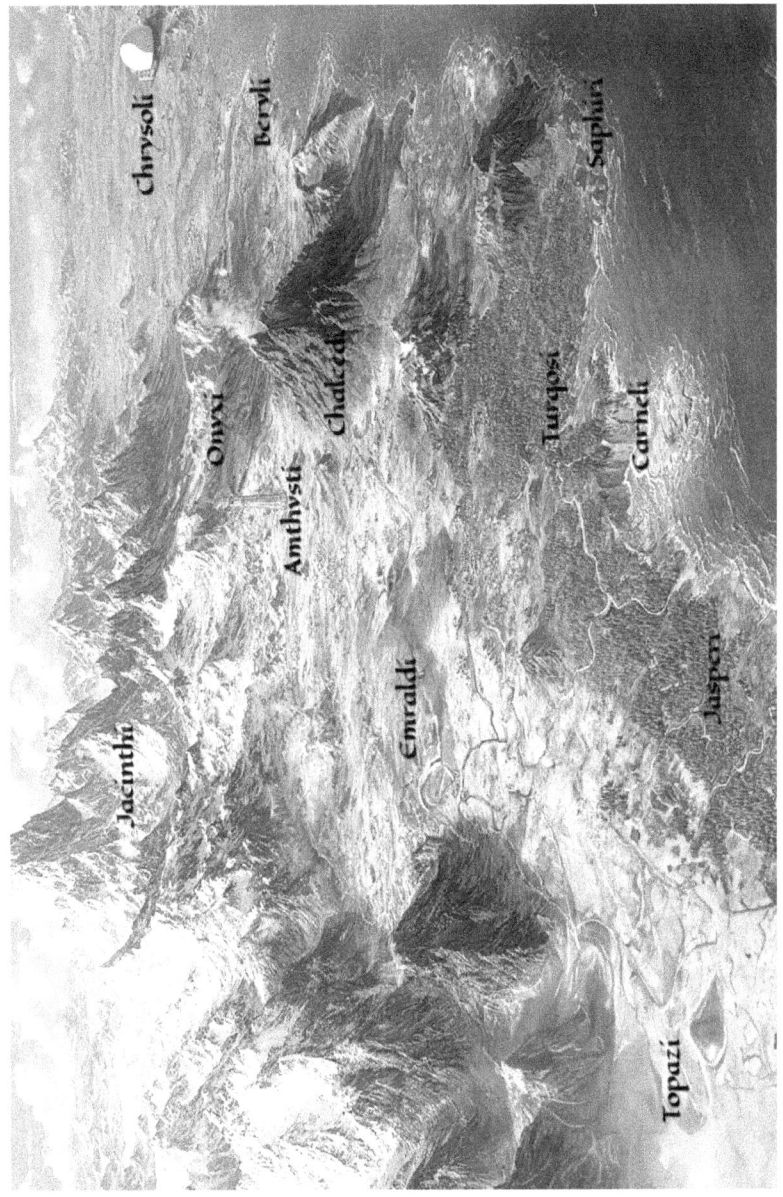

THE CHARACTERS

The Whisperers

Watchers (singers of the Music)
>   Weaver – sings the story of the Way Wards
>   Extoller – sings about the wonders of the Forever
>   Exalter – sings about the goodness of the Forever
>   Magnifier – sings about the many acts of love
>   Proclaimer – sings announcements of altering events
>   Messenger – sings a warning cry
>   Teller (the leader) – sings the story of the Forever

Metanoi (influencers)
>   Phosi – bringer of revelation
>   Gnosi – bringer of insight and knowledge
>   Sophosi – bringer of wisdom
>   Elegosi – bringer of alternatives, options, choices
>   Kitisi – bringer of creativity and imagination
>   Kratosi – bringer of strength
>   Chariti – bringer of love in the heart
>   Eleutheri (the leader) – bringer of freedom

'Ro (heart-movers)
>   Spa'ro – stirs joy
>   Ma'ro – stirs the deepest heart's desires
>   Na'ro – stirs courage to remain on the difficult path
>   A'ro – stirs passion to be filled with Music
>   Sa'ro – stirs healing and hope
>   Pa'ro – stirs peace
>   Cla'ro (the leader) – stirs the true expression of self

Bellator (warriors)
>   Paxor – shields the Way Wards
>   Munior – fends off attacks

Impetor – takes the offensive against enemies
Parator – prepares for battle
Admonitor – warns of approaching threats
Luxor – illuminates, exposing dangers and traps
Veritor (the leader) – provides truth to protect hearts

The Dark Ones

Skia Skotos – (formerly called Phaini) The Dark Lord, self-proclaimed god of the second world, ruler of all evil

His Minions

Pseudos – god of lies and the false sense of self
Hedraios – god of settling, immobilizing, and paralysis
Ademoneos – god of hopelessness, anguish, and despair
Aischunos – god of shame, condemnation, and hypocrisy
Phobos – god of fear, power, and control
Zelos – god of jealousy, envy, and comparison
Phagos – god of gluttony and self-gratification
Pleonexos – god of greed, using, usurping, and stealing
Diastrephos – god of perversion, seduction, and lust
Nothrotos – god of sloth, laziness, and avoidance
Thymos – god of wrath, anger, indignation, and unfairness
Thanatos – god of death (Skia Skotos' general)

The Child of Light

Kindred – (formerly called Kindra) "Light-bringer"

The Way Wards

Jasperi (tree dwellers)

Amadah – "Forest water"
Nikani – "Dear friend"
Kai – "Tree in the wind"
Alatha – "Beautiful one"
Sonta – "Trustworthy"
Itai – "Sturdy oak"
Papina – "Vine on a strong tree"

Emraldi (grasslands dwellers)
Aleshanee – "Playful"

Topazi (desert dwellers)
Fala – "He fights"
Sewati – "Curved claw"
Seri – "Desert tribe"

Jacinthi (high mountain dwellers)
Angeni – "Wise one"
Catori – "High spirit"
Hanai – "Spirit fighter"
Isusa – "White stone"
Kacina – "Spirit elder"
Meda – "Prophetess"
Nadie – "Gentle wisdom"
Chevei – "Warrior"
Kwania – "Gracious"

Saphiri (ocean dwellers)
Misa – "Rippling water"
Towila – "Joined together by water"
Leytia – "Shell"
Kantila – "Sings"

Onyxi (cave dwellers)

Enla – "Solitary"
Yiska – "The darkness has passed"

Carneli (cliff dwellers)
    Kilchi – "Red boy"

Amthysti (tower dweller)
    Ogima – "Chief" (inhabited by Skia Skotos)

Chalcedi (aerie dwellers)
    Cholena – "Little bird"
    Chatan – "Hawk"

Turqosi (wetlands dwellers)
    Leenha – "Stream"
    Lise – "River rising"
    Eteena – "Rich land"

Beryli (gulf dwellers) – the Lost Clan

Chrysoli (plains dwellers)
    Kola – "Friend"
    Leoti – "Flower of the prairie"
    Tocho – "Great lion"
    Tadita – "Runner"
    Lonan – "Thundercloud"
    Kasa – "Fur-cloaked"
    Miakoda – "Under the moon"

CHAPTER ONE

The Jacinthi

Kwania howled as two sets of claws pierced the skin beneath her feathers and dragged her back from her only hope of escape. Her fellow slaves had crawled through the hinged metal-covered slot used for accepting new slaves—all except Taka, who lay in a pool of blood from the gash across her throat. One of the masters stuck his muzzle through the opening and let out a thunderous roar after the fleeing slaves. Kwania could only hope they made it to some cover before the masters sent out a hunting party to recapture them.

"Tadita, take two others with you and search for them," one of the masters commanded.

"Aye, Tocho," The one called Tadita unbolted the massive door and three of the masters loped from the cramped room.

The leader bent down close to Kwania's beak. "You will make payment for all of them. And it will cost you most dearly."

"We've lost hundreds!" another of the masters bellowed.

"We will get them back." The words reverberated against Kwania's chest. "Gather a larger force to join Tadita. She will have scouted their location when you reach her. Surround the runaways and return them. Kill any who resist."

"Aye, Tocho"

"Now, as for you." Tocho's long, glistening fangs dripped in Kwania's face. The claws dug deeper as the master yanked her forward. "Back to the camp!" Dragging Kwania in the dirt, he strode before the remaining force out of the back room, across the main room, out the

13

door to skirt the collection of outbuildings, and across the open fields toward the encampment. Kwania's battered wings ground into the dirt beneath her, shedding feathers along the trail to the center of camp. There, Tocho deposited her at the feet of a cluster of the masters, murmured a few terse instructions she couldn't hear, then left to enter a nearby building.

The masters bound her wrists with a rope and hoisted her up the pole holding the meal bell, her arms stretched above her head. Some of the slaves who remained behind started wandering from the large building where the leader had disappeared and gathered in small groups to observe the Jacinthi prisoner's fate. Several masters prowled around the base of the pole, spitting and growling at her.

When Tocho returned, he gestured to one of the guards, who stood on his hind legs and positioned his claws next to her throat. "Witness what happens to the disobedient."

Kwania remained silent. She didn't want to give the masters the satisfaction of seeing her terror. Tocho nodded, and the guard dug his claws into her neck.

Kwania whimpered, but the leader was not satisfied. He gestured to the guard again. The outstretched claws raked down her chest, ripping out feathers and leaving large welts that welled with blood.

"Disobedience is punished." Another nod from Tocho brought another stab of pain as the master tore her belly.

Courage, child. A strange, inexplicable peace washed over Kwania. She pulled herself up by her extended arms, raising her head to meet the leader's eyes.

"I see rebellion remains in you." Tocho sneered. "We will see how long it lasts." He waved a paw at the masters circling beneath Kwania. They launched themselves at her, ripping and tearing at her until a pile of bedraggled and bloody feathers covered the ground. Somehow, Kwania didn't cry out, despite the pain, and when the onslaught was done, she lifted her head slowly and stared down the leader.

A few of the slaves murmured amongst themselves. Tocho's glare silenced them, but the meaning was not lost of Kwania. They seemed to feel empowered by her response to the torture. The leader narrowed his eyes at their restless shuffling, frowned, and let out a thunderous roar. The masters' howls got louder and their strikes against her sarkikos grew more vicious. Her blood dripped and pooled below her feet. The edges of Kwania's vision began to fade to gray, and her head fell to her chest.

Tocho raised his paw. The masters' hackles were raised, and bloodlust shined in their eyes, but they didn't disobey their leader. They panted and snarled, then resumed their pacing around the pole. "Resistance to the order will not be tolerated." Tocho's booming voice pierced Kwania's thick veil of semi-consciousness. She managed to lift her head slightly, trying to focus on the crowd of slaves, but the weight of her head was too much for her to support, so she closed her eyes and allowed herself to float into the gray-black abyss.

She regained consciousness when her arms were untied, and she dropped to the ground in a heap. The angle of the sky light had changed dramatically, so she must've been left hanging on the pole for a long while. A master hoisted her up and carried her limp sarkikos to the barracks, threw her on a cot, and chained her leg to the frame. So alone. She assumed the rest of the slaves were still out in the fields. When she tried to sit up, her sarkikos screamed in protest, so she dropped back onto the cot, lying as still as she could. The entire surface of her skin was aflame, like in her lab when she had accidently spilled a caustic chemical on her hands.

Her lab. Oh, the solitude, the excitement of discovery, the joy of purposeful labor, the challenge of seeking beyond what was known, consumed once more by inquiry instead of despair. How she missed her solitary lair and her quiet existence. Her eyes misted over, but she blinked the tears away. She couldn't afford to give in to her emotions, not now. She had to think.

As the crimson beams of the falling sky light hit the openings high on the wall that served as windows for the barracks, something drew Kwania's attention. It was odd how the light seemed to be pulsating, almost like the light waves were fluttering in a breeze, which she knew wasn't possible. The flood of memories of her life as a scientist prompted her to investigate, but her tortured sarkikos wouldn't cooperate, so she was forced to consider explanations with the limited data at her disposal. She already knew something strange was happening with the sky light. She had seen that when she was still on the high mountain with her kind. Could this odd pulsing be related to the distortion she had seen in her studies, the expansion and contraction of the sky light's surface? If it was, the oscillation had considerably worsened. Was this a harbinger of things to come for her world?

She needed to study the phenomenon, to see if her fears were founded. But how could she? She was a slave, not a scientist anymore. Kwania shook her head, banishing that thought. She would not accept this label of slave as her identity. She was still a scientist. She was still a Jacinthi of the high mountain. This realization strengthened her resolve, and she pushed herself up to sit on the edge of her cot. A wave of nausea made her head swim, and gray fog clouded the edges of her vision, threatening to take her back to oblivion. Taking a deep breath, she struggled to stand, unfurling her battered wings behind her to help her balance. It felt like a million knives were slicing into her, but she refused to give in to the pain.

She grasped the edges of the rail-like ladder at the foot of her cot, then climbed up, rung by rung, pausing often to breathe and steady herself, bracing for more agony. The chain clanked against the rails and bent her foot with its weight. When she reached the top bunk, she collapsed forward onto the cot, spent. Ragged pain shot through her as the rough cloth covering the board-thin mattress scraped against her sarkikos, and she could feel blood seeping from the open wounds on her chest into the fabric. Still, after several beats, she lifted her head again, looking up to the open slits to try to see the sky light.

Because she knew better than to look directly at the sky light without her equipment, she was forced to wait until it began to sink below the horizon. She gave a quick, sideways glance every few beats until less than half of the sky light remained visible, then she leaned forward as far as she could to examine it. To Kwania, the falling sky light looked like a plumanate, knotted and bumpy, protrusions erupting from the surface. A halo, yellowish against the purpling sky, encircled the pulsing orb. As she watched, the edge of the sky light shrank back into itself, like a frightened hopper retreating into its hole, then vomited out flames and yellow gases, adding to the mist surrounding it.

A strange voice resonated in her chest. She looked around the barracks, even though she knew she was alone, and she wasn't hearing the voice with her ears but was feeling it in her sarkikos. It was an odd sensation.

The Tempor is thinning. Your sky light will end. You must act.
"Wha...?"

"Heed my words," Pa'ro declared. "The Tempor is thinning, and you are correct. The sky light is dying."

"Dying." Kwania looked around the empty room. "The sky light is dying." Her hands felt like blocks of ice, her stomach a black hole. Had they avoided the planet's destruction at the hands of the Chalcedi only to experience the same outcome by their own sky light? "I must tell someone." She couldn't understand her urgency, because she knew nothing could prevent the disaster she thought was coming. Still, she felt she had to tell them, and she needed to get word to Angeni, somehow.

Kacina's ancient texts had described the end of all things. Had it finally come to pass? Would she never see her beloved mountain again? Would she die a horrible death in the company of cruel masters and pitiable slaves? Kwania tried to push herself back toward the rickety ladder, but the pain in her beaten flesh combined with her terror and despair overcame the little strength she had left. She fell back onto the cot and wept.

As the room darkened in the waning sky light, other slaves began to shuffle into the barracks. No one spoke to Kwania. No one chose to take the bunk beneath where she lay sobbing.

The masters rang the bell before sky light's rising, and the grumbles Kwania heard made it clear her fellow slaves blamed her for the shorter sleep cycle. She tried to sit up, but a sky fall of rest had only stiffened her battered sarkikos and worsened the pain. As the other slaves were gathering up their gear, a master barreled into their room, roaring orders and snapping at hides to get the slaves moving. Seeing Kwania still in the cot, the master strode to the foot and snatched her chain. Kwania squawked, and the master pulled harder until he dragged Kwania off the bunk. She fell with a sickening thud.

"Move it!"

Kwania lifted her head, her voice a rasping croak. "I need to speak to..."

The master's paw struck the side of her head and slammed her face back into the dirt floor. Kwania knew she was being reckless and foolish, but the words she had heard the prior cycle rang in her ears— *you must act.* "Please."

The master bent and unlocked the chain. "Silence, slave." His breath, wet-hot against her ear, sent a chill of panic through her. What was the leader's name? Tosi? Tachi? Her mind swirled in a fog.

"Tocho," Pa'ro's whisper prompted.

"Tocho! I must see Tocho!"

The master swiped his claws down her side. "You scum, how dare you speak his name!"

"I—I have an urgent message for the master. He must hear it. It has to do—with the survival of your pack—the survival of the whole planet."

"What could a slave have to say to Tocho worth hearing?"

"Pardon, great master—but I am a—a scientist among my kind."

The master snorted. "A scientist! That's a new one."

"I am, master. Please, what I have to say is—urgent."

"Get up! Get to work." The master snatched on her wing for emphasis.

Kwania moaned, as much in frustration as in pain. She pushed herself up to kneeling and groveled before the master. "Sir, I..."

"Not another word from you, or you'll hang again."

Kwania's tremulous breath echoed in the silent barracks. The master was poised to grab her if she spoke, his muscles rippling under his golden fur. She knew she had pushed beyond reason, so she grabbed the edge of the lower bunk and stood, sluggish and wavering. The master gave her a quick shove toward the door, and she stumbled, weaving as she made her way across the barracks.

As she exited, she gave a glance toward the horizon, where the edge of the sky light was just beginning to show. She turned back to the master, walking behind her. "Look." She gestured toward the horizon. "Do you see it?"

A rumble rose in the master's throat, and he raised his paw again.

"Wait—just look. It costs you nothing." Kwania pointed again. "Do you see the odd yellow film over the sky light? This is unnatural." The master glanced, almost as if against his volition. His eyes widened. "It is a harbinger of further destruction."

"The Chrysoli have been spared the plague of destruction seen by all other species. We are chosen for survival."

"Not if there is no planet."

"The Chrysoli will emerge as the preeminent species..."

"You are not listening."

"...as it has always been. Move!"

Kwania turned and hobbled toward the fields. As she stopped to pick up a spade, the master walked away, but when he turned, she saw him taking a surreptitious glance at the sky light. She could only hope she had gotten through to him enough for him to bring the strange occurrence to Tocho's attention.

In the fields, Kwania went through the motions of digging in the packed dirt, but her strength was gone, so she used the beats to try to observe the phenomenon. Her shovel gave her a semi-reflective surface on which to catch the sky light's image and chart its course across the sky. The spade also made a convenient object to block the sky light's mass where she could observe the distorted rim, the ejections vomiting from the surface, and the hazy mist growing around the orb. The eruptions appeared to be increasing in frequency. Kwania made a mark with a stick for each eruption. She needed to quantify the speed of increase.

Kwania was glad she was ostracized from the others. It meant they left her alone in her work. But soon, the other slaves began to notice her odd maneuverings.

"You," a Topazi hissed. "Slacker."

19

An Amthysti punched her idle shovel with his own. "You will get us all in trouble."

"Trouble-maker." The Topazi huffed and poked her tortured back with his claw.

One of the Jasperi pointed. "Haven't you done enough to us already?"

"What's going on?" The master who guarded them marched over to the group of grumbling slaves.

"We work," the Topazi muttered.

"Then get back to it!"

Kwania pretended to dig her trough until the master was well away, then resumed her counting. By the coming of the sky fall, she had etched hundreds of lines in the ground, but had made no progress on her trough.

The Jasperi who had questioned her earlier walked by and noticed her strange marks in the dirt. "What are you doing?"

The Jasperi were always so curious, like Amadah. Thinking of Amadah brought her friends, Angeni, Meda, Kacina, and Nadie to Kwania's mind, stirring a mist of tears and a renewed urgency to convince the Chrysoli leader to listen. "I am observing."

"You'd better be making headway on your trough, or the masters will have a go at you again." The Jasperi hesitated. "What are you observing?"

"The sky light."

"Why?"

"It is changing. Do you see it?"

The Jasperi gazed toward the setting sky light. "Looks the same to me." She shrugged.

"Look at the yellow haze. Do you see it? That's new." It felt good to be teaching someone again, even if it was just for a beat.

"Huh." The Jasperi cocked her head. "Strange."

"Yes, it is Expulsions from within the sky light are creating the haze. If you watch the sky light as it falls, you will see it."

The Jasperi grunted again and walked away. Not everyone appreciated science. Kwania was used to it. In a few beats, the Jasperi was back, and she started digging on Kwania's trough. "Thank you," Kwania whispered.

"Don't thank me. I just don't want to get in trouble again because of you." But the Jasperi gave a slight smile, then gestured with her head toward the sky light. "What's it mean?"

Kwania sighed. "It could mean something very, very bad."

The Jasperi leaned on her shovel. "Like how bad?"

"End of the world bad."

The Jasperi frowned. "From that?" She gestured again toward the sky light.

Kwania couldn't help but smile. What seemed to the Jasperi so disconnected and distant from their world was actually the key to their survival, but she didn't understand. "If the sky light—explodes, well, we will all die."

"Explodes?"

"Or implodes."

"Implodes! What does...?"

"I am observing right now. I do not know yet what it means."

The Jasperi closed her eyes, sighed, and smiled. "So—you don't know."

"No."

"Good." The Jasperi picked up her shovel.

"I do know this is not supposed to happen."

The Jasperi grunted and bent into her work, checking periodically for the master's location. Kwania continued her counting until the bell calling the slaves to come back rang. As the two trudged back toward the encampment, the Jasperi leaned close to Kwania. "What'd you learn?"

Kwania shook her head. "I am still gathering data."

"But—what do you think?"

"A scientist does not speculate without adequate data to support her hypothesis."

The Jasperi wrinkled her nose. "What?"

"Never mind. I need to look at the numbers."

"Oh." The Jasperi stalked off ahead of Kwania.

21

The other slaves pushed and shoved by Kwania and caught the Jasperi, who murmured to them and jerked her head at Kwania.

"Wait, what is your name?" Kwania called out.

The Jasperi didn't respond. Kwania remembered how her friends who had escaped had told her the slaves don't share names, but they had finally been willing to open up to her. Now some were free, she hoped. Or perhaps being hunted and killed. Her heart sank at the thought.

"You!" A master at the top of the rise called out. "Get away from that slave!" The Jasperi pointed to herself as a question. "Aye, you. Get away from her. And you, scum, no talking to other slaves."

"My name is Kwania." She watched the Jasperi as she scurried away, but the Jasperi didn't reply. When Kwania reached the top of the rise, the master grasped her in his paw, threw her over his back, and carried her to the barracks, where he flung her on the cot and chained her once again.

"You won't eat with the others. No more inciting rebellion for you."

"Will I be eating at all?"

The master snorted. "If your guard thinks you are appropriately remorseful."

So, the master who had spoken to her at sky rise would be returning. Kwania's heartbeat quickened. Had he considered her request? "I am remorseful." She lowered her eyes.

"Ha! No, you're only scared of being punished. I heard you calling out to that Jasperi slave after I instructed you to stop. Perhaps I will punish you for it."

"I am sorry, master. I was not inciting rebellion. I was only sharing my name."

"No names here." The master marched out of the barracks.

Kwania bent down and scratched numbers in the dirt floor, then plotted the numbers on a rudimentary graph. As she expected, the frequency of eruptions was slowly but steadily increasing. Her frustration grew. She needed her instruments to gather the data she needed if she was going to project the course of the phenomenon. She had no way to measure the volume of the eruptions, the intensity of the explosions, or the condition of the sky light's surface. Then, there was the yellow fog now surrounding the sky light. How far would it extend? What was its chemical makeup? What would it do if it reached the atmosphere? Would it thicken and block the life-giving rays of the sky light from reaching the world?

If she could get to her cave on the high mountain, she could answer these questions. Seeds of another escape plan stirred in her mind, but she knew if captured again, she would be killed on the spot. She also knew, if she tried again, she would go it alone.

The barracks door creaked open and the master who guarded her earlier entered. Something about his movements caught Kwania's attention. He was furtive, looking back over his shoulder as he shut the door gently, crouching as he scrambled across the floor to her cot. Before he could speak, Kwania pressed him. "Master, please, I..."

"Silence." He glanced around again. "Just listen." Kwania nodded once. "I've been watching. I don't like the looks of it. What's happening?"

"I do not know. Without the instruments in my lab, I cannot measure adequately."

"But if you had instruments?"

"I believe I could determine the cause and project the course of events."

The master looked toward the door again. "If I take you to Tocho, how would you convince him? What would you say?"

"Look." Kwania said, pointing to her etchings on the dirt floor. "This graph is a picture of the number of surface eruptions I could count during the cycle. See how the number is growing? It is not getting better—it is getting worse."

"You would show this graph to Tocho?"

"If you allow me to see him."

The master hesitated, pacing before her bunk, a low growl rumbling in his chest. Then, he shook his large head, his mane whipping the air. "No. Tocho will never trust the word of a slave. He will believe you seek to save your own skin."

23

"He can see with his own eyes I am not lying."

"No, it's too great a risk."

"Please, master, in your wisdom, take me to Tocho," Kwania pleaded. "What is there for you to lose? If Tocho does not believe me, he will simply punish or kill me."

"Tocho could very well punish me."

"I will take full responsibility. You could, in fact, be rewarded for your quick action if what I have to say captures Tocho's ear."

Silence again, then after several beats, the master pulled Kwania off the cot and unlocked her chain. "Come on, then."

Relieved, Kwania bowed low. "Thank you, wise master."

"Come on," the guard roared, pacing.

Kwania scurried across the yard, crouching behind the master, her head low. The pole loomed above her, and she cringed as the masters' blows seemed to strike again through the memory. Was she setting herself up for another beating?

"Peace be still," Pa'ro soothed. "Speak with reason. Make your case. Convince them."

"What good will it do?" Kwania whispered to no one.

"Quiet," the guard snarled.

"You must have faith," Pa'ro continued. "Things are changing rapidly now. The orb is on the move. Kindred marches against the imposter. The Chrysoli have a role to play. You must convince them to take the correct side."

"Sides?" Kwania received an open-pawed slap across her beak for her question. She remained silent during the rest of their walk across the courtyard to the great hall.

"I'm taking this slave to Tocho," the guard announced to the two masters standing before the entrance.

"Why bring a slave before Tocho?"

"What affair is it of yours?" He gave a demanding wave of his paw, and the masters opened the large double doors, revealing a huge, domed hallway constructed of dark okechan. Kwania stared at the massive hall and puzzled over how creatures who lived on open plains managed to secure such large amounts of wood from other regions, but the master shoved her roughly through the doors, bringing her attention back to the imperative to convince the leader the sky light was dying.

"Speak only when Tocho gives you leave."

"Peace," Pa'ro whispered. "Peace." Kwania straightened her back, her steps slow but purposeful, and her heart gaining confidence with each stride. She could explain the science. He would recognize the disruption to the sky light once she pointed it out. Surely, the master would listen.

"Wait for Tocho to acknowledge you." The guard's whispered instructions echoed through the hall. "Don't do anything to offend, because if you do, you will face more than Tocho's wrath." The guard gave Kwania a warning glare, then opened the door at the end of the hallway.

This door led into an oval chamber, once again domed, with large buttresses at intervals around the chamber. Kwania marveled at the architecture, which she hoped indicated a level of intelligence and sophistication she had yet to see from the masters. Against the far wall, a raised platform held an ornate, velvet-covered reclining couch, low to the ground, and on the couch lay Tocho. A small group of masters stood before Tocho, gesturing and talking all at once. Tocho appeared bored with their quibbling, but he raised his massive head when Kwania entered, followed by her guard.

"What is this?" Tocho snarled. "Kola?"

"Tocho." Kwania's guard bowed, his snout touching the ground.

"Why is this slave in my courts?" Tocho's tone dripped with disgust.

"Tocho, this slave claims to be a scientist among her kind. She says she has important science to share with you. I would not disturb you with such things, but she showed me some—evidence that convinced me you needed to hear her words. With all the destruction going on everywhere else on this world, I thought you might consider what she has to say."

Tocho sat upright. "Isn't this the slave who caused the uprising?"

"Aye."

"And why would I trust any words from this creature?"

"I wouldn't either, Tocho. She has caused you great hardship by leading the slaves into rebellion. But when she showed me..." Kola scraped his paws across the stone floor.

"What did this slave show you?"

"The sky light, master."

"She showed you the sky light."

"Aye, Tocho."

"Something that is there for you to see every cycle, plain before your eyes. Are you an idiot?"

"Nay, Tocho. You are right, of course, the sky light is plain before us, but because it's always there, we don't really pay attention to it, do we? She also showed me numbers on a graph."

"Numbers."

"Aye."

"Numbers of?"

"Eruptions on the surface of the sky light."

Tocho's brow creased. He appeared to consider Kola's words for a few beats, then nodded once and waved the other masters away. They scuttled to the side of the chamber to watch as Kola brought Kwania forward.

"What is it you have to say, slave?" Tocho's anger with her still boiled near the surface.

Kwania bowed low as she had seen Kola doing. "Great Master, I would take you to look at the changes in the sky light."

Tocho waved a paw impatiently. "Just speak what you have to say or get out of my sight."

"Master, I have observed the surface of the sky light has been distorted. Eruptions are spewing great amounts of matter out of the sky light, and now, a yellow haze surrounds the sky light, created from all that matter ejecting from the surface."

"And what difference does all this make to me?"

"If the sky light explodes or implodes, all life on this planet will be destroyed. If the sky light continues to erupt and the haze thickens and grows, it could mean life as we know it is over. We might have to learn to live in semi-darkness. It would certainly change how we grow food, if we could grow food at all."

"Well, that certainly could become troublesome, or it could mean nothing, but what do you, a slave, propose to do about it?"

"Master, I humbly ask, if you would allow me to use some of the implements of your scientists to do further study?"

"Our scientists are quite capable of doing their own study."

"I am sure that is true, Master, but my specific area of expertise is the study of the sky and beyond. My entire life has been spent in those pursuits. Do you have a scientist who has studied the sky as their specific focus?"

Tocho frowned and remained silent. Had she been unwise to challenge the knowledge and experience of the Chrysoli? She saw them as prideful, believing in their own superiority in all things. She opened her mouth to recant, but Kola spoke before she could. "Tocho, have our researchers mentioned the changing sky light to you?"

Tocho's gaze shifted to Kola. "They have not."

"This slave has brought it to your attention. Doesn't that give her at least some credibility?"

"Hmmmm." Tocho's exhale rumbled in his chest. "I will consider this. Take her away."

"Wait!" Kwania spoke before she thought. Tocho raised himself from his lounger to pounce, as Kola grabbed Kwania and shoved her behind him. Tocho roared, his massive head swinging from side to side.

"I'll punish her insolence, Tocho," Kola promised, pushing Kwania toward the door. "Thank you for considering her words despite her poor attitude."

"Teach her respect." Tocho's roar rattled the walls, but he had reclined again when they reached the exit.

"Fool!" Kola shouted, once the doors to the inner chamber were closed. "You could've gotten us both killed!"

"I apologize. I did not mean to cause you any trouble. You have been helpful to me. I do appreciate it."

"Then, listen to me! If Tocho does come around, he will want to see you again. You must show respect and restraint. He won't tolerate backtalk from someone as lowly as you. Remember your position."

Kwania did remember. She was a Jacinthi of the high mountain. She was a scientist, esteemed and respected by colleagues. She was a friend, confidant, and advisor to the wisest and most powerful creature in this world. And she would never, never consider herself a slave.

CHAPTER TWO

The Jasperi

Nikani raised his head as the gong sounded for the start of the celebratory meal in Ogima's throne room. Nothing was going to make this event tolerable, but he knew he had to attend or face dire consequences. Ogima would not be slighted or ignored. Perhaps if he found Meda, they could at least commiserate.

Nikani wandered from his cave, crossing the open area where Meda often sat in contemplation, but he didn't see her. He avoided the other Jacinthi who were making their way to the chamber, their excitement making him slightly nauseous. Waiting until the last beat, he loitered outside until all the other high mountain residents had disappeared, then he slunk inside and plopped down in a seat at the back corner. That's when he saw Meda. She occupied the other far corner, looking as miserable as he felt. He stared at her, trying to will her to look his way. When she finally did, he proffered a cursory wave and shook his head. She nodded once in reply.

Ogima entered the room, his cloak sweeping behind him, bracketed by two of his Chalcedi sycophants. He mounted the altar and raised his hands. "My loyal subjects, I welcome you. You will take a beat, fall to your knees, and thank me for my provision." He folded his arms and waited as the rustling sound of movement filled the chamber. Nikani ducked his head to the level of the kneelers, but he refused to kneel. His annoyance was bubbling into anger.

Glancing over at Meda, he saw that she, too, wasn't kneeling. Good for her. He tried to signal her, but her attention was focused on Ogima, probably afraid she would be seen and called out for her disobedience.

Throughout the chamber, everyone else had fallen to the dirt. One of the Chalcedi began to chant. "We give thanks to Ogima, the Lord most powerful, King of kings and God of gods. We praise you!" The congregants echoed the call. "We give thanks to you, oh great one, for providing so abundant a harvest for your creatures." Once more, those kneeling before Ogima's throne repeated the words. "All glory to you, all praise to you, for you are the greatest and most powerful of all, Great Lord Ogima, our rightful King. All hail!" The final "all hail" vibrated the stones and echoed off the walls of the chamber, and finally, Ogima seemed satisfied.

"Now, my little ones, I offer you—a meal fit for a king!" The group stood to their feet as one and cheered as the Chalcedi servants brought out platters and trays of food. An indescribable stench filled the chamber. Nikani, who was still seated, pulled his neck cloth over his nose and mouth and tried to peer around the crowd before him to see what was causing the putrid smell, but he couldn't see what was on the platters.

It was then Nikani heard a cry of horror. It was Meda. Nikani stood to see Meda, her hand over her beak, revulsion creasing her face. She turned her head, vomited, and fled from the chamber. Nikani spun around to find what Meda had seen. Before him, table after table had filled their plates and were gobbling down the food like a Carneli after the hunt.

Then, Nikani saw it. Corpses. They were eating corpses. Nikani stared at Ogima and the Chalcedi in horror. They were eating other creatures, the creatures killed in the falling of the fire from the sky. The Chalcedi had dug the dead from their hillside graves and were serving them up as food.

Did no one else see it? Surely, Sonta wouldn't eat rotting meat, and certainly not an Emraldi or Onyxi—he had traveled with them and survived because of them! Nikani searched the chamber and found Sonta, gnawing on a bone covered in flesh. What was happening here?

As casually as he could, given what was before his eyes, Nikani turned to a Jacinthi at his table. "What are you eating?"

"Is it not delicious? Only our Lord could create these kinds of delicacies in our ravaged world."

"Yes, but what is it?"

"Datura fruit, from the river lands," the Jacinthi said, clicking his beak. "Delicious! Do you want some?" The Jacinthi held out the supposed fruit, and Nikani saw what the Jacinthi was actually eating looked like someone had gouged out several milky white eyeballs and spooned them onto the plate.

Nikani bolted from the chamber, gulping in fresher air and trying not to retch. He ran toward his cave, determined to leave the horror, no matter what it took.

As he ran across the open area, he saw Meda, perched on her usual rock, her sarkikos convulsing with her weeping. "Meda," Nikani called, "we've got to get out of here."

Meda turned, and he saw she had pulled handfuls of feathers from her face in her distress. He ran to her side and put a hand to her ravaged face. "We can't stay here."

"No."

"Let's go. Together."

"But what of my clan?"

"You saw what they were doing! They're bewitched or something. They thought they were eating fruit from the river lands!"

"Ogima has deceived them. He has altered their minds and perverted them. We must help them!"

"We can't help them! He has them under his control." A horrible thought rose in Nikani's mind. "You don't think he's been—feeding—feeding us—the dead—all along—do you?"

Meda just looked at him. Now, it was Nikani's turn to vomit over the side of the cliff. "I am grateful I have refused the food he provided on principle. Now my eyes are opened, and I finally see the truth."

"I may never eat again." Nikani moaned and heaved until nothing else would come up.

Meda stood. "I must try to help my friends."

"If you go back in there, you'll be punished or worse. You know Ogima noticed us leaving. We can't stick around any longer."

"I cannot just leave them to this fate."

"We'll have to find some other way to help them."

Meda thought for several beats. "We will hide and wait for the meal and celebration to be completed. I will approach my kind one by one, and you do the same with yours. If anyone can be reached, we will take them with us. Once we have spoken to all, we will leave this mountain with whomever will come, never to return."

"It's very risky."

"Yes, but it is right."

Nikani lowered his head and sighed. "I don't have any hope of them listening, and we're risking getting turned in to Ogima. He'll kill us both. He can't afford to give us the chance to awaken the others to what he's doing."

"I know." Meda sighed. "But I do not want to become what I am seeking to escape. If I abandon my friends without trying to reach them, how am I any better than Ogima?"

Nikani set his mouth and nodded. "You're right. Come with me. I've an excellent place to hide. No one knows about it." Together, they climbed up the side of the mountain to Nikani's cave to wait out the ceremony.

As the noises from the festivities died down, Nikani, his face and head covered, crept from the cave to look down on the others as they exited Ogima's chamber. They stumbled out in small groups or in twos and threes, weaving across the open area, often supporting one another.

Some appeared in an altered state, babbling and waving their arms or flapping their wings in ecstasy. A few had to be carried, seemingly unconscious. Meda slunk to his side.

"What's wrong with them?"

"Drugged, perhaps? Or just the effects of Ogima's mind control?" Meda shrugged.

"If they're drugged, they'll never listen to us!"

"We may need to wait longer, to give them the chance to recover."

"We can't afford to wait! Ogima will have Chalcedi out looking for us. And they'll find us, eventually."

"But, as you say, they will not hear us in this state of mind."

"Please, Meda, let's go. While we still can."

Meda looked at Nikani, shook her head once, and turned back toward their hideout. Soon, the mountain was deathly quiet and cloaked in darkness. Meda and Nikani huddled deep in their cave to wait out the sky fall.

Chapter Three

The Carneli

Kilchi strained against the vines binding him to the sphere, until the cords cut into his flesh and drew blood. Above him, Chevei cried out, flapping furiously but losing altitude. Yiska and Enla, pulling by his side, grunted but didn't complain. They were stronger than they seemed, Kilchi realized. Without them, all would be lost.

The path leveled, and Kilchi found himself back in the chamber with the living water pool. With a grinding rumble, the pathway receded behind them as Amadah shrieked. "Find a boulder! Quickly!" But it was too late. The entrance to the cave closed with a loud thunk.

Amadah sank to her knees before the wall of the cave, screaming. "Fala! Fala!" She beat against the wall, then began searching for a crack. She clawed at the edges of the stone. "Help me! Help me get it open!"

Misa wrapped her arms around Amadah but said nothing.

"Look around. Is there a song? A clue? Something to tell us what to do to save him?"

Yiska made a cursory search of the area, but Kilchi suspected what had happened was exactly what the cave wanted to happen and there would be no further instruction.

"I don't see anything, Amadah" Yiska rubbed his large paw down her back. Amadah sobbed, scratching at the wall. Her chest and shoulders heaved, and her breath rasped in her throat, until finally she leaned her head back and howled.

The rest of the group surrounded Amadah. Even Chevei came down and touched her shoulder. Kilchi understood Amadah's pain. He had lost Misa for some cycles and believed he might never see her again. Amadah's loss was permanent, though, and Kilchi couldn't imagine the anguish of losing any hope of seeing Misa again.

After a few beats, Chevei murmured, "We need to keep going."

Enla glared at the Jacinthi. "Give her a beat, for sorrow's sake."

"The mountain could come down at any beat. We cannot afford to remain here." Enla's stare hardened into a growl, and Chevei backed off.

But Kilchi realized Chevei was right. How long could Fala last in the cold, dark cave before he succumbed, fell off the pressure plate, and exploded the bomb? He leaned close to Misa. "Should we carry her?"

"Her and the sphere?" No one spoke after that.

Amadah's weeping was inconsolable, her fingers and fists bloodied from her futile attempts to reopen the pathway. Still, she beat against the wall, screaming out her torment. At one point, she turned to the group and bellowed, "Do something!"

Misa and Aleshanee enveloped Amadah, who collapsed into their arms. Again, no one spoke. There was nothing to say.

Aleshanee murmured something only Amadah could hear. Amadah nodded, and her wailing began to turn to quiet tears. "But I promised him I would never leave him again."

"You and Fala are together forever. Remember?"

"Forever." Amadah mouthed the word again. "Forever."

Misa squeezed Amadah in her arms. "Let us honor Fala's sacrifice and save the sphere for which he gave himself." Amadah looked through Misa, her eyes swollen and red, her face streaked with dirt and tears.

"She's in shock." Enla moved to Amadah's side and took her arm. "Let's help her up." She, Aleshanee, and Misa gathered Amadah up and lifted her to her feet, but Amadah continued to stare at nothing. Her mouth gaped, her eyes unblinking, and she wavered as if about to collapse again, but her friends supported her weight until she was able to find an uncertain balance.

"We have to go," Chevei insisted. "Look there. I see light beyond the waterfall."

Kilchi looked. Chevei was right, there was a glow coming from behind the living waterfall that wasn't there when they were first in this chamber. "Is it a way out?"

Chevei fluttered his wings and disappeared through the flowing stream. "It leads outside, beyond the mountain."

"What a relief." Yiska breathed a shaky sigh. "I don't think we could've carried that thing back up the way we came in."

"We can't leave," Amadah rasped.

"Yet, leave we must," Misa whispered, stroking Amadah's back.

"No. No, we can't leave him. He'll..." Amadah gulped and gasped for air. "He's all alone."

"What would Fala say to us?" Enla asked.

"I imagine him saying, 'Go. Save world.'" Yiska gave his best imitation of Fala's guttural speech.

"I think he would say, 'Fala's choice. Go and do what must be done,'" Kilchi suggested.

"Too many words." Enla mouth broke open in an ever-so-slight smile.

Kilchi puffed through his nose and grimaced. "You're right."

"He'd say, 'Fala's choice. It is the way.'" Aleshanee's smile was tinged with mourning.

"That's it," Kilchi agreed.

Chevei returned. "Kilchi, get back in the harness. It is not far to the exit, then a level path beyond the mountain through woods to the plains. We can make it."

"The cycle is now to leave this place," Misa purred in Amadah's ear. "What Fala desired is this."

Amadah hung her head but turned to take her place beside the sphere, her tears dripping on its smooth surface and trailing down its side. Aleshanee took her position on the other side, with Misa trailing the rear. Enla and Yiska pulled the vines over their heads, and with Kilchi began the arduous task of moving the sphere toward the waterfall.

As the first sprays of water touched the sphere, Misa cried out. Wherever the droplets landed, a warm glow infused the sphere. All but Amadah stared into the sphere, entranced by the light swirling within its depths.

Kilchi noticed thin streaks of darkness where Amadah's tears had fallen and had the thought the living water could help Amadah. "Amadah, take a step into the waterfall. Drink a sip of the water."

Like a puppet with no will of her own, Amadah took a few steps forward until the water poured over her head. She cupped her hand, caught a little water, and drank it. The rest of the group joined her.

As the water cleansed the dirt and tear stains from her face, she began to cry anew, but these tears were not desperate, wailing, wrenching cries. Now, Amadah's weeping sounded almost peaceful. Kilchi felt his own throat tighten, and a well of tears flowed down his muzzle. One by one, each of the members of the little band began to weep, even Chevei. They embraced one another as they stood in the living water and allowed their grief to flow freely. No one seemed to feel the urgency to leave that had just compelled them forward.

After many beats, Kilchi bent down and took another drink. He felt the soothing warmth of the water flow through his sarkikos to the tip of his tail, and his weeping abated.

"The way is lit," Luxor, the Bellator Whisperer who guided them through the cavern, proclaimed. "Let us be on our way."

"Look at the sphere." Kilchi pointed. Where before the drops had created a swirling glow deep within the sphere, now bright light beamed from it. Even the dark remnant of Amadah's tears was gone.

"Fala would say..." Amadah paused and took a deep breath. "He would tell me—we are bound." A wisp of a smile touched her face. "Forever."

38

"Taking some of the living water with us would be wise." Misa trailed her fingers through the pool, catching the tiny flecks of glimmering light in her fingers. "Also, for my clan."

"So they can walk on land?" Kilchi asked. Misa nodded.

"And some fruit from the tree, too." Enla suggested.

"We need something to hold it all that isn't too hard to carry." Yiska massaged his shoulder where the harness dug inti his flesh. "We already have a heavy load."

"Imuba leaves," Amadah murmured. "When I was leaving my forest to go to—the desert—where I met..." she swallowed. "I used imuba leaves to cover my feet. They are large enough and strong enough to hold the water and would easily carry the fruit."

"What do imuba leaves look like?" Kilchi asked. "Where would I find them?"

"They look like large, shiny, oblong, dark green boats. You would find them on the edges of a forest or under a clump of tall trees."

"I will be back soon." Kilchi shrugged off the harness and bolted out of the cave. At the opening, Kilchi stopped and scanned the area. Chevei was right, the path was level and straight. The wooded area was not dense, so he wondered if he would find Amadah's imuba tree here. She mentioned the edge of a forest, so he ran through the woods until he reached the start of the open plains, and there, scattered among the trunks of trees, he found plants with the leaves she described. He plucked the leaves, then gathered up some string-like vines to tie the leaves closed and carry them as a sling across their backs.

He hurried back to his friends, and each took a few leaves to use as containers. Enla and Aleshanee tied the edges of the leaves together, while Yiska made loops from the vines and tied the loops to the leaves. The result was a set of lightweight, makeshift carriers. Misa and Kilchi filled several bladders with living water, Chevei picked pieces of fruit for each to carry, and everyone hung the loops around their necks.

Once again, they were ready to go, but Amadah gasped as if she'd been holding her breath too long. "Wait." Everyone stopped and looked at her. "Isn't there anything else we can try? Anything?"

No one replied. Kilchi understood she already knew the answer.

Finally, Aleshanee reached for Amadah's hand. "We need to go."

With a nod, Kilchi strained against the harness. Yiska grunted on one side and Enla on the other as they ground the sled across the stone. Several beats later, the little group reached the opening and stepped into the sky light's glow.

"We are free," Chevei cawed. As the sphere rolled out from the cave, a blinding beam shot from it into the sky.

"Uh oh," Kilchi moaned. "It's going to be hard to hide ourselves with that light showing the whole world where we are."

"Remaining here is not possible," Misa declared.

Chevei circled above them. "Try pulling it into the trees."

Kilchi, Enla, and Yiska pulled the sled into the wooded area, trying to find a copse of trees dense enough to block the beam. The light danced amongst the branches. Chevei called down to the group. "I fear the light can still be seen."

"Do not fear the light, only the darkness," Luxor whispered.

"We don't have anything to cover it, we can't leave it here, and we can't stay this close to the mountain. The bomb could explode at any beat."

"We'll just have to risk being seen," Aleshanee said.

"Taking the sphere directly across the plains, through Amadah's destroyed forest, and on to the high mountain is a fool's errand," Misa stated. "Remaining within the trees until we reach once more the sea of the Beryli, where my pod now lives, is shorter and safer. Going the shorter route is one which provides us more creatures to help carry the load and more options for how to reach the high mountain."

"Misa makes a good point." Kilchi knew Misa was desperate to return to her clan, especially after her experience in the cave. "With living water to drink, her clan could walk on land and help us carry the weight."

"But I thought we were to take the sphere straight to the high mountain," Enla argued.

"Taking it to the high mountain after we reach others to help us is wiser."

"Chevei, what's the closest route to the sea?" Kilchi called. Chevei pointed beyond the mountain. "Is there a path we could navigate while carrying the sphere?"

Chevei dropped the vine attached to the sphere and circled higher above the tallest trees, then swooped down to join his friends. "The path will be difficult and slow-going through the trees, but I see a way that leads us to the sea."

"And away from this mountain?"

"Well away."

"That's it, then." Aleshanee shuffled to her position beside the glowing sphere.

Kilchi noticed Amadah had not spoken or moved away from the sphere since they left the cave. He padded to her side and nuzzled her hand. "Ready?" Her glazed, empty stare let him know she would never be ready to leave this place and perhaps would never be the same again. His head down, he returned to his harness with Yiska and Enla, while Chevei picked up his steering vine in his beak and soared above them.

Misa moved to the front of the group and, using a large, flat stick, she did her best to flatten plants and dislodge rocks from the path they forged through the trees.

As they trudged through the woodland, Aleshanee began to hum a mournful tune, then started to sing:

"Hear our lament, Great Love;
Listen to our cries, Forever.
In the sky light rising, we seek you;
As the sky light falls, we wait for you.

41

For the cycles vanish like smoke,
Our hearts are withered like grass.
In our distress, we groan aloud,
And mingle our words with tears.

Our lives are like a shadow,
Our hearts are brittle dust;
Hear the groans of our grief,
And lift us, lift us up.

No one made a sound as the echo of Aleshanee's song died away. Heads down, they slogged on. Kilchi's load of grief seemed much heavier than the sphere. The beam from the sphere continued to flicker in the treetops, a beacon exposing their course and location to anyone who was looking. Kilchi hoped no one was.

Chevei acted as both lookout and navigator from his vantage point above the trees. The trek was arduous and unbearably slow-going, requiring frequent stops for rest and repositioning of the cumbersome sphere. They were loath to drink the living water, knowing they needed enough for all of the Saphiri so they could walk on land. With so much exertion, everyone was becoming dehydrated.

The other big problem was sustenance. They didn't want to use the fruit from the living tree for food, recognizing if someone was injured on the journey, they had no other means of healing their wounds. No one had eaten for several cycles, and nothing edible presented itself in the forest. They were all needed to move the sphere, so no one could leave the group to forage or hunt—not that there would be anything to hunt anyway. With all these factors weighing on them on top of losing Fala, a somber pall hung over the group. No one spoke.

Behind them, a hollow-sounding whump shook the air, then the ground began to tremble and roll. Another sound, this one a screaming, grating clamor, reverberated around them. They turned to see a massive plume of dust belch into the air, and Kilchi knew the detonator had

42

triggered and the mountain had collapsed in on itself. Without a sound, Amadah crumpled to the ground, unconscious.

More grinding followed, and thunderous waves rippled through the ground. Without warning, a chasm ripped open behind them like an unfurling flower, racing toward the sphere. Kilchi howled. "Move!" He yanked against the harness with all his strength. Yiska and Enla roared as they scrambled desperately to outrace the crumbling dirt.

Aleshanee darted behind the sphere and grabbed Amadah beneath her arms, dragging her away from the chasm just before it consumed her. The sphere wobbled and rolled, barely remaining on their rickety sled, until the widening hole caught up to the right brace, and the limb began to slide into the chasm.

Chevei screeched and beat his wings with fury, straining to hold the sphere atop the makeshift sled. But as the sled tilted toward the widening hole, the sphere started to roll. Glancing back, Yiska saw the sphere sliding toward the chasm, and without hesitation, he jumped onto the sled and wrapped his long arms around the sphere.

"Noooo!" Kilchi grabbed for Yiska, but he was too late. A yelp, a sizzle of burning fur, and Yiska was blown back off the sled. Kilchi couldn't stop to check on his friend, for the sphere started moving again. "Pull!" he barked. Misa grabbed Yiska's harness and added what strength she had as Enla and Kilchi swerved the sled away from the chasm, snatching the right skid from the edge of the hole in a cloud of flying dirt.

The chasm cut a jagged path ahead of them, consuming brush and trees along the way until it was beyond their sight. The little group remained scattered along the ground like so many leaves before a gust of wind. Aleshanee and Amadah lay in a tangled mass among some bushes, Enla, Kilchi, and Misa face-down before the battered sled, and Yiska on his back near the edge of the chasm, his eyes wide and unblinking, staring at nothing, his mouth open in a silent scream.

"Is everyone safe?" Chevei circled down from above them.

Kilchi sat up and embraced Misa as Enla rolled up onto her haunches and lumbered to Yiska's side. She gasped, falling to all fours, then she bellowed a mournful howl that shattered the air the same way the explosion shook the ground. Kilchi and Misa walked slowly to her side as Chevei landed near Yiska's head. Chevei reached down and examined Yiska, feeling his snout and chest for some sign of life, but after a few beats, he closed his eyes and shook his head.

Behind them, Aleshanee cried out, "Yiska!"

"He tried to stop the sphere from falling into the chasm," Kilchi explained.

"He touched the sphere?" Aleshanee whispered. Kilchi bowed his head, and Aleshanee covered her face and sobbed.

Dazed, Amadah struggled to sit up. She stared blankly at her friends, but it took several beats for her to speak. "Aleshanee?"

"Yiska," was all Aleshanee could manage in reply.

"Is he dead?" Amadah's voice was as hollow and empty as the air around them.

Before anyone could respond, another rumble built beneath their feet. Kilchi bounded to the sphere, but the rest of the group froze, grief and exhaustion paralyzing them. "Help me!" Kilchi barked. No one moved.

The ground rolled, widening the chasm, and Yiska's sarkikos slid over the edge. Enla lunged and grabbed for a hold, but she couldn't keep her grip. Yiska tumbled out of sight.

Misa grabbed Enla and pulled her back from the expanding hole before she followed Yiska into the abyss. Now, the group mobilized. While Misa dragged Enla to her place in the harness, Chevei grabbed his vine and took to the sky. Amadah and Aleshanee hurried to the sled to hold the sphere in place, and Kilchi led them as they pulled the sled deeper into the woods, away from the rift.

"Chevei, which way?" Kilchi wanted to get clear of the new crevasse the explosion created as quickly as possible. Chevei pointed, and the struggling group heaved the sled across rocks and over brush, but without Yiska's strength, they gained little ground.

"Failing." Misa leaned over, her hands resting on her new knees as the sled ground to a halt.

"Let me pull." Amadah stepped forward, but Kilchi shook his head.

"Aleshanee can't hold onto that sphere all by herself. And we can't afford for that thing to roll off the sled. We'd never get it back on."

"What are we going to do?" Enla asked, her voice still tremulous with weeping.

"This is all my fault." Amadah's head sunk to her chest. "My fault."

"Don't say that." Aleshanee was uncharacteristically vehement. "None of this is any of our faults."

"If I had been on the sled, steadying the sphere..."

"Don't."

Enla folded to the ground. "I can't."

Kilchi was sympathetic. Enla had just lost her best friend, and Amadah her bound mate. But he knew they had to leave this area—and soon. "We don't have a choice. We have to keep going." As if to emphasize his statement, the ground started to rumble again.

"Awaiting at the sea is our help," Misa reminded them.

"If we can just make it there." Kilchi picked up his harness. "Come on. The sooner we move, the sooner we find help."

"I don't think I can do it," Enla whispered. "Not without Yiska." Her weeping intensified.

Misa laid comforting arms across Enla's shoulders, leaned in close. "Dying for the sphere's sake did Yiska. Honoring of his sacrifice is going on." Enla looked into Misa's eyes. "For his sake."

"For his sake," Enla murmured and rolled to her paws.

"Let's go." Kilchi pulled the sled in Chevei's direction.

"Lacking in strength, I fear." Misa sighed.

"It's all good. We'll make it. We have to."

The group worked without speaking. Their progress was excruciatingly slow. Chevei resorted to flying circular patterns to keep from having to try to remain stationary overhead. They had to stop often to clear rocks and debris blocking their way. As the sky light started to descend below the horizon, Kilchi knew it would be impossible to continue in the darkness, so he called for a halt.

Chevei descended to join the group. "The light from the sphere is going to be an even bigger problem after sky fall."

"Aleshanee, could you and Amadah collect fronds and leaves to try to cover the sphere?" Kilchi asked. Without replying, the two bearers stepped off the sled and wandered into the woods.

Misa wandered over to Kilchi. "Lifting spirits seems to be needed. Becoming our own worst enemies through hopelessness."

"You're right. But I have no idea how to do that. Amadah was always the one who kept us on track. Now..."

"Having little reason left for hope," Misa finished for him.

"Yes."

"Aleshanee always helped Yiska—and me—to keep hoping, even when things seemed impossible." Enla gulped and started crying again.

"Not having the chance to say how saddened we are by Yiska's loss. A tragedy for us all."

"I am the only Onyxi left alive now. I have no one. I'm alone."

"You have all of us," Kilchi protested. "We are your clan now."

"Remaining is love in this world for you." Misa wrapped her arms around her friend's thick neck.

"I wish I could go back, back before the fire fell from the sky, back before Yiska and I walked out of our cave. We thought we were unhappy then. We wanted to leave, to find something greater in the world than playing stones and collecting water. Now look at us."

"Going back is impossible. Making a different choice means you would both be buried in the hill cave. Having purpose is your being here with us, as did Yiska."

"To die? That was his purpose?"

46

"Yiska was instrumental in getting us here. And his sacrifice saved the sphere from falling into the chasm." Kilchi shook his head. "We would never have made it this far without him."

"Yet, he's still dead, left to rot at the bottom of a cleft in the ground, just as if he was buried in our home cave. It doesn't make sense."

Amadah returned, carrying an armful of leafy branches. She arranged the branches across the top of the sphere and along its sides. Soon, Aleshanee added the brush she collected to fill in the gaps around the limbs. Although not completely blocked, the light from the sphere didn't shine like a sky light anymore.

Amadah plopped down next to the sphere. "I'll take first watch."

"Are you sure?"

"I'm sure I won't be sleeping any beat soon anyway, so yes, I'll take watch. Besides, I need to make up for what I did to Yiska."

Enla padded to Amadah's side. "You can't blame yourself for Yiska's decision."

"But if I had been there..."

"It might've still rolled, and he might've still tried to stop it. Yiska was brave—and strong—and..." Enla dissolved into tears again.

Amadah, Aleshanee, and Misa embraced her, and with Kilchi and Chevei beside them, they allowed their grief to overtake them—grief for Yiska, for Fala, for their circumstances, for their clans, and for their world.

Chapter Four

The Topazi

Fala slumped in the dank darkness of the cave, his sarkikos failing him despite his best efforts to be still on the pressure plate. Was Amadah far enough away from the mountain that, if he fell off, she would remain unharmed? Was the sphere safe? Fala accepted his fate, but he wanted to be certain his group was well away from the mountain before his inevitable collapse into unconsciousness, and whatever was beneath the plate exploded. However, he didn't know how to measure the number of beats he had been alone in the cave or how many beats it would take the group to reach the exit. So, he tried to hold on.

The cold crept into his bones, and he felt his heartbeat slowing, his eyes narrowing, his mouth drooping open. He would sleep soon, and then it would be over. He tried to force himself to focus, but his thoughts scattered like grains of sand in a swirling wind. "Not yet." He heard his words slur. "Not yet."

"Fala." A whisper echoed in his ears. He tried to open his eyes and lift his head to see, but he couldn't move. Everything was frozen. "I'm here."

All Fala could manage was a guttural grunt. A thin light reflected off the muddy ground beneath him. He tried again to raise his eyes, trying to see the source.

"I'm here." Somewhere in the fog of his mind, a glimmer of recognition shimmered like the golden light at his feet. Then, he felt a touch, and a warming glow spread through his sarkikos. "Hello, dear friend."

49

Fala looked up into the deep pools of her eyes. "Kindra."

"We are going now."

Fala felt himself float above the pressure plate. A blossom of fire poured from beneath the plate, but it appeared to move in slow motion, as if Tempor itself had been stretched. Fala looked at Kindred. "Where?"

"We are going to the First World."

"Amadah?"

"Amadah is safe. She has taken the artifact beyond this mountain."

"Amadah comes?"

Kindred shook her head. "It isn't yet the cycle for Amadah to return to the First World."

"Fala stays. Bound to Amadah."

Kindred placed her hand on Fala's claws. "You cannot stay, Fala."

"No."

"Do you remember when I touched Amadah, and she rose from death?"

Fala nodded.

"Where do you think she was before she returned?"

Fala paused. "First World?"

Kindred nodded. "Do you remember how she said she wanted to go back?"

"Except for Fala."

Kindred smiled. "You're right. She remembered her love for you."

"Fala stays."

"Amadah understands the reason for your sacrifice was love for her."

"No. Fala comes back. Like Amadah. This is love."

Kindred was silent. The warmth of her love for Fala poured over him like the living water. He felt as if he were bathing in it. Before his eyes, a hole ripped in the wall of the cave and dazzling light poured out. Fala's nictitating membranes drew closed. Kindred carried him to

50

the opening, and Fala saw a kind of beauty he had never seen. A gleaming waterfall, like the living water of the cavern but somehow more alive, tumbled off a brilliant purple mountain. Green, brighter and more vibrant than the thickest Emraldi grass, coated the fields below the mountain, without blemish. The sky light was white, not red—a clean white, the light from it too intense to examine. The sky was the color of Misa's hair but with more depth and texture, swirling with varying shades like the waters of the falls. Fala couldn't breathe.

"You would choose to stay, if you could?" Kindred asked.

"Stay with Amadah, yes."

"Great pain and hardship would come."

"Amadah will have pain? Hardship?"

"Yes."

"Fala must stay with Amadah. Bound."

"You cannot protect her, Fala. Your presence would only hurt her more."

"Fala protects bound mate."

"She must walk her own path."

Fala growled at Kindred. "Fala walks on path beside Amadah. We are bound."

"You will remain bound on the First World."

"No!"

"Fala..."

"Amadah needs Fala. Crying for Fala."

Kindred sighed. "You still see with desert eyes. You hold onto the old ways, even now."

"Kindra can make Fala stay. Kindra can do this."

"You do not know what you are asking. You cannot see the whole. You don't care what comes to Fala, but do you care what comes to Amadah?"

Fala stared at the belching fire beneath him. Finally, he choked out, "Yes."

"Does Fala trust Kindred?"

"Yes."

"Then listen to me. If you remain, as you request, Amadah will have her pain plus the greater pain of seeing you suffer."

"Amadah suffers more without Fala. Like Fala without Amadah. Bound mates together. Forever."

"When you love someone, it is hard to bear when they suffer." Kindred waved her arm across the landscape revealed by the opening. "Do you see what awaits you?"

"Fala sees no Amadah."

Kindred sighed. "You were willing to die for her sake before. Why not live in the First World for her sake now?" Fala's mouth tightened into a firm, thin line. "I will not force you to come with me, Fala, but I ask you again to trust me. Will you trust me?"

"Fala stays with bound mate. It is the way. Kindra makes it so."

Kindred sighed again, and a tear glistened on her cheek. "Very well. It is your choice." The two of them spiraled slowly toward the flames. As Fala watched, the fire receded, sucked back beneath the pressure plate as if the Tempor had reversed its course. Instead of depositing Fala on the pressure plate, Kindred placed a delicate foot on it. Her gown swirled as she settled onto the plate, leaving Fala standing on the muddy earth beside her. "Go." She pointed toward a curve in a far wall. "Around that bend, I will open a doorway for you."

"Kindra..." Fala began.

"I will remain to give you the chance to get well away from the mountain before it collapses."

"No! Kindra dies again?"

"I return to the First World. This is the choice you made, Fala."

Fala bellowed, "Fala dies. Amadah suffers. Kindra gone. What kind of choice this?"

"The choice of pain for a cycle of pain. Who will you choose to suffer?"

"Fala."

"And suffer you will." Kindred wept. "Now go."

Fala let out an anguished howl, released Kindred's hand, and scuttled toward the curve in the wall. As he rounded the bend, he saw a dim glow in the distance. He hurried along the passage, pausing once to glance back toward the darkness where he left Kindred, then he stepped through the opening into the light.

CHAPTER FIVE

The Jacinthi

Angeni startled awake. She was shocked to find the sky light high above. She felt like a dense fog surrounded her head, and her sarkikos ached across every metric from wingtip to talon. What had happened? She didn't recall going to sleep in Ogima's chamber; in fact, she assumed Ogima would be enraged if he found her here, since this was his throne room. When she thought about it, she couldn't remember much of anything after the celebratory meal was served.

The stone beneath her vibrated, and she realized what had woken her from her slumber. A rumbling thunder rose from the valley. Angeni struggled upright and tottered out of the chamber, expecting to find storm clouds approaching. Instead, the sky light's rosy glow lit the valley. Looking down, Angeni saw a gaping black crack etching its way across the valley. The thunder, growing in volume, shook her mountain so much, stones began to rattle down its face and clatter around her. She hurried back into Ogima's chamber. "Wake the Lord! Wake him!"

One of the Chalcedi, who was supposed to be standing guard but who had also lapsed into unconsciousness, roused, and hearing Angeni's cry, he squawked and scuttled toward Ogima's quarters. But Ogima had heard the thunder rolling across the valley and was already entering his chamber. "What is that noise?"

"The land quakes and splits in two," Angeni cried.

Ogima turned to the Chalcedi. "Get the other guards and go awaken everyone. We must bring them to safety."

"Oh, Lord, I am so glad you are with us," Angeni cooed. "You care so for your clan."

"Of course, I do. Why aren't you helping?"

"Right away, Lord." Angeni bowed low and backed out of the chamber, then fluttered to the sleeping quarters of her Jacinthi and their Jasperi guests. "Wake up! Awaken! Come! The Lord has called for you. He brings you to safety!"

Sonta, Itai, and Isusa were the first to stumble from their quarters. Angeni pointed them toward Ogima's chamber. Kacina, Nadie, Hanai, and the other Jacinthi wandered out slowly. "Where is Nikani?" Angeni gestured for them to follow Sonta. "Has anyone seen Meda?" Hanai shrugged.

"No, Angeni," Kacina replied.

"Where could they be?" She flew back toward the chamber and saw Catori circling high above the valley. Ogima must've sent him to scout the quake. Angeni decided to join him. After all, she was the leader of the clan, serving Ogima, of course.

She approached Catori and settled in the fly beside him. "Have you seen Meda or Nikani?"

"Look." Catori, not answering her question. pointed instead to the farthest end of the valley, where the hills of the Onyxi used to stand tall, and beyond that to what was once the fertile, rolling fields of the Emraldi, now a blackened wasteland. A massive split tore through the center of the valley, with webs of smaller crevasses tearing through the ground on either side.

As the thunder rolled and the ground shook, the split widened and crawled nearer to her mountain. Whole sections of land collapsed into the deepening hole in clouds of dust. Boulders and rocks skittered down the front of the mountain to the valley floor as the mountain shook with the force of the quake.

"You must tell Ogima," Angeni shouted. "I will find our missing friends." Catori circled once more to survey the tableau, then made haste back to Ogima. Angeni flew back to where she expected to find Meda, perched on her favorite outcropping meditating. Hopefully, Meda would have some insight into Nikani's whereabouts, because Angeni didn't know where he usually lived. She had witnessed the two of them speaking more than once.

As she neared the mountain, she thought she saw movement and a flicker of color higher up, so she flew up to investigate and saw Meda taking off from the mountainside. "Meda! Meda!"

"Angeni, I was coming to find you."

"Do you see what is happening?"

"What is it?"

"Quakes split the ground." They landed high on a ledge. "How I wish Kwania was with us! She could explain this occurrence."

"Oh, yes. I miss her so."

"As do I. Where were you? I have been looking for you."

"And I you. Are you aware of what is happening in this camp?"

"We are all in grave danger. Ogima has called everyone to his throne for their protection."

"No, I do not mean the quakes. I mean in the camp. I mean the celebration."

Angeni frowned. "It was a wonderful celebration. What do you mean?"

"Did you see everyone leaving late after the meal was well done?"

Angeni hesitated. "No—I..."

"They could hardly walk. Many had to be carried. All acted as if their minds were altered, like the Chalcedi often appear."

"What is this nonsense? No one in our clan would..."

"Where were you after the celebration? I did not see you coming from the chamber."

"I..."

"Angeni?"

"I—slept in the throne room."

Meda raised her brows. "Alone?"

"Of course." Angeni tossed her head and ruffled her feathers. "I was tired and remained in the throne room in case I was needed."

Meda's eyes narrowed, but she let it drop. "How do you explain what I saw? And the food. Do you know what you were eating?"

Angeni smiled and closed her eyes. "Delicacies from the river lands and the sea. Ogima provided..."

"Dead sarkikos."

"What?"

"Ogima provided corpses. Both Nikani and I saw it, but all others appeared to believe as you do, that they were eating delicious food."

"Meda, you have lost your senses."

"No, Angeni, you have lost yours. Please listen to me..."

"I will not. I will not have you disparage our Lord in this manner."

"He is a liar and a fraud."

"How dare you!" Angeni gasped.

"Angeni, you know me. You have known me for my entire life. How long have you known this Ogima?"

"He has given..."

"He has deceived you."

"You are wrong."

"I am not. Angeni, do you even remember learning about the Dark Ones? Do you remember how they deceive? Do you recall Aleshanee and what she taught you?"

Angeni blinked twice but then shook her head. "I will not listen to any more of this heresy. You will come with me now to Lord Ogima and throw yourself on his mercy."

"Angeni. Would you give your friend, one of your dearest friends, over to be tortured and murdered?"

"He would never..."

"He already has. You must hear me."

"I will not listen. You—you have been tricked by the Dark Ones. It is you who must be awakened. Come. I will plead with Ogima. He will listen and forgive your insolence, and he will help you awaken from your insanity."

"I will not go with you, Angeni."

Angeni grabbed Meda's arm. "You will."

Nikani scrambled down the embankment behind them and pushed Angeni off the ledge. She lost her grip on Meda, fluttering her wings to regain altitude, but when she returned to the ledge, Meda and Nikani had vanished.

Saddened, Angeni flew back to the chamber where the rest of her clan gathered. Everyone was talking at once, but Ogima rapped a stone on his dais. "Silence!" He lifted his hands. "No need for panic or concern. Nothing is beyond my power. I have the situation in hand. You will all be safe here until the quakes pass. Now, settle down. Find a place to sit comfortably, and please keep your talking to a minimum. I despise your incessant chatter."

As commanded, the large group moved around the chamber until all were seated. Angeni approached Ogima's throne. "Lord, I am aggrieved to inform you that we have two defectors: Meda and Nikani. I found them high upon the mountain, but they refused to come with me to safety. Meda spoke about you in a way—well, I would not repeat what she said."

Ogima's face darkened as Angeni detailed what had happened. When she concluded with Nikani's attack, Ogima rose slowly and thundered, "He dared attack you? My servant?"

"I am sure it is all a misunderstanding, Lord. Meda would never..." She was interrupted by the floor of the chamber shuddering. It tilted, and bits of stone clattered down the walls. Several voices screamed. Ogima, his eyes fixed on the roof of the chamber, yelled for Chatan, his Chalcedi guard, and scurried from the chamber under Chatan's wings.

The stone floor continued to convulse, as if the mountain swayed on its foundations. Angeni wondered if the crevasse had reached the base of the mountain, but she couldn't leave her clan to see. Ogima clearly wanted her to handle the situation in the throne room while he went out to take care of the quakes. Angeni stepped up on the dais and imitated Ogima, raising her hands and calling for calm, assuring them all would be well. "Ogima has gone to deal with this crisis himself. When this is over, we will owe him our very lives."

"Are we safe here?" one of the Jacinthi asked.

"Ogima says we will be safe here. So, you have nothing to fear. He has the situation well in hand." The floor tilted again, and with a loud crack, it split it two.

Now, everyone was screaming, and a few rushed for the exit despite Angeni's pleas to remain still and calm. But Catori stepped into the doorway, spread his massive wings, and held up a hand. "You will remain here, as Ogima instructed."

"We'd be safer in the open than in a closed space," Sonta argued.

Catori pointed. "Sit." The Jacinthi and Jasperi dropped back, then drifted to places as far as possible from the crack down the center of the stone, whispering and grumbling amongst themselves.

One of the Chalcedi lit the smudge pots at the base of Ogima's altar, and the room began to fill with a thick, acrid smoke. Soon, the inhabitants of the high mountain were lying around, some across each other, their eyes drooping. Angeni's expression was beatific, having forgotten all about their terror of a few beats ago. Ogima was wonderful. Life was good.

Chapter Six

The Turqosi

Leenha rapped on the door where the Turqosi brought slaves for the masters and received food and materials as payment. She had no slaves this trip. She had been recovering from wounds she'd received in the battle against the Beryli, and creatures to capture were in very short supply. She'd not caught the scent of the Carneli or his group in many cycles. But her army still had to be fed. She pulled the braided rope, then pounded the door again. She would not be denied her due, even if it meant bringing her army against the masters. Her clan was starving.

The hinges on the door creaked, and a gruff voice said, "You're late."

Leenha gestured to the scars and sores over her sarkikos.

The master looked past Leenha and frowned. "Where are our slaves?"

"Food," Leenha hissed.

"Slaves?"

"Food first."

"We offer no credit," the master growled.

"Starving."

"Too bad for you." The master chuckled.

Leenha spat, and the master howled as the acidic sputum seared through his fur. "You will pay for that, you wretched creature!" The master roared and shoved open the door to grab Leenha, which was what she wanted all along. She slithered in between his legs, slicing his underbelly with her claws along the way. At her whistle, the rest of her army, led by Lise, attacked the master, swarming over him like antlings

61

over a bead of sap. The master howled, grabbing Turqosi in his huge paws and slinging them against the wall, but he was blinded by their spit and soon collapsed beneath their relentless tearing and biting.

Leenha stood over the dead Chrysoli with a satisfied sneer, spit once more on the master's face, and hissed, "Food." The Turqosi ripped open the master's chest and stepped aside for Leenha to partake first. She pulled the ribs apart and dove into the meat, gesturing for her army to join her. Soon, the bones were picked clean.

Leenha gestured across her throat, and the army slithered out of the room and beyond the wall, racing across the open fields toward the deep brush. However, she caught the scents of many different kinds of creatures in the grassy plains, so she called for a halt. As they were trained, her army fell into a protective formation around her as she sniffed the ground. She smelled Jasperi, Topazi—Carneli? Was it the impressive Carneli specimen she had coveted? If so, she would follow the trail and have him for her own. Then she caught a whiff of Chalcedi and hissed. Enemies! Strange. What were these creatures doing together? What were they doing out on these plains?

Lise whistled and pointed. The taller grass where she stood was tamped down, as if many footfalls had walked there. Leenha joined her and gestured for a scouting party. They would follow this trail and find out what these creatures were up to.

Nearby, Leenha found evidence of Chrysoli tracks—two, maybe three. Were they with the larger group or following them? Could it be some slaves had escaped from the Chrysoli encampment? That would explain the unusual conglomeration of species. Why else would enemies have come together? But this was a strange cycle, so the expected no longer applied.

The scouts followed the tracks to the edge of the heavily wooded area. Leenha held up her claw, and the scouting party fanned out to search for the trail in the brush. Soon, she heard Eteena click to the left of her position. The rest of the Turqosi took up their positions behind Eteena, who, nose to the ground, took the lead through the heavy undergrowth. Leenha snorted. Where the creatures had trod was flattened, bushes trampled and limbs broken. Clumsy creatures. If they were afraid of being followed, they showed no sign of it. Foolish creatures. Her army moved silently through the brush without disturbing a single leaf. If Turqosi didn't want to be found, no one would ever find them.

Once again, she picked up the Chrysoli tracks. At least they moved with more care. So, the Chrysoli were following the other, larger group, making it likely those creatures were escaped slaves. Leenha snorted again. If the Chrysoli caught up to the slaves, which they would with such an obvious trail, the slaves wouldn't stand a chance.

A seed of a plan formed in Leenha's mind. The Chrysoli had offended her, which was unacceptable. She would not stand for that to go unpunished, and one master as a meal didn't suffice. Her army could tip the balance in favor of the slaves. Two or three Chrysoli would be no match for her warriors. Plus, the slaves would be fighting for their lives, so they could be at least some help in the battle. Losing all those slaves would be a real strike against the Chrysoli. She could teach them about denying her food when she had served them so well for so long, and she would make sure they knew who had hurt them by leaving the two or three Chrysoli hunters blinded and laid open by her claws for the other masters to find.

Leenha clicked, and Eteena and Lise were by her side. She gestured her plan, and her two generals slid their tongues across their teeth in approval. As they scurried to their soldiers to convey Leenha's desires, Leenha slithered ahead, scouting for the slaves' position. It didn't take long for her to find the three Chrysoli crouched behind thick bushes overlooking a narrow river. The slaves huddled by the river, where they had stopped to drink water and rest. Fools. The slaves were out in the open, exposed and vulnerable. Was there not one strategist among them?

She backed away and rejoined her scouts, quickly describing the setting. They would wait for the Chrysoli to strike, leaving them also exposed, then they would descend on the Chrysoli, surround them, and destroy them.

Lise scuttled back to the main force and led them to the outskirts of the clearing. Moving like specters, her army spread in a semicircle around the river scene. They didn't have long to wait. The three masters crept down the embankment, barely rustling the brush, until they were within pouncing distance. As they tensed their haunches to go in for the kill, Leenha raised her claw, and her army scurried forward to the Chrysoli's former position. And when they leapt, Leenha screeched the attack call. The slaves, hearing the cry, raised their heads, and seeing the Chrysoli masters coming for them, they scattered. Leenha's army swooped in from all sides, ripping the masters' hides, clawing at their bellies, and blinding them with their spit. The slaves didn't have to lift a claw to defend themselves.

"Food." Leenha gestured to the fallen masters, but the slaves remained huddled in small groups, clutching each other. Leenha sighed. She didn't think these pitiable creatures would be much help if her army had to stand against the whole of the Chrysoli fighters. "Eat," she insisted, waving a claw toward the corpses. "Make strong."

A Chalcedi flyer among the slaves pointed to the masters and shook her head. "No."

Leenha frowned. "Fools." She gestured for her army to consume at will. Then, Leenha approached the Chalcedi who had spoken. "Debt," was all she said.

"We are in your debt," the Chalcedi agreed. "My name is Cholena. These creatures were all slaves of the Chrysoli, but we escaped."

"Chrysoli come," Leenha warned.

Cholena grimaced. "We know. I fear they won't give up so many slaves easily."

"For revenge," Leenha added, pointing to the dead masters.

"The masters are vengeful. Why did you help us?"

"Chrysoli refuse Turqosi food, having plenty," Leenha explained. "Offense."

"I see."

"Correction." Leenha gestured toward the dead Chrysoli.

"Now that your opportunity for correction is taken, will you move on? Or are you willing to continue to help us?"

"What benefit?"

"The masters may seek revenge against you as well," Cholena suggested. "We are stronger with greater numbers."

Leenha sneered. "No fighters."

"We could be taught. We are willing."

Leenha shook her head, turning away. "No fighters."

"Wait. Please. Please help us. We want to free our fellow slaves from the masters, but we don't know how."

This information gave Leenha pause. What a strike against the Chrysoli that would be! She turned back to Cholena. "Why?"

"Why? Why what?"

"Why free others?"

"Because they are our friends. Because they don't deserve to live as slaves for the rest of their lives. Because the masters are cruel. Because children are there who have never known freedom. Because it's wrong."

"No gain."

"What?"

"What benefit?"

"We want to free them because it is the right thing to do, not for our benefit."

Leenha scoffed. "Foolish reason to die."

"And payback for an offense isn't a foolish reason to die?"

"No Turqosi die."

Cholena sighed. "You could've died."

"Slaves will die."

"I know. But maybe fewer die on both sides if we help each other."

Leenha slashed her hand across her throat.

"Help train us, then. You are obviously skilled. You can help us learn so fewer of us die in the raid."

"No."

"Look," Cholena argued. "You know the Chrysoli won't back down. They'll come for us, and they'll come for you, too. Wouldn't it be better to take the offensive and take the fight to them on our terms?"

"Turqosi will not be found."

"Then you'll starve."

The Chalcedi was right. Food supplies on the rest of the planet were dwindling to nonexistent. Without supplies from the Chrysoli's massive farms, her army would slowly starve to death, and Leenha was not of a mind to continue their former ways of supplying slaves to masters who didn't show her proper respect. Besides, populations to take as slaves were as scarce as food. It was possible joining with these slaves and taking over the Chrysoli lands were her best options for survival. "Do as told," Leenha insisted. "No question. No argue. My way."

"We will listen to you and follow your lead."

"Respect."

"Of course."

Leenha stared at the ground for several beats, considering all options to see which was best for her army. Ultimately, she decided more was better. Without a word, she scuttled to Lise and Eteena and gestured her decision. When she saw Cholena, despondent, walk back to her group of slaves, she signaled for Lisa and Eteena to follow her and slithered over. "First," she shouted, "no standing in open." She gestured rapidly, and Lise and Eteena herded the slaves into two groups. "Follow."

The slaves appeared confused, but Cholena, smiling, nodded to them and motioned for the others to follow. Lise led one group to her section of Leenha's army, and Eteena led the other group to her side. "Follow," Leenha called out again. The slaves mingled with the Turqosi army, and when Leenha gave the signal for the spear formation, the Turqosi pulled the slaves into the proper alignment, then dragged them through the narrow river and into the brush on the opposite bank.

Cholena remained by Leenha's side. "This isn't the way to the encampment."

"Lose scent," Leenha explained as they waded the river. "And trail."

"I see," Cholena whispered.

"Never in open. Double back."

"Smart."

"Training."

"Yes. Thank you."

Leenha smirked. The slaves would make good fodder for the initial attack against the Chrysoli. She would have them rally the rest of the slaves against the masters. They might even do some damage. Then, after they were killed, her warriors would come in and clean up what was left, take over the masters' land and food, and press any surviving slaves into the service of the Turqosi. And all would be as it should be.

CHAPTER SEVEN

The Jacinthi

Meda grabbed Nikani in her talons and dove off the ledge.

She knew they had to get out of sight quickly, before Angeni sounded the alarm, so she ducked into a crevasse in the face of the mountain and waited. Quakes continued to send pebbles and stones rattling down the mountainside, so Meda pressed Nikani against the stone and took the brunt of the falling debris on her back.

"We can't stay here," Nikani whispered.

"I know."

"What are you waiting for?"

"I am waiting to see if Angeni sends other Jacinthi after us, or if Ogima sends the Chalcedi to hunt us down."

"Wouldn't it be better to get as far away as possible?"

Meda gestured toward the valley. "We have a broad, open expanse to cross before we reach any adequate cover. It would be best if we waited for sky fall unless that proves impossible."

"So, we wait here until sky fall or until some flyer starts looking."

Meda nodded. "Let us hope Ogima has greater concerns than two runaways."

As they waited, the valley beneath them roiled and split open like rotted fruit falling to the ground. Meda managed to control her urges to cry out as rocks grazed her, but Nikani expressed increasing concern. "You can't let the stones damage your wings, or we'll never escape. Trade places with me."

"You are much more vulnerable to damage. My feathers offer some protection."

"But we need your feathers more than I need my skin. Move." Nikani pulled Meda until she took his place against the wall of the crevasse. Then, he ducked his head toward Meda and allowed his back to be exposed to the rock falls.

When the sky light settled on the horizon, Nikani's back looked like Ogima had whipped him bloody. "Oh, my!" Meda exclaimed when he turned toward the valley.

"I'm fine. Let's go. I don't think anyone is coming, at least not yet."

Meda collected Nikani, being careful to avoid his wounds, and took off straight down the mountain to the tortured valley below. She tried to keep to the shadows as much as possible, hoping the encroaching darkness would cover their escape. As she turned to cross the valley floor, she asked, "Where should we go?"

Nikani grunted. "I say we go back to the Beryli shore to find our friends. We never should've left them to begin with."

Nikani had friends to return to, but Meda's kind were all on the high mountain, her home. Would she ever see her home again? Her clan? She knew their decision to flee from Ogima was final, no turning back. Even if they managed to get away without being seen, she was sure Ogima would not abide such disobedience without consequences. Meda sighed. "The Beryli, then."

She beat her wings with a fury she had rarely employed, pounding against the air with speed born of desperation and some degree of terror. Her imaginings of what Ogima would do to them if he found them fueled her strength. She wanted to make it beyond the hills and grasslands to the remnants of the Jasperi wood before they rested. Nikani's extra weight meant fatigue would come sooner than usual, but she knew she had to press on or risk capture, so she pounded away, straining her neck toward the goal as if it would hasten their arrival.

Nikani pointed out the jigsaw of rifts across the valley. "Look at that!" he shouted into the wind. The ground continued to buckle and shift every few beats, as if the planet was a discontented hatchling seeking a more comfortable perch. Meda wondered what had set off the quakes. Kwania would know—but she was lost to them. So much had been lost. Meda's eyes misted, but she gulped down her feelings and blinked the tears away. She knew she couldn't afford to indulge her hopeless thoughts, or they would never survive.

Darkness settled around them like a black cloak, and she flew on, relying on her internal sense of direction to guide them. They could no longer see the ground below, but they continued to hear the rumbling spasms.

"Do you think we're far enough away to stop and rest?" Nikani asked.

"I will not risk it." Meda redoubled her efforts. Nikani must've sensed her strength waning. Her wings ached as she had never felt before, even when she carried two of the visitors up the side of the mountain.

She had never been among the largest or strongest of her clan— Catori and Chevei vied for that title. Now, Catori used his strength to serve Ogima, and Chevei was—lost, like Kwania. What good was a Jacinthi prophetess? Strength was needed, strength and cunning and knowledge. At least Nikani was strong, for his species. What did she bring? What worth did she have to anyone?

"The darkness will hide us. I think we could rest for a few beats," Nikani urged.

"Are you tired?"

"No, I'm..."

"Then we keep going."

"What are you up to, little dove? Where are you going? Ogima seeks you even now."

Who was that? Meda snatched her head left and right but saw no one.

You were wise to leave when you did.

"You are a fool," Phobos hissed. "What possessed you to believe you could stand up to the likes of Ogima? You are weak. You are small. You are insignificant."

You might listen to Nikani and rest now. You will feel stronger after rest.

"Great idea! Rest and let the Chalcedi catch up to you!" Phobos cackled.

"We cannot rest," Meda murmured.

"That's right, little dove. Fly on. Fly fly fly. As fast as you can until you drop from the sky."

Do not listen. Strength of sarkikos is not the only kind of strength. I know of no one with a stronger spirit. Why do you think you were able to discern the real menu Ogima was serving? You knew in your spirit it was wrong, even before you could perceive it with your eyes.

"Too late, though, wasn't it? Too late for Angeni. Too late for Nadie and Hanai and your other friends. You have always been too late."

You were the first to see through Ogima's façade, and you warned them. Remember the warnings you gave to Angeni? That she did not heed them is due to Dark Ones, not you.

Dark Ones. That's who she was hearing. Was the other voice one of the ones Aleshanee called her friends?

"Always too little, too late. Isn't that right, little dove? You call yourself a prophetess, but you were always falling short. Angeni was the real prophetess. You call yourself wise, but you were, once again, not wise enough. Isusa and Kacina were much wiser than you. You call yourself loving, but as usual, you were not loving enough. Nadie loved more deeply than you ever could. You fancy yourself having knowledge and insight, but compared with Hanai, even your knowledge falls short. Never enough."

"Why, then, did Hanai and Nadie and Isusa and Kacina and Angeni fall under the spell of Ogima?" Sophosi challenged, her strong voice echoing in Meda's heart. "I speak truth."

Meda's chest expanded as she breathed in Sophosi's words. She clinched her beak, nodded, and tightened her grip on Nikani. "We will rest. I believe we could both receive benefit. Help me locate a place of concealment."

By the tiny sky lights, Nikani was able to discern what appeared to be a rock outcropping, likely pushed up by the quakes. "Do you think it would be safe to hide there, with the quakes and all?"

"We will chance it." Meda circled the rocks for a final look before landing among the shadows. She didn't hear the Dark One's voice again, but Sophosi remained to soothe and strengthen them for the cycles to come and guard them should Ogima send Dark Ones or Chalcedi to claim them.

Sleep was impossible for the two runaways, as the ground continued to heave and roll beneath them, but Meda did manage to rest her wings. Before the sky light rose, she gathered up Nikani and set out once again for the Beryli sea.

"You may want to fly low," Sophosi whispered, "in case the Chalcedi are seeking you in the sky." So, Meda hugged the tortured ground. Heavy, dark clouds gathered, and she was able to use the rising winds to glide and spare her wings.

As a purplish glow kissed the horizon, high above them, soaring through the building clouds, Meda caught sight of a Chalcedi flyer, clearly on the hunt. She believed the flyer was too far away to catch sight of them along the darkened ground, but to be safe, she landed in a rockslide from a fallen Onyxi hill. Meda and Nikani crouched in the shadows between the rocks until the flyer moved on. "He appears to be heading toward the Chalcedi aerie."

"Why go there?" Nikani wondered.

"I do not know."

"I guess we're lucky he isn't heading to the Beryli sea."

"Perhaps he is not searching for us but has a purpose for going to the far mountain."

"Looked like he was searching to me."

A few beats later, as Meda readied to take off with her charge, Nikani hissed, "Wait!" Another Chalcedi was flying nearby. They hid behind the rockfall again, waiting for the flyer to pass. "If this is what it's going to be like, we're never going to reach the Beryli."

"Surely Ogima will not leave the high mountain undefended. Protecting his person is more important to him than finding two runaways. After all, what can we do to him?"

"I have fantasies," Nikani whispered. Meda couldn't help but chuckle at the little Jasperi. He had a warrior's heart, even if his sarkikos belied his ability.

The gloom caused by the thickening clouds helped with their concealment, but it also made it increasingly difficult to spot any Chalcedi who might be hunting them. Nikani squirmed. "Let's go. I'm sick of waiting here. We haven't seen another flyer in many beats."

Meda clicked her beak and sighed, but collected Nikani in her talons and took off, keeping low to the ground as before. "Keep a sharp eye."

Sparks shot through the clouds, lighting them a dazzling white, then a crackle and booming like an explosion vibrated the air. More sparks, followed by more roaring clashes and strong gusts, shook Meda, making it difficult to maintain her course. She lowered her head against the force of the wind and pulled Nikani closer to her chest.

Suddenly, balls of ice the size of boulders began to pummel them from the sky. The ice spheres smashed against the ground at high speeds, leaving craters in the mud and flattening the burned-out husks of trees remaining on the landscape. "We must find shelter!" Meda cried, deftly dodging another ice ball. Nikani held on with all his strength as Meda ducked and twisted through the maze of flying ice.

Nikani spotted an indentation in what remained of a hill whose face had sheared off and pointed Meda toward it. Before they reached the cleft, however, Meda was struck by an ice ball. She tumbled in freefall, losing her grip on Nikani, who flailed and screamed as he fell straight to the ground and out of Meda's sight. Meda smashed into the side of the hill in a crumpled heap.

CHAPTER EIGHT

The Jasperi

Amadah stretched her aching limbs. Her heart thudded like it was beating through tree sap. Her eyes felt like she had been buried in a Topazi sand dune, but a warning echoed in her heart. They needed to move. They needed shelter.

Eleutheri and Na'ro gently urged their wards to awaken and gather themselves. The darkening clouds foretold of the next rage of their world against its inhabitants. It was imperative the sphere be protected, or all was lost. "We can lead you to a safe place, one you know," Eleutheri whispered to Amadah.

"We need to go." Amadah tried to sound forceful and assured, but her words came out as more of a hoarse grunt than a directive.

Misa nodded and stood, nudging Kilchi, who groaned and yawned before rising. Enla and Aleshanee were wrapped together in a dead sleep, and neither seemed willing or able to move.

Amadah knelt beside Aleshanee. "Our friends are saying we must go." With that, Aleshanee lifted her head, her eyes blinking against the rising sky light.

"Unhhh." Enla moaned and flopped her large paw over her head.

"Enla, wake up. We have to leave now," Aleshanee whispered.

"Our friends are taking us to a safe place. But they say we have to leave now."

"I can't," Enla muttered, turning away from her friends.

75

"We need you, Enla. We can't carry the sphere without your help."

At Amadah's words, Enla burst into tears, rolled into a ball, and hid her face in her paws.

Na'ro surrounded Enla with light and whispered soothing words to her heart. When Enla's sobs had abated, Na'ro said, "Come, now. Come back to us. Yiska frolics in the light. Have no fear, he is safe."

"Wha...?" Enla sat up slowly.

"Yiska lives now on the First World, dear heart. He has adventures as he always dreamed, and great joy as he always wanted."

"Yiska lives?"

"You will see him again," Na'ro assured her.

"It...how is it possible?"

"You must trust and hope. As Yiska would."

"What did you say?" Amadah's chest tightened, her breath short and quick through her nose. "What did you say about Yiska?"

"He—he lives?"

"Yiska is alive?"

"Our friend says so."

"How can that be?"

"We must go. The beats are short to reach safety. We will speak of this later," Eleutheri replied.

"I don't understand..." The edges of Amadah's vision clouded, and the landscape around her seemed to spin away. She heard her name as if spoken through a hollowed-out log, ringing in her ears. Then, she felt hands and paws touching her, and she realized she was on her back, staring up at the sky. "I—I think I fainted."

"Faint you did," Misa confirmed.

Amadah bolted up. "Easy now, easy." Kilchi nuzzled her to lie back down, but Amadah wouldn't be contained.

"Could Fala be alive? Is it possible?" But the Whisperers were silent. "Tell me!"

"We must go," Eleutheri repeated.

Chevei lifted his vine. "Let's go." As he took off. Aleshanee took her place beside the sphere as Kilchi shrugged into his harness. Misa took Yiska's place. Enla, moving as if in a fog, shambled to her spot and collected her harness.

"Come, Amadah," Aleshanee called. "Search your heart. You know of what they speak."

But Amadah felt no reassurance. She remained with only brief flashes of her experience of death—not like Aleshanee, who seemed to remember it all. To Amadah, the First World was more like a strange dream than reality, sensations and vague impressions with no substance. She wasn't sure it was a place—more like an idea.

Aleshanee brought Amadah back to the present. "Our friends say Kindra led us to this cave, before she became Kindred. Do you remember?"

"She and—Fala," Amadah's voice faded away.

"They found a cave with water, where they hid stores of food."

"I remember..."

Eleutheri whispered, "You will be safe and have provision there. But we must hurry. Follow Luxor's light."

Amadah saw a flash ahead, through the brush, and pointed. "This way." Kilchi strained against the harness, and they began their laborious trek through the undergrowth.

"You are turning away from the Beryli sea," Chevei cawed from above.

"We follow our friends," Aleshanee called out to him. She smiled as she heard Chevei's muttering complaints. "Nothing changes," she whispered to Amadah, shaking her head.

"Everything changes. I wish it wouldn't. I wish we could go back, back to my forest, back to before..."

"Amadah, you would never have met Fala," Aleshanee pointed out.

"Then I wouldn't be in so much pain."

"Losing the joy of the love you shared to avoid the pain of loss is a greater loss still," Misa observed.

"I wouldn't trade anything for meeting Misa." Kilchi glanced at the Saphiri laboring beside him in the harness, his eyes alight with love.

"Even your entire species?" Amadah snapped. Kilchi lowered his head and pulled the makeshift sled in silence.

"Amadah, that was cruel," Aleshanee whispered.

"He should think before he speaks."

"You know what he was saying. Kilchi meeting Misa was the only good thing he could take from the terrible disaster we have all experienced. Meeting Fala was your one good thing."

"What about you? What was your one good thing?" Amadah asked bitterly.

"I have many. I have seen the First World. Plus, I had no one in my clan who cared for me. They all thought me a foolish, silly child. Now, I have dear friends who love me. You are one of them. And I am very glad I met you."

Amadah began to weep again.

The group struggled forward in contemplative silence, as the clouds above them darkened and roiled, mirroring the ground's tremors of the previous cycle.

"Looking storm-like," Misa observed.

"We must hurry," Eleutheri urged again.

"Can you go any faster, Kilchi?"

"Trying." Kilchi grunted. Sparks shot across the sky, increasing their urgency. Finally, after what seemed interminable beats, they pulled the sled out of the undergrowth into an open area.

A short distance ahead, Amadah saw a familiar rise. "This is the place."

"How can we get this sled up that hill?" Kilchi cried. "It's hard enough to move it on this broken ground."

"Chevei, could you fly it up the hill, maybe with the two of us rolling it, if we took it off the sled?" Amadah called.

Chevei flew down and landed next to the sled. "I do not think it is possible. It is too heavy, and the land is too steep."

"What do we do now?" Aleshanee sent her question into the air.

"Hide the sphere in the cleft at the base of the hill," Luxor replied. "Here. Quickly. Then, follow me up to the cave."

"We cannot leave the sphere untended!" Chevei argued when he heard the plan. "One of us will need to remain with it to guard it."

"We can't. There isn't room in the cleft for the sphere and one of us," Amadah pointed out. "Plus, we can't risk someone else accidently touching the sphere."

"The sphere will be safe during the storm," Eleutheri assured Amadah. "But you will not be if you are in the open. You must hurry and follow Luxor."

"Our friends say the sphere will be safe until the storm passes. Let's roll it in." Amadah and Aleshanee tied the vine ropes around the sphere, and Kilchi, Enla, Misa, and Chevei used the ropes to roll the sphere off the sled and near the split in the face of the rise. As Kilchi pulled with his rope, Amadah and Aleshanee pushed the sphere. It gathered enough momentum for Amadah and Aleshanee to push the sphere into the fissure.

"You are out of beats. Move!" Luxor commanded. The group scrambled up the hill, following Amadah over the hill and down the other side.

"There!" Amadah pointed to a barely visible opening in the next hillock. At that moment, sparks split the sky and massive balls of ice plummeted to the ground, pounding holes in the dirt around them. Luxor spread her shield over them as they slid the rest of the way down the hill, climbed up the knoll to the opening, and one by one crawled inside.

The cave was small, dank, and humid from the trickle of water running at the back of it, but the parched group didn't seem to mind. They took turns drinking from the tiny stream until they felt refreshed.

Aleshanee uncovered the stores Kindra and Fala had hidden in the cave. "We have food!" She passed items around to each member of the group.

Amadah remained near the mouth of the cave, looking out at the destruction wrought by the continuing ice storm. Aleshanee approached her tentatively and offered her some food. Amadah turned with a rueful smile. "Even now, Fala provides for me." Her eyes brimmed as she took a bite.

Although relieved to be out of the pelting ice, refreshed with water, and filled with food for the first cycle in many, the group's mood was somber. No one tried to talk over the cacophony of the storm. The wind howled outside the opening, and sparks danced across the sky, followed by thunderous booms that rattled the rocks and hurt their ears, and the ice balls slamming against their hillock was like being inside a beating heart.

Amadah could almost see Fala crawling to the cave, handing little Kindra one item after another through the opening to save their food supply. Her mind skipped across her memories, and she could see him silhouetted atop a rock, the lookout for the group. He never seemed to tire. She saw him sliding effortlessly across the dark field to confront the flying creatures they later learned were the Jacinthi of the high mountain. Once again, she saw his claw grasping down into the sand to find purchase so he could pull her out and save her life. She felt his sarkikos covering hers as she wept for the loss of so many in her clan. It was so tangible, so real to her, she reached to clasp his claw in her hand, but found only air, and her tears flowed anew.

CHAPTER NINE

The Chrysoli

Tocho stepped onto the portico, his golden eyes fixed on the clouds descending toward the Chrysoli dome. "Kola." Kola scampered to his side. "These clouds are strange. What say our weatherseers?"

"I will return with their report." Kola hurried toward the large building housing the scientific research center.

Tocho strode to the observation platform, usually meant for watching over their slaves, and climbed up to take a closer look at the sky beyond the dome. Flashes of jagged light cut through the clouds, followed by a roar that shook even their impenetrable covering. He knew from experience their dome was resistant to strikes, so that didn't concern him, but something was making his chest tight. He paced the platform and grumbled against Kola's delay.

Finally, Kola, accompanied by Miakoda, the weatherseer, came into sight. Tocho whistled sharply, then gestured for the weatherseer to join him on the platform. As Miakoda stepped off the stair, Tocho snapped, "You gave us no warning!"

"We have never seen anything like—it could not be predicted!" Miakoda trembled.

"And why is that?" Tocho's voice lowered to a dangerous rumble.

"We had no warning signs! Our sky sensors registered nothing until the clouds were already upon us. The pressure gauges dropped precipitously with no hint of impending storm activity prior."

"Explain how this is possible."

81

"I cannot explain." Another flash above them caused Miakoda to startle.

The clouds lowered until they engulfed the dome in a shroud. With the exception of the light from the sparks, the Chrysoli stood in complete darkness. Then, out of the darkness, something slammed against the dome, followed by another and another. Miakoda shrieked as one of the objects crashed into the dome, leaving a jagged crack above her head.

"Get everyone inside," Tocho roared. They bolted down the stairs, Kola running to ring the bell, while Miakoda hurried back to the science building, and Tocho bellowed instructions to his guards. The noise from beyond the dome was deafening. Tocho realized the slaves in the fields would never hear the ringing of the bell, and he couldn't afford to lose more slaves, so he directed two of his guards to the fields to bring the slaves back to their barracks.

Tocho kept a wary eye on the dome as he watched his pride rushing to and fro around him, trying to get to their homes. He saw the slaves from the nearest fields running beneath the whip of their guard as a deluge of objects pummeled the dome above them. Feathered cracks appeared in the dome under the onslaught. "To the barracks!" he roared, but his voice couldn't overcome the terrible pounding. His ears ached from the unrelenting din.

He heard Kola scream, "Look out!" At the same beat he heard a loud crunch above him. He looked up just as a section of the dome collapsed toward him, then everything went black.

CHAPTER TEN

The Dark Ones

Phobos sidled up to Ogima, who paced in his chambers, wringing his hands and mumbling under his breath. "I found the runaways, Lord."

"And?"

"One of the hated light ones was with them."

"And?"

"I thought I was reaching the Jacinthi. She was wavering, I swear it. Then, the light one spoke to her and..."

"You lost?"

"I know where they are, Lord," Phobos asserted quickly. "I can lead you to them. We can bring them back, no problem there!"

"I've sent an idiot to do my work," Ogima muttered. "You cannot turn one Jacinthi? What about the Jasperi?"

"He did not seem to hear, Lord."

"The god of fear could not stir fear in a Jasperi CHILD?"

"Lord, the light one..."

"Never mind. I'm upset enough. Chatan came back with the report that the Chalcedi mountain has collapsed, I assume because of the same ground tremors threatening this mountain. This wrinkle was—unexpected."

Phobos appeared relieved the blame had shifted from his shoulders. "Unexpected, Lord?" he simpered, rubbing Ogima's nose in his failure.

"Something strange is afoot, but how can I know what is happening, strapped in this sarkikos. I'm sick and tired of being stuck in this pile of bones!"

"I'm with you, Lord. I miss your magnificence, the glory of your presence, the wonder of..."

"Oh, shut up! I'm irritated enough without your groveling."

"Lord Ogima!" Angeni burst into his chambers, uninvited.

Ogima opened his mouth to berate her and considered throwing her into the flames rising in the center of the cave toward the oculus in the ceiling but stopped himself, took a breath, and purred, "What is it?"

"Dark clouds with sparks in them lower over the high mountain. I believe we should bring everyone to safety inside the throne room."

"Very well then, handle it."

"I will, Lord." Angeni bowed and backed out of the entrance.

Ogima looked at Phobos. "First quakes, then the mountain collapses, now storms? What is happening?" At that beat, Ogima heard screams outside his cavern. He rushed to the entrance to see his subjects running pell-mell across the open area, and large balls of ice shattering around them. Creatures screaming and running, sparks sizzling, thunder booming, ice pounding against stone—the chaos was overwhelming, the noise deafening. Ogima's lips curled above his teeth. He couldn't help himself, he so loved turmoil and terror.

"Lord..." Phobos hissed.

"Right. To the throne, everyone! You will be safe there, I promise you!"

Creatures were being struck by the falling ice, but they seemed to be helping each other, so Ogima felt no compulsion to render aid. He thought about remaining in his cave to wait out the storm, not wanting to risk this sarkikos, but then he considered what a relief it would be to be shed of it and decided to walk amongst his subjects, exuding confidence and eschewing fear. He turned to Phobos. "Whip up their fear to terror levels, while I demonstrate my power over the elements."

"At once, Lord." Phobos sneered and darted among the fleeing creatures. "It is over! The end has come! Death! You won't make it!

You will die a horrible, twisted, painful death! You will be struck down! All is lost!"

The howls and screams rose to a crescendo, and the chaos worsened, just as Ogima planned. Where the ice hit higher on the mountain, rocks loosened and tumbled, adding to the cacophony. Ogima walked out into the throng, instructing everyone to get to safety, pointing and gesturing directions, urging calm while claiming his throne room had powerful shielding that would protect them. Once everyone was safely ensconced, Ogima stood guard at the entrance. "I will shield you!" He waved his arms in the air as if he could control the winds.

After many long beats, once the ice storm started to abate, Ogima strode to the edge of the protrusion overlooking the valley. He lifted his hands and called out to the storm. "I am the Lord of all, protector of my clan, the most high God. You will obey my commands. You will not harm another of my subjects, I command it."

Pseudos, Hedraios, and Ademoneos flitted from subject to subject, extolling Ogima's virtues and his power, and the helplessness of the clan without him. When Ogima returned to the throne room, all were on their knees, foreheads on the dirt, hands outstretched, praising his name. Ogima pranced around the cavern, touching lowered heads and allowing his subjects to touch his feet.

"The ice fell all around him but did not touch him!"

"The very winds obey him!"

"He saved us from the terrible storm!"

"Heal my wounds, great Lord!"

"I must rest and consider the meaning of this storm," Ogima called out to his worshippers. "You may remain here until the darkness has passed." He went to Angeni. "Tend the injured, and I had best not hear of anyone dying. Show me you can handle something on your own."

"Of course, mighty Lord." Angeni bowed low.

Ogima gestured for his Dark Ones to follow him back to his chambers. "I fear remaining in this sarkikos has left me blind and deaf. I need you to be my eyes and ears. I believe the creatures here are sufficiently brainwashed to remain loyal to me, and I can always have the Chalcedi dose their food should the thought of rebellion rear its head. Phagos, stay behind to control the Chalcedi. The rest of you, go out into the land. Find all the creatures remaining alive, observe them, stir up bitterness and hopelessness and discord as you can, then report back to me on any movements or plans."

"Yes, Lord."

"Thanatos, you are tasked with observing the land itself. See what is happening abroad and tell me what you observe. The land itself appears to be in rebellion. I must know what to expect next. Start with the Chalcedi mountain."

"I will, Lord."

"I am most interested in the Chrysoli. How are they vulnerable? What are their weaknesses? How can we exploit them and bring them into the fold?"

"They are my wards, Lord. I will monitor them and report," Pleonexos replied.

"And I must know the status and location of the child and the two witnesses and their followers." Ogima glared at each Dark One in turn.

"The child has vanished, Lord. I swear it!" Phobos whimpered.

"Yet, the hated light ones remain! Believe me, she lives, and she is here, somewhere. Find her and her followers!"

"Yes, Lord."

CHAPTER ELEVEN

The Onyxi

$\mathcal{E}$nla didn't relish feeling stuck in a cave. Now that she knew what it was to be out and roaming free, she felt trapped in the confined space. So, as soon as the ice stopped falling, she stuck her head out of their little hole. Sporadic sparks continued high within the clouds, and the wind ruffled her fur, but the danger appeared to have passed.

"I'm going down to check on the sphere," she told the others.

"Do you want company?" Kilchi asked.

"No, I'll go alone." She lumbered down the hillock. "I imagine I'll be going it alone from now on." She wondered if Yiska could hear her from his comfortable home on the First World. Deciding it was worth the chance, she said, "I miss you. You were—are—my best friend. What am I going to do without you?" She listened for a response as she crawled back up the neighboring hill, but silence pressed around her. After such a loud storm, the quiet felt eerie.

From the hilltop, she could see their makeshift sled, still where they'd left it at the base of the hill—and it was bashed to bits. The ice had done its work. Enla groaned. "Now what?"

A groan echoed back to her. Strange. She sat down, deciding it would be much easier to slide down the hill than climb down. Before she could begin, another groan wafted up on the wind. "Was that the wind?"

She thought she heard a sound like a squeak. "Is something out there?" A surreal image of an injured Yiska crawling out of the crevasse, dragging himself across the open field to find his friends, flashed across her mind. "Yiska?"

Nothing. What was wrong with her? She must be imagining things to dispel the dead silence. She started her slide, but midway down she heard an unmistakable moaning noise. She dug her claws into the rocky dirt and skidded to a stop.

"Who's there? Show yourself." Silence.

Enla considered returning for Kilchi or Chevei. This could be a trap, someone coming after the sphere. She vowed she would never divulge the location, no matter what they did to her. Yiska had died to protect that sphere. She wouldn't dishonor him by failing to keep it out of the wrong hands.

But why go for help? She was so used to relying on Yiska as a steadying presence, she felt like she needed his strength to make it, but what she really needed was to prove she could handle things on her own. At least to herself. "I'm coming down. Don't try anything."

Rather than sliding, Enla stood in her Onyxi way and waddled down the hillside, scanning left and right as she went. Far off to the left, she spotted what looked like a wadded blue blanket. Trembling, Enla angled toward the object, slowing her steps down to a crawl. She wasn't sure what she was seeing until the object moved, and she thought she recognized the shape of a wing. Was it a Jacinthi? Who would be so far away from the high mountain?

Forgetting her misgivings, Enla scrambled down the hill, almost falling on her face twice. She began to make out feathers, and she thought she saw the shape of a tail. The bluish color let her know it was indeed Jacinthi, not Chalcedi. "It's Enla. Do you remember me? Who are you?"

The Jacinthi lifted her head with another loud moan. "Enla?"

Enla thought she recognized the feathered face. "Meda? Is that you? How did you get here? What happened?"

"Storm," Meda managed to squeak out. "Hit by ice."

Enla scurried as fast as an Onyxi could to Meda's side. "Are you badly injured? Anything broken?"

"I do not know." Meda groaned. "Everything hurts."

"You fell from the sky? How horrible!"

Meda gave one wing a single flutter, testing for broken or cracked cartilage. "Help me roll over."

Enla hesitated to use her clumsy paws to push Meda off her side, but Meda asked for help again, so Enla closed her eyes and shoved as gently as she could until Meda was face down on the hill. Meda ruffled her other wing and breathed a sigh. "I do not believe anything is broken on my wings."

"Can you sit up?" Enla asked.

"Help me, please." After a few awkward, failed attempts, Enla was able to raise Meda onto her talons. Meda sat for several beats, her breaths whistling through her beak, before she opened her eyes and smiled at Enla. "I believe I am in one piece, just badly bruised. Alarm contorted Meda's face. "Nikani!"

"Nikani? Amadah's friend? He's here?"

"I was carrying him when we were struck. He fell further down the hill."

"Are you good here if I go see if I can find him?"

"Yes, go, please go. Oh, I could not bear it if he..."

"Don't think that. I'll find him." Enla rumbled the rest of the way down the hill, then ranged, first toward their demolished sled, then back the other direction until the hill curved such that Meda was out of sight. She found no sign of Nikani, so she extended her search onto the open field. Nothing. Enla decided to enlist her group's help. Amadah would want to know her friend was here, although Enla wished she could report good news to Amadah. She certainly had received enough bad news for one cycle.

Enla crawled back up the hill to Meda. "I can't find him. My group is in a cave, on the other side of that second hill." She pointed. "You wait here. I'm going to go get them so we can all search for him. Are you good?"

"Yes, please go. Stillness helps with the pain, so I will wait here for your return." Meda closed her eyes.

Enla nodded and took off for the little cave where her friends were concealed. As she approached the opening, she called out,

"Amadah! Nikani and Meda are here!" She heard muffled exclamations from within the cave. "Come on! We need to find Nikani!"

Kilchi was first to exit the cave. "What are you talking about?"

"Meda and Nikani were caught in the ice storm. When Meda was struck by an ice boulder, she dropped Nikani, and now I can't find him."

"Is Meda hurt?"

"Yes, but she says nothing is broken."

Amadah exited the cave. "Where did she drop him?"

"Meda is on the face of the first hill, down that way. I think she must've dropped him further out on the field than I looked, because he wasn't anywhere near the base of the hill."

Amadah was already scrambling over the hill as Enla finished her explanation and was out of sight before Kilchi and Enla started moving to catch up.

Misa stuck her head out of the opening. "Kilchi?"

"Nikani and Meda," was all Kilchi said as he bolted to the top of the hill.

"Meda was injured, and I can't find Nikani," Enla explained..

Aleshanee and Chevei stepped from the cave, and Misa turned to Chevei. "Flying above is best for a search." Chevei nodded and took off to glide over the open field. Misa ducked in the cave and grabbed one of the makeshift containers holding the fruit from the living tree, then she and Aleshanee joined Enla walking over the ridge and up and down the next hill. When they caught up with Kilchi, he was checking Meda carefully for wounds. Misa offered Meda a bite of fruit, which she accepted gratefully, and after one bite, Meda rose.

"I feel as if I was never injured. How is this possible?"

"Receiving special healing powers on our journey is now for your benefit," Misa replied.

"I will want to hear your story, but now I will join in the search for Nikani." A rush of wind, and Meda was airborne.

Chevei and Meda made broad circles overhead. Enla spotted Amadah running across the open space beyond the base of the hill, and she hurried to join her in the search, calling Nikani's name, but they had no success. The thought crossed Enla's mind that Nikani, injured, might have hidden himself to prevent capture or worse, so she returned to the base of the hill and crouched on all fours to look for fissures large enough to contain a small Jasperi. Her search brought her back to the crevasse holding the sphere, and there she spotted two small feet, barely visible near the edge of the opening.

"Nikani! Nikani, it's Enla. Amadah is here." But Nikani didn't move or speak. The blood drained from Enla's head, and her claws dug into her paw pads. What if Nikani had unsuspectingly touched the sphere? He would be dead, just like Yiska. "Nikani!" she screamed, frantic. She dared not reach in and move him, lest she drag him into the sphere and kill him—if he wasn't already dead.

Amadah ran toward Enla, Kilchi, Misa, and Aleshanee close behind. "Where is he?"

"There." Enla pointed, panting. "We can't move him, or he'll touch the sphere. What if…"

"Aleshanee, help me." Amadah ducked into the fissure, wrapped her arms around the sphere, and heaved against it. Aleshanee stepped around to the other side and pushed, but the sphere barely budged.

"Could you slide Nikani out safely?" Kilchi asked.

"I'm not sure. He's tucked back deep in here, and I'm afraid he might brush the sphere."

"We need help," Aleshanee said.

Kilchi dashed to the crushed sled and snagged a length of vine in his jaws, taking it back to the crevasse. "Here." His breath whistled through clenched teeth.

Aleshanee took the piece of vine, and she and Amadah tied it around the center of the sphere. Then, Kilchi took the vine in his jaws again, dug his claws into the dirt, and pulled, his haunches rippling with the strain. Amadah and Aleshanee continued to roll the sphere from within the crevasse. Misa bent down to smooth the ground before the sphere, hoping it would help the sphere move. When the sphere slid a fraction of a metric, the vine snapped, and Kilchi screamed, "Look out!" The sphere rocked back into the crevasse.

"This isn't working," Aleshanee groaned.

"I'll pick up Nikani and use my sarkikos to shield him from touching the sphere," Amadah said.

"What if he's injured, and picking him up makes it worse?" Kilchi asked.

"We'll just have to chance it." Amadah squeezed around the sphere to where Nikani's legs protruded from behind it. "Aleshanee, help me."

Aleshanee slid beside Amadah. Enla couldn't get the image of Yiska, eyes and mouth wide in terror, staring at the sky, from her mind. "Is he—dead?"

"I don't know."

Chevei and Meda landed near the group huddled around the opening. "Nikani?"

"He's in there, but we don't know yet if he…" Kilchi paused, then said, "Chevei, between the two of us, do you think we could pull the sphere out of the hole?"

"Perhaps."

Kilchi ran to grab another piece of vine, which he handed to Amadah. "Wrap it around the sphere. We're going to try again. You two, steady it."

Amadah encircled the center of the sphere with the vine, handed Chevei the end, then handed Kilchi the other end "Let's try it."

Chevei gave a strong beat of his wings as Kilchi strained again against the sphere's weight. Amadah pushed while Aleshanee positioned herself between the sphere and Nikani, in case the sphere rocked back again. Still the sphere wouldn't budge.

Meda took to the air and joined Chevei pulling on the vine, then Enla stepped in and pulled with Kilchi. Finally, the sphere began to creep forward. Once they managed to get it rolling, they were able to pull it free from the crevasse. The light beamed from the sphere, bathing the sky.

"What is that thing?" Meda gasped as she and Chevei landed.

Aleshanee came out of the crevasse, followed by Amadah, carrying a bloodied and unconscious Nikani. She laid him gently on the ground. Kilchi put his snout against Nikani's nose to check him for breath. After a few beats, he lifted his head. "I think he's still breathing."

Relief washed over Enla like a cold rain. Misa knelt beside Nikani and dripped some juice from the fruit into his mouth. In a few beats, his eyes started to flutter.

"Nikani?" Amadah leaned over her friend. "Nikani, it's me, Amadah."

"Amadah?" Nikani croaked. Amadah clutched Nikani to her chest.

"Praise the light, touching the sphere you did not," Misa breathed. "Eat this." Nikani bit into the juicy fruit.

"How did you end up in that hole?" Amadah asked.

Nikani munched the bite of fruit. "When Meda was struck by the ice, I fell and landed on the side of the hill and rolled down to the bottom. I managed to crawl into the hole to get away from the falling ice. I guess I blacked out after that. How did you find me—us?"

"We were in a cave on the hill beyond, escaping the ice storm, too. We put the sphere in the fissure to keep it safe."

"What is the sphere? Where did you find it? What is its purpose?" Meda's questions tumbled out like water down a mountainside.

"We have a lot to tell you." Amadah sighed. "A lot has happened since we last saw you."

"Amadah—I—I'm so sorry. I'm sorry I left you. It was a terrible, terrible mistake." Nikani lowered his head.

"I'm just so glad you're alive."

"I, too, am grieved I left with the others. We have much to tell you, also, about Ogima and the high mountain." As Meda shared their story, rage and sorrow, disgust and anguish, and wonder and terror flowed freely.

"I—can't express how sorry I am for—about Fala." Nikani couldn't seem to meet Amadah's eyes. Amadah spoke no words as she turned away to climb back to their stores over the hill. Nikani watched, tears filling his eyes.

"We have supplies—food and water," Kilchi explained. "I'll go with her to bring them down."

"I'll come, too," Enla said. Aleshanee, Misa, and Chevei remained with Meda and Nikani.

"Amadah, are you good?" Enla asked as they caught her. Again, Amadah remained silent. So, Kilchi and Enla walked to the cave on either side of their friend without another word.

They piled the supplies on Kilchi's back, and Enla and Amadah shrugged the water containers over their shoulders. As they left the little cave to return to their friends at the base of the hill, Kilchi's expression was grim. "We have some problems to solve." Amadah grunted in agreement. "What will we do without the sled?"

"We needed a better way to carry the sphere anyway," Enla said. "That sled was too hard to move and too slow."

"Well, we have two flyers now, so that'll help. Maybe they could carry it if we made a sling for them."

"It's awfully heavy for just two. We'll have to work together."

Kilchi sighed. "I'm fresh out of ideas."

"At least we have food and water now." Enla didn't feel the positive attitude she tried to express. To her, their situation was hopeless, and without Yiska, who could restore her hope?

They walked the rest of the way down the hill in uneasy silence, the tension of their impossible predicament and the gravity of their losses weighing them down more than the heavy loads they carried.

Nikani was standing when they reached the bottom of the hill. The fruit had done its work, and he suffered no ill effects from his tumble.

"I've been explaining to Meda and Nikani about the sphere." Aleshanee grimaced. "And they've been sharing about Ogima's stronghold on the high mountain. We're going to have trouble getting the sphere where it needs to go. Apparently, he is living in the cavern with the opening to the sky, where Angeni had the altar."

"Where we thought we'd take the sphere," Enla said.

"Yes."

"That's bad."

"I don't know this Ogima. What's he like?" Kilchi asked.

"It is Ogima—and it is not Ogima." Chevei's brow furrowed.

"Ogima was a groveling, pitiable creature when I first met him," Amadah said. "But the ruler of the Dark Ones controls him now."

"The one who killed us," Aleshanee whispered.

"He does a lot of stuff to make himself appear very powerful." Nikani made a sour face.

Meda took up the story, "However, Nikani and I were able to discern they were tricks and deceptions as much as any real power. He uses strange substances to control his subjects and convince them they are seeing what he wants them to see."

"If your plan is to take the sphere to Ogima's stronghold, you need to know how to move within the mountain. I can help with that." Nikani's half-smile didn't last long. "There are hundreds of interconnecting caves honeycombing the mountain, and I've explored most of them."

"Going on to the Beryli Sea to get more numbers seems to be the best plan still," Misa said.

Enla shook her head. "We are closer to the high mountain from here than from the Beryli Sea."

"We haven't solved the problem of how we're going to move the sphere yet, so we can't go either direction until we have a plan. Any ideas?" Kilchi asked.

No one spoke for several beats, then Nikani spoke up. "What if we create a method for rolling the sphere instead of having to carry it?"

"How? Amadah and I tried to roll it and couldn't, and we're the only ones who can touch it," Aleshanee replied.

"No, we need to use...hmmm—create like a steering...let me think for a beat." Nikani paced back and forth, gesturing in the air as if drawing something with his hands.

"We had a sled before, but it was rough going. And since Yiska..." Kilchi's head dropped to his chest. "Well, we lost one of our strongest members."

"I am not the strongest amongst the Jacinthi, but I will assist in any way I am able," Meda offered.

Nikani stopped his pacing. "You could still use the same idea you had with the sled, but instead of the sphere being on the sled, you'd let the sphere sit on the ground, between two—poles. They'd need to be long enough, but then you could use the front pole to steer and the back pole to push. The sphere would roll along the ground." He seemed to be warming to his idea. "And, with two flyers, they could be attached to the poles from above using those same vines and help to keep it rolling."

"Interesting." Chevei looked to the sky. "I believe I can imagine your design. The problem is we have no poles."

"Tree trunks."

"And where do we find trees?" Chevei gestured around the open spaces surrounding them, the low brush in the distance in one direction, and the hills in the other.

"There are plenty of burned out, fallen tree trunks in the Jasperi forest."

"You're speaking of dividing our group again." Enla shook her head. "Because we can't carry the sphere to the Jasperi forest to get the trunks, so some of us would have to go and leave the rest behind with the sphere. I'm not comfortable with that. And how long would it take to get there?"

"By flight it would take less than one cycle to get there and back." Chevei gestured to Meda. "Meda and I could go."

"But what if something happened to you? What if Ogima captured you? We wouldn't have a way of knowing until it was too late to help you. I can't—I won't lose anyone else." Enla crossed her arms across her chest with a grunt. As far as she was concerned, her word was final.

Aleshanee stroked Enla's arm. "It isn't up to you who lives and who dies, Enla. You have no control over such things. What we're trying to do is dangerous. At some point, we will have to face Ogima."

"And I know just what I'll do when we face him." Nikani's eyes narrowed to slits.

96

Aleshanee raised her hand to silence Nikani. "And when we do, some of us will be called to the First World. But we're trying to save this world from forever destruction, and that's worth it."

A tear slid through the fur on Enla's cheek.

"Fala died for it." Amadah's voice cracked, and she swallowed hard. "Yiska died for it. We all may die for it. But if we don't do it, the whole world will die. I say Chevei, go with Meda, gather some tree trunks to act as poles, and let's give Nikani's suggestion a try. If it works, we will take the sphere directly to the high mountain. Unless someone else has another idea?"

No one spoke. Enla knew Amadah and Aleshanee were right. She needed to be strong and brave, like Yiska. But her paws trembled, her stomach roiled like the ice storm clouds, and her heart felt ripped open like the ground after a quake. She didn't know if she could make it, not without her Yiska—not alone.

"You are not alone," Na'ro whispered. "You are surrounded by friends who love you. And we are here to guide you and help you."

"Are we doing the right thing?"

"We're doing what we have to do," Amadah replied.

Enla looked at Amadah, who was standing again, her eyes clear, her mouth set. If she could do it—Enla nodded. "I'm ready."

Chevei turned to Meda. "Are you ready to fly?"

"I am ready."

"The poles need to be at least five metrics long," Nikani said.

"Five metrics," Chevei repeated, and he and Meda leapt into the air with a strong beat of their wings.

"Come back to us!" Enla called as they gained altitude and disappeared into the clouds.

Then, Aleshanee sang:
> "Love and faithfulness meet together,
> Hope and peace join hands in strength.
> The Forever goes before us
> And prepares the way for our steps.
>
> The Great Love is our light,

Why would we fear?
The Great Love is our strength,
Who can make us afraid?

When evil comes against us,
It is our enemies who will stumble.
For the Forever will keep us in His shelter
And set our feet upon the high mountain."

"Will the Forever, Aleshanee? Will our feet be set upon the high mountain?"

"Hope will not put us to shame."

"Hope, then." Enla sighed. "I choose hope."

CHAPTER TWELVE

The Chrysoli

Kola bounded to Tocho's side. The master lay still, a section of the dome pinning him underneath its bulk. "Help me! The master!" He motioned for the guards who were herding the slaves to their quarters to come to his aid.

"Move it!" one of the guards screamed, whipping the slaves toward the broken piece of the dome. They encircled Tocho, grabbed the edges of the glass, and lifted it. As a loose piece of the dome clattered down on top of them, they dropped the shard and scrambled away. Two slaves were crushed. .

Kola roared in frustration. The idiot slaves had dropped the heavy glass back on Tocho. He snatched the whip from the guard's hands and beat the backs of the slaves bloody. "Pick it up! Pick it up!" The slaves shifted the dome piece a few metrics away from Tocho's prone form, then dropped it before they fled to their quarters, their guard bellowing orders and snapping at their heels as they ran.

In a flash of golden fur, Kola was by Tocho's side, checking his breathing and listening for his heartbeat. His breaths were shallow, his heart rate rapid. Looking at the remaining guard, he growled, "Get the medichi. Quickly."

"Aye." She bounded off to the science building. Beats passed, and Kola was beginning to despair as Tocho appeared to be worsening, when he spied the guard running toward them, followed by two other figures dodging falling shards and ice balls. It was the medichi, and the slave, Kwania. What was she doing here? Kola growled under his breath as she approached the master.

"I can help." Kwania pawed up and down the master's limbs and chest. "I see no open wounds."

The medichi knelt beside Tocho. "He is bleeding internally." The medichi pressed against his abdomen. "We must get him into surgery. Are you a trained medichi?"

"I can assist," Kwania replied.

"Help carry him!" Kola barked at the guard.

"Carefully. We don't know if his spine is injured."

Kola used his sarkikos like a stretcher, lying on the ground beside Tocho, while the guard, Kwania, and the medichi lifted Tocho and placed him on Kola's back. They held him in place as Kola padded toward the science building, trying to avoid swaying or bouncing the unconscious sarkikos while avoiding the falling balls of ice and shattering pieces of dome. It seemed an impossible task.

Once inside, Kola deposited Tocho on a stretcher, and he was wheeled away, the medichi and Kwania on either side. Without waiting a beat, Kola rushed back outside. Someone had to take charge while Tocho was down, and he was the most likely candidate.

The ice continued to pound the dome. Cracks snaked throughout its surface, and huge sections of glass continued to fall. A number of slaves, struck by glass or by balls of ice coming through the broken areas of the dome, lay around the open yard like discarded trash. Some slaves continued to run in from the fields. Kola knew he would find more slaves injured or killed on the fields. It was an unimaginable disaster.

"The crops?" he called to the guards running behind the slaves.

"Flattened."

Their leader was seriously injured and could die. Their protective dome was obliterated and useless. Their crops were destroyed. An ice ball fell nearby through a hole in the dome, and Kola realized he needed to get inside until the storm subsided. He decided to check on Tocho, because if the master didn't recover, it would fall to Kola to clean up this mess, and he didn't relish the task.

Inside the science building, he barked, "Surgery?" to a Chrysoli scientist rushing down the hall.

"Follow me. He pushed through two sets of double doors into an antechamber with a floor to ceiling glass wall overlooking a room filled with tubes, tables, and mechanistics. Tocho was on one of the tables, surrounded by several Chrysoli and Kwania. The antechamber was filled with observers, scientists of various types who had heard their master was wounded and who were either there to gawk or mourn or cheer, depending on their experiences with Tocho.

Kola approached Miakoda, the weatherseer. "How is it looking?"

"There is so much blood. The medichi is working quickly, trying to repair the damage before too much blood is lost to save him. But the Jacinthi slave has made a strange suggestion." Miakoda pointed. "See how she taps the blood of that young Chrysoli scientist and sends it through tubing into the hide of the master? She claims it will replace the blood he has lost without harming the young Chrysoli."

"How odd!"

"I've never heard of anything like it. If it works, it will be the reason Tocho lives, because the internal damage is severe."

"You've been working with Kwania, the slave, on looking into the sky light's changes. What have you learned?"

Miakoda sighed. "I've learned I know very little about the sky light. Kwania has knowledge beyond any Chrysoli. Tocho was wise to listen to her warning."

"What has she been doing in the lab?"

"She is using our equipment to measure changes in the sky light's diameter and shape, the yellow film surrounded it, and changes to our atmosphere, which she claims could account for the strange weather patterns we've observed lately."

"How could the sky light change our weather patterns?"

"According to Kwania, the sky light directly affects our weather and our atmosphere, even though it is far away. She has studied these effects for all her cycles. She has great knowledge, which she shares freely, although only a slave."

"What does she propose we do about it?"

"She has made no suggestion yet. But, Kola, look at her creativity in an area where she is not the expert of her kind. Imagine what she can do in the field where she is the expert."

At that moment, Kwania was removing the tube from the young Chrysoli and transferring it to a second volunteer. "It looks like she's sticking the tube into the sarkikos directly." Kola watched with a mixture of fascination and disgust.

"She punctures the skin until she finds a blood source."

"And that's not dangerous?"

"She says it is not."

Kola's eyes narrowed. "As you say. If Tocho dies, she dies with him. If he lives, she will be elevated in his eyes, perhaps even freed."

A slave guard rushed into the antechamber, his head on a swivel until he spotted Kola. "Master, the slaves!"

"What about them?"

"The flyers are escaping!"

"Stop them!"

"We can't! They fly freely from the dome. There are too many of them for us to stop them all, and those we try to stop overpower us. They even take the youngling flyers. Some are carrying other, smaller species with them when they go. What should we do?"

Kola's chest tightened. He glanced at Tocho, prone on the table with his sarkikos laid open, and imagined the punishment he would render when he woke to find his slave population further depleted. Kola couldn't let this happen. He stared at the ground. "Enlist the other slaves, particularly the ones who serve as trustees, to capture and contain the flyers."

"The other slaves cheer their escape. They won't help."

"Threaten them with punishment if they refuse. They'll help you then."

"Aye, Master." The young guard dashed from the room to carry out Kola's orders.

"Don't fail, or the punishment will be yours," Kola called after him.

"Aye."

Kola turned to Miakoda. "Keep me posted on Tocho's recovery. I must attend to these rebellious slaves." Kola followed the guard from the antechamber and onto the open area, where he spied his guards wrestling with a particularly large Chalcedi. Kola diverted his course to a storage area, where he collected coils of rope to take to the guards. All flyers would need to be secured to a guard or to a stake from now on, until the dome was repaired.

Kola realized he needed to get the engineers working on the repair immediately. Not only could the slaves escape, the entire Chrysoli population was vulnerable to attack as long as the dome was open to the outside world. Kola couldn't let that happen.

CHAPTER THIRTEEN

The Topazi

Fala, so used to being assured and strong, felt as ragged as a frond buffeted in a sandstorm. The collapse of the mountain told him Kindra had gone to the First World—because of his choice. Now, it was as if the whole world had shattered, releasing chaos into the air like a swarm of acridids in the desert. The solid ground rolled like the waves he had observed on the water; sparks cracked the sky like the egg of an aging Topazi; ice boulders rained out of the empty air. All Fala could do was hunker down under a rock overhang and hope it did not collapse on top of him as he waited for the world to stop its wailing.

For he knew these events were his fault, too. The world was mourning the loss of its light. With Kindra gone, what hope was there for his bond mate? Had he doomed Amadah to a torturous death? Had he doomed the world to a hideous end? Kindra had warned him, but he wouldn't listen. The only thing left for him to do now was to find Amadah and protect her from whatever new sleep terror the world offered up next.

When the ice boulders stopped falling and the sparks stopped shooting down from the sky, Fala set out on all fours, racing across the plains at his best speed, heedless of the destruction around him. All he knew was he had to reach the high mountain before Amadah and his friends tried to place the sphere. The world in its current state would never allow her to succeed. "Forgive Fala," he murmured as he ran, hoping Kindra could somehow hear him.

He ran without rest until sky fall, then he scouted for water and something to eat. As he was sniffing the ground, he caught a familiar scent some distance away: Turqosi! Fala melted into the ground and slithered toward the source of the scent. Then, he caught the smell of Jasperi. Was Amadah captured by the Turqosi? He resisted his urge to assault the Turqosi encampment, deciding he could best help Amadah by stealth instead of force.

Other scents assailed him: Chalcedi, Emraldi, Carneli...it was his group. Wait, was that...Topazi? It was. Impossible. He was the only Topazi remaining. Fala crept toward an overgrowth of brush where the scent seemed to originate. The place was as quiet as a stone, and nothing moved. Was he imagining the scents? Or perhaps the world was playing its tricks on him as punishment.

No. There it was, a slight movement among nearby bushes: a lookout, walking the perimeter, just as Fala would've done. He crouched beneath some weeds until the Turqosi came into view and walked near enough, then he pounced, pulling her back into the bushes without making a sound. He remembered the blinding spit they used as their defense, so he slammed the Turqosi face-down, wrapped his massive claws around her throat, and put his snout against her head. "No sound," he hissed. She stopped her writhing and gave a single nod. "Jasperi in camp?" She nodded once. "Amadah?" The Turqosi shrugged. "Topazi?" She gave a single nod. "Other Topazi dead. How possible?" He positioned his claw at the ready to slice her neck open. "Speak. Quiet."

"Slaves," she whispered.

Fala frowned. Slaves? Topazi would never agree to be slaves. And how would Turqosi be able to hold Topazi captive? "Liar."

The Turqosi shook her head. "Fala I know. From before. No lie."

"Tell Fala about slaves."

"Slaves escape. Chrysoli masters. Turqosi help."

"Turqosi help Turqosi,"

"We help fight Chrysoli."

"You have Topazi slave?"

"Was slave. No more."

"And Jasperi?"

"Was slave. Yesss."

So, it wasn't Amadah. Fala could keep the Turqosi captive until he skirted the camp, then release her and keep going toward the high mountain. But he wanted; no, he needed to see his own kind, to see if they had needs, before he left them to the Turqosi, whom he knew were untrustworthy. And Amadah would demand he look to the needs of her kind as well, if she were here. "Take Fala into camp. Show." He allowed the Turqosi to rise, while keeping her face turned away and his claws digging into her throat.

The Turqosi moved slowly and silently through the brush to the edge of the encampment with Fala behind her. Seeing the many different creatures scattered around the ground sleeping, Fala stopped short, his eyes wide. He didn't see one Topazi, he saw many. His kind, alive. A strange warmth and sense of home infused his breast. It was a feeling he thought he would never have again. He also saw many Jasperi and Emraldi and Amthysti and Carneli and even a Chalcedi—the Chalcedi looked familiar. Was it Cholena, the Chalcedi who was sent away by Hanai? How had she come to be a slave of the Chrysoli? Did she know what happened to the rest of the group who left the Beryli Sea? Were they now slaves?

Amadah's face loomed, consuming all thought, and every muscle in his sarkikos tightened, readying to run, to get to his bound mate before it was too late. "Who leads?"

"Leenha."

Fala remembered Leenha, a vicious, dangerous enemy. He thought she had been killed by the Beryli. These escaped slaves were in danger, but so was Amadah. No matter what Amadah would say about helping these creatures, he was not bound to them. He must help his bound mate, and his friends who had saved his life as he had saved theirs. He leaned close to his captive. "Tell Leenha Fala saw. Tell her Fala comes for slaves." The Turqosi nodded, relief evident in her eyes, but Fala also saw a new fear. Was it fear of repercussions from Leenha for letting him escape or fear of Fala's return stirring in her? "Tell Chalcedi same. Speak it."

"Tell Leenha and Chalcedi Fala was here and comes."

He dragged the Turqosi with him back through the overgrowth and around the encampment to the opposite side. "Sleep," he whispered, tightening his grip on her throat. He held her until her sarkikos drooped in his arms, then left her in the brush and ran full speed toward the high mountain and his bound mate.

CHAPTER FOURTEEN

The Dark Lord

Skia Skotos, now known as Ogima, fumed, his essence chafing at the constriction of the borrowed Amthysti sarkikos, his mind blackened and boiling as if filled with acid. His servants were imbeciles. How long could it take them to find a smattering of wandering creatures? If he was out of this sack of blood and bones, he would've already found and killed them all, and the world would once and for all be his to rule. Instead, he was forced to wait on idiots to do his work for him, and the Tempor was not on his side.

He needed to destroy something soon, or he would forget his grand plan, leave this sarkikos, and wreak havoc on them all. He considered a public execution, but the two apostates had not yet been found, and he couldn't conjure a good reason to kill any of the creatures cowering in his throne room. He almost wished one of them would speak against him, so he'd have an excuse. He wanted to taste death. He would have to settle for corruption.

"Chatan!" The Chalcedi who guarded his door stepped in and bowed. "Bring me food! This sarkikos needs it."

"Yes, Lord." Chatan disappeared briefly, returning with what appeared to be a haunch of a large creature. It was difficult to tell what kind because of the decay. "We'll need to scout for more of the dead soon, Lord," Chatan reported. "The supplies are getting low."

"Do it now. We must keep these fools satiated lest they wake up and decide to rebel."

"Why would they, Lord? You feed them. You give them pleasure. What more do they need?"

"Two have already left! I need my army intact and willing to fight when the cycle for battle comes, not disgruntled and deserting me!"

"They'll be ready, Lord."

"You had better make it happen, or it will be your head!"

Chatan lowered his beak to the ground. "I swear it, Lord, by all I have, I'll have them ready to fight."

"Use whatever enhancements you need, even if it means they begin to fight each other. I need them vicious and hungry for blood."

"Maybe starving them would be a good idea, Lord. It might make them angry."

"I don't want them angry at me, you stupid creature. I need them mad at those out there who would stand against me!"

"I'm sorry, Lord. I'm stupid, but I see now."

"Get them ready to fight."

"Yes, Lord."

Pleonexos materialized before the Dark Lord. "Most excellent news, my King. The Chrysoli are vulnerable. Their dome has been severely damaged by the falling ice, their leader is injured and may die, and their slaves are running away. They are ripe for your picking."

Finally, some good news. "Their food supplies?"

"Their fields were devastated by the ice storm. They have food in storage, but it will not last forever."

"Watch for me. As their stores get low, report, and I will lead my army to overtake them. And I will not have to risk my numbers to do it. The Chrysoli will come into the fold willingly because I will offer to feed them. They will be desperate enough to give up their self-governance in exchange for a sense of security."

"These creatures always do, Lord."

"What of the slaves? Where are they going?"

"They scatter, Lord, but one group appears to be coalescing. And get this—they are under the leadership of a Chalcedi and have joined forces with the Turqosi."

"A Chalcedi?" Ogima paced and flailed his Amthysti hands. "The Chalcedi are mine!"

"Not this one."

Ogima's eyes narrowed. "Who is this Chalcedi?"

"They call her Cholena."

Ogima's rage darkened the chamber. "I destroyed her. How is this possible?" Pleonexos floated silently as Ogima threw any objects he had handy against the stone walls and ranted against the hated light ones. "This is their doing. Well, we will just see about this. Chatan!"

Chatan scurried into the chamber. "Lord, I was just leaving with the Chalcedi to collect more food. I'm sorry it has taken me too long, but don't punish me. The Chalcedi can be very hard to motivate when they're..."

"Forget the food. We'll put to the test your claim my army is ready for the fight. We are going to war. And I myself will lead you."

Chatan clicked his beak in delight. "Who will we destroy, my Lord?"

"Cholena and anyone who follows her."

"Cholena? I thought she was dead."

Ogima sneered. "Apparently, our death decree was premature. Call Angeni! It's high cycles she and her lot earned their free lunches."

"They're going to war with us? Can they fight?"

"Just do it! Do not question me again."

"Yes, Lord." Chatan bowed and slunk from Ogima's chamber.

"Go to the Chrysoli," Ogima ordered Pleonexos. "I want to know the beat their food supplies are on the last dregs." Pleonexos vanished. "Thanatos! Return to me. Thymos! Hedraios! Ademoneos! Pseudos! Phobos! Come!"

One by one, the summoned Dark Ones materialized in his chamber. Assuming they were being called for punishment, they groveled and simpered, speaking over each other in their attempt to divert blame for their failure to find the child, her wards, or the two witnesses. "Silence!" Ogima howled. "I do not want to hear your excuses! We have a new task at hand. We are going to war!"

Relieved they were off the hook, the Dark Ones smacked their lips, cavorted around the chamber, and cackled with delight at the prospect of war.

"Who do we destroy, great one?" Phobos asked.

"The Chalcedi called Cholena has taken leadership over a group of escaped slaves from the land of the Chrysoli. The Turqosi have taken up with them, and I will know why. We will capture them—as many as will come with us. Those who resist, we destroy. But Cholena—she is mine. No one is to touch her but me. Is that clear?"

"Yes, Lord."

"Hedraios, Ademoneos, and Phobos, you are the advance party. You will stir their terror, their despair and hopelessness, and their paralysis. By our arrival, I expect to find a quivering mass of jellified creatures unable to resist us."

"We will accomplish it, Lord." Ademoneos clapped her hands in delight. "They will be practically suicidal when you come. I promise it!"

"I'll have them quaking from top to bottom," Phobos cried.

"Their thoughts will be stuck like they just paraded their minds into quicksand!" Hedraios added.

"Thanatos, you will lead Thymos and Pseudos beside my army. You will make them believe they are skilled and brutal warriors, barbaric, and so filled with rage they go berserk in the battle. I want these slaves to cower before me. And I want Cholena to witness my complete domination over all she leads."

"They will be mad with rage, Lord," Thanatos promised.

"Go! Go now! Begin your work!"

The Dark Ones dematerialized as Angeni walked into the chamber, bowing as deeply as she could. "Lord?"

"Angeni—" Ogima made his voice as smooth and cool as cream kept in a mountain creek. "Dear, dear Angeni."

Angeni's wings lowered, her clenched hands opened, and her face brightened. "Yes, Lord?"

"I have a very important assignment for you, my dear. You are chosen. You will be my spokesperson."

Angeni gasped, her surprise and delight genuine. "I, my King?"

"I will array you in crimson robes adorned with jewels, befitting your high office, the prophet leader of the high mountain. You will speak on my behalf. Come here, dear." Angeni sidled up to Ogima, who wrapped his arm around her. "Picture it, Angeni. You, in full regalia, standing tall, an imposing figure above a group of—slaves."

Angeni gasped.

"Yes, slaves. I have discovered a horrible truth. The Chrysoli, whom I imagined would be our allies, I have found have been keeping—I can hardly bear to say it—slaves to do their labor for them."

"Lord, that is an abomination!"

"Oh, yes. I have found a few brave souls who escaped from the clutches of the Chrysoli, but who stand little chance of surviving on their own. The Chrysoli will surely seek them, and if recaptured, they will be tortured or perhaps even—murdered."

"No, Lord!"

"Yes. So, you must convince them to join with us, here on your mountain. You will tell them of my great works and my power, and you will explain our lifestyle here in such a way, all will want to come. And for those who seek to make it on their own—well, you know we will need to take them, for their own good! You see the need, right, Angeni?"

"Oh, of course. We cannot leave them to the Chrysoli, even if they do not understand their danger."

"One you know is among them—the Chalcedi called Cholena."

"Cholena! You have found her!" Angeni seemed genuinely excited.

"Yes, yes. She leads this ragtag group, so you will need to convince her, first and foremost, how important it is for her group to join with us." Ogima shrugged. "We cannot have her swaying the others to remain free and vulnerable to the Chrysoli. And you know Cholena is a contrarian by nature. Remember?"

"She is, Lord?"

"Yes, you recall when all other Chalcedi followed me—I mean, followed Chatan—Cholena refused."

Angeni flinched. The image of Cholena, struck down by the spark from the air for her refusal to kill Amadah, flashed before her. A sickening twist in her stomach almost brought up her last meal.

"What is it, Angeni? You appear ill." Ogima gave a subtle flick of his hand, and a pleasing wisp of fog wafted before Angeni's eyes.

"No, Lord. I remember Cholena—as she was." She breathed in the fog.

"Very well, so you know you will need to be very persuasive." Ogima swept his hand, and another billow of the sweet-smelling mist surrounded Angeni's head. I believe in you, Angeni. You are the one I know I can count as my follower forever. Is that right, Angeni?"

Angeni inhaled deeply. "Lord, I will follow you to the very ends of the lands, through good cycles and difficult, no matter what others may do or say." Her voice took on a distant, monotone quality. "You are my King."

"And you will do whatever I say?"

"Of course, my Lord."

"You are my prophet and my queen."

"Yes, my Lord."

"You will not let me down."

"Never, my Lord."

"Remember your prophecy, that all creatures would come to live in harmony on the high mountain?

Angeni stared dreamily to the oculus and the sky beyond. "Oh, yes, my Lord."

"You will make it all come to pass."

"I will."

"Yes, and you will gather them all to you as a dove gathers her hatchlings to her breast."

Angeni wrapped her wings around her sarkikos, enraptured by the sky.

"Go, now, and prepare your speech. I will send one of the Chalcedi with your raiment. Then, you will gather the rest of your clan together to take the journey. They will stand behind you, ready to help you in any way necessary, as will I."

With that statement, Angeni's eyes focused and came down from the clouds to Ogima's face. "You are coming?"

"Of course! This task is too important for me to remain here. All will come, for we will succeed! At all costs!"

"No matter what it takes."

116

Chapter Fifteen

The Jasperi

Amadah choked down her grief like she was swallowing a rotted koloochee fruit whole. It sat rock-hard in her stomach, pressing against her throat and threatening to heave back up, but she couldn't afford to allow herself to feel. Too much rode on their success. Too many counted on her to be strong.

Nikani and Chevei busied themselves with preparing the poles to transport the sphere. The rest of the group sat together, quietly conversing, but Amadah couldn't bear that either, so she remained separate and alone. Fala had introduced her to the idea of a bound mate, something she never imagined she would want. She had rejected Nikani's advances out of hand, always reminding him they were just friends. But now, having had a bound mate, her heart longed for connection. The feeling reminded her of being in Fala's desert with no water, a desperate, cloying need, like a compulsion, but this feeling went much deeper. Her whole being ached for it, until she thought she might go mad.

"Ready to move the sphere," Nikani called.

"We're going to be out in the open, with no covering, no hiding places, nothing to block the light from the sphere from being seen." Kilchi wrinkled his snout. "It's a huge risk."

"There's nothing we can do about it. Unless you can think of another way to move the sphere?" Amadah lifted her brows hopefully.

"Let's get on with it." Nikani had decided Kilchi and Enla would be attached to either end of the pole behind the sphere, pushing it

117

forward, while Nikani and Amadah would take the steerage in the front. Misa would walk in front of the sphere, clearing the ground of obstructions, and Aleshanee would walk beside it, in case it needed to be repositioned, while Chevei, attached to the front pole by a vine, would fly above to provide additional guidance. Meda would act as scout for the most unobstructed and level route to the high mountain.

Amadah and Aleshanee held the orb steady while Nikani bound Enla and Kilchi to their pole and positioned the pole behind the sphere. Then, Amadah and Misa held the steering rod in front of the sphere while Nikani used some thick vines to bind the poles to each other on either side of the sphere, to keep the sphere centered between the two logs. He then tied a long vine to Chevei and bound it to the center of the front pole. Once completed, Nikani took his position on the front pole and Chevei took to the air.

"I will call out right or left from above." Meda took off behind Chevei.

Their contraption was cumbersome and odd-looking, and Amadah was convinced it wouldn't work, but as Kilchi and Enla pulled forward on the back pole, the sphere rolled, just as Nikani predicted. It took a while for the foursome to get their rhythm and pacing, but they were soon moving along at a decent speed.

"Left!" Meda called, and Amadah pulled her end of the pole back. It worked! The sphere glided to the left. "Straight!" Meda called. Amadah moved parallel to Nikani, and as he claimed, the sphere leaned against the thick vine and righted its course. They were forced to stop frequently to clear the path ahead and to rest, for the poles were heavy.

"This is working much better than the sled," Amadah said to Nikani. "I'm glad you're here to help us."

Nkiani looked around at the other members of the group, lying in a loos circle around the sphere. "We're a strange kind of procession. Who would've thought, all these different kinds of creatures, working together, when not that many cycles ago, we didn't even come into contact with each other?"

"We had no choice."

The group labored through the valley. Meda warned them when they were approaching rifts from the many quakes, and they were often forced to circumvent the chasms or find a new direction to turn the sphere. She tried to steer them around rises, but the number and height of rolling knolls was increasing, making the going difficult. Finally, Meda circled down to land before the group. "We cannot maintain this direction. Just ahead, many of the hills have fallen, leaving piles of boulders Misa will not be able to move. Also, there is a massive chasm transecting the area ahead and I cannot find a nearby way to cross it. I believe we must turn and take a path parallel to the high mountain, to find open land we can traverse."

"Let's rest here and eat," Amadah said. "Then, we will make our turn. Meda, were you able to scout out the new course?"

"I will now."

"No, rest and eat first. We have quite a way to go. We all need to preserve our strength. In this case, rest is a weapon."

Seeing everyone collapse after they put down their poles told Amadah she was right. In fact, she might've waited too long to call for this rest. She knew she would need to be diligent about pushing the group too hard. Since she was running away from the aching weight of her grief, stopping was torture for her, but for the others, who were pushing toward a goal instead of running from pain, rest was not only a relief, it was a necessity.

Aleshanee and Misa distributed the food and water. Once again, Amadah took her meager supplies away from the others to a nearby rise. She climbed to the top, and from there, she was able to see what Meda had warned was coming—collapsed hills, tumbled rockslides, and a huge crater zigzagging across the entire area with webs of crevasses shooting off from the crater in both directions. Fala had taught her to always be aware of her surroundings, so she scanned the area for potential hiding places or sites of a possible ambush. Then, she settled down to eat, watching her friends from above.

A brilliant flash, and the rose-colored sky was suddenly bathed in yellow and orange, as if the air itself was on fire. A strong gust carrying a blast of intense heat followed. Amadah scrambled down the knoll to rejoin her friends, who were lying on the ground, trying to cover their faces against the scorching wind. "Over here!" She waved her arms, but couldn't keep them up. Her exposed skin on her face and arms felt like it was on fire. She knew she had to get them underground somewhere, or at least shielded from the main force of the blast. "This way!"

Keeping their heads covered, the group scuttled along the ground, following Amadah's cries. She was forced to close her eyes against the blinding white around her. The hot wind roared in her ears, gathering speed. The small patches of weeds still trying to regrow after the great burning from the object that fell from the sky withered, some even flaming for a moment before they blackened and burned out.

The howling, scalding wind caught up the dust and loose soil in its path. When Amadah called to her friends again, her mouth was filled with dirt, choking her. She figured they could no longer hear her calling, so she leaned into the wind, trying to run to them, but it pressed back against her. She could barely move. The stinging dirt, acting as tiny projectiles, peppered her, each one searing her skin. She waved one arm in front of her, hoping she would bump into one of her friends, but she had no idea where they were or where she was. Her foot caught on something protruding from the ground, and she fell face first and tumbled the rest of the way down the knoll.

She felt someone grab her arm, then she was dragged across the scalding earth. Shouts and screams mixed with the roaring wind. Every metric of her sarkikos felt aflame. When she opened her eyes, excruciating pain seared them closed again. Her arm was released, and she was shoved forward, tumbling a couple of turns before coming to rest on what felt like cooler ground. She risked opening her eyes again. The blinding light was gone, replaced by a twilight darkness. She was in a hole or a chasm. Scanning around her, she counted her friends. "Is everyone—did everyone...?" Her throat felt like the bark of a pinacea tree.

"Making it to safety, yes, but injured," Misa whispered.

Amadah looked up at the Saphiri standing over her. Misa appeared untouched by the severe heat. "How did you...?"

"Having thick scales to protect against the deep waters. Needing to care for the wounded now. Take this." Misa handed Amadah a small piece of the fruit from the living water cavern. "Hoping one bite is enough, for we are going through our supply much too rapidly."

"I'm fine. See to the others. Quickly." She could hear their moans and cries, and she, like Misa, hoped the healing fruit would be enough.

As Misa turned away, Amadah's eyes flew open, and she bolted upright. "The sphere!"

"Forced to leave the sphere, I am afraid."

"No!" She struggled to her feet, intending to run from their little cave and ensure the sphere's safety, but after one step, she collapsed in a heap.

"Allow the fruit to do its work," Misa urged her, while tending to the others.

Amadah then surveyed her group, and guilt flooded through her. How could she be so concerned about an object, even one so precious and vital as the sphere, when her friends were in such terrible condition. Aleshanee looked burned to a crisp, her wings in tatters. Meda's pale blue feathers were edged in black, curling up like wood shavings in a flame. Enla, who lay outstretched face-down, had huge sections of her fur burned completely off, revealing red, blistered skin beneath. Kilchi, too, had lost patches of fur to the fire, but he seemed to have fared better than Enla and was helping Misa with her task.

Behind Kilchi, Amadah saw Nikani and Chevei, both lying flat on their backs. Kilchi was squeezing juice from a piece of fruit into Nikani's slack mouth. "Nikani!" Amadah tried to rise once again, and once again, failed.

"Stay down," Misa commanded. "Having them in hand."

So, Amadah sat back, closed her eyes, and waited. After many beats, a soothing balm flowed from deep within her, moving slowly outward to her extremities, as if the oil from myrta leaves was spreading over her, but from the inside of her skin. It was a strange feeling.

Gradually, she felt her strength improve. When she opened her eyes, they no longer burned, her skin returned to its natural fern-green tint, and her face stopped feeling like it was on fire. She could hear others moaning, but not in pain. They groaned with relief as the healing juices of the fruit restored and revived them. Soon, they were all stirring. Amadah stood. "I must go check on the sphere."

"Wiser to allow me," Misa pointed out. "Burning from the sky may still occur."

Amadah nodded, and Misa, after checking everyone else's status, climbed out of their little hole. "Remaining terrific heat. The sky darkens."

"The sphere?"

"Seeing it intact, where we left it."

Kilchi asked, "How about our poles?"

"Not seeing from this distance but going to see."

It took many beats for a winded and despondent Misa to return. "Not knowing how to tell you, poles and vines are—gone."

"Gone?" Kilchi sucked in his breath between his fangs.

"Burned to ash are they."

"We have no other way to carry the sphere, and no materials available to create a new way." Meda groaned.

"Oh, no! What're we going to do now?" Enla wailed.

Chevei fluttered his wings. "Everything we try fails. It is as if this whole expedition is cursed."

Despair flooded through Amadah like icy water, washing away her last shred of hope and sucking it down into the dirt beneath her feet. The long, heavy silence was deafening.

"Perhaps it is." Aleshanee's voice sounded small after the exclamations of the others.

"What do you mean, Aleshanee?"

Aleshanee cleared her throat. "We keep trying to do this task— our way, using our own ideas, our own strength, our own resources. Perhaps this task is one we aren't supposed to do alone."

"You mean, we should go find others to help us?" Kilchi shook his head. "Who could we trust?"

122

"No one." Misa sighed. "Traveling now to the Beryli Sea and my father is no longer an option, taking longer than we have food supplies to sustain us."

"You've forgotten our friends." Aleshanee cut her eyes to the sky.

"Which friends?" Kilchi asked.

"Our friends who helped us in the caves."

Kilchi puffed through his nose. "The ones we can't see?"

"Our friends helped us get through the maze in the cavern, but, Aleshanee—they aren't—real—I mean, they're real, but we can't touch them, and they can't touch us. They can't move heavy objects like the sphere. At least, not that they've shown us. They encourage us and give us ideas and light our path, but they can't move mountains." Enla ducked her head, almost like she was afraid she'd hurt Aleshanee's feelings.

"And if they can, why haven't they helped us before now?" Kilchi growled.

"They have helped us so very much, more than you know."

"More magical thinking," Chevei muttered under his breath.

"You said yourself everything we try to do falls apart. It's an impossible task; yet, we keep trying to do it ourselves, our way. Maybe there's another way."

Chevei stood and paced. "What way? Ask invisible beings I cannot see or hear to just move it where it needs to go? Then say thank you very much like all we have been through is just fine? Like Kilchi said, if they could do that, why did they ever need us? They could have retrieved it from the cave themselves. Why drag us into this? If they are real, why not zap the sphere to the mountain and be done with it? Why not stop this catastrophe from happening in the first place?" He paused, shaking his clenched fist in the air. "Why did they not save Fala and Yiska?"

Chevei's tirade reverberated in the dead silence of the chasm. Every head down and every eye focused on the ground, no one spoke for what felt to Amadah like a full cycle. Finally, Aleshanee sighed and started to hum a somber tune.

Defeat after defeat. Amadah scanned the bowed the shoulders of each individual and recognized the losses they had experienced were taking their toll. Her loss carved gashes in her very being, so she imagined the others felt the same depth of pain.

Aleshanee's mournful notes caused everyone's eyes to glisten with a building flood of tears. Then, Aleshanee sang:

> Sky light's rise and sky light's fall
> We cry out in our despair.
> Given more than we can bear,
> Following an ancient scrawl.
>
> Do you even hear our call?
> Tumbling deeper in the pit.
> Steadfast hearts refuse to quit,
> Sky light's rise and sky light's fall
>
> Sky light's rise and sky light's fall
> We can't escape; our eyes grow dim,
> Our situation deadly grim,
> Evil's plot our steps forestall.
>
> Whispered hopes hard to recall.
> We walk closer to our death.
> Trouble steals our very breath,
> Sky light's rise and sky light's fall
>
> May sky light's rise and sky light's fall
> Find us where your message sends
> Reached before our sky light ends
> And evil's darkness buries all.

Her final note trembled in the silence for a beat, then faded. Amadah looked at each one in turn. "We have nothing left. So, what do we have to lose?" She looked up to where she imagined their friends were, hoping they would respond. "We are lost. We can't do what you asked. We need help. Help us. Please."

Aleshanee joined Amadah's plea. "My friends, what do we do? All our efforts have failed. Is it truly hopeless? Help us!"

Misa lifted her arms. "Reaching for the Light. Help us."

"I—I'm sorry." Enla's words choked in her throat.

"Listen, I know you helped us in the caverns, but I haven't seen hide nor hair of you since, and honestly, I'm angry. Why have you abandoned us?" No one argued with Kilchi or quieted him.

"I am unsure, and I do not understand. But I know I felt warnings in my heart while I was on the high mountain, warnings against Ogima and warnings not to share his table. Was that—you?" Meda looked at Nikani and nodded.

Nikani cleared his throat. "I'm pretty sure you helped us escape, didn't you? Amadah believes in you, so I do, too. Would you help us again?"

Everyone glanced toward Chevei, who shook his head and folded his arms. "I stand by my question. Why did they not save Fala and Yiska? That is all I have to say."

"Do you claim to understand the ways of all things?" A deep voice boomed, echoing through their tiny hole. "Do you live outside Tempor? Do you know the beauty and majesty of the First World? Were you among the Whisperers when the Divinethos divided the worlds? Have you seen all life and know the nature of each precious being? Speak, Chevei, and I will listen."

Chevei cowered against the dirt wall of their hole. "I—no, of course I do not know…"

"Indeed, you do not. Now, you listen, and I will speak, and I will show you what was, what is, and what is to come." A pulsing sphere appeared in mid-air, rotating with increasing speed, light swirling in its depths. It looked like a miniature version of the sphere they had carried from the cavern. It grew so bright they were forced to shield their eyes. A beam shot from the sphere toward the sky, and another sphere appeared at the end of the beam, this sphere glowing blue and green and amber and rose. The beam seemed to draw the colorful sphere closer to the bright one, and as the colorful sphere came down, the group could see familiar shapes within the colors—mountains, waterfalls, green valleys, golden fields, a bright beauty their words couldn't describe. The colorful sphere reached the bright one, and as they touched, the spheres merged, becoming one, larger sphere. Brilliant beams shot from the sphere in all directions, the beams of light hitting each member of the group.

Amadah's sarkikos exploded in sensation. She could taste color and smell sound. Notes of music danced across her skin and behind her eyes. She closed her eyes and leaned her head back, adrift in an ecstasy she found vaguely familiar, yet more complete than anything she had ever experienced. Nothing and no one existed beyond her consciousness. Her sarkikos screamed to express what it felt. She couldn't hold still any longer, so she began to twirl and dance. She felt as if she was floating in mid-air.

"This is what you seek. This is why you live and die." Amadah heard Veritor's voice inside her head, not through her ears. The voice vibrated in her chest and resonated through her cells. "Yiska knows why he died. Yet, you ask why as if it is your life and not his to give. Know this: he gives it freely with great joy."

"Stop!" Chevei cried. "I cannot bear it!"

Amadah looked for Chevei and found him crumpled in a heap, shivering, his wings enfolding his head as if to ward off an attack. She weaved her way through her other friends, engrossed in their own experiences, and knelt by Chevei. "Don't fight against it. Let it come."

"I cannot. I cannot bear it."

"Yes, you can. Let it cleanse you. Release your control."

"I cannot. I will not." Chevei wrapped his arms around him and clutched his hands, as if he were holding onto a tiny raft in a tidal wave.

"Is your self-determination worth so much to you that you would sentence your world to destruction?" Veritor boomed.

"Please stop..."

"What you witness was, is, and will be the Great Rejoining. Will you hinder? Will you choose to be your own divine? For, hear me, if you listen to fear and hold onto self-determination, you are standing with darkness, and all is lost. Or will you stand in the light and give yourself to the one, true Divinethos, the Forever, the First before all, worthy of all glory and honor and praise?"

"Chevei, choose the light."

"It hurts," Chevei moaned.

"It hurts because you cling to your control. Listen to our friend who speaks truth. I feel nothing but pure joy in the light. You can, too."

Chevei's wings slowly relaxed and settled behind him. Amadah placed her hands on either side of his head and brought her eyes in line with his. "Look at me." When he met her eyes, she continued. "Let go. Release your hold." Chevei opened his hands and allowed his arms to fall to his side. Then, Amadah rose and offered her hand, which Chevei finally grasped. She pulled him up and stepped aside.

The beam from the sphere hit Chevei in the chest, and he cried out, bowed his back, and threw back his head as the light pulsed and enveloped him. His wings unfurled and he started to rise from their little hole, captured in the rapture of the light.

Amadah smiled and turned back to the sphere. She reached out her hands and embraced it, and the light infused her. Suddenly, she knew things she couldn't know, things that hadn't happened yet but had happened long ago. She saw everything as if she had never seen it before but felt as if she knew all. "Hold the sphere!" she called to her friends.

One by one, they joined Amadah around the sphere, at first touching it tentatively, then embracing it. "Ahhh, the First World," Aleshanee breathed.

"You remember." Amadah marveled that Aleshanee carried the memory of this experience with her.

"I always have and always will."

"Now, listen, and I will speak," Veritor said. "You have each given yourself to the Divinethos and seen and touched the First World, taking its light into you. Now you may all hold the sphere without fear of consequence. Together, you may carry the sphere to its place on the high mountain, as long as you all work together. You will no longer need tools or implements, for the Forever will strengthen you for the task. Now, take the sphere to its home and rejoin the worlds.

"Take heed of my words! The Dark Lord is on the move. He parades in the open as one in command of all things. Keep to the hills and walk where you cannot be seen. If you are successful, you will reach the high mountain and find it empty and ready for the sphere to be placed and the worlds to be rejoined. But beware! If you are not successful, the path to the high mountain is fraught with pain and terror, and lives will be forfeit and lost to the darkness. Fall not under his spell. Know this: control breeds control. When the Dark Lord displays his power, do not respond in kind, or you will fail. Remember what you have learned this cycle.

"We walk beside you, as we always have and always will. Listen for our whispers. Do not allow other voices to drown our words, for to do so leaves you blind."

"You mean the Dark Ones," Aleshanee said.

"Yes, dear one. The Dark Lord has sent out his minions in force. Do not think yourself immune simply because you have touched the First World and received its light."

"But how will we know the difference?" Kilchi asked.

"Trust the Forever, and your heart will hear the Music," Veritor replied. "Listen now. What speaks the Music?"

They closed their eyes and listened as one, still holding onto the glowing sphere. Aleshanee spoke for the group. "The Music sings of hope and great joy, of every tongue bursting into song in praise of the Forever and the Great Love, of standing before the throne on the First World as if born anew."

"Is that all?" Veritor asked.

"No," Amadah replied. "I hear a harmony line in minor key, a mournful song of travail and..." her breath hitched, catching in her throat, "a—and—death—the death of love, and—um—darkness lying prone and rising—both somehow—and terror and pain and loss beyond bearing." She moaned. "Is this what will happen?"

"It is what may happen, should hearts grow cold."

"Please don't let it be so."

"The choice is yours and yours alone," Veritor said. "We speak. You may listen. You may not. Your hands hold the sphere; yet, the Music still sings in harmony." Veritor paused,. "Remember always: it matters what you choose."

"We won't choose darkness," Aleshanee cried. "We won't let our hearts grow cold."

As quickly as it came, the gleaming sphere vanished.

"That gives me a chill." Kilchi shook his coat with a shiver. "It's like our friend was saying we're going to choose the harmony line."

"No." Amadah was thoughtful and quiet in her spirit. "I believe he was saying we could choose either way, and the warning is to let us know we need to guard our hearts and our choices. We must remain in the light. Everything depends on it. Now, let's go get the sphere."

CHAPTER SIXTEEN

The Turqosi

Leenha kept her army positioned near the river. The water was her habitat, and she planned on using it. When they marched, she would frequently cross over and double back to check for any Chrysoli who might be following—and for Fala, who, as far as she was concerned, was even more dangerous than the Chrysoli masters. Since she heard from Eteena that Fala was coming for them, she hadn't rested, nor had she allowed the army to rest. When they weren't marching, they were training. She knew Fala hated the water, and the Chrysoli masters avoided it for anything more than drinking, so being at the river gave her an advantage. Leenha was not one to forego any advantage.

More escaped slaves joined their ranks each cycle, but Leenha now had the problem of younglings. Cholena demanded they not be killed, and Leenha relented with the understanding the slaves were responsible for their care and feeding, but she informed the slaves if the young ones slowed them down or got in the way during battle, they would be the first to die, by her hand. She saw Cholena's horrified look, but she didn't care what the Chalcedi thought of her kind. She didn't plan on being friends.

The sky light was on the decline when a strange flash lit the sky. Leenha didn't wait to see what caused it. With a single gesture, she commanded the Turqosi army to dive into the river. They disappeared in the brown waters, leaving the slaves in the encampment to fend for themselves. The sky's brilliance pierced through the murky water, and

Leenha could sense the temperatures of the water rising. The surface of the water chopped, buffeted by a strong wind.

Screaming and screeching slaves dove into the river around her, churning the waters even more. Leenha gestured for her army to swim downstream, away from the panicked slaves, then she rose near the surface for a beat to assess their situation. A few slaves remained on the land, mainly Topazi who were burrowing into the mud near the river's edge. Many of the slaves couldn't swim, which to Leenha was ludicrous, and she determined it advantageous for her army if they died in this newest onslaught. She could see the brush surrounding their encampment wilting in the oppressive heat, and water evaporating from the river at an alarming rate before she descended again to the river bottom to wait it out.

Was this another falling object from the sky, or some new horror the powers had devised against her kind? All Leenha knew was her kind could not survive out here, vulnerable to the capricious whims of the powers of this world. She needed to possess the Chrysoli dome, and their bountiful lands. And possess it she would.

CHAPTER SEVENTEEN

The Jacinthi

Kwania gaped, eyes wide, from within the stone walls of the Chrysoli science building as the chaotic scene unfolded outside. The lenses she used to protect her eyes as she took measurements of the sky light allowed her to witness what the naked eye could not see. A giant explosion on the surface of the sky light propelled massive amounts of superheated material toward their world's atmosphere, and as it hit, it burst into flame and caught the upper atmosphere on fire. The fire danced across the sky as far as she could see, heating the air to intolerable levels.

It was indeed fortunate the ice storm had forced the slaves indoors, and the masters had yet to organize repair crews to work on the dome or salvage what crops they could, mainly because Tocho was still in intensive care, for Kwania believed the flesh of anyone outside would be burned beyond healing. She caressed her wings, imagining the kind of damage this firestorm would do to them. What a strange feeling, to be thankful she was a captive to a culture with structures that could withstand such heat and wind. Her friends on the high mountain would survive if they were in their caves, but if they were outside, or flying—she couldn't bear the thought.

Miakoda interrupted her worst imaginings. "What is it, do you think? Another strange weather event?"

"No, the sky light experienced an explosion. I was taking measurements and observed the explosion when it occurred."

"And the explosion caused this?"

"Yes, it ejected a tremendous amount of..."

133

"Kwania!" a gravelly voice roared.

"Master Kola seeks you," Miakoda murmured.

Kwania hesitated. She desired to continue to observe, to try to predict what would happen next, but she dared not refuse his call, so she fluttered from her perch to the doorway where he stood. "I am here."

"Is this the explosion you told us would happen?"

"No, master. This is a precursor of that explosion. The final explosion will be significantly worse. This world will not survive it."

"Precursor? Explain."

"These events are the result of an explosion from the surface of the sky light. Now imagine the entire sky light itself exploding and all the force and energy of that explosion hurtling toward us. That is what we are facing. Our world will be engulfed in the explosion and destroyed."

"Worse than this?"

"This, multiplied by ten billion."

"Can you do something?" Kwania just looked at Kola. "What's going to happen next?"

"I am unsure. I believe the upper level of our atmosphere may be burning off, which will mean a dramatic change in our climate and weather patterns. On the other side, it could be the residue from the burn off leaves a thick layer of smoke and debris above us, blocking the sky light's rays and darkening our world, causing other dramatic and unpredictable changes to our climate. This is all unprecedented, so I do not know what to expect, other than to expect massive changes in life as we have known it."

"What should I do to prepare the pride?"

Kwania shook her head. "Even if your dome was intact, it would not protect you against the upcoming explosion. As to the current situation, all I can suggest is keep everyone indoors until we determine how the environment will respond to this new event."

"Tocho, when he recovers, will expect me to have taken care of things in his stead. I can't tell him I did nothing!"

"Then allow me to continue my observations and measurements. I will report to you as the situation unfolds."

Kola's glare let Kwania know he chafed at her response, but he stalked away without another word. With a gentle flap of her wings, Kwania returned to her perch, where Miakoda continued to take measurements. "The temperature appears to be declining."

"That is good news."

"Look at the sky."

Kwania lifted her lenses. As the atmospheric fire burned out, the sky appeared to be darkening. "Thoughts?" she asked Miakoda.

"Smoke and haze." She swung a large instrument toward Kwania. "Look."

Kwania bent to look through the instrument. "As I feared." A dense layer of grey blanketed the usually rosy sky. The sky light itself looked like a fuzzy brown ball, its edges smeared by the fog. As they watched, thick clouds gathered above them.

"Evaporation during the firestorm," was all Miakoda said as she pointed to the clouds. "Soon, it will rain, and it will be raining for quite a while."

"The problem is, without the sky light's rays, plants will not grow. Whatever food supplies you have stored will have to sustain us all for the foreseeable future."

Miakoda groaned. "Which means Tocho will likely forbid feeding all slaves."

"We will die!"

"He won't care."

"That is awful! Could the slaves at least be allowed to glean from the fields what little is left after the ice and fire?"

"To give to the masters, sure. For themselves? I doubt it."

"I will speak with Kola."

Miakoda shrugged and went back to her observations. Kwania fluttered over the main room, searching for Kola in the throng of Chrysoli, but she didn't see him, so she landed by the door to the medichi area and strode into intensive care. As she expected, Kola was there, conferring with Tocho, who lay on his side on a large gurney beneath bright warming lights. She walked boldly up to the two Chrysoli.

Tocho lifted his head slightly and growled, prompting Kola to turn. When he saw Kwania, his eyes bulged. "What are you doing in here?"

"I need to speak with you. I have additional information."

"Speak quickly, slave."

"Smoke darkens the sky; clouds build at an alarming rate. These events will have a direct impact on your ability to grow food in the future."

"Get out!" Tocho barked, his voice as coarse as gravel.

Kola leaned close to Tocho. "Tocho, this is the slave whose quick thinking and knowledge saved your life."

Tocho grumbled something under his breath but didn't command Kwania again.

"So, what do you mean, direct impact?" Kola asked.

"It is likely food will no longer grow until the haze dissipates. If it does."

"So, what we have is all we will have."

"Yes, Kola."

Kola turned back to Tocho and whispered in his ear. Tocho growled and shook his head, then waved his paw and turned away, ending their meeting.

Kola walked out with Kwania. "What did Tocho say?" she asked.

"He told me to handle it."

"How will you handle it, Master Kola?"

"Strict rationing."

"What about the slaves?"

Kola stared at Kwania. "What did you think? That I would feed a bunch of useless slaves over my own kind?"

"I am one of those useless slaves."

"You aren't useless to us. Don't worry, you will eat, at least enough to keep you alive."

"Not if the other slaves do not eat."

Kola growled and snapped, nipping Kwania on the arm. "Don't be a fool! You will eat what I provide."

136

"I will not, unless you feed the remaining slaves. Or, you may set them all free, and I will remain and help you prepare for the crisis."

"I can't just let them go. Tocho would never approve."

"You make no sense! You say they are useless to you, yet you will not free them. Why? If they serve no purpose for you, and you are just going to let them starve, free them!"

"We'll use them to repair the dome, as long as they are able to work."

"They cannot work if they do not eat."

"They can for a while. Then they are free to die off."

"You wretched creature! Have you no belief in the value of life?"

"Our lives." Kola's head tilted back, nose held high as he shook his mane.

"But not all life. You are selfish, callous, horrid, hateful—you are the ones who are unworthy to live!"

"Watch your words with me. You are not immune to my whip."

"Go ahead!" Kwania blurted. "And after that, you may enjoy figuring out how to survive without any knowledge or understanding of what is transpiring. I wish you the best in that foredoomed endeavor."

"You are getting very uppity for someone whose life is in my hands." Kola issued a warning snarl.

Kwania threw her head back and chortled, while Kola stared, looking dumbfounded. "You have no power over me. You imagine yourself this all-powerful, superior creature. But you cannot take my heart or my soul. You cannot control my thoughts or my feelings. You are weak. You are nothing." With that, Kwania gave a quick flap and returned to her perch, leaving Kola standing with his mouth open and his threat to punish her unsatisfied.

"What was that all about?" Miakoda whispered.

"A lot of bluster with no teeth," Kwania answered. "I told Kola if he does not feed the slaves, I will not eat either. He insinuated he would force me to eat. I wish him the best."

"You'd die to save a bunch of slaves?"

"You would not?"

"Of course not."

Kwania turned to face her new companion. "They are living creatures, just like you."

"They aren't at all like me."

"They may appear different on the outside, but I promise you, from a scientific viewpoint, we are all very much the same. If you devalue one life, you devalue them all. You devalue your own."

"The slaves exist to serve the masters. When they can no longer serve, they no longer deserve to live."

Kwania snorted. "Then you do not deserve to live either."

Miakoda's nose and brow wrinkled. "No, I'm saying you deserve to live because you still serve!"

"You believe we are only worth what we produce?"

"Of course."

"Is the same true for the masters?"

"Look around you at all we have produced and continue to produce. See all we create? We are creators, the highest category of creature known."

"Then every living creature is the highest category, because all creatures have the capacity to create new life."

"That's different, and you know it!"

"I do not. Creation is creation, is it not?" Kwania glared at Miakoda. "Who decides what stands as the so-called right kind of creation to be worthy of life? You? Tocho?"

"All masters do."

Kwania shook her head. "How arrogant you are. What if I determined Tocho was no longer worthy of life and refused him the blood transfusion? After all, he was not producing anymore when he was injured. Why not just allow him to die?"

"Honestly, we probably would've let him die," Miakoda admitted.

"Because you could not save him or because he no longer served a purpose?"

"Because, if he recovered but remained damaged, he would be a drain on the pride."

"And if you were the one lying on that table wounded?"

"I would expect to die."

Kwania paused, shook her head again, and stared for several beats at the platform where they were standing. "I feel sorry for you."

Miakoda bristled, her mane standing up. "*You* feel sorry for *me*?"

"I do," Kwania said softly. "I may be just a slave in your eyes, but I know my value and worth. I know who I am, and it has nothing to do with what I produce for my clan, or for you. I have intrinsic value in my being. You rely on what you do to prove your worth, but my worth is an unchanging truth and does not rely on the winds of circumstance to prove it." She sighed. "I pity you."

"Keep your pity," Miakoda exploded, "and leave this lab at once!"

Kwania looked up at Miakoda and sighed again. "You would send away your greatest resource to protect your arrogance? To do so would be foolish. But I will leave if you insist."

Miakoda swished her tail and gestured toward the exit, so Kwania dropped her special lenses, glided down to the bottom floor, pushed open the door, and walked toward the slave bunkhouse to join her fellow slaves.

CHAPTER EIGHTEEN

The Topazi

Fala raced through cycles of light and darkness, across open fields, through burnt landscapes, and around chasms left by quakes, with one thought in his mind—reach the high mountain before Amadah. The mountain, shrouded in mist, was coming into view before him in the distance, when the air above him seemed to catch fire and the intense heat drove him underground. He burrowed deep under some loose dirt to protect himself from the blast.

Despite the torrent of fire, wind, and dust raining down above him, Fala trembled, not with cold or fear but with impatience at the delay. Images of Amadah hanging from the pole before the Chalcedi horde, tortured by mysterious sparks of light, rose before him. He could not, would not, let her go through something like that again. Kindra's warning whispered in his mind's deep recesses, but he wouldn't let that happen either. He refused to be the cause of pain for his bound mate, whatever it took.

After what seemed like a whole cycle, the chaos quieted, leaving a thick, oppressive heat and dark clouds boiling up from beyond the mountain. Fala clawed his way out of his burrow, coughed some dirt from his mouth, and started his run again.

The heat made the air shimmer, distorting objects in the distance, but Fala thought he saw movement between him and the mountain. Whatever it was appeared massive and seemed to hover mid-air. Was it a mirage? Was someone there? He slowed and pressed his sarkikos against the ground, then slithered behind a nearby rockfall.

141

Soon, Fala heard distant sounds, squawks and caws and indistinguishable voices, and he knew what he had seen was not a single object but a mass of beings moving as one—the Chalcedi horde. Rage and hatred bubbled in Fala's chest like the morass in the Topazi mud pits. He risked a peek around the rocks, long enough to see the group was moving slowly and was still some distance away. He also saw their numbers meant attacking them would be foolhardy, so he decided to follow them, watching for an opportunity to catch them unawares and pick them off one by one.

At his next glance, he recognized the mass was more than Chalcedi. He saw white and deep blue and purple and light blue, the feathers of the Jacinthi. Were they captives? They appeared to be flying freely, side by side with their enemies. Fala had to know, to try to understand, so he crept to the top of the rocks of his hide, hoping his coloration and the distance of the horde would camouflage him.

His throat tightened when he saw flashes of green amid the many flyers. Amadah! Was he too late? Was she already captured by the horde? Fala was about to throw caution to the wind and attack when he recognized some former members of his group from the Beryli Sea. He saw Hanai with Sonta riding his back. He saw Isusa carrying Itai. He recognized Kacina and Nadie, flying willingly beside Chalcedi warriors. Then, he saw Angeni, wrapped in scarlet and gold, and astride her rode none other than Ogima, the betrayer.

Fala crouched down among the rocks, pondering what he witnessed. Somehow, for some unknown reason, the ones who left his group by the Beryli Sea were now in league with their enemies. It was clear they were willing participants, not captives, and it appeared Angeni held a position of some honor or power. Fala couldn't fathom what he saw, so he landed on the one positive—he didn't see Amadah among the masses, nor did he see any others from his group, so he was not too late to save his bound mate. It also meant Amadah and his group had not yet reached the high mountain with the sphere.

Fala decided to follow the horde. He needed to see if they were on the hunt for Amadah, or if they had other evil purposes in leaving their stronghold. Because of their large numbers, and the fact they were flying, he was able to keep them in sight even at some distance, staying in the hills and hiding in the fallen rocks. The darkening sky helped conceal him in shadow. So, Fala became the hunter once more, as was the heritage of his kind, slinking and scurrying and slithering through rockfalls, beneath ridges, and along crevasses, while Ogima's horde flew through the valley toward the open plains.

He crept along, parallel to the horde's path, always keeping Angeni's bright robes in sight. He had gone some distance when his acute hearing picked up noises beyond the hills he traversed. Whoever or whatever made those noises were close by, closer than the Chalcedi. Quickly, he squeezed into a crack between two large rocks and waited. The sounds seemed to be coming from behind his position. Had he missed some Chalcedi breaking off from the group? Had they spotted him and were now hunting for him?

Scraping footfalls caused him to slow his breath and heartbeats, while he checked the horde to see if they were responding to the noises. They didn't seem to hear, so Fala assumed these noises were coming from behind the hill, hidden from the view of the Chalcedi and Ogima and beyond their earshot. He pulled himself from between the rocks and slithered to the top of the hill, always keeping a watchful eye on the horde. When he reached the top, he noticed a glint of light at the base of backside of the hill, moving slowly toward him in the shadows, but he couldn't make out the source.

Fala had a decision to make—risk losing sight of the Chalcedi to see who or what was moving below or ignore the potential threat below and continue to follow the horde. With one more glance toward Angeni and Ogima, he decided he would be able to easily regain contact with the horde—they were traveling in plain sight—but whatever moved below appeared to be attempting to hide their movements, so he started picking his way down the hill, moving from boulder to boulder to hide his approach.

When he thought he was close enough to see what was making the noises, he poked his head up from behind a rock, and some distance away, approaching his position, he saw the sphere. Amadah! It was his group! They looked like antlings beneath the bulk of the sphere, cradling it in their arms, moving in concert, but he could make out the distinctive shapes of wings and the dark blur of black fur. Where was his Amadah? He scuttled the rest of the way down the hill, no longer caring if he was seen or heard, then raced along the base of the hill toward them.

One of his group must've caught his movements in the darkness, because they lowered the sphere. He saw their wide eyes, white in the shadows, and knew he had frightened them, so he slowed and waved his claw. Still, he didn't see his Amadah.

Finally, stepping out from behind the sphere, he saw the glow of her auburn hair and the deep green of her skin. He waved again, and at that moment, a scream pierced the silence.

Instinctively, Fala dropped to the ground, scanning over his shoulder to see if the Chalcedi were coming for them.

"Fala? Fala!" It was Amadah. She was running to him.

Fala bolted as fast as he could to her side, clamped his clawed hand over her mouth as he reached her, and dragged her closer to the base of the hill, deep within the shadows. "Silence."

She engulfed him in her arms and burrowed against him as if she were trying to climb into his skin. "You should be dead."

"Chalcedi." Fala pointed beyond the hill.

The rest of the group rushed to Fala's side, touching him as if he weren't real, pawing at him, embracing him.

"Chalcedi." At Fala's word, everyone hunkered down. Kilchi and Chevei hurried back to the sphere and rolled it closer to the base of the hill.

"How touch sphere?" Fala asked.

"It's a long story. Oh, I can't believe it! I just can't believe you're here! How? How is it possible?" Amadah clutched him as if she feared he would disappear like smoke.

"Kindra came. Now gone."

"Gone? Gone where?"

"Fala's fault," he choked out.

"She came and saved you?" Enla asked.

"Stood on plate."

144

"She took your place." Enla smiled. "Of course, she would."

"When the mountain collapsed, I thought..." Amadah's fresh tears flowed. She buried her face against his chest.

"Fala here now. Never leaving Amadah. We are bound."

Amadah wept. "I never thought I'd hear you say those words again. We are bound."

"We are bound."

"Forever."

"Forever."

They held each other as the rest of the group watched, some sharing tears of joy. Finally, Fala looked around the group. "Yiska?"

"He's gone, Fala," Enla said. "He died protecting the sphere."

Then, Fala caught a glimpse of Nikani, and he stepped back, taking a defensive posture.

Amadah looked up at him, and seeing his glare toward Nikani, she smiled. "Nikani has come back to us. He saw Ogima for what he was."

"Ogima." Fala spit the name like he had something bitter in his mouth and pointed. "Ogima marches with Chalcedi. Flies with Angeni."

"Angeni has indeed been turned," Meda said. "Nikani and I tried to reach her, but..."

"So, Ogima is here?" Nikani interrupted. Fala pointed again, and Nikani's eyes narrowed. "I promised next cycle I saw him I would kill him."

"No, Nikani, we're taking the sphere to the mountain," Amadah said. "We must stay the course."

"He's right here, Amadah. Within reach. What if you go ahead, and I will catch up to you?"

"We must stay together. Remember? We have to work together, or we fail."

"We can wait until they camp, I can sneak in, kill Ogima, and get out before anyone knows I was there. Then all our problems are solved. With Ogima dead, the Chalcedi would have no one to lead them."

"You would risk the sphere falling into Ogima's hands to get revenge?" The whites of Enla's eyes glowed in the darkness.

"Not revenge!" Nikani argued. "Don't you see? He's the source of all our problems. Fala, you see that, don't you?"

Fala seethed at every mention of Ogima's name. "Betrayer. Liar. Murderer. Fala kills Ogima."

"No!" Nikani shouted, then remembered where they were. "No, he's mine."

"This is exactly what our friend warned against." Aleshanee grasped Nikani's arm and shook him, as much as her little hands could muster. "Control breeds control. Hate breeds hate. Don't respond in kind. Remember?"

Nikani sighed. "I'm sorry, it's just such a good opportunity. He's so close, and he's vulnerable out here. We never had a real chance to get close to him before."

A shadow passed across the hill. Fala looked up and saw four Chalcedi flyers circling overhead. A loud squawk told him his group had been spotted. "Hide!" he hissed, but the Chalcedi dove toward them and were upon them, grabbing in their talons those who tried to run.

Fala spread himself over Amadah, hiding her from their sight. Nikani twisted and bucked in the Chalcedi's grip, batting against their legs in a futile attempt to get free. Chevei and Meda took to the air to battle against the two Chalcedi who had Aleshanee and Misa in their clutches. Kilchi and Enla made it to the sphere and were rolling it away when one Chalcedi grabbed for it. An earsplitting screech and the smell of burning feathers, and the Chalcedi tumbled to the ground, dead. No other Chalcedi tried to retrieve the sphere or the two who were moving it away.

Apparently satisfied with their catch, the Chalcedi flew over the hill to return their prizes to Ogima, with Nikani, Aleshanee, and Misa still in their talons. Meda and Chevei gave chase to the crest of the hill, observed where the Chalcedi took their friends, then they returned to their group.

Fala rose and helped Amadah to her feet. "Is everyone alright?" Amadah asked. No one was injured, so she called everyone to gather around the sphere. "We have no choice now. With three of our members captured, we can't continue on our journey to the mountain without them. We must confront Ogima here."

"Foolish," Fala replied. "Greater numbers. Only advantage is stealth."

"So, Nikani's plan? Sneak into their camp?"

Fala nodded. "Fala goes."

"I'm going with you," Kilchi insisted. "I won't leave Misa's fate in someone else's hands."

Fala nodded. "Best choices, Fala and Kilchi. Equipped for stealth. Experienced hunters."

"You're not going anywhere without me," Amadah insisted.

"You need to consider this—Ogima now knows we are here, and he will surely send his forces back to collect up the rest of us," Chevei pointed out. "He does not abide being crossed."

"Meda, Chevei, do you think Ogima will kill them?" Kilchi asked. "Torture them?"

"He is capable of both, but if I know Ogima, he will have his eyes set on a bigger prize." Chevei glanced at the sphere.

Meda agreed. "The Chalcedi will report what they saw, which includes telling Ogima about the sphere and its power. He will want that sphere, which means I believe he will use our friends as bait to lure us to his camp in hopes of making a trade—our friends for the sphere. If they are damaged, he defeats his own purpose, so I do not think he will kill or torture them—yet."

"But we cannot trust any deal he offers. He will promise, but he will never deliver."

"We won't let it come to that." Amadah reached out her hand to the sphere, almost as if she thought touching it would give her answers.

"We must find someplace to hide the sphere from him," Enla said. "We can't risk him getting his hands on it."

"Nor can we risk getting caught ourselves," Meda said.

"We're trying to figure out an impossible situation on our own again. Aleshanee would tell us to ask for help." Amadah looked up into the darkened sky.

"Fala scouts hide." He darted to the base of the hill.

"Wait, Fala," Amadah called.. "Let's ask for help first."

"Who helps? No one but us."

"That's not true. We have our friends to help us, like Kindred helped you."

Fala's brow furrowed, but he trusted Amadah, so he waited. Enla reached out her paws, open as if to receive. "We need your help again. We got ourselves into another mess and don't know how to get out."

A beam of golden light from the sphere highlighted a circle on the ground before them. Fala gawked as Eleutheri, clothed in a golden cloak and light shimmering around her, rose from the circle and spoke. "You are able to overcome with the help of the Forever. I encourage you to remember and follow your path."

Another beam, this one like blush roses, colored a circle on the side of the hill, and Na'ro appeared, sitting on a boulder. "Have courage, my loves. The path may be difficult, but you are strengthened by the Forever and the Great Love. Do not lose your way."

"You will want to protect the sphere, first and foremost," Eleutheri encouraged.

"How do we protect the sphere?" Amadah asked. "I guess that means finding a hiding place for it the Chalcedi can't find."

"Wisdom, my loves," Na'ro replied. "Follow wisdom."

"What is wise in this case?" Enla asked.

"Listen to ones with knowledge," Eleutheri replied, and the two glowing figures disappeared.

The remaining members of the little band looked at each other for several beats. Then, Kilchi nodded. "Well, I believe Fala knows the most about setting up a hide."

"If Fala finds a hidden cave, I can explore inside to find the best places to hide the sphere," Enla offered.

"That's it, then," Amadah said. "Fala and I will find a hidden cave. Enla, come with us. When we return, we'll hide the sphere, and then we'll figure out how to get our friends back."

"I could be scouting out the Chalcedi while they look." Kilchi glanced back in the direction the Chalcedi had disappeared.

"I know you must be impatient to get to Misa, Kilchi, but we'll need you to help us carry the sphere. Fala is strong enough to take the place of our missing friends, but he can't touch the sphere, so we'll still need you."

"Why Fala not touch sphere?"

"Because you've not gone to the First World," Amadah explained.

"Fala saw First World. With Kindra."

"How is that possible? You..."

Kilchi groaned. "Come on! Let's move. I don't want Misa in Ogima's clutches one beat more than absolutely necessary."

Fala, Enla, and Amadah scoured along the base of the hill for any crevasses that might lead into a cave system, but with so many rockfalls and collapsed sections of the hill, they found nothing. Fala felt an unrelenting pressure to move, to hurry, to succeed. His Amadah was vulnerable, and the value of the sphere, for which he almost died, was immeasurable. It meant life or death for the whole world.

Finding nothing at the base, Fala moved up the knoll, climbing over boulders in hopes that one of the cave-ins would reveal an opening into the heart of the hill. Enla and Amadah remained at the base, afraid to slow Fala down. Frustration boiled in Fala's belly. He found nothing.

He scurried back down the hill. "Look other side." He pointed to another knoll rising behind them. This hillock was smaller and evidenced even more damage from the quakes and slides, so Fala was forced to move slowly as he searched in the rubble for a cave entrance, but his careful search paid off as he discovered a crevasse hidden from view behind a huge slide of rocks. Fala whistled for Enla and Amadah, who clambered up the hillock. They ducked into the crevasse, picking their way around piles of large bones clustered near the entrance.

"Are these Onyxi?" Amadah whispered, her obvious concern for Enla creasing her brow.

Enla picked up a large, twisted tusk. "Banask. Massive animals. They used to roam the hills, terrorizing any Onyxi who dared set foot outside their caves. They probably sought refuge here from the blast and fires of the falling sky light, then were trapped by the rockslide." The tusk clattered to the ground. "I guess they're all gone now. Like the Onyxi." She disappeared into the cave and reappeared several beats later with a smile. "There is a perfect place farther in to tuck the sphere away out of sight, even if the Chalcedi happened to find this entrance."

So, the three hurried back to the waiting group. Together, they lifted the sphere, with a little more difficulty than before, and carried it across the small valley to the hillock. The struggle to get the sphere up to the crevasse took much longer than Fala hoped. At several points, Kilchi had to get behind the sphere and push while Fala pulled from the front to drag it over rockfalls. Once, the sphere started to slide off the edge of a boulder down the hill. Kilchi managed to brace it against the rock while the rest of the group scrambled to pull it back up to a stable position.

Finally, they pulled the sphere up and over the rockslide that hid the crevasse and rolled it through the opening, crunching the banask bones under its weight. Enla led the group through twisting tunnels to a curved inset. The sphere slid into the cavern like the inset was carved out specifically to hold it.

"Now what?" Enla asked.

"Hide. Wait for dark. Kilchi and Fala go, free others."

"I'm going, too," Amadah said.

"Stealth against greater force."

"I can be stealthy. No arguments. I won't be separated from you again."

"Would it not be better to all go together? It seems advantageous to have more numbers with which to fight the Chalcedi," Meda observed.

150

Kilchi's fur bristled along his neck and back at the mention of the Chalcedi. "We don't want to fight the Chalcedi. We want to take them by surprise and pull our friends out from under their noses."

"Do we hide here to wait for you?"

"Hiding in the same location where we secreted the sphere is unwise. If we are to follow wisdom, wisdom dictates locating a different hiding place." Chevei's head swiveled seeking better ground for their hiding place.

Amadah groaned. "I can't believe this! We had the perfect opportunity to reach the high mountain while Ogima and his army were gone. We could've avoided them and completed our task. Now we're stuck having to deal with freeing hostages and probably fighting Ogima and the Chalcedi." She looked at Fala, her face furrowed with pain. "And you just came back to me, just to face another terrible danger. Will it ever end?" She reached out and grabbed his clawed hand, pulling him to her.

"Best protection is attack."

Amadah closed her eyes and nodded. "Get it together, Amadah. Now isn't the cycle for self-pity. Let's find another hiding place. Then, when the sky light falls, we will go get the others."

CHAPTER NINETEEN

The Dark Lord

Skia Skotos raised Ogima's hand to call for a halt. He had spotted his Chalcedi flyers returning from their reconnaissance, and it looked to him like they brought company. Delightful! His Chalcedi and Jacinthi fluttered down to an open field, and Angeni gently lowered the sarkikos he inhabited to the ground before the horde as the three scouts deposited their captives before Ogima.

"Where is the fourth?" Ogima folded his arms.

Chatan bowed his head. "They killed him. Killed him with a crystal ball."

"What. Are. You. Saying?"

"He touched this huge crystal ball they were holding, and it fried him like an egg on a desert rock."

Ogima frowned, then turned to inspect the prisoners. He recognized Nikani instantly. "The little runaway. So good of you to rejoin us."

Nikani gave a snarl of his own and pulled against the Chalcedi holding his arms, wrenching and twisting and kicking until the Chalcedi jerked his arms almost out of socket.

"And what have we here?" Ogima preened before Aleshanee. "One of the witnesses. Your demise was exaggerated, I see. Where is your partner?" Aleshanee beamed a placid smile but said nothing, so Ogima moved on. "A Saphiri, but one that is not quite a Saphiri. My my, it looks like some magic has happened without my knowledge. How did you manage that trick, sweetling?" Following Aleshanee's lead, Misa said nothing, lowering her eyes from Ogima's piercing glare.

Ogima turned back to Chatan. "The rest of them?"

"We had to leave them, Lord Ogima. They had two Jacinthi with them, plus a Topazi and a Carneli, so if you give me leave to take more fighters, we'll go back and capture the rest."

"You're saying you weren't able to defeat two feeble Jacinthi flyers?"

"They weren't feeble, Lord! Chevei was one of them!"

Hearing this news, Ogima's face darkened like the skies above them. "Chevei. Back-stabbing, insolent—he will pay with his life. Angeni!"

"My Lord?"

"One of your Jacinthi betrays us! What do you have to say for yourself?"

"Lord, I..."

"Chatan, who was the other Jacinthi?"

"Meda, Lord Ogima."

"Well, Angeni? How do you explain two deserters from your Jacinthi charges?"

"I cannot, Lord." Angeni groveled on the ground before Ogima.

"Get up!" Ogima barked, disgusted. "You are supposed to be my queen. Stop acting like a youngling!"

Angeni scrambled off the ground, brushed off her glittering robes, and bowed. "My King, I cannot explain why anyone would desire to leave your protection and care. Only a fool would do so. They must be fools."

"Do you hear that?" Ogima chortled to his captives. "You are in a company of fools. Does that make you fools? I believe it does."

"The way of fools seems right to them, but the wise walk a different path," Aleshanee sang softly.

Ogima chuckled. "I am sure you fools do believe you are doing what is 'right,' as if you know what 'right' is. You are pitiable creatures." Skia Skotos sneered, twisting Ogima's face into a grotesque mask.

Aleshanee giggled.

"By the way, what is this crystal ball Chatan described? A weapon of some kind? Magic, hmmm?" Ogima tickled Misa under her chin. "Come now, tell Ogima what he wants to know."

Aleshanee continued her song:

> "Walk with the wise and become wise;
> But walk with mockers and suffer.
> For fools die for lack of sense,
> And their folly yields more folly.
> The wise inherit great honor,
> And the peace of the wise is their crown,
> But fools receive only shame,
> And their own mouths do them in."

Ogima no longer found this song amusing. He swiped his open hand across her face, almost knocking her down. The pearlescent color of the little Emraldi's face deepened to a muddy brown where she was struck. Nikani screamed and bucked in the Chalcedi's tight grip. Misa raised her head high, appearing almost regal as she stood, hands pinned behind her back. "One of you will tell me of this magic weapon that burns with a touch, the easy way, or the hard way. I care not. Chatan!"

"Yes, Lord Ogima."

"Take several flyers, and take Catori with you, and go find the rest of them. I want the other witness!" He grabbed Chatan's chest. "And bring me that crystal ball! I don't care what it costs. I want it!"

Chatan cringed. "I will, Lord." Hee called Catori and several flyers to his side, and they took off for the hills.

"Angeni, you will make these creatures talk! Show me you deserve the honor I have bestowed upon you! Get the answers I seek."

Angeni bowed, then faced the creatures she had once called friends. "Aleshanee, it is so good to see you."

"Angeni, I truly wish I could say the same." Aleshanee rubbed her cheek.

"We set our camp here and wait for Chatan's return with the other prisoners," Ogima proclaimed. "Set up shelters for your Lord and his Prophet."

Chalcedi scurried to unfurl colorful, fringed canopies, which they erected side-by-side on the open field. "Come with me, my friends," Angeni cooed to the three prisoners. "We will talk. I am sure we can come to an understanding."

As Nikani was ushered past Angeni by his Chalcedi guard, he spit on her robe. Angeni appeared genuinely surprised by the affront. "Cover his mouth!" The guard shoved a piece of cloth so deep into Nikani's mouth, he started gagging.

Ogima grabbed Angeni's arm. "Get answers for me, or pay the price with them."

"I will, Lord, do not fear. I know them all very well. They will tell me everything you desire to know."

CHAPTER TWENTY

The Chalcedi

Cholena gathered the uninjured, escaped slaves together, setting up a triage and treatment area to care for the ones with injuries from the burning of the sky. The worst injuries were burns, with some species showing blackened skin and some showing huge blisters. Those who were able to remain in the river escaped the brunt of the scorching heat and wind, including all of the Turqosi, who appeared unharmed, and who also showed no interest in helping those with injuries.

Cholena's experience distributing different substances for a variety of purposes to the Chalcedi flock served her well in this circumstance. Using the burned bark of the river trees she found fallen along the bank to make a salve, she smeared the balm on the blisters to soothe the pain and had the injured chew on pieces of bark, too. She sent a few Jasperi to catch and skin fish from the river, and when they returned with the fish skins, Cholena laid the skins over the blackened burns and wrapped the wounds with cloth she ripped from slaves' clothing. She held out little hope for these creatures' survival, but she had done what little she could to make them more comfortable.

The Turqosi were getting restless, she could tell. Leenha, the Turqosi leader, sent a scouting party out shortly after the heat waned and the sky turned grey. Cholena was fairly certain when the scouting party returned, the Turqosi would be ready to move, no matter the condition of the injured slaves. Cholena would have to take a stand for their sakes. After promising she would obey Leenha's orders, she wasn't looking forward to that confrontation.

Although it was becoming difficult to tell, Cholena thought the sky light was starting to fall when the scouting party returned. She risked leaving the wounded untended and sidled up to hear the scouts' report. Unfortunately, the scouts used Turqosi hand signals to share most of the information. The scouts were animated—excited, or perhaps distressed? Cholena gleaned something about large coverings or tents, and at one point, Eteena pointed to Cholena, then made a gesture indicating very large numbers, meaning a lot of Chalcedi. Apparently, the Chalcedi were in the area, but tents? Tents were useless to her kind. What was happening?

When their report concluded, Cholena stood before Leenha. "What did they find?"

Leenha glared at her as if her question was a distraction and an imposition, but she responded by pointing toward the open plains and foothills of the high mountain. "Many. Camped."

"Who are they? Where are they from? Not the Chrysoli?" Cholena looked behind her, apprehensive.

Leenha swiped her webbed hand across her throat, her version of "no." "Chalcedi, Jacinthi, Jasperi. Together."

It wouldn't be the group from the Beryli Sea, because she was the only Chalcedi with them when she left. "Did the scouts tell you anything about them?"

"Danger," was all Leenha offered. "Scout."

"I would like to go with you." Leenha slashed her throat again, but Cholena pressed. "These are my kind. I can help you figure out what they're doing."

Leenha considered Cholena's words, nodded once, then gestured for her to follow. With a single gesture, the Turqosi army formed three columns. One column veered left, crossed the river, and disappeared into the thicket on the opposite side. A second turned a hard right in the direction of the Chrysoli dome. The other, led by Leenha herself, with Cholena beside her, veered right, moving toward the low hills rising gently from the plains. The Turqosi moved as one being, without a sound, sliding from rock to boulder like a ripple lapping the shore. Cholena tried to scrunch down close to the ground to mimic their movements and fold her wings around her sarkikos to quiet the rustling sound, but it was impossible. No matter what she tried, she still made noise, and Leenha kept glaring at her. If she could fly, she would be soundless like the Turqosi, but Leenha refused to allow her to take off.

In the distance, out on an open field, Cholena saw the tents referenced by the scouts—massive, colorful canvas cloths, stretched over poles, elaborately decorated and fluttering like wings in the breeze. She saw Chalcedi milling about, some flying overhead, acting as sentries. And then she saw what looked like Angeni, with her coloration at least, garbed in bright red robes with golden braids, walking with—was that Nikani, the one who shunned her? And little Aleshanee, Amadah's friend who was dead and then alive again? And what looked like a Saphiri, but walking on legs?

As she and the Turqosi drew closer, she could see the three creatures walking with Angeni were held by their arms by Chalcedi and were being shoved along. So, they were captives. Yet, Angeni didn't look like she was being forced against her will. If anything, she seemed to be directing the Chalcedi. Why would Angeni allow her friends to be captured? Cholena couldn't make any sense of what she saw.

Then she saw Ogima, and her heart froze in her chest. He also wore exquisite robes of swirling colors, and what looked like a jewel-encrusted hat, which caused glimmering reflections on his face, making it match the swirl of color of his robe in the waning light. He bellowed and swung his arms around, directing the movements of the Chalcedi. Cholena couldn't imagine what could've happened during her stint in the Chrysoli slave camps to result in this strange tableau playing out before her.

She glanced at Leenha, who appeared strangely tense. Cholena tried to make a questioning gesture to see what Leenha planned to do, but Leenha continued to stare at the mass of creatures in the camp, perhaps gauging the risk of making contact against the chance of getting captured if she tried to avoid them. Cholena wished she could tell Leenha what she knew about Ogima, a slimy, selfish worm of a creature, but it would have to wait.

What was Angeni doing with Ogima and the Chalcedi? Ogima, who had almost blown up the entire world. The Chalcedi, who had killed Angeni's friends. Leenha made a gesture, and the Turqosi column on this side of the camp hugged the ground and slid into the tiniest of cracks and crevasses from which they could observe the goings-on in the camp. It looked like Leenha had decided to risk observation for now, but she clearly didn't want to be seen. Cholena perched behind a tumbled boulder leaning against a slide of smaller rocks, a perfect hiding place for her large form.

After the sky light fell and the camp appeared asleep, Leenha crept up to Cholena, placed her long snout against her ear, and hissed, "Sssspy."

"You want me to spy?" Leenha nodded yes. "To go in the camp and..." Leenha nodded. "No, I can't! They all know me and will recognize me. They will punish me, probably kill me for what I've done." Leenha raised one hand in question. "Before I was captured by the Chrysoli and made a slave, I joined with a group who fought against the Chalcedi and Ogima, the Amthysti. I deserted my kind. They would kill me for it."

"Ssssay ssslave."

"No, I turned on them before I was made a slave, and they know it."

"Ssssay realized wrong, tried return, captured."

"I don't think they would believe me. Angeni, the Jacinthi in the red robes, knows I remained with the others until the group split at the Beryli Sea. She knows I left and that I didn't leave to go back to the Chalcedi. She'll tell them I'm lying."

"Ssssay ssslavery opened eyesss."

Cholena paused. She could imagine a scenario where the Chalcedi would understand being with her kind would be better than being a slave. They were pragmatists in many ways. But what about Angeni and the others from her group by the sea? What would they believe?

Leenha waited, her sleek forehead wrinkled in anticipation. Finally, Cholena relented, perhaps her curiosity getting the best of her.

"I could say I escaped from the Chrysoli, and I was looking for my kind since the aerie was destroyed, and I have information on the Chrysoli and how to defeat them. They might overlook my past actions if I offer them something they see as useful."

Leenha nodded once as if the decision was made. She pointed toward the camp and nudged Cholena to leave the protective cover of her boulder. "Report here." She slithered away.

"Will you rescue me if they decide to take me captive instead of listening to me?" Cholena whispered as Leenha moved away, but Leenha only shrugged.

Cholena sighed. "Well, I guess I'm on my own once again." She slid from behind her boulder and took off, flying into the Chalcedi encampment like she belonged there.

She was spotted almost immediately by one of the flying sentries, who spiraled down to her side and ordered her to land.

"I have returned to join with you." But the Chalcedi who escorted her showed no interest in hearing her out. She brought Cholena straight to Angeni's tent.

Angeni was perched on a raised dais, with her three captives kneeling on the dirt in front of her and a Chalcedi guard alongside. Her Chalcedi guard interrupted Angeni mid-sentence. "Another traitor captured."

Recognition dawned in Angeni's eyes. "Cholena, my dear. I'm glad—and surprised to see you."

"I was captive of the Chrysoli and held as a slave, until I escaped."

"Is that so? My my, how awful for you. Lord Ogima told me the Chrysoli kept slaves."

Lord Ogima?

"This is the very reason we left the high mountain. We heard some slaves had escaped and were encamped on the plains, but Lord Ogima knew immediately we had to help them. He said the slaves would be murdered by the Chrysoli if we did not."

"This is true, Angeni. The Chrysoli are a vicious, murderous species with no regard for life."

161

"Why come to our camp, my dear?"

"I wanted to rejoin my kind after so long away." Cholena looked down, hoping her portrayal was convincing. "I had nowhere else to go."

"I see."

"And I have good information for you about the Chrysoli. I know the layout of their buildings, where they house their slaves, where they store their food, their defenses, anything you want to know."

"Very well, we welcome you to our camp. I will take you to Lord Ogima so you may pledge your fealty and worship him. First, however, I must finish my talk with these...oh, yes, you've met them! Do you remember Aleshanee?"

"I do." Cholena lowered her head in acknowledgement. Aleshanee's mournful eyes, gazing back at Cholena, gave her pause. What did Aleshanee know that Cholena did not?

"And Nikani and Misa? You know them also."

"Yes."

"Perhaps you might give them some encouragement to share in the safety and security and protection of those who worship Lord Ogima. Once you pledge yourself to him, of course."

"Um—sure, I can tell them about him."

"We know all we need to know about him already," Nikani spit out. "Save your breath."

"Nikani, now is not the cycle for holding grudges. Now is the cycle for healing. You must forgive." Nikani grumbled something unintelligible. "So much anger," Angeni sighed.

"Like Ogima," Aleshanee murmured.

"What? Oh, no, no. You do not understand! Lord Ogima is not angry like Nikani. He desires the best for us all. His striving for perfection and his ideals push him, and he in turn pushes us to achieve our best. He is passionate, yes. But not angry."

"Except for when he's killing anyone who doesn't agree with him." Nikani tossed his head with a sneer. "Like he's going to kill us."

"Lord Ogima is not going to kill you, Nikani. How ridiculous!"

"Angeni." Aleshanee hummed softly and gently. "Do you recall our friends?"

"Your friends, Amadah and the rest of your group? Yes, of course."

"No, I mean our friends who spoke to us. Your friend who came to you and took you from your sarkikos to see the survivors of the object from the sky. The light?"

Angeni blinked. "Yes, I do recall such an experience."

"Do you also remember the Dark Ones? The ones who fought against our friends. The ones we were told to resist?"

"Yes. Horrid creatures."

"Angeni, Ogima has control over the Dark Ones."

"How silly you are! Lord Ogima will fulfill the prophecy and bring all creatures to the high mountain, just as my friend showed me." Angeni closed her eyes and turned away from Aleshanee, then spoke to Cholena's guard. "Cholena needs to be cleaned up for her meeting with Lord Ogima. Take her from here and help her to prepare."

Cholena was shoved through the tent's opening into the darkness and pulled to a water station in the center of camp. "Clean yourself," she commanded, pointing to the water. Cholena splashed herself with water, preened, and fluffed her feathers. When she was escorted back to Angeni's tent, the three prisoners were gone.

"Very nice." Angeni smiled. "Let us go now to Lord Ogima. You must bow to him, only speak when he requests an answer from you, and as you leave, back away from him, never turning your back. You must refer to him as Lord Ogima or my King. Do not provoke him. He will know if you are lying, so be truthful."

Angeni requested audience. As they waited, Cholena rehearsed her story, keeping as much truth as she could without betraying her fellow slaves or the Turqosi.

Finally, Angeni was allowed to enter. She bowed, so Cholena followed her lead. Ogima stood upon a dais like Angeni's, his hands clenched behind his back, his face like stone.

"My Lord, we have a petitioner who desires to join with our camp. She says she has information about the Chrysoli which could be to our benefit. I present to you Cholena."

163

Ogima's smile rippled across his face like a writhing serpentus. "Cholena," he said expansively, opening his arms wide. "How special. You have returned to us."

"Yes, Lord Ogima."

Ogima paced the dais. "Correct me if I am wrong, but as I recall, you turned your back on your Chalcedi brothers and sisters. Is that correct?"

"Yes, Lord Ogima, but..."

"And now, we are to trust you will not betray us again?"

"If you please, Lord Ogima."

"And we are to trust the information you give us on the Chrysoli?"

"I was their slave. They are monsters. If you can stop them and free the rest of the slaves..."

"If?"

Cholena hesitated. "When you free the rest of the slaves, I want to help you."

"And that is why you are here? To—help me?" Ogima paused in his pacing, expanding the word, 'help' to multiple syllables.

"Yes, Lord Ogima."

"Really. And why would you want to help me? You did not want to help us before."

"I—I've seen how horrible it is to be a slave, and I wanted..."

Ogima thrust his head forward, seething. "What exactly do you want from me?"

"I want to help."

"I do not believe you are here to help. Tell me the truth, Cholena."

"I—I had nowhere else to go."

"Is that so? I heard something quite different."

A flash of panic raced through Cholena's chest. "What did you hear?"

"I heard you and your slave followers have taken up with the Turqosi and are on the march."

"To free the other slaves!" Cholena insisted.

"Or to attack my camp!" Ogima screeched. "Seize her! She is a liar and a betrayer and cannot be trusted! Put her with the other prisoners! I will decide her fate at sky light's rising."

Cholena was grabbed and wrestled to the ground, her wings bound to her back and arms to her side, then dragged by her talons to a mudpit behind the tents. At a single caw from her guard, several Chalcedi approached, leering at her. They were holding broad boards or whips tipped with tiny, razor-sharp metal plates. Cholena was shoved into the pit, as the Chalcedi encircled her. Their whips cracked in the air, and they pounded their wooden planks against the ground, working themselves into a frenzy. Then the first board whacked her chest, and the game was on. She was bounced back and forth across their circle like a ball in a child's game of catch-and-toss. As the metal tips bit into her flesh, Cholena couldn't help but cry out, which brought gales of gleeful laughter from the Chalcedi. The circle tightened as their implements pounded her back and ripped her flesh, driving her into the muddy ground.

Her vision started to close in, as if a fog descended around her head. Her yelps and squeals sounded distant, as if from someone else, until she was no longer able to cry out. At that point, the Chalcedi stopped, their fun over. Her guard dragged her to a metal pen set up behind Ogima's tent. She saw her friends through half-closed eyes, her vision further blurred by blood seeping into them. Aleshanee, Nikani, and Misa, mud-covered, huddled in the back of the pen. Aleshanee lay across Misa's legs, her face swollen, her wings hanging in tatters, as Misa gently stroked her brow. The Saphiri's blue color wasn't visible through the red and brown smears of blood and mud and bruises. Nikani sat on his haunches apart from the other two, clutching his knees to his chest and muttering to himself, his face a twisting mask of rage and pain.

Grabbing Cholena by the ropes binding her, the Chalcedi guard threw her into the pen and left her, face-down in the muck.

Chapter Twenty-One

The Chrysoli

Kola padded up and down the hall outside the intensive care area as he waited for the medichi tending Tocho to make her report. He was already weary of command, something Tocho more than took in stride, he loved it. Kola knew his strength was working behind the scenes, following through on assignments, and carrying out orders, not directing others. He always had a rumbling of doubt, questioning, and disagreement in his gut with Tocho's decisions, but he willingly followed his orders rather than carry the burden of responsibility. Now, depending on the medichi's report, Kola might become the responsible one, the one that others grumbled against.

The large door creaked behind him, and Tocho's medichi pushed through it. Her vacuous eyes told Kola everything he needed to know. "Well?"

"Tocho is damaged," she reported, her voice flat.

"Isn't there anything to be done for him? Surgery?" Kola felt an icy tendril snake up his spine.

"The damage is too extensive to repair."

Kola stared at the floor for several beats. The medichi was waiting, shifting from paw to paw, expecting Kola to issue the order, but Kola couldn't bring himself to say the inevitable words. "Wait here." He stalked from the science building and across the yard, moving blindly, as a specter, unaware of where he was going or why he chose to go there, until he found himself standing in the open doorway of the slave quarters.

167

He watched the slaves cower away from the door, trying to make themselves invisible behind bed frames and under blankets, and he felt the same mortified feeling he always felt when dealing with the slaves. He scanned the bunkhouse for the Jacinthi slave, Kwania, finding her hunched in a corner, her wings folded over her head. "Kwania!" he barked, trying to exude authority he didn't feel or want.

She rose slowly, making her way to the door, her eyes down and her tail feathers dragging in the dirt. She didn't speak but stood in silence, waiting for his command. He hated it. "Come with me." She shuffled along behind him as he led her outside. "May I ask you a question?" He stopped and turned to face her. She met his gaze. "Why didn't you fly away like all the other Jacinthi slaves? The dome is open— your wings are not clipped. Why are you still here?"

"I will not abandon the other slaves to their fate." She sounded so much stronger than he felt.

"But you can't do anything for them. Why not save yourself?" Her withering look silenced him, so he turned and walked on toward the science building. When she failed to follow, he gestured stiffly, reasserting his command posture. As they entered the building, he glanced at her. "Tocho needs your help."

He half-expected her to scoff and ask why she should do anything for her captor. Instead, she said, "What does he need?"

Kola's shame deepened. "Our medichi has determined Tocho is damaged and beyond repair. I need to know if you have some—skill we don't possess that could help him."

"I will need to examine him."

"Come with me." Kola and Kwania, now walking side-by-side, passed by the still-waiting medichi without a word, pushed into intensive care, and approached Tocho's stretcher. Kwania started to feel along Tocho's hip but startled back when Tocho growled and snapped at her.

Kola leaned down to meet Tocho's eyes. "Tocho, I brought help."

"Just leave me alone," Tocho growled, and Kola knew the medichi had already reported her findings to his leader.

"Don't give up. Not yet. Kwania may know…"

"A slave? Go away."

"She saved your life once already."

"For all the good it did me."

"Let her try."

Tocho breathed a staccato grumble but submitted to Kwania's examination. She poked and prodded, eliciting yelps and some howls of pain, then she flipped him to his other side, and starting prodding again. Finally, she felt along his spine, feeling bone by bone, notch by notch, until she reached his tail.

"I believe, with the right equipment and extensive therapy, I could possibly repair the damage. But I do not know if the equipment I need is available here."

"Tell the medichi what you need." Kola rushed from the room and returning with the medichi.

"Do you perform focused light-assisted surgery?" Kwania asked. "And do you have the capability to perform joint replacements?"

"I'm not familiar with either procedure," the medichi said. "Focused light? To do surgery? It sounds preposterous."

"It is minimally invasive and speeds recovery."

"We have nothing like that. And to replace a damaged joint? How would you do that?"

"You cut out the damaged joint, take the same joint from another sarkikos, and replace the damaged one with the new one."

"Impossible! You would be mixing souls. Who knows what would come from such a thing?"

"We have done it with good result," Kwania replied.

"You've already mixed his blood with another. Now you want to mix in someone else's bone? He won't be Tocho anymore."

"He will still be Tocho, just with another bone in him."

"This is strange magic, Kola," the medichi said. "Tocho would not like it."

"Do not speak for me," Tocho grumbled. "I'm not gone yet."

"Apologies, Tocho." The medichi backed away.

Kwania bent over Tocho. "I may be able to help you, but it will be a long and difficult recovery, and nothing is guaranteed. I would have

169

to design and develop the tools I need to perform the focused light-assisted surgery, but I believe Miakoda could help me using equipment from her research. I would need your permission to replace two of your joints with ones from a deceased Chrysoli."

"Disgusting. I don't want pieces of a dead sarkikos inside me."

"Consider the alternative," Kola whispered.

"What difference would it make? The slave said it isn't guaranteed to work, and the recovery would be long and difficult, which means I would no longer be the leader of the pride."

"But you could return as leader after your recovery," Kola reassured him.

"Who would willingly give up leadership once they knew the pleasures of it?" Tocho heaved a rattling sigh. "It would mean a battle, and unless I misunderstand the slave, I would be poorly equipped to win a battle once she was done with me."

"I would willingly relinquish leadership back to you after your recovery."

"You say so now..."

"At least you would still be alive."

"Would I? Not by my definition of living."

"It is a chance," Kwania intervened. "As it is now, you will never be able to walk again."

"That won't matter."

"What do you mean?" Kwania asked. "Of course, it will matter to you."

"He means he'll be dead," Kola explained.

"Why? None of his injuries are fatal."

"Chrysoli who serve no useful purpose to the pride are taken outside the dome and left to die."

"That is barbaric! Do you see no intrinsic value in life at all? Even your own kind?"

"Your ways are not our ways." Tocho moaned with pain. "We do what's best for the pride."

"How is losing a strong leader best for the pride? Just because you cannot walk..."

"I can only lead if I'm strong." Tocho coughed, then moaned again. "I'm ready, Kola. Take me out."

"No!" Kwania placed her arm across Tocho. "Please! Give me the opportunity to save you." Tocho turned his head away.

Kola frowned. "Tocho, do you want to ask Leoti her desires?"

"I know her desires."

"But Tocho..."

"No."

"Do you want to see her before you go?"

"I don't want her to see me like this."

"This is ridiculous!" Kwania exploded. "You will not take this creature out onto the plains and leave him to die."

Kola's face darkened. "You forget yourself, slave."

"You are the one who invited me here and asked for my help. Let me help!"

"The decision is mine to make." Tocho lifted one side of his mouth into a semblance of a snarl, but quickly let it droop over his fang.

"Tocho, I plead with you. Let me try. You have nothing to lose. If I fail, then you may choose to surrender and die. But if I succeed, you have the chance to live a long and productive life, a life with meaning and purpose. I am sure, if Leoti is your mate, she would choose life."

"You don't know Leoti, so don't speak as if you do. She acts for the benefit of the pride, as do I."

"Kola, you sought me out to give Tocho a chance, so you must believe this decision is a horrible waste of life. Tell Tocho you do not agree with his decision. Tell him he is wrong."

Kola did disagree. He wanted to tell Tocho he was wrong, to tell him to try, to live, but as he tried to speak, his throat constricted, and nothing came out but a guttural grunt.

Kwania squawked in exasperation and leaned down in Tocho's face. "Coward! A courageous creature would take the chance. A truly strong creature would go through the pain and effort of recovery. A brave creature would stand up for life instead of giving up. You are not courageous, strong, or brave. You are a coward." Tocho growled deep in the back of his throat. "Is that how you will be remembered? Tocho, the coward, who refused to fight for life? Tocho, the coward, who forgot about his pride for an easier path for himself? Tocho, the coward, who abandoned his mate?"

Tocho lifted himself and swiped his paw across Kwania's face, striking her to the ground. "Remove this slave from my presence," Tocho commanded, then flopped back on his stretcher, his breaths labored.

Kwania pulled herself up quickly and started to dig her fingers into his spine. "You have furthered the damage, you fool," she snapped. "We must go to surgery now, or he will die on this table."

Kola stood, staring blankly for several beats, before saying, "Take him." Tocho moaned as if in protest. "On my authority."

Kwania nodded once, then pushed the stretcher through the double doors and back into the surgery suite. "Get the medichi and Miakoda," she called as the doors swung closed behind her.

Kola sent the medichi into surgery, then rushed out into the main area of the science building and called for Miakoda. "Hurry! Get to the surgery. Kwania operates on Tocho." Satisfied Miakoda would obey his orders, Kola left the science building and hurried to the Master's hall, where he would call Leoti from her chambers to be present when Tocho woke from surgery. If anyone could command Tocho, it was Leoti.

Kola crossed the compound, pushed past the guards without a word, and entered the domed, okechan hallway. "Leoti!" he roared, hoping she was on this floor. "Leoti!"

A sleek, golden head with chocolate, almond-shaped eyes, poked out from behind one of the antechamber doors. "Kola," Leoti murmured. "How pleasurable to see you." She moved with a sensual glide from the chamber, her muscles rippling beneath her skin, her fur the rich color of honey. Her eyes narrowed. "Have you come to lay your claim?"

"I come to bring you to Tocho's side."

Leoti stopped short, her eyes wide again. "Tocho's side. He recovers?"

172

"He is in surgery."

"I was told he would not recover." She purred, her voice lush and thick like sugared buttercream. She brushed against his side and nuzzled his cheek. "Which leaves me a very important choice to make." She chuckled, a deep, raspy sound. "Do you have an opinion about my choice, Kola?"

Kola's legs wobbled beneath him, and his heart pounded. "You are premature. Tocho lives."

"But not for long, I hear."

"We don't know that."

"But you want that, don't you, Kola?" Leoti crossed in front of him, stroking her back across his neck, then she flicked her tail into his eyes. She looked back over her shoulder, chuckling again. "I see you do." She rubbed against his other side, completing her circuit of his sarkikos with a playful nip on his hindquarters.

"Tocho needs—encouragement. He needs you to tell him you want him to live."

Leoti threw her head back and howled. When she caught her breath, she asked, "Why would I want damaged goods?"

"He may yet recover."

Leoti tossed her head is dismissal. "He is broken. I don't want broken." She rubbed her fur against his. "I need someone strong, vibrant, alive—powerful." She drew out the last word, meeting his eyes, their faces almost touching, then she blinked once and moved away. "Unless you aren't those things."

"I'm loyal and true. Loyal to Tocho, and ready to see a better cycle for the Chrysoli."

Leoti gave a throaty chortle. "Every male envisions himself as the one who revolutionizes the Chrysoli way of life. You claim loyalty to Tocho yet can't wait to change everything to bring a new cycle. Are you a revolutionary, Kola? Do you seek to change the Chrysoli ways of life and death?"

"We must return to Tocho. He needs you."

"Tocho needs to go ahead and die and have it over," Leoti snapped. Her moods flipped like the tip of her tail. She purred and licked Kola's cheek. "Then we can—" she licked again, "—pursue life."

Kola steeled his weakened knees and lifted his head out of her reach. "I am going. Will you come?"

Leoti sighed, her face furrowing into a pout. "Don't you desire me?"

"Of course I desire you. But you are Tocho's until he dies, and Tocho still lives. I would not betray his trust."

"What about my trust?" Her lithe sarkikos wound around him like a coiling serpentus. "What about my desires?"

"Tocho needs your support, your comfort, and your help. His recovery will be long and difficult."

Leoti sneered. "I am just as likely to suffocate him as help him. Let's leave Tocho to his slow, difficult death. If you join with me, the throne is yours. Will you take your queen?"

Kola's exasperation exceeded his longing. He turned, and with a flick of his tail, stalked down the hall toward the double doors. "Wait," Leoti called. Kola turned back, and Leoti walked stiffly toward him. "I will go. But if he is not repaired in full, he will die. Tocho would wish it, and you will not stand in the way of the natural order of things."

Kola and Leoti made their way back to the science building and into the surgery suite, where Kwania stood over an unconscious Tocho, flanked by Miakoda and the medichi. Their hands were deep inside his flesh and coated with his blood. Leoti made a retching sound, turned tail, and fled from the room. "Progress?" Kola asked.

"I fear Tocho has crushed the central nerve in his back with his movements. Repairing the fractured bones will in no way guarantee the damage to the nerve will self-repair. There is nothing I can do beyond set the bones and hope."

"What about the joints you were to replace?"

"Tocho was struggling to breathe, so continuing with the joint replacement is not possible now. If his central nerve does not repair itself, he will not walk or breathe on his own again, so the joint repair would be superfluous."

Kola sighed. "Stop the surgery."

"I have not completed..."

"Stop. Now. Tocho is, for all intents and purposes, dead."

"We must wait and see..."

"How often have you seen a central nerve repair itself?"

"Well, I have not, but..."

"Neither have I. How about you, medichi?"

"Our studies say the central nerve cannot repair once damaged, very much like the brain, which once damaged, does not recover."

Kola nodded. "This is the very reason the Chrysoli make special provision for those damaged beyond repair. No Chrysoli wants to live without the ability to move, to think, to contribute to the pride."

"You call murder 'special provision'?" Kwania shrieked.

"Each chooses how his or her life ends. We honor each other in this manner," the medichi explained.

"You do what is convenient, not what is right," Kwania huffed. "I will not stop before we see if Tocho survives on his own."

"Remove the breathing device," Kola insisted.

"The device is keeping him alive."

"I know."

"I will not."

"Miakoda, escort Kwania from the surgery. Medichi, remove the device. It was Tocho's wish."

Miakoda bound Kwania's arms and shoved her away from the table and out the door as the medichi pulled the breather from Tocho's throat. Tocho gave a final gasp and gargle, then expelled a long breath and lay still.

Kola lowered his head. "Cover him. No Chrysoli will see him like this, butchered like game on a table. When Miakoda returns, take him to the fire pit and burn him. We will tell the pride Tocho died with dignity on the plains, and no one will ever report differently. Do I have your word?"

"Yes, Master Kola."

Kola left the surgery, sent Miakoda to help the medichi, then unbound Kwania's arms. "Thank you, Kwania." She glared at Kola.

175

"Thank you for trying to save Tocho's life. Thank you for showing me the importance of each individual. Thank you for modeling how to care for those who treat you badly. Thank you for demonstrating to me the power of hope."

Kwania stared, mouth agape, for a few beats, then lowered her head. Kola was shocked to see tears dripping onto the stone floor. "You weep for Tocho?" He glanced at Leoti, silhouetted in the doorway, beckoning him with her eyes. "Even his mate does not cry for his death. Why do you weep for him?"

"I weep for the waste and the loss, for the frustration of powerlessness, for the horror of this place. I weep for us all, for death comes from the sky, and there is nothing we can do to stop it."

Kola stood in silence, processing her proclamation. Then he murmured, for her ears only. "I make you a promise. I will release the slaves who desire freedom. I will feed those who wish to remain. And should you choose to remain here, I will allow you free reign and all our resources to study and prepare us, if you can, for what is to come."

Kwania, tears still glistening in her feathers, looked at Kola and nodded. "Thank you."

"Will you remain with us? Will you help us prepare?"

"I will."

Chapter Twenty-Two

The Jasperi

Amadah, Fala, and Kilchi crept in a wide circle around the Chalcedi encampment, counting the guards, many of whom were sleeping. As they reached the farthest end of the camp, behind the area where the large tents billowed in the sky fall breezes, Amadah spotted a familiar sight, a pen similar to the one in which the Chalcedi held her captive at the aerie. "Look, Fala. See the metal pen behind the tent? Can you see if anyone is inside it?"

Fala slithered forward a few metrics, then gestured for Kilchi and Amadah to come. "Three, or four."

Kilchi sniffed the air. "Two guards."

"That must be them," Amadah whispered. "How do we get them out?"

"Fala and I take out the guards, you release them from the pen."

"Must be silent." Fala slashed a claw across his throat to communicate his method of attack.

"I will take mine down by the throat to keep him from calling out," Kilchi said. "But Amadah, you've got to keep our friends from making any sound, too."

"I will tell them to be quiet. How do I open the pen if it's locked?"

"Take key from guard." Fala gestured toward one of the guards, and Amadah spotted the ring of keys dangling from a cord around his neck.

177

"Then let's go." The three, hugging the ground and moving slowly, stole up to the pen and the two guards standing beside it. Fala's went down first, but before the second guard could cry out, Kilchi was on his throat, ripping it with his teeth.

Amadah placed a finger on her mouth and whispered to her friends in the pen. "Quiet. We're getting you out." No response. Amadah hoped these shapes in the dark were her friends. She made her way to the door of the pen, where Fala gave her the key he'd pulled off the guard. She opened the gate and felt her way through the mud to the back of the pen, where she found four creatures lying in a pile. "Sssshhh. Can you stand?"

"Injured are all, some worse," she heard Misa whisper.

Kilchi and Fala joined Amadah in the pen. "Are you hurt?" Kilchi asked Misa.

"Walking is possible, not for Aleshanee."

"Fala carries." Fala reached out his long arms. Misa gently placed Aleshanee in his arms. He cradled her to his chest and carried her from the pen.

"Nikani?" Amadah asked.

"Here." His small voice cracked.

"Can you walk?"

"I think so."

"Also here is Cholena," Misa said.

"Cholena? How...?"

"Captured and injured was she, like we. Unconscious now, I fear."

"We must try to revive her. She is too large to carry."

"Cholena, wake now. Rescue is come." Misa stroked Cholena's bronze feathers, and she stirred. Amadah breathed a sigh of relief.

She helped Nikani to his feet, while Kilchi assisted Misa. Then, the two of them lifted Cholena. As they walked from the pen, Amadah said, "We must hurry, as much as possible. Sky light will come soon, and we're dead if we're seen."

"I'm not leaving without killing Ogima," Nikani's hunched body straightened, and his head swiveled, looking for Ogima.

"Nikani, look at yourself. You couldn't kill a stinger fly in this state."

"I'm stronger than I look," Nikani insisted, then stumbled.

"Don't be hard-headed. The most important thing is to get away and take the sphere to the high mountain. We can complete our task without a fight if we go now while the Chalcedi are still here. Then, Ogima won't matter."

"He matters to me."

"Quiet," Fala hissed, lowering to the ground. Everyone dropped into the grass. A Chalcedi guard strolled nearby, then turned and entered the larger of the two tents.

"That was close," Kilchi whispered. They struggled to stand again, then resumed their slow and painful journey around the encampment.

As they passed the larger tent, Nikani pulled away from Amadah and half-dashed, half-limped toward it. "Nikani!" Amadah hissed, but he was gone from sight.

"Take Aleshanee." Fala handed her to Amadah. "Get others out. Fala finds Nikani."

Amadah grabbed Fala's arm, digging her fingers into his scales. "Please, be careful. I can't bear to lose you again."

"Fala comes to Amadah."

"We'll wait for you in the rocks." Amadah hurried to catch up to Kilchi and the two leaning heavily on his back.

Some of the guards who had been sleeping as they made their way into camp were now stirring in the approaching sky light's rise, making their escape torturously slow. Without Fala's keen hearing and superior sight to help them, they were forced to crawl along the ground most of the way, hoping against hope they wouldn't be seen.

Whenever they heard movement, they stopped, flattened against the dirt, and remained still. So, the trip back to their hide in the rocks took much longer than their approach, and the misty gray sky light had risen when they reached their hide.

Enla met them at the opening. "You found them!"

"Take Aleshanee," Amadah grunted, her speech pressured. "Give everyone the fruit. I'm going to Fala."

"Where's Fala? Was he captured?" Enla gasped.

"I hope not. I have to find out."

"Wise is this to leave?" Misa asked.

"I have no choice."

"Amadah, what do you want us to do?" Kilchi asked.

"Wait for us here." Frantic, Amadah dashed onto the rocks, scrambled down the hill to the flatlands, and started the slow, creeping approach among the fallen rocks toward the encampment.

Amadah was about to turn out onto the open field to approach the camp when something or someone grabbed her leg and yanked her down. She had enough presence of mind not to yelp, and when she flipped over, she clutched a rock in her raised hand to attack whatever she found.

A Turqosi, the one she remembered from the Beryli battle who was injured in the fight, stood in her face. She thought her name was Leenha, the leader of the Turqosi. Fala had dealt with before.

"Fool." Leenha hissed and spewed a wad of toxic spit on the ground. She snatched the rock from Amadah's hand and dragged her by her legs into a hole between two large rocks. Amadah sat up, her mouth agape at what she saw—a large number of Turqosi were huddled en masse behind the large rocks. Leenha put her webbed hand to Amadah's mouth. "Sssshhh."

Amadah's frenzied mind could only formulate one thought. "I—I have to get to Fala."

Leenha rolled her eyes and susurrated. "Ssstay." With a single gesture to her Turqosi, she slid from behind the rock without a sound. Two of the other Turqosi held Amadah down, and despite her squirming and wrenching against their slimy hands, they managed to keep her from leaving.

Leenha returned after several beats. "Well?" Amadah pressed.

"No Fala. Small green thing."

"What? What are you saying?"

The Turqosi hissed and rolled her eyes again. "Captured green boy."

"Oh, no! They recaptured Nikani?"

Leenha shrugged.

"But you didn't see Fala?"

Leenha turned to the Turqosi and gave a series of gestures. The Turqosi responded by spreading out, and to Amadah's eyes, it appeared they simply disappeared into the rockfall. Turning back to Amadah, Leenha pointed in the direction of the hide where Amadah's friends were waiting. "Go."

Amadah shook her head vigorously. "I must find Fala. And help Nikani."

"Too much noise!" Leenha kicked Amadah's feet.

"Will you help me?"

Leenha's hissing sounded like her version of a laugh, so Amadah stood. "Fine, I'll go alone."

"Fool. Too many." Leenha pointed toward the camp. Then, she jabbed Amadah in the chest. "Caught."

Amadah sighed. She wasn't thinking clearly. As much as she hated to admit it, Leenha was right. If she went in alone with the sky light risen, even though the sky was a dark grey, she was sure to be caught. Just like the game tipping rocks, she could see one action lead to another and another that ultimately left her entire group in Ogima's hands, the sphere lost, and in the end, the world destroyed. "I'll go back. But my group has to save Nikani and find Fala, or all is lost. Are you sure you won't help us?"

Leenha waved her hand in dismissal, so Amadah snuck from behind the large rocks and wove through the rockfall to the cave where her friends were waiting. They raised their heads, their eyes expectant and hopeful when she entered, but she had nothing but bad news. "Nikani has been recaptured. I didn't see Fala."

"Ogima is sure to kill Nikani since the rest of us escaped," Aleshanee said.

"He will be angry." Cholena's brow furrowed. "I think he was looking forward to killing me."

181

"What're we going to do?" Enla asked.

"We need help. They have greater numbers, so we can't possibly win in an open battle. I met some Turqosi on the way to the encampment, but they refused to help us."

"We couldn't trust their help anyway. They tried to kill me!" Kilchi exclaimed.

"But they didn't kill me when they had the chance, for some reason. And I don't know why they were lurking outside Ogima's camp."

"I know what they're doing." Cholena sighed. "They're scouting the camp. They consider Ogima a danger to them."

"Which he is. Why wouldn't they help us, then?"

"The Turqosi do things their way and don't really work well with others. I escaped from the Chrysoli, along with a large group of other slaves, and the Turqosi would only allow us to join with them if we agreed to come under her command. We were desperate, so we agreed."

"That's a story we need to hear, but right now, we have to come up with a plan to save Nikani and find Fala. Since the Turqosi won't help us, what about the Saphiri? Misa?"

"Helping us they would but taking too long to arrive."

"What if Chevei and Meda flew you to them?"

"Still, having to swim or walk back will be too late for Nikani and Fala."

Amadah wrenched her neck backwards and shook her clenched fists.. "We can't just sit here while Ogima kills Nikani! And I have to know where Fala is! How did we make such a mess of this?"

"Amadah, we can ask our friends," Aleshanee offered. "They will help us."

"You have indeed made quite a mess of things." Luxor's voice echoed off the stones surrounding them.

"Be kind, Luxor," Sophosi interrupted.

"I only speak truth."

"Now, you must consider what your best course would be, with your circumstances as they are." Sophosi paused. "You must not make your choices based on emotion alone, as Nikani did, but on wisdom and sound judgment."

"Remember what you learned from Veritor," Luxor added.

"Our hearts have grown cold." Aleshanee sighed and shook her head. "We allowed control to breed control and fear to breed fear in us. Now, we experience the consequences of our choices."

"That means we're on the harmony line." Kilchi moaned.

"Hatred brings death," Luxor intoned. "You must put aside all hatred if you are to fulfill your task."

"Ogima makes it difficult to put aside hatred," Meda grumbled.

"If you do not, you are no better than he," Luxor replied.

Kilchi cringed. "Ouch."

"What is the best course?" Amadah asked, fearful of what the wise Whisperer would say.

"You know the answer," Sophosi replied.

Amadah studied the ground and refused to respond. So, Aleshanee said, "We must return to the melody line, where hope and great joy may be recovered and songs of praise ring out to the Forever and the Great Love."

"That means taking the sphere to the high mountain straight away," Kilchi said." But how can we, without all of us to help carry the sphere?"

"Before Fala's return, how many carried the sphere?" Sophosi asked.

"Eight of us."

"How many carried it after Fala came and the others were captured?

"Six."

"How many now?"

"Seven." Kilchi looked around at the remaining members of the group. "We could do it."

"I won't." Amadah turned her back on the whispering voices.

"Amadah..." Aleshanee began.

"I won't!" Amadah stomped from their hide, her hands clenched and tears brimming. A breeze lifted her hair as she hit the opening. She looked up and froze. Several Chalcedi flyers, along with a Jacinthi, flew up and down the range of hills. Had they seen her? If she didn't get back inside, they would find her group, and it would be her fault. What a fool she was. She ducked into the cave, hoping she hadn't been spotted. "Chalcedi flyers," she whispered to her friends as she reentered the cavern. "A Jacinthi is with them, searching for us."

"Probably searching for the sphere," Chevei corrected.

"We can't leave for the high mountain as long as they're out there searching," Enla pointed out.

"We can't rescue Nikani, either." Kilchi uttered a low growl.

"And Fala can't get back to us. He may be in hiding somewhere nearby, and we'd never know, because he would never expose our position by risking coming back to us." Amadah moaned. "We're trapped here, at least until they leave or the sky light falls."

Meda's face fell to her chest. "Poor Nikani. I would be surprised if he lasted to sky fall."

Amadah wrapped her arms around her head. She had failed in every way possible, and her best friend and her bound mate were going to pay the price.

As if reading her mind, Luxor whispered, "Your world will pay the price if you do not come back to the light."

"What can I do? Tell me! Tell me how to come back to the light!"

"What is love?" Sophosi asked.

"I'm in no mood for your philosophical questions. Just tell me what I have to do."

Aleshanee stepped in front of Amadah and touched her arm. "Emotion is clouding your reason, Amadah. Our friend's question is the one that matters. What is love when it is true? Love is sacrifice, like Kindra's sacrifice, like Fala's sacrifice in the cave of the sphere. We must fix our eyes on the purposes of the Great Love, even if it means sacrifice."

"Sacrifice Nikani? Sacrifice Fala—again? How much more sacrifice will this quest demand from us?" Amadah covered her eyes and wept.

"All," Luxor whispered.

A heavy silence descended over the group like a thick blanket. No one moved beneath its dark weight. Finally, Amadah stood, folding her arms. "There's more than one way to sacrifice. If true love is sacrifice, then I choose to sacrifice myself. I will offer myself to Ogima in trade. My life for theirs."

"What'll you do? March into Ogima's camp and say, 'here I am, take me instead'?" Kilchi asked.

"Something like that."

Enla sucked in her breath, lifted her head, and smiled. "I have a better idea. Banask horns."

Chapter Twenty-Three

The Turqosi

Leenha watched the green girl disappear beyond the rockslide, then returned to her hidden soldiers. Using gestures, she put Lise in charge. With Cholena no longer in play, she needed information, so she was going to scout the Chalcedi encampment herself. She kept her plan to look for Fala to herself. Turning a mighty warrior from enemy to friend seemed a smart play, and if she could help Fala, she knew he would become her ally. She also knew his loyalty would never waiver, so she determined to find a way to put him in her debt. She'd considered if helping the green girl might put Fala in her debt, but decided it was to her advantage to help Fala directly, so she sent the Jasperi on her way.

Leaving her soldiers behind, she slid from the rocks, her slick skin adapting to the color of the field, so she became indistinguishable from the grey of the dirt and the sky. She moved silently but with great speed, matching the flow of the wind across tufts of waving grass. No Chalcedi, whether on the ground or in the air, would ever see her.

She reached the edge of the camp and searched for cover, which was easy enough for her to find with the many piles of useless junk the Chalcedi carried with them. Leenha snorted in disgust at the lack of preparedness and exorbitant waste of Ogima's army. If they didn't have superior size and numbers, her armies would defeat him soundly. As it was, she would wait and see what opportunities presented to her.

Ogima appeared to be readying for a celebration of some kind. The little green boy was hoisted up at the top of a pole before the larger tent. Leenha was gratified to see his spirit remained unbroken, even though his sarkikos was damaged. She might find the Jasperi useful allies, too, if she could turn them. Ogima had dressed the green boy in garish clothing with a floppy hat covering his curls. Again, Leenha marveled at the waste. If she held a prisoner who served no use to her, that prisoner would be dead, end of their story. She couldn't fathom the reason for Ogima's games. Leenha believed it would lead to Ogima's downfall. As it was, the one the green girl called Nikani was hurling insults and curses toward his captor and continuing to struggle against his chains, despite the impossibility of his predicament. Leenha was impressed.

Movement caught her eye, to her left behind the large tent. She squinted her eyes but could only sense a presence without a clear shape. Fala, Leenha assumed. She knew he was skilled at stalking, for she had been taken by surprise by him once before. She considered going to him, knowing he wouldn't risk exposure by fighting her, but decided she would wait and see what played out before revealing her presence.

Chalcedi were draping colored strips of cloth between the tents and off their edges. Two of the Jacinthi were painting a banner with large letters: WELCOME FRIENDS. Other Chalcedi were setting up torches at random places in the camp. Torches made sense to Leenha. If this were her camp, she would want to lighten the dim grey of the sky light, so she could easily spot intruders. They seemed to have another purpose in mind, however, because once the torches were lit, the Chalcedi gathered around them and danced wildly, screeching and cawing like they were possessed of some madness. The noise was grating.

Leenha saw a billow of tent fabric and knew Fala was making his move during the chaos. She paralleled his movements, still waiting to discern his plan. He reached the front edge of the tent, and the pole where Nikani was flailing and screaming. Leenha positioned herself behind the opposite side of the tent. Finally, she made out Fala's distinctive shape as he stood and reached as high as he could to grab the chain holding little Nikani in place. Nikani saw Fala but was smart enough not to call out to him, continuing instead his barrage of insults. The chain clinked against the pole as Fala tried to untwist it, so Fala dove back behind the tent to see if anyone heard.

Leenha knew Fala could use her help. She envisioned him holding her up to unbind the chain easily, instead of risking the noise and difficulty of unwinding it from below—if he would welcome her help. She was rising to move to his side when Fala stood and yanked repeatedly on the chain, creating a clamor of metal on metal. Leenha crouched low and shrunk back, checking the open field for anyone who overheard the noise. She was certain of one thing: she would not be captured for trying to help her sworn enemy. Fala was on his own.

The chain was loosening, and Nikani wriggled to pull himself free, but just as he dropped into Fala's arms, several Chalcedi poured from Ogima's tent and tackled Fala to the ground. Nikani rolled away and jumped up to run. One of the Chalcedi grabbed him easily. Fala fought viciously, injuring several Chalcedi in the process, but he was too badly outnumbered. Using the fray as cover for her escape, Leenha backed away slowly. Just then, Ogima, resplendent in his raiment, paraded from his tent to stand before the prone Fala. Leenha paused, thinking she might glean some information from hearing Ogima address his new captive.

"Well now, what have we here? Stealing my bait, are you? We cannot have that, now, can we? How can I catch my little fish if you steal my bait?" Ogima crooned, quite obviously pleased with himself. "Of course, in reality, you just *took* my bait, hook and all, and I caught you in my little trap, and now I have even better bait for an even bigger fish." Ogima chortled. "Thank you! You followed my script perfectly!" He waved his arms at those decorating the camp. "Continue your preparations! We must be ready for our guests!" Pointing at the guards holding Fala and Nikani, Ogima said, "String them up!" He clapped his hands like a child with a new toy. "I am going to enjoy this."

Just then, a single, mournful note, something akin to a strong wind blowing through a hollowed-out log, echoed from a distance. It was followed by another blast, coming from a different direction, and then another and another and another, until a cacophony, like the honking of a thousand geese skimming over the moors of the riverlands, reverberated throughout the camp. Leenha cringed at the bellowing noise, as did the Chalcedi, then she scampered through the tall grass toward her hidden soldiers.

Even the Jacinthi appeared frightened by the strange occurrence. As the last note faded, a voice boomed from beyond the camp. "Ogima! Let them go!" Leenha craned her neck to try to find the source of the voice, but she saw no one.

Ogima's eyes narrowed. He hissed at one of the nearby Chalcedi. "Find them!" The Chalcedi took to the air to circle the open fields beyond the camp.

"Ogima!" This call came from the other side of the field. "You will let them go!"

"Go! Go!" Ogima insisted, waving more Chalcedi into the air. "Who dares command me?" Ogima screeched, his voice echoing across the plain.

Directly across from Ogima, a third voice bellowed, "Let them go!"

"I will let them go, in exchange for the sphere I covet."

"You shall never hold the sphere," one voice roared.

"You shall never have the witnesses," another voice cried.

"Let them go!" a different voice thundered.

"Watch me!" Ogima turned to the Chalcedi guarding Fala and Nikani. "Hang them up, high, where they can be seen. I will shock them until their flesh hand from their bones, and we will see how these challengers handle such a sight."

Fala bucked against the hold of the Chalcedi, and they were forced to try to wrestle him back to the ground. At the same moment, Nikani stomped with both feet on the exposed talon of the Chalcedi holding him, then kicked the Chalcedi in the stomach. Gasping for air, the Chalcedi loosed his hold. Nikani broke free and grabbed a sword from one of the Chalcedi wrestling with Fala. With surprising quickness, Nikani darted up and shoved the sword deep into Ogima's side.

Ogima's shriek was so piercing, Leenha fell to the ground and covered her earholes. Blood spurted from the wound. Ogima stared, dumbfounded, at the sword protruding from his sarkikos, gaped at Nikani, then collapsed like a sack of bones.

The camp fell deathly silent for several beats, Chalcedi and Jacinthi staring at each other in shock. Then, a single, mournful voice penetrated the silence with a high-pitched squeal. "Noooooooo." Angeni raced across the open field to Ogima's side.

Nikani sprinted toward the rocks, but Angeni brayed, "Kill him!" and his Chalcedi guard took to the air. A new cry resounded across the field as Amadah rushed from her cover toward Nikani, but she was too late. The Chalcedi ran Nikani down, lifted him in the air before Amadah, and broke his neck like he was cracking a limb on a sapling tree. Amadah's knees folded beneath her.

Cholena, hidden within the dark grey clouds above the center of the camp, plummeted toward the ground, scooping up Amadah in her talons before she returned to the clouds. Chevei and Meda, also flying in the clouds, swooped toward Fala, dragging the Chalcedi off of him one by one and tossing them aside, but the Chalcedi recovered quickly. Brandishing their swords and clubs, they swiped and whacked at the Jacinthi until they were forced to retreat. The Chalcedi proceeded to follow Ogima's final orders, binding Fala with Nikani's chains and lifting him to the top of the pole, where Fala twisted and thrashed, to no avail.

Angeni examined Ogima. She pressed his neck with her fingers, then put her head to his chest. After a few beats of silence, she threw back her head and wailed again, writhing and tearing her scarlet robes. Then, she dipped both hands in his wound and smeared his blood across her face. The camp degenerated into chaos, Chalcedi and Jacinthi alike rushing around but going nowhere, some clamoring for blood and others screaming in fear. The Jasperi huddled together in a trembling knot.

Angeni continued her unintelligible wail, then she lifted her hands over her head. "The King is dead. They have killed our Lord." She prostrated herself on top of Ogima's dead sarkikos, weeping and pounding the ground with her fists. Her display brought similar wailing and screeching from the Chalcedi, who strutted around beating their chests and shaking fists in the air.

When Angeni finally rose, her face was contorted with rage. "Hear me, Amadah and all who follow her." The camp fell into a thick, oppressive silence. "You will pay for what you have done. I will hunt you to the ends of the land, across the skies, under the waters. Wherever you hide, I will find you. And you will die." Her last word echoed in the silence.

Murmurs of "Ogima is dead" rippled through the camp. Ogima's followers stared at each other as if they were strangers. No one knew what to do. It was as if they all lost any semblance of a will of their own.

"We will hunt them down and they will die monstrous deaths." Angeni lifted a fist into the air. "But we must first honor our fallen Lord. We will honor him as the Jacinthi honor their dead, with a grieving ceremony and worship."

"He was Amthysti, not Jacinthi," one of the Chalcedi muttered angrily.

"I am the Lord's true prophet. I know what he would have wanted." Angeni collapsed over him again, her cries a gasping, howling cacophony of anguish. "How has it come to this? Why did I not see this coming? Why did I not warn him?"

As Angeni's tears continued, Leenha noticed the Chalcedi staring at Angeni, their eyes narrowed and their glances suspicious. Leenha watched with renewed interest. Would there be a coup, now that Ogima was dead? Leenha could see herself stepping neatly into the void left by Ogima's demise and Angeni's decomposition.

Angeni apparently noticed their glances, too, for a tiny flicker of fear flashed across her face when she raised her head. Leenha knew the Chalcedi were wild and unpredictable, and needed to be controlled. With Ogima dead, Angeni would have to keep them on a leash, if she didn't want to lose her position.

Angeni stood, collecting herself. "We must tend to Ogima and prepare his sarkikos. My Chalcedi, gather anything you can find that will burn, the decorations, brush, anything made of wood. Take down the tents if you must. We will build a fire the likes of which this world has never seen to honor our fallen Lord."

Angeni's decree spurred the camp and Leenha to action. The Chalcedi rushed to tear down cloth banners, pull up wooden stakes, break down furniture inside the tents, and collect any limbs and brush they could find. They tore down the silks from the tents, leaving Fala hanging on an empty pole. They scurried across the camp and beyond, collecting armfuls of decorations and bringing limbs, twigs, and brush back in their talons. While the Chalcedi darted across the camp, Leenha stole the rest of the way across the open field to the rocks and her soldiers.

Angeni pointed to a slight depression in the ground. "Here is where we will build his pyre!" Soon, the growing mound of detritus reached almost as high as Fala's pole.

Leenha gestured for scouts to gather the other two columns together and conceal themselves nearby to wait for her call, then she settled down to watch the strange scene unfolding in the camp. Perhaps there would be an opportunity for her to call her army forward and attack the Chalcedi while they were leaderless and distracted by grief.

Once the pyre was complete, at Angeni's direction, Hanai and Nadie prepared Ogima for display. They wrapped him in black linen for his shroud, leaving his face uncovered for the viewing. Nadie fashioned a pall from his colorful cloak, while Hanai used Ogima's bed to make a bier.

With somber care, Sonta and Itai set about constructing an altar of stone. The search for stones in the valley was laborious, but Angeni made it clear Ogima would demand an altar like the one he had on the high mountain. Everyone in the camp hunted for stones for Sonta, and some Jacinthi flew back toward the mountain to carry stones from its base to the camp. Sonta and Itai arranged the stones on the higher ground before the pyre, building it up so Ogima's sarkikos would overlook the flames once the fire was set.

Once Angeni was satisfied, she arranged the entire camp in two lines before the altar. Six Chalcedi soldiers carried Ogima's bier and placed it on the altar before the fire.

"Kacina, write a tribute befitting our Lord," Angeni commanded.

Kacina pulled out her ancient texts and scoured them for lines she felt captured Ogima's essence. While she studied and wrote, Angeni sent the rest of the camp to collect gifts to place on Ogima's bier. As they returned, she said, "Stand erect, and do not move or speak. Spend these beats contemplating Ogima's greatness and wonder and power. Give thanks to him for all he did for us. If you must weep, kneel and shed your tears upon his altar."

Many wept and groveled upon the stones, while others stood as still as dead trees, staring but seeing nothing. When Kacina signaled she was ready, Angeni picked up the one remaining torch and flourished it overhead. "Come together, all who loved our Lord. Pay homage to his magnificence and splendor. Bow before him and offer your gifts. Weep and tear your robes and feathers in your desperate grief."

A line formed behind Angeni and moved in a solemn processional before the bier, each creature stopping to kneel and to lay objects upon Ogima's chest. Some lay across him to weep; others collapsed to the ground and had to be carried away so the next individual could worship. Both Jacinthi and Chalcedi tore their feathers and arranged them around his sarkikos, forming a bizarre brown wreath dotted with purple, blue, and white. One of the Jacinthi started to sing a song of mourning, as was the Jacinthi custom, but Angeni silenced them with a harsh rebuke. She knew Ogima hated music and would not want to be honored in such a scandalous way.

Once all had placed their gifts upon Ogima, Kacina stepped forward and read:

> "Listen to the clamor from beneath the mountain,
> The uproar of the multitude gathered together!
> Pain and anguish grip them;
> They writhe like laboring females.
> A cruel cycle, with wrath and fierce anger,
> Making the land desolate.
> The sky light will not show its light,
> On the terrible cycle of the death of the Lord.

194

The realm of the dead is astir to greet him;
All pomp has been brought before his grave.
How you have fallen, oh glorious one,
Cast down, he who brought clans together at his feet.
You said, 'I will raise my throne into the sky;
I will sit upon the mountain throne;
I will ascend above the clouds.'
But they brought you down to the realm of the dead.

Those who mourn say, 'He made the world tremble,
But he was pierced by a sword.'
Wail, those who love the Lord.
Howl, those who follow his ways.
For what was fertile now lies desolate;
What was plenty is in ruins.
Wear ashes and prostrate yourself with weeping,
For he is fallen and is no more."

As Leenha watched the spectacle unfold, fascinated at this turn of events, she considered the impact of Ogima's death, everything from the void in power it left over the Chalcedi to the opportunity it presented with the Chrysoli. She even considered freeing Fala and throwing in her lot with Amadah and her ilk, for she heard Ogima bargaining for a magical sphere they possessed, and she wondered if that sphere held the key to her army taking power.

Would the Chalcedi continue on their journey to the Chrysoli plains, and if so, was it to conquer them or ally with them? What was Amadah's magical sphere, and what did it actually do? Should she confront the Chrysoli while they were weak, before the Chalcedi arrived? Should she attack the Chalcedi now, while they were leaderless and vulnerable? In the end, she decided to wait and observe how circumstances played out to best position her Turqosi to rule over all creatures and lands.

As Angeni threw her torch into the towering funeral pyre, and the flames licked up the pyre into the sky, Leenha disappeared in the shadows, her narrow tongue sliding across her mouth in anticipation of what was to come.

CHAPTER TWENTY-FOUR

The Onyxi

Enla smothered Amadah against her furry chest, wrapping her long, thick arms around her. Amadah's sarkikos felt like a limp rag. Enla knew something of how Amadah felt, having lost Yiska, her only connection to her former Onyxi life, but Amadah had lost not only her childhood friend, Nikani, but her bound mate as well. Her pain must be unbearable.

The rest of their group stood in the opening of the cave, watching the strange processional before Ogima's corpse.

"What are they doing?" Kilchi asked. "The Carneli were not sentimental about death at all. To us, it's just a part of life."

"Angeni leads a Jacinthi celebration of Ogima's life," Chevei explained. "The fire represents the passing to a new form."

"What new form? Dead is dead." Kilchi tossed his head, his fur rippling along his back. "And I'm glad Ogima has ended."

"Never good is death, for beautiful is all life," Misa said.

"Not all life."

"Ogima's death changes everything. The Chalcedi will be leaderless and without direction. We can try again to free Fala." Chevei's speech was pressured, and he couldn't look Amadah in the eye. Enla figured he must feel guilty for leaving Fala behind.

"I believe we must take the sphere now to its place on the high mountain." Aleshanee closed her eyes, and tears glistened along the edges. "We should've done so before these terrible things happened."

"I have failed." Amadah buried her face in Enla's chest. "In every way, I've failed you all. I failed Nikani." His name caught in her throat, and her breath hitched several beats before she could continue. "I failed Fa..." She gasped out a sob.

"No, Amadah. Don't think that way." Enla stroked Amadah's hair. "You didn't fail."

Amadah pushed back from Enla's grasp. "All of this is my fault. Nikani is dead, Yiska died because I didn't remain with the sphere, now Fala is going to die—if only I had listened! If only I had controlled my emotions when I saw Fala—returning to us—alive—had I not called out, the Chalcedi wouldn't have found us. Had I kept my hands on Nikani, as I should've, he'd still be alive. I knew what he was thinking, and I still let go. I failed him. I failed you all." Amadah fell against Enla's chest again, her shoulders heaving. Her moans made Enla's chest ache and throb, but nothing she did seemed to comfort Amadah's terrible grief.

"Stop this." Aleshanee's quiet voice was unusually stern. "This way of thinking will not change what has happened or bring back our loved ones. We have all lost so much, and it is no one's fault. All we can do now is complete our task." Aleshanee walked over to Enla and touched Amadah's back. "Come now. No more speaking of fault or failure. Our task is still before us."

"Aleshanee!" Enla gasped, her eyes wide. "Give her a cycle, for sorrow's sake."

"I do not feel sorry for her. Pity serves no one. Pity is not love. If we love our fallen, we will honor their sacrifice and complete what they died to fulfill."

"You are not usually so heartless," Meda murmured.

"The cycle for grieving all we have lost will come, but not now."

"You all go ahead without me." Amadah's voice was muffled by Enla's fur. "You'd be better off anyway, and I can't leave Fala to die alone."

Aleshanee yanked Amadah around and grabbed her face in both hands. "You would compound our problems by doing the very thing you claim you see as your fault?"

"Stop it!" Enla cried, pulling Amadah away from Aleshanee as if she could shield her from the words.

"Not understanding, Aleshanee, so unlike you is this," Misa said.

"None of you understand." Aleshanee's eyes glinted like metal, her teeth clenched. "The Music is changing; our chances to fulfill our quest are running out. If we linger here much longer, it will be too late. This is why we must hold our grief and complete our journey. We can't wait any longer."

"Go, then!" Amadah exploded. "I'm not stopping you."

"Amadah, we can't." Kilchi spoke softly. "We need everyone to be able to carry the sphere."

"Having still a long way to go," Misa added.

"Nikani knew the paths inside the mountain leading to the peak. Now, we have no one to guide us, and trial and error are cruel teachers." Meda heaved a heavy sigh. "It may take us much longer than we imagined, without Nikani's help."

Amadah glared at them each in turn. "We. Have. Failed. Why can't you accept that?"

"To accept such a belief is to accept we will never rejoin the First World, and to never see the First World again is worse than death."

"Maybe we don't deserve to see the First World again." Amadah's eyes flashed as she met Aleshanee's gaze.

Aleshanee whirled and marched from the cave.

Enla gaped at Aleshanee's retreating back. "Let me talk to her." She followed Aleshanee, leaving Misa to console Amadah.

The fire's glow against the glowering sky formed a surreal image of light and darkness, life and death. The light flickered across Aleshanee's face, giving her a golden radiance, and her wings fluttered like delicate flower petals in the breeze.

"I understand," Enla began, "we have to finish the task or the whole world dies. I get it. I'm not trying to fight you, Aleshanee. I'm just trying to love Amadah the only way I can."

Aleshanee continued to gaze across the expanse at the Chalcedi gyrating around the fire, and the Jacinthi and Jasperi clasping hands and rocking in unison, their moans creating an odd bass counterpoint to the crackling of the flames.

"Come back inside," Enla urged. "I believe if we can give Amadah the chance to rest, sleep if she can, she will be able to see the urgency."

"Something is about to happen." Aleshanee hummed, her voice distant as if from a dream.

"What?"

"Bring them out. Especially Amadah. She and I must witness what is to come."

"What is it?"

"Quickly. The darkness approaches."

CHAPTER TWENTY-FIVE

The Dark Lord

Skia Skotos stared down at Ogima's displayed sarkikos, disgusted. Such a weak vessel, so easily damaged and destroyed, and now he was forced to do his work by influencing others instead of taking matters into his own hands. The instant that Jasperi ingrate's blade pierced Ogima's flesh, Skia Skotos fled the sarkikos, leaving Ogima to experience the ignominious defeat and excruciating pain on his own. What a shock it must've been for Ogima, to awaken from the depths of his psychosis to find himself bleeding out at the hands of such a little creature.

The crowd of creatures paying him homage below was gratifying, he had to admit. The problem he faced was starting anew, convincing a bunch of stupid, concrete creatures that his voice in their heads was the voice of Ogima. Scanning the chaos below, he noticed Angeni taking command. While this was good in many ways, and she was doing what he had groomed her to do, it chafed him to know she would be the one they would follow from now forward. He enjoyed the admiration. More than that, he relished the raw power and control.

His work was far from complete, although he believed the cursed child had been dealt a severe blow. He floated down and whispered a directive to Angeni, but she did not appear to respond. Did she not hear him? Or was she drunk with the power she now possessed? Some tortured dreams might resolve this momentary lapse on her part. If he had to kill Angeni and find another prophet—the delay to his plans might provide the sphere bearers just the opening they

201

needed to win the cycle, just when he had them reeling. No, that would never do.

He whispered his directions again and still received no response in acknowledgement or action. Frustration churned within him like the strange thunderclouds forming above the encampment. He would've never believed he would miss the sensations of a sarkikos. He so despised the fatigue, the forced sleep, the hunger, and the pain, that he failed to realize the pleasures of the taste of real food or the physical stimulation of the kill. On top of those losses, he was being ignored, a situation he found utterly intolerable.

The seed of an idea formed in his mind. At first, the idea revolted him, but he massaged it, tended it, and fed it until it blossomed within him, and he knew with blinding clarity what he must do.

CHAPTER TWENTY-SIX

The Jacinthi

Angeni's heart burned like the pyre whose flames touched the clouds. Rage and anguish roiled around each other like a ball of serpentus younglings, newly hatched and seeking to establish dominance. At present, anguish was losing, and rage was winning. She kept eyeing the betrayer, hanging from the very pole which once supported the shelter of her master. Ogima wanted his skin hanging from his bones. It almost seemed too kind a punishment for such a heinous crime; however, Angeni prided herself on her loyalty, so she would follow Ogima's wishes.

Her gaze turned to the young Jasperi, Nikani— or what was left of him, lying spread like one drawn and quartered, his neck at a horrific angle. She imagined traveling down his throat into the blackness of his heart and squeezing it until it crumbled into dust.

Dust. Angeni had almost forgotten the ashes. "Everyone! Listen. As the fire dies, reach into it and take a handful of ash. Smear the ash on your face and the rest of your sarkikos, and do not wash the ash from you for the span of six cycles. In this way, we carry the death of our Lord on our persons, a reminder of the gravity of our loss and our devotion to our Lord."

"Angeni, the fire remains quite hot," Kacina said.

"It would serve us all to taste just a touch of the pain suffered by our Lord in the brutal, unprovoked attack." Rage won in Angeni that round. She thrust her hand into the flames, feeling her skin blister and crack, and pulled out a handful of grey-black ashes. Edges of her skin blackened before her eyes, but she refused to acknowledge the pain. Ogima had suffered much worse at their hands. As his Prophet, she was willing to suffer as he did, even unto death. She smeared the hot ash over her feathers until she appeared as black as Ogima's shroud. Her huge, round eyes, glaring out of the black, demanded the same from the others. Soon, the camp was filled with shadow specters, dancing and whirling and groveling around the pyre.

A whisper rose in her mind. "Burn the medichinals." She hesitated. They might need those substances. She did not fancy wasting them; besides, she enjoyed partaking herself. So, she waited.

Again, an insistent, "Burn them now," flitted through her mind. She decided the voice belonged to Aleshanee's Dark Ones, trying to rob their group of their pleasures, and dismissed the idea.

Suddenly, the pyre flames burst forth in an explosion of intense heat, climbing beyond the lowering clouds, as if someone had thrown an accelerant on the fire. The mourners cowered beneath the conflagration, as a voice thundered from Ogima's bier. "From desolation and despair comes forth ecstasy. From treachery and darkness comes forth strength. Behold, and tremble before my mighty power." Angeni felt as if she moved through molasses as she turned toward Ogima's sarkikos.

The bier shivered. The pall slipped from across his shroud. Angeni screamed as the sarkikos lifted slowly into the air, prone at first, then tilting up to reveal Ogima's eyes, wide and aflame like the pyre. The shroud fell away as he lifted his arms. His sarkikos was changed. All imperfections were cleansed, his skin shining like gold. His thickened muscles rippled as he thrust his hands toward the sky. Blue-white sparks sprang from the ends of his fingers and kissed the clouds. He brought one hand down, pointing five fingers toward the pyre, and jagged sparks blasted through its center. Ash and debris rained down on the mourners, who scattered like so many leaves before a wind, feathers, hair, and skin burning from the cinders.

"Kneel!" the voice thundered. Angeni collapsed, prostrate on the ground, her face buried in the remnant of ash. She dared not look to see if others followed her lead, for sparks were shooting just above her head and striking Chalcedi and Jacinthi alike. Anyone not sprawled flat on the dirt received the sting of Ogima's wrath.

"Angeni." Ogima's voice reverberated, drawing her name out like poetry. "Rise." Careful to keep her eyes down, she stood. "Come forth." She walked as slowly as she could, following each tentative step with a lengthy pause. But Ogima seemed patient, maybe even pleased with her reverence. She hoped so.

"You will be my voice. You will speak only my words. Those who follow you follow me. Those who disobey you, die." The final word echoed across the plain.

"Yes, my Lord and Master."

"There will be no more mourning, no more wailing and gnashing of teeth, no more sorrow or pain or suffering. From this sky fall forward shall we celebrate the glory and wonder of my greatness. Let this cycle be marked as the Cycle of Rising, for I was dead, and now I live."

A euphoric cheer rose from the crowd, causing the very ground to tremble, as an icy wind settled over the camp and chilled them to the bone.

CHAPTER TWENTY-SEVEN

The Whisperers

Veritor wept. His ward, Angeni, was lost to him forever. He witnessed the wildness descend over her eyes like the slamming of a door, and the fevered ecstasy which vibrated her soul and set it aflame with hatred. In a few passing moments, he held onto hope—when Meda spoke truth before fleeing the high mountain, when Skia Skotos overplayed his hand and brought a flicker of doubt to her mind, when Angeni recalled Cholena's acts of bravery and kindness. But his whispers went unheeded, and the moment passed, and now Angeni was lost.

Veritor allowed his grief to wash through him as the Music rang in mournful strains of the anguish of the Forever. Yet, hope still remained for the quest, solitary notes beneath the chorus of grief, almost hidden but not snuffed out. The Music urged Veritor to leave the scene, that no more whispers would be heard there, but he hesitated, reluctant to abandon his ward, his love for her throbbing against the song, urging him to try just once more, and to try again and again, as futile as a youngling's finger attempting to crush a diamond stone. For Angeni's walls she built, methodically and resolutely, around her heart were as diamond stones now, untouchable, unbreakable, immovable.

So, leave he did, returning to the wards cowering in the mouth of a cave overlooking the tableau on the field, shivering less from the cold than from disbelief and no small measure of fear. He called for all Whisperers to come to his side, for the success of the quest teetered on the edge of a cliff. The wards would need the combined influence of all Metanoi, the unwavering love of all 'Ro, and the might and power of all his fellow Bellator lest the slightest stumble send them plummeting to their end. As the Whisperers gathered, Veritor directed them to stand behind their trembling wards and exude warmth and peace to calm their thoughts, but they, too, had heard the mournful song. Soon, the wards were sobbing, a grief they could not quantify or specify seasoning their terror.

"They must collect themselves. Speak to them of hope." Sa'ro and Pa'ro stepped forward, touching the wards to allow their light to flow through them, whispering of the peace and splendor of the First World, and the hope of the rejoining. A quiet calm began to settle over the wards. Aleshanee was the first to speak.

"We have borne witness to the Great Lie. Remember what you have seen so that you may testify against what will be spoken about this cycle."

"What did we see, Aleshanee?" Enla asked.

"A corpse appearing to rise but remaining a corpse. The Dark Lord pretending to hold the power of life but only sowing death. A dead sarkikos disguised as a living creature being used as a puppet so the Dark Lord could continue to deceive those who follow him and could bring more followers to him with claims of signs and wonders. You saw a counterfeit, an imitation of Kindred's power with none of its light. Ogima's corpse will mortify, but still the Dark Lord will use it and disguise the corruption with tricks and illusions, and he will use Angeni as his mouthpiece."

"Heinous is this, and horrifying to behold," Misa murmured.

"We must listen now to our friends. They are here with us to help us, but we must hear them and follow their guidance, or I fear all will be lost."

Luxor bathed the little band in the warm glow of her light, while Ma'ro stirred the memory of their encounter with the sphere, and Elegosi encouraged them to choose as Aleshanee suggested.

"Let's stand together to listen." Amadah reached out her hand to take Enla's paw. The group formed a circle, holding each other close.

The cave settled into a quiet stillness, not the oppression and weight of the silence that fell over Angeni's camp, but the tranquility of love and connection that needed no words. Veritor whispered into the silence. "The course is now set. The tide has turned, and the way is now narrow and much more difficult. Darkness has closed many paths to you. Still, one path remains, and hope still sings beneath the sorrow. Step from this path, either to the right or to the left, even one step, and the quest fails. Walk this treacherous road, and you will find suffering and loss, desolation and despair, torment and anguish along the way. But at the end of it, the worlds are rejoined."

"What is our path?" Amadah asked.

"The Dark Lord is no longer hindered by physical eyes. You cannot take the sphere directly to the high mountain. If you bring the sphere out of hiding now, the Dark Lord will see, shed the stolen sarkikos like a cloak, which is all it is to him now that he is no longer indwelling it, and possess the sphere, and all will be lost. You must leave the sphere behind."

"Leave the sphere?" Kilchi cried. "I thought the sphere was the whole point."

"You will return for it once the turning of the cycles has come near its end. For now, you must go to the sphere and conceal it. You must disguise its hiding place such that the Dark Lord's minions will not spy it or even suspect its location. Go quickly, while they are distracted by his—theatre—and safeguard it beyond discovery."

"Then where will we go?"

"A battle approaches—and yes, it will be combat as you've not seen since the division of your species, but more importantly, it will be a battle for souls. You must gather as many as will come to the side of the light before it is too late. You will go first to the escaped slaves, for they are most vulnerable to the Dark Lord's offers of security and safety. Tell them of the Forever and lead them into the light of the Great Love. Cholena will lead you to their location.

"Then, you must proceed with all haste to the Chrysoli. If you do not preempt the arrival of the Dark Lord, the Chrysoli will surely fall into darkness. However, we have a weapon unseen by the Dark Lord—

an ally to our cause in their midst, one who has been, unbeknownst to her, leading the Chrysoli into the ways of the light. She will prepare their hearts to receive our message, and as it stands, she is our only hope, for the Chrysoli are by nature a stubborn and prideful species who desire domination, something the Dark Lord willingly offers. You must convince them his offer is pretense, and what he really brings them is subjugation.

"Your final gathering will take place at the sea, where Misa will offer the Saphiri living water and bring her father and clan back to the Light. Be assured, we will be with you every step of the way on your journey. Guard your steps, for you walk a thin path bordered by sheer cliffs on either side."

"And what of Fala?" Amadah held her breath.

Veritor's heart ached for Amadah, whose love was deep for the Topazi. The Music told him a great brokenness would come upon her before she found her strength. "You must leave Fala's fate in the mighty hands of the Great Love."

"I can't just leave him. Please...don't make me do that. Anything but that."

"I do not have the power to make you do anything. Yet, I urge you to heed my words. Fala is not abandoned or alone. Should you choose the course of trying to release Fala from his suffering, the only path yet remaining to us will fall into darkness, and this world will be lost. Either way, you will carry a great and heavy burden, and your soul will break beneath its weight before you find redemption. Which burden will you choose to bear?"

"I can't choose between two unbearable choices."

"And yet, choose you must. Will you trust Fala to the Forever or take his fate into your hands?"

Amadah's face writhed in agony, and her fingers scratched her neck and chest until beads of blood dripped from the wounds. "You cannot leave me with such a choice. You're cruel—horrid—what you ask is unspeakable." Her clawing hands moved to her face, leaving long gouges along her sodden cheeks.

Aleshanee reached up and took Amadah's hands. "Dear friend, we're here for you. Please don't harm yourself anymore. Let us help you."

"Our friend says the decision is mine alone."

"But we stand as one." Aleshanee reached up and touched Amadah's lacerated cheek. "We love Fala, too." Enla wrapped her arms around her friend, and the others collected around them, adding their arms and wings to the enfolding warmth.

Finally, Veritor broke the silence. "You must conceal the sphere before Ogima's enraptured spell is broken, and the Chalcedi are dispatched to search for you and the sphere."

The group loosened their embrace and lingered to see Amadah's decision. Her head was down, and the muscles in her neck and back knotted. Her jaw bulged as if holding her mouth clenched in a vise grip would prevent her choice from escaping and becoming reality. It was Aleshanee who broke through the tension. "What would Fala tell you to do?"

Amadah lifted her head and looked at each of her friends in turn. All knew the answer but waited for Amadah to give it voice. "Fala would say..." she paused and swallowed, her throat working to release the words, and when she spoke again, her voice had become a rasping, tormented shadow of itself. "He would say—save world. It is the way."

CHAPTER TWENTY-EIGHT

The Chrysoli

Leoti prowled the open fields, watching as hordes of slaves made their way to the exits Kola had opened in the dome. Most of the flyers had already fled when the dome collapsed. Now, Kola had, for some reason, decided to free the rest of the slaves.

"We can't feed them," was Kola's rationale, when Leoti questioned his decision. "They'll be useless to us."

"If they're useless, they should die," Leoti countered, but Kola was set on his course and wouldn't listen.

Other Chrysoli stalked among the slaves, growling at them, some even swiping at them with their claws or slapping them down. If Kola was near and saw them, he punished the affronted Chrysoli instead of the worthless slaves. Leoti found this untenable.

Kola was to be her mate, now that Tocho was dead. As the first female, it was her right. But she found now she didn't want him and schemed to find a replacement. Whoever she chose would be the new leader. Lonan was her main choice, but to take over and have her as his mate, he would need to fight Kola. Lonan wasn't going to be too keen on the idea in their current circumstances. Plus, Kola was a formidable opponent, almost rivaling Tocho in strength and ferocity. Leoti was hoping this new, softer side of Kola would prove his downfall.

Kola had been spending a lot of his cycles consulting with the Jacinthi slave, Kwania, another affront to Leoti's sensibilities. Leoti buried deep within her the pang of hurt and rejection, opting instead for

213

indignation over him consorting with a lower creature, which she openly and loudly shared with anyone who would listen.

The pathetic slaves dragged themselves beyond what was left of the dome, some with younglings in tow. Who would rebuild their dome now? Who would sow the fields and reap their crops? Who would rebuild their damaged buildings? Surely, Kola didn't expect her to dirty her paws. If that's what he thought, she knew none of her class would comply.

Leoti shivered. A cold wind was sweeping in from the west, and the dome provided little protection from the elements now. She had come to the fields to fuel her anger and perhaps toy with some of the slaves before they left, but the frigid air drove her back to her keep. She found Kola sitting on Tocho's throne, meeting with several key Chrysoli from engineering, mechanistics, and science. To Leoti's dismay, Kwania stood among her kind, that insolent, officious, meddlesome creature. Leoti snarled as she moved to her place on the platform beside Kola, causing Kwania to take a step back, to Leoti's great satisfaction.

"We must make plans for the rebuilding of the dome," the lead engineer was saying, but Kola shook his head.

"The first priority must be food. Our stores are woefully inadequate, and the crops in the fields were destroyed by the ice storm. How long will it take to regrow the fields?"

"We won't be able to regrow the fields," one of the scientists said. "We have no more slaves to plow and plant."

"We'll have to do the plowing and planting, if we want to eat."

"You can't be serious," Leoti interjected.

"Of course, I'm serious. Food isn't going to magically appear on our tables."

"You have a bigger problem than who is going to plow and plant," Kwania said. "The weather changes are going to make it impossible for food to grow. The cloud cover, the storms, and now the cold—nothing will grow in this."

"If we repair the dome, will food grow?"

"Not without the sky light's rays coming through the dome. Until—or unless—the dark clouds clear, nothing is going to grow."

"Options?" Kola's request was met with silence. "The best scientists and engineers in Chrysoli history can't figure out how to grow food?"

"We could leave this land and seek warmer climate," one of the younger scientists offered.

"Fool! Leave our land? Chrysoli land is our heritage, our birthright, our strength and power." Leoti's voice was shrill as she began to pace before the groveling attendants. "Kola, dismiss these useless creatures and bring in our warriors. They will know what to do."

"Fighting will not solve our food shortages, Leoti."

"If we don't have enough food, we'll send our warriors to take what we need from others!"

"You would leave others starving rather than seek to solve your own problems?" Kwania murmured.

Leoti bared her teeth and hissed through them. "Be careful, slave. You look quite tasty to me."

Kola sat bolt upright. "Leoti! Leave this chamber immediately!"

Her eyes narrowed, her tone menacing. "How dare you..." She slid from the platform, eyeing Kwania the whole way as she strode from the chamber. She decided to seek Lonan. When he heard what Kola was planning, she was sure Lonan would make Kola pay.

Lonan was lounging with several of the other fighters in one of the side rooms off the main hallway, perhaps waiting to be called before Kola to make their report. Leoti oozed into the room like honey dripping from a comb, cutting her eyes at Lonan, whose tongue lolled in response, quite a gratifying reaction after Kola's dismissal. She spoke to the other warriors first, feigning disinterest in Lonan as she wove her way in and around the prone forms. His tail flicked, and he thumped his massive head onto his paws. At that point, she knew she had him.

"Lonan," she purred. "I've a bone to pick with you."

Lonan raised his head. "What've I done?"

"Kola meets with weak, facile Chrysoli, and even a slave, to decide the fate of our pride, and you are not there to defend my honor."

"Kola is going to call us..."

"Is he?" She rubbed her long frame against his thick hide. "It sounded to me like all the decisions were being made without you."

"What decisions?"

"Like, who is going to get to eat."

"What?"

The other Chrysoli began to grumble under their breath. They certainly seemed annoyed at Leoti's news. Good.

"And who is going to work the fields and rebuild the dome and do all the slave labor." Leoti drew out the word 'slave' to emphasize what Kola apparently thought of his fighters.

"He can't mean to send us to work the fields?"

Leoti shrugged. "It sounded that way to me—before Kola told me to shut up and made me leave."

"He said what?"

Leoti nodded knowingly. "You see how he favors the lesser? He listens to the advice of the slave, Kwania, over his own soldiers. He frees the slaves, rightfully owned by the Chrysoli, and consigns his own kind to labor in the fields. He refuses to send the sick to the plains, as is their right, forcing them to die without honor or to live in infirmity, unable to contribute to the pride. He even mentioned leaving our lands behind to be ravaged by other species."

The warriors were all standing now, joining her in storming back and forth, shaking their heads, and pounding their paws with each new declaration. "He changes all the ways of our ancestors," Lonan roared.

"He has no honor," Leoti agreed. "To elevate those who are lower to an equivalent status—it is despicable. He would destroy our pride way of life and undermine our power."

"The Chrysoli have always been the strongest, wisest, and most powerful species on this world."

Leoti shook her sleek head. "No longer, once Kola finishes dismantling our entire structure and systems. Are you going to let him destroy everything we've worked so hard to build?"

"We will go and confront him." Lonan looked to his cohorts for agreement.

216

"If he didn't listen to me, what makes you think he will listen to you? I am, after all, the first female. No. You must fight him for the seat of power."

"Fight Kola?"

"Yes, fight him." After bunting and sliding her sleek hide along Lonan's, Leoti hooded her eyes. "And if you win, I am your prize."

She watched Lonan's fur ripple along his back. She had aroused his excitement. But would it be enough to motivate him to fight Kola? The quiet stretched out much longer than she'd hoped.

Finally, Lonan spoke. "We'll all go and confront him. Perhaps this is all a misunderstanding. We must give him the chance to correct himself. After all, he was Tocho's choice."

"You doubt me?"

"I don't doubt what you think you heard."

"What I *think* I heard?" Perhaps she had miscalculated by choosing Lonan.

"We will all go." Lonan gave a final nod. "Then we'll see."

Leoti made her displeasure known, striding away from the group with her nose high and her back to them. Cutting her eyes back, she noted Lonan's deflated posture and smiled. He wanted her for his own, and that would turn the wind in her favor.

Kola was still meeting with Kwania and the scientists when Lonan barged into the chamber, followed by his fellow warriors. "I will call you in shortly." Kola waved a paw in dismissal.

"You will speak to me now, Kola. Leoti claims you expect your warriors to do the work of lowly slaves. She claims you listen to the Jacinthi slave over your own kind. She claims you speak of leaving our land behind. She claims you allow injured and sick to remain, refusing them their right to die with honor. What do you say in response to her accusations?"

Kola glared at Leoti, who met his gaze with a haughty sneer. "Leoti failed to explain our situation to you, Lonan. We have limited food stores. Nothing will grow without the sky light, even if we had our dome, which we do not. Unless the climate changes again, what we have in storage will have to sustain us all for who knows how long. Trust me, it won't matter who is doing the work or who I allow to remain for long, because we will all starve to death soon."

"So, send the weakest to the plains, as is our heritage, so the strongest will survive!"

"Who will choose who to send to their death? You? How will that choice be made? By strength? Intelligence? Contribution to the pride? Are you willing to risk I might choose you as unworthy of survival?"

"Of course, you would not choose me. I protect the pride."

"Are you protecting the pride from starvation, which is our present threat? I think not! Which makes these scientists, who are working on a solution to the crisis, the most valuable members of the pride, and warriors the least valuable."

Lonan gaped at Kola, and the other fighters squirmed, backing a step away from Lonan. Leoti didn't like the way this 'confrontation' was going.

"Before you decide to judge who will live and who will die, you'd better be willing to send yourself to the plains. If not, be silent and let us do our work." Once again, Kola dismissed Lonan, who, with his head down and his tail tucked, left the chamber.

Leoti stood her ground, shaking in her fury. "You've not heard the last of this. You will pay for your insults to the first female."

"Perhaps your cycle as first female is over," Kola snarled.

"You wouldn't dare!"

"Don't test me."

Leoti bolted from the chamber, her mind churning with rage. Kola would pay. She would make sure of it.

CHAPTER TWENTY-NINE

The Topazi

Fala strained against his chains as the spectacle unfolded below him. Blasts of fire and sparks almost blinded him from seeing Ogima's dead sarkikos elevate above the funeral bier, but Fala heard the dead creature's booming voice echo through the valley. A gentler voice whispered inside his mind—Kindra's melodic tones—and he was surprised to find her words drowned out Ogima's speech, so at the end of it Fala wasn't sure what Ogima said.

"Do not be deceived. Ogima is dead. The Dark Lord, the one who murdered your Amadah, has taken Ogima's empty sarkikos and is wearing it like clothing. His followers will believe he lives, for they want to believe. They see what they want to see and are blind when it suits them. But look, Fala. See with my eyes."

Fala looked and saw a hideous yet formless figure, black with shadow, with the suggestion of dark wings protruding from Ogima's sarkikos. The apparition appeared to be moving Ogima's limbs as if dark smoke on the wind lifted them. The burning rage in Fala's chest matched the flames the figure exploded over his followers.

"Imposter. Liar. Murderer. Fala kills."

"No, Fala. The Dark Lord is mine to destroy."

Fala opened his mouth to argue but realized her words had soothed his fury. For some reason he couldn't understand, he trusted Kindra would deal with the entity, and her manner of addressing him would be absolute. Despite his aching limbs and perilous situation, Fala smiled, satisfied.

219

The Chalcedi, Jacinthi, and Jasperi seemed to be fooled by the spectacle of a sarkikos rising and were celebrating as if some great victory had been won. They passed around smoking pots and inhaled the foul-smelling vapor. Then, Fala saw Angeni approaching, her eyes wide and gleaming like the greenish rock Amadah found in the desert after the sky light fell from the sky. Other than her eyes, Angeni was cloaked in the shadows of the growing darkness.

"Usurper," she hissed. "All you have ever done is take from me—you took the respect I was due, took my position as leader, and thought you had taken my Lord. But you failed. Look upon your failure, creature. The Lord lives." Angeni cackled and whooped, waving her arms in the air as she spun and danced around Fala's pole.

"Angeni is sick, Fala," Kindra whispered. From deep within, a flood of compassion Fala didn't know he had in him welled and flowed out in salty tears.

"Weep!" Angeni screeched. "Weep and cry and wail, for you have accomplished nothing, and now you are doomed."

"Fala weeps for Angeni."

With a flap of wings, Angeni rose to stare, face-to-face, at Fala. Hatred oozed from her eyes like the thick, black sludge the Topazi often found when they dug deep into the sand. She brandished a knife, its edge glinting with the remnant of flames. "You will weep for Fala."

Fala thought it odd her voice sounded more like a Carneli than a Jacinthi.

Angeni slashed with the knife, but Fala refused to cry out. Again and again, she sliced, but still Fala held in his tongue.

Screeching, Angeni held the knife against his throat. Fala met her eye and saw her blink, then she pulled back the knife. "No. No, it is too soon. You have not suffered enough to satisfy my Lord. I will return soon, and you will know pain like you have never known, and I promise you, you will weep and wail and beg me to kill you." Angeni fluttered away to rejoin the Chalcedi as they gyrated around Ogima's sarkikos.

Smoke from the pots the Chalcedi were inhaling thickened the air with a sickly-sweet smell. Fala's eyes burned with it, and he started to feel nauseous, but he struggled against his chains, nonetheless. He focused his mind on one thought—Amadah was free. As long as she was free, he could bear whatever these creatures had in store for him.

Two Chalcedi, reeling from the effects of the substance they inhaled, unwrapped his chain from the pole and lowered him until he claws were almost touching the ground, then wrapped the chain around him so it was impossible for him to move. Angeni returned, along with several more Chalcedi.

From behind them, the Dark Lord's voice boomed. "Show him our displeasure." One by one, the Chalcedi punched him, hitting his ribs, gut, and face.

"Soon, you're gonna be purple instead of brown," one of the Chalcedi cawed, laughing at her own joke.

"A big, purple monster," another agreed.

They vomited into their mouths and spit it on Fala, then began another round of beatings. Fala closed his eyes against the pain to travel to memories of Amadah sleeping against his chest, Amadah sitting with him among the rocks as they waited for the Beryli to approach, Amadah standing watch with him in the valley before they met the Jacinthi, Amadah crying on his shoulder for Sani and her clan, Amadah rising under Kindra's touch and saying, "We are bound" as if it was the only thing she knew in this world. He was jolted from his memories when a Chalcedi shoved his sword in Fala's side, saying, "For our Lord! How do *you* like it?" Still, Fala refused to cry out.

Angeni grabbed his face and thrust her tiny beak against his nose. "I have heard the Lord speak about your bound mate. He says she will die soon. He has seen it. She will suffer for your actions, then she will die. The sphere will be the Lord's and Amadah will lie dead by his hand."

"Hold in your tongue," Fala hissed.

Angeni smirked. "Ahhh, a reaction. Perhaps I will send the Chalcedi to fetch Amadah now, so you may witness her torture and watch her die."

Fala writhed against the binding chains, only to receive more blows in response. With the final blow to his head, his vision faded to black.

He didn't know how long he had been unconscious when he finally raised his head, bleary-eyed and stiff, his sarkikos screaming like it was on fire. The Chalcedi had left him for more entertaining pursuits. He saw Angeni consulting with Ogima's sarkikos, looking quite foolish to Fala's eyes, as if she was a child being entertained by a puppet show, thinking the puppet was real.

While he was unconscious, an icy wind had poured into the valley from the high mountain. He realized, before long, drowsiness would soothe his pain and sleep would end his suffering. Fala made his peace with his fate. Amadah was still alive and free, for he now knew if she had been captured, he would've been forced to watch her torture and witness her death.

Either the Dark Lord or Angeni noticed Fala awaken, for Angeni strode over to him and smiled. "You are back among us, I see. Are you ready for some more punishment?" Something about Fala's countenance caught her attention, possibly his head lolling on his thick neck, or his glazed eyes with his nictitating membranes half-closed. She slapped him across the face, to no effect. Frowning, she muttered, more to herself than to Fala. "You have not lost that much blood. What is wrong with you?"

Fala offered her a woozy smile, then closed his eyes to let himself sink into oblivion. He felt her hands on his chest, poking and prodding. Then, through the haze, he heard Angeni's muffled voice scream. "Wood! Quickly!"

In his head, Fala cried out, "No!" but all he heard, as if from a long distance away, was a moan. Rustling noises, Angeni barking orders, and footfalls blended into a mélange of torment for Fala. He just wanted to sleep. Soon, a crackling sound and smoke penetrated his haze, and a growing warmth touched his feet and legs. He opened his eyes to see a small fire blazing near the base of his pole, and he realized Angeni was not going to let him go just yet.

"Now, then, that is better. We cannot have you leaving us too soon."

Fala's tongue still felt thick. "Wethcue."

"No one is coming for you, Fala. No one cares for your suffering, except, of course, the Lord and me. We care deeply that you suffer." Angeni cackled at her irony. "Get nice and warm, now. We want your blood flowing when we begin again."

As the fire warmed his sarkikos, Fala's pain intensified. He tried to squirm against the chains, but the metal squeezed him to the pole, cold against his back. For the first cycle in his life, Fala wondered if he was strong enough to bear what surely was to come.

"Are you ready, Fala?" Kindra's calm voice bathed him with a different kind of warmth, a strange peace blocking the pain searing his sarkikos.

"Ready?"

"Ready to come with me to the First World."

"Amadah..."

"Do you trust me?"

"Fala trusts Kindra."

"Will you give Amadah into my hands? Will you allow me to care for her and protect her in your stead?"

Fala paused, his longing for Amadah warring against his deep desire to go with Kindra. As if she could read his thoughts, Kindra whispered, "Do you believe I am able to care for her, that perhaps I hold even more love for her than you can hold in your heart?"

"Kindra is love."

"Yes, Fala. The Forever reveals this truth to you."

"Kindra loves Amadah."

"I do."

"Fala loves Amadah."

"I know you love her, Fala. Do you love her enough to release her to me?"

"Let go is not love. Bound forever."

"Do you remember what I told you in the cave? You are bound forever on the First World. Yet, here, Amadah's task remains. As one of the witnesses, she must bear the sphere to its place on the high mountain. Many trials remain before her task can be completed, but

Fala, you were not meant to be present for these trials. Your presence is a distraction instead of a help for her."

"Fala never hurt Amadah."

"Not intentionally, no. But you saw her pain when she was forced to leave you. She suffers now for having left you behind and fights against what she knows she must do."

"Amadah hurts because of Fala?"

"Of course, she feels pain, having seen you suffering, and because she cannot save you."

Fala cried out in his anguish at the thought of hurting his bound mate. Angeni, who was waiting nearby, darted back to his side. "Finally, the mighty Fala breaks! I knew I could break you."

"Fala helps Amadah." He ignored Angeni and her attempt to get another reaction.

"You cannot help Amadah anymore than you can help yourself!" Angeni screeched. "She will die very soon."

"You know how to help her," Kindra soothed.

"Go."

"Yes." Fala could feel Kindra's gentle, sad smile.

"I do not obey your commands," Angeni yelled. "I am the one in command!"

"Ready." Fala exhaled a long, rattling breath.

"Come, take my hand." Fala saw a small, brilliant point of light. The glow grew before his eyes, and within the bright sphere of light stood Kindra, her arm outstretched.

"You want more? You have not had enough? I will give you more!" Angeni's fury shot from her eyes like scarlet flames, matching her ruined robe, as she reached her knife out to cut his flesh, but Kindra's hand moved past Angeni's to envelope Fala's claw. Before Angeni could slash with her knife, Fala lifted from his limp sarkikos like a swirl of sand in a windstorm and floated toward the familiar dazzling brilliance. The last sound he heard was Angeni's frustrated roar.

CHAPTER THIRTY

The Chalcedi

Cholena shoved a boulder into the crevasse which now housed the sphere. Chevei pushed another boulder forward, lifted it, and plunked it down on top of Cholena's, followed by Kilchi, then Enla, and finally, Meda. Amadah, Aleshanee, and Misa arranged smaller rocks around the huge boulders to give the appearance of a rockslide. They dribbled rocks and dirt on the pile and scattered more in front of the entrance. When they finished, they all agreed their work would fool anyone searching for a hiding place for the sphere.

"How do we find it when we return?" Kilchi asked.

"Marking the spot with something only we would recognize will work," Misa replied.

Enla scrambled over the rocks. "I'll climb above and dig a path into the hill. To anyone else, it'll look like the rockslide caused the damage, but to us, it will act as an arrow showing us the way to the crevasse."

While they waited for Enla's return, Kilchi said, "Tell us about the slaves, Cholena. What's their attitude? How willing do you think they'll be to come with us?"

"Well, assuming the Turqosi don't get to them first, I believe they will listen to me. We were planning to go back to the Chrysoli dome anyway. All I have to convince them to do is talk to the Chrysoli instead of attack them."

"Are they wanting revenge for the cycles of slavery?"

"Some, but most want to free the remaining slaves."

"We can do that."

"Other than that, all they want is the chance to live their own lives in freedom."

"Do you think they'll help us in a fight against the Dark Lord?" Aleshanee asked.

"How would the slaves feel about fighting side by side with those who kept them in chains?" Kilchi added.

Cholena shook her head. "Fighting in an all-out war might be a hard sell. They're frightened and tired and hungry, and some are injured."

Aleshanee kicked some more pebbles toward their manufactured rockslide. "It's more a question of their survival."

"Yes, but will they believe us?" Chevei asked.

Cholena nodded. "They trust me. I'm one of them. I think they'll believe me since I led them safely out."

"Cholena takes the lead in talking with the slaves," Aleshanee declared. "We must move quickly. We need to reach them before sky light rising, for I believe the Dark Lord will send his Chalcedi forth at the rising, and we must reach the slaves before he does."

"And if we're going to beat him to the Chrysoli, we need to get to the slaves and move on. Fast." Kilchi pawed at the dirt and stared up the hill, watching for Enla.

Misa laid her arm across Kilchi's back, as if for support. "Depending on so many variables is our path. As our friend said, narrowing is our chance."

"We've no beats to waste," Aleshanee agreed.

Cholena's face brightened. "We have three fliers. Why don't we take to the clouds, like we did when we attacked the Dark Lord's camp? Wouldn't that be a lot faster than walking?"

"But the Dark Lord will send out fliers, as well." Chevei snapped his beak. "They may already be in the clouds and could spot us."

"Aleshanee thinks not until sky light rises."

"Cholena, this is a good idea. We could carry those who cannot fly and avoid having to climb over boulders and around the rifts in the ground from the quakes." Meda nodded and clasped her hands. "I feel hope for our mission I did not feel before. We may be able to precede the Dark Lord and reach the Chrysoli first."

Aleshanee's pressed her lips into a thin line. "We'll use the Dark Lord's own weapons against him. The darkness he ushered in will cover our escape and hide us on our journey across the plains. But we must hurry!"

"The slave camp has more fliers." Cholena shrugged her wings. "Although many of the slaves are weak and some are wounded. And there are young ones."

"Children?" Amadah choked out.

"Yes."

Amadah buried her face in her hands and rubbed her eyes, muttering, "children," under her breath.

Meda shook her head. "Do not worry. We can leave the weak and wounded to care for the children and take them to safety, allowing the strongest to join us without concern."

"I'm back!" Enla slid down the hill and plopped down beside them. "I made it look like the rocks scraped a swath in the dirt, and it points right to our crevasse."

"Great work, Enla. The fliers are going to carry us to the slaves." Aleshanee pointed to her friends, each in turn. "Chevei, carry Kilchi and Misa. Cholena, you carry Enla. And Meda, you can carry Amadah and me."

Kilchi hesitated. "I'm a little heavy. Sorry."

"I have been carrying boulders. I am certain you are not too heavy for me." Chevei motioned for Kilchi. "Climb on."

"Maybe you should carry me in your talons." Enla wrung her hands nervously. "I'm afraid I'll fall off."

Cholena smiled. "I can do that."

Aleshanee fluttered up and landed on Meda's back. "Come on, Amadah. Let's go." But Amadah didn't move. "We have to go now."

Amadah's jaw tightened and her brow furrowed with the effort to hold back her tears. "I know, but..."

"Can I help you climb on?" Enla offered, her voice soft and gentle.

"I just..."

"Listen to Fala's voice, Amadah. You know what he would tell you."

"I—I know I'm...but—if I go, I have to accept..."

"He's really gone."

Amadah squatted down and wrapped her arms around her knees. "I can't..."

Aleshanee threw back her head and shook her fists in the air. "We don't have beats for this. Meda, pick her up."

Enla glared at Aleshanee, then reached her long arms around Amadah. "Come on, Amadah. I know this is hard, but you can do it. You're the strongest creature I've ever known."

"If I was strong, it was because Fala was strong."

"And he is still with you. How often have I heard the two of you say you are bound forever? Do you think some Dark Lord can break that? No matter where Fala is, he is with you. Use his strength, like you always have."

Amadah loosened her grip on her legs. Meda coaxed her to stand and Enla gave her a boost up onto Meda's back. She settled in behind Aleshanee, who gave the word. "Let's go!" The group took off into the dark clouds above the valley.

Cholena took the lead position, with Meda and Chevei trailing to her right and left. She would dip down to the edges of the clouds on occasion to check her position, and it wasn't too long before she spotted little dots of light like tiny sky lights in a pitch-black sky scattered across the area beside the river where the slaves were encamped. She signaled Meda and Chevei, and they circled down. As they neared the pools of light, they saw the lights were small campfires, and around the fires huddled groups of former slaves.

Cholena landed some distance from the encampment, so they wouldn't frighten the slaves. "I'll go to the camp first, to prepare them for your arrival, then you approach."

As she approached the outermost campfires, she called out, "I've returned, and I have news." The slaves, who were lounging near the fire, rose to greet her.

"Cholena! We have news, too. Many slaves have joined us since you left, and more keep coming every cycle. They say the Chrysoli are setting them free."

"Freeing them willingly?" Cholena was shocked.

"Yes, they say it is so. Some escaped through the damaged dome, but others have been released."

"This is very good news indeed! I have some good friends who are coming to join us, and they have important information to share. They're of many different species, just like us. They desire us to join with them."

Hearing Cholena's voice, other groups of slaves approached to hear her news. "Are they many?" one of the slaves asked.

"They're only a few, but they bring knowledge we need and help in ways you can't imagine."

"What of the Turqosi?"

"The Turqosi aren't with us."

"Did they abandon us?"

"I don't think the Turqosi can be trusted. We are better off with these friends. Look, here they come."

Aleshanee led the rest of the sphere bearers into the camp. The slaves were quiet, waiting to hear what they had to say. Cholena felt her heart thump in her chest. What were the slaves going to think?

"My name is Aleshanee. I am from the Emraldi. This is Amadah, of the Jasperi; Enla, of the Onyxi; Kilchi, of the Carneli; Meda and Chevei, of the Jacinthi; Misa, of the Saphiri; and you already know Cholena. We..."

Before Aleshanee could continue, Kilchi gasped. "Carneli! I thought I was the last of my kind!" He bounded forward to a group of Carneli and began to nuzzle them in the way of his species.

Beyond Kilchi, Aleshanee spied several Emraldi, who had fluttered forward from the river. Tears welled and spilled on her shiny cheeks. "Emraldi. I can't believe it."

Amadah froze. Turning to look where she was staring, Cholena saw a host of Topazi, standing two by two around a large fire, away from the group and far from the edge of the water. "Oh, Amadah," Cholena moaned. Amadah didn't respond to the large group of Jasperi who gathered around her, touching and hugging her but kept her eyes fixed on the Topazi.

The celebration was short-lived, as Aleshanee recovered herself and cleared her throat. "I know how exciting it is to see our kind, still alive, when we believed for so long, we were the only ones remaining. But we must tell you what we know and prepare to leave."

"Listen, my friends," Cholena called. "Listen to Aleshanee."

"This world is in great danger. All the signs you see, the darkness, the storm of ice, the quakes, the falling light from the sky—these are all precursors of the danger."

"Cholena?" a Chalcedi slave asked.

"She speaks truly."

"We have a way to stop the danger. The Forever, the one who created this world, has given us a powerful weapon to use to stop this destruction. But a Dark Lord has set his mind against us and seeks to destroy us before we can use our weapon to save this world.

"You, too, face a grave threat from this Dark Lord who leads a large army. He plans to lead his troops into a great battle against us. He is coming this way and will try to convince you to join with him. He will promise you safety and food and protection. But he is a liar and a murderer. He has captured, tortured, and killed members of our group. If you remain here, he will claim to give you the choice to join him or not, but if you don't agree to take his side and join his army, he will slaughter you. We ask you to come with us before it is too late. We fight on the side of the Forever against the Dark Lord. We bring light against the darkness."

"What of the Turqosi? Will they come? Who do they fight for?"

Cholena answered for Aleshanee. "The Turqosi remain at the Dark Lord's camp. I don't know what they will choose. If you agree to come with us, we will go to the Chrysoli and invite them to join..."

"The Chrysoli!" a Jasperi slave cried. "Our captors?"

"We must warn the Chrysoli about the Dark Lord's armies and give them the opportunity to choose as well."

Grumbling broke out among the slaves, and several turned away to walk back toward the river.

"Listen to me," Cholena called. "I am one of you, and I have no love for the Chrysoli. But I have heard the words of those who speak for the Forever, and they say we must tell all creatures about the Forever and warn them about the Dark Lord."

"You want us to willingly walk back into their camp to be recaptured!"

"No! You said the Chrysoli are freeing the slaves. If they are, they won't try to capture you or harm you. We are hoping, instead, they will agree to join us on the side of the Forever."

"The Chrysoli only serve themselves!" another slave said.

"They'll have the choice to accept what we say or go the way of the Dark Lord," Aleshanee said. "But it is right and true to give them a real choice, which the Dark Lord won't provide. After we speak to the Chrysoli, we'll gather the Saphiri from the oceans to join us."

"Join us they will," Misa affirmed.

"And although the Dark Lord will have greater numbers and strength, he doesn't have the Forever on his side. If we follow the Forever, we will win the battle and stop the world's destruction.

"You'll hear rumors about this Dark Lord. Rumors that he was dead and rose again, that he is all-powerful and all-knowing, but these things are not true. He is a liar and a cheat. You'll need to know who he is in your heart, so you won't listen to his lies. He is cunning and slick and will try to convince you to come to his side with pretty promises of things you all want. But please, don't listen to him. He never does what he says he will do."

"We need food! We're starving!"

Meda raised a hand in the air. "He promised the Jacinthi food, and most of them believed him and took his side, but when the Forever opened my eyes, I could see the food he brought was really made from dead corpses of creatures just like you. But he deceived the other Jacinthi, and they ate his food."

"They ate sentient species?" a Jacinthi cried.

"Yes, because the Dark Lord deceived them."

231

"Disgusting." "Heinous." "Horrifying." The slaves muttered to each other, shaking their heads.

"You must understand, the Dark Lord is terrible, and capable of even worse deeds. He will try to make you believe he is your friend, just like he did with the Jacinthi, but he isn't!" Cholena bowed her head. "I was with him from the start. I even helped him almost destroy everything. But when I saw how horrible he really was, I left him. That's when I was captured and made a slave. Now, I've seen his lies continue. I know his plans. We must stand against him and his armies. We can't let him win, or the end of the whole world will follow."

More murmurs, as the slaves considered Cholena's words. "You're saying you want us to fight against this Dark Lord? With fewer numbers? If he's so strong, we'll all die."

"Better die than live like slave," a Topazi said.

"Die fighting or die later," another Topazi agreed.

Amadah burst into tears, pushed through the group of Jasperi gathered around her, and ran from the fire. The slaves stared after her, then glanced at each other, fear growing in their eyes.

"What's wrong with her?" one of the Jasperi whispered.

"Amadah has suffered a great loss and mourns," Meda explained. "You do not see fear in her, but sorrow."

"We must leave this place before the Dark Lord arrives. Will you join with us?" Aleshanee pleaded.

"The Turqosi were many, and they knew how to fight. Why join you, when the Turqosi promised they'll return and teach us. They were going to lead us against the Chrysoli instead of seeking to join with them. I think I like their plan better."

Cholena squawked. "I told you, they can't be trusted. If you think the Chrysoli only help themselves, the Turqosi are twice as self-serving. I believe the Turqosi are likely to take the side of the Dark Lord, believing it benefits them more. They will use you and spit you out when it serves their purposes. It's exactly what they did to me, and I was almost killed by the Dark Lord as a result."

This revelation brought another round of murmurs among the slaves, then one of the Jacinthi stepped forward. "We hear you talk of this Forever, but we do not see or hear anyone but you. How do we know what you say is true? How do we know this being you claim to hear, but we do not see, will help us?"

"We've all heard the voices of the ones who serve the Forever, and we've all seen their light. We testify to what we've seen." Kilchi looked at the Carneli slaves. "For Carneli, more than two witnesses are proof."

"Topazi believe with eyes," one of the Topazi grumbled.

"Own eyes," another Topazi agreed.

"I was bound mate to Fala, a Topazi, who saved my life and I his." Amadah's voice rang from the darkness. "Fala heard and saw and believed. Do you doubt Topazi?"

"I see no Fala."

"You see no Fala because the Dark Lord..." Amadah's words caught in her throat. "He murdered my bound mate, just as he will murder you if you remain here and don't join us."

The group of Topazi whispered among themselves, then one stepped forward. "Bound mates speak one tongue. Believe Topazi Fala."

"So, you believe us?"

"Topazi believe."

"The rest of you?"

"We don't want to fight," a Jasperi said. "Isn't there another option?"

"The Dark Lord is coming," Aleshanee reiterated. "He won't be bargained with. He won't listen to reason. He cares only for power."

"If you don't choose to join us, you won't have a choice at all. You'll be forced to join the Dark Lord, or you'll die, and he'll make you fight on his side." Kilchi looked pointedly at the Carneli.

"We just want to be left alone, to live the rest of our lives in peace."

Aleshanee sighed. "You're not listening. If we don't complete our task, this world is going to end. You won't have a life left. Do you understand?"

"The Dark Lord is trying to stop us. Will you help us stop him?" Kilchi asked.

"We Carneli refuse to be slaves again to anyone, the Chrysoli or this Dark Lord. Or to you."

"If you join us, you will not be slaves but will be free creatures, free to choose how to live your own life," Kilchi assured the Carneli.

"Topazi join."

"If what you speak is true, the only logical course would be to stand with you, for the other option leads to total destruction. The Jacinthi agree."

"As do the Amthysti."

"We will join with you," one of the Emraldi said.

"I don't know." The Jasperi, who appeared to speak for her group, dug at the ground with her feet.

Amadah moved back into the circle of light from the fire. "I know your thoughts. The Jasperi have always been cautious creatures, averse to any risk, but you can't take council of your fears. Not this cycle. I want nothing more than to give up, but I—I can't let myself entertain such thoughts. You can't hide from this. You can only choose a side."

"Tree hiders," one of the Topazi hissed.

"Scurriers," another Topazi echoed.

"Hold in your tongue," Amadah barked. "If we divide, we fall. We must stand like bound mates." The Topazi bowed their heads in acceptance. "Now, we are leaving. Collect what you need and douse your fires."

"Topazi need fire," one of the Topazi said. She pointed to the air. "Cold."

Amadah walked over to the group of Topazi. "You are called?"

"Seri, bound mate to Sewati."

"Seri, if Topazi leave the fire, you die?" Seri nodded. "If you leave the fire, how long?"

"Sleep comes, then Topazi die. Soon," Sewati replied.

"You know how far you have walked from the Chrysoli compound. If our fliers carried you back to the compound, would you make it?"

Sewati shrugged. "How fast fly?"

"As fast as you need us to fly," Cholena said.

Seri looked at Sewati. "One chance better than none."

"Worth risk." Sewati nodded once.

"Our fliers will carry the Topazi ahead to the Chrysoli compound," Aleshanee said. "Those among you who are fliers and uninjured may help carry them as well. Once you arrive, find a safe place to build a fire for the Topazi and wait for us. The rest of us will march to the Chrysoli compound." She looked to the Jasperi. "Are you coming?"

"No."

Cholena threw up her hands. "You know me. I brought you safely this far. Why won't you trust me now?"

"You ask too much of us."

"No more than we ask of anyone else. How is it preferable to remain here, where the Dark Lord is sure to find you? He'll torture you to find out where we went. Don't you see that?"

"We'll hide from him," the Jasperi said.

Amadah, her voice, lifeless and flat as a brine pool, said, "There are no more trees for any of us."

CHAPTER THIRTY-ONE

The Turqosi

Leenha stared, dumbfounded, while the rest of the Turqosi cowered, hugging the ground or sliding into whatever holes they could find. She had observed with her own eyes the blade pierce Ogima. She had watched his blood pour out on the ground. The creature was dead, of that she was sure. Yet, there he was, flying above his bier, sparks flying from his hands, speaking—what was she seeing? What magic was this? Was it real? She watched Angeni grovel before the apparition and scurry to follow his orders. She saw the camp break out in celebration, as if something astounding had occurred. It certainly appeared *they* thought it was real. If it was real, it was the evidence of genuine power, and Leenha wanted it.

She slithered to where Lise and Eteena had assembled her army. Leenha gestured for them to take a few scouts and fan out on either side of the camp. She wanted to get a closer look, to see if some trick was at play. But both of her generals balked, something they had never done before, their eyes white with terror. Leenha curled her lips back, her tongue flicking toward them, but they still refused to leave their hide, so Leenha shot her claw across Eteena's face, slicing it open. Before she could strike Lise, both bolted toward the Chalcedi camp, splitting before they reached the perimeter to go to either end.

Leenha glared at her armies, making sure each one saw her eyes and caught her meaning. She would brook no disobedience. However, her armies were transfixed by the drama playing out in the camp. They, too, seemed to be wondering at the magic they were witnessing, but she

237

could tell they were more terrified than fascinated, as she was. Her tongue slid across her mouth, desire bubbling up from her gut. This creature could bring life from death, and she wanted to possess his magic.

The Chalcedi appeared crazed, but then again, so did Ogima. Leenha couldn't hear anything over the cacophony, so she chafed as she waited for her generals to report. At long last, Lise returned.

"He lives?"

Lise nodded, then gestured the plans were to celebrate until sky light rising, then move against the Chrysoli. So, Ogima planned to challenge the masters.

"Slaves?" Lise made a sweeping gesture, indicating Ogima planned to collect them on his way to the dome. Leenha pointed to herself and the army with a questioning gesture, but Lise didn't know if Ogima had any plans for the Turqosi. Leenha's eyes narrowed. With this kind of power, she didn't want to become one of the casualties in Ogima's wake. Better to get out in front of this and offer her armies to stand beside him.

Eteena returned a few beats later with the same report—no mention was made of the Turqosi, but the Chrysoli would submit or die. Leenha calculated, she could be viewed as a great asset, and therefore highly valued, should she go to Ogima by choice rather than by force. She spun her hand in the air, and her armies gathered behind her. They crept forward to the edge of camp, moving as one, soundless in the darkness. As the ink-black sky started to fade to an ashy grey, Leenha lifted her fist, and she and her armies marched forward to present themselves before the risen one.

Three Chalcedi swooped before the Turqosi and commanded them to a halt, but Leenha waved her hand with a dismissive sneer. "We come to Ogima, not Chalcedi." She gestured for her armies to continue their march. They pushed their way past the Chalcedi toward the stone altar where Ogima stood, receiving the lavish praise of his followers. When Ogima spotted them, his face seemed to darken, but Leenha noticed his facial expressions were dulled somehow, as if his muscles were not responding. Still, Ogima looked displeased—whether with her or with his Chalcedi guards, she didn't know.

Leenha decided boldness was her best course, to assert her position as an equal. "Ogima." She didn't expect his thundering response.

"Who stands unbidden before the Lord?"

Strange. Ogima spoke, but his mouth didn't move. "Leenha and the Turqosi armies."

"You presumptuous creature, grovel on your face and address me as your Lord and King!"

Leenha would do many things, but groveling was not one of them, even for self-interest. She held her head high and crossed her long, thin arms. "I offer service."

"Kneel!" Ogima howled, sending a flurry of sparks toward her army.

"Turqosi obey only Leenha."

"And if I kill you, who will they obey?"

"No one."

"Then you will all die by my hand."

With a single gesture, Leenha scattered her armies to encircle Ogima's altar, then unfurled her frill in its full glory. "Only fools kill offered army in war."

"You are bold," Ogima muttered with some apparent admiration. "But all who follow me will address me as Lord or King and show me the proper respect I am due."

"For Turqosi, respect is earned."

"I demand what is mine!"

"Show reason to respect. Listen."

"Speak, but if what you say does not please me, you die."

The armies crouched, ready to pounce, but Leenha shrugged. "Turqosi massacred Beryli, larger, stronger, now all dead."

"So? The Beryli were a lazy, useless species."

"Good fighters."

Ogima considered her words, then nodded. "Continue."

"Turqosi not slack-brained Chalcedi, weak-boned Jacinthi, frightened Jasperi. Turqosi powerful. Like Ogima."

"Ah, so you acknowledge my power."

"You acknowledge ours," Leenha challenged.

"I acknowledge your audacity, but I am running out of patience."

"Ogima fights Chrysoli with Chalcedi, Jacinthi, Jasperi, Ogima loses."

Ogima rose up from the altar, white sparks shooting from his sarkikos, eyes aflame. "How dare you! I never lose!"

"With Turqosi, Ogima winssss." Leenha's lips curled, her eyes bright.

"So, give me your armies to command."

Leenha gave a sharp shake of her head. "I offer service. Armies obey Leenha."

"If they serve me, they obey me."

"King needs general."

"What?"

"King needs general leading armies."

"And I suppose you will be my general?"

"Yesss."

"Chatan is my general, and he obeys me."

"Chalcedi slack-brained fools."

Ogima paused, and Leenha saw she struck a nerve. So, perhaps Ogima was worried his Chalcedi, while strong, would do something stupid to undermine his cause. She wondered what the Chalcedi had done before to create this concern. "General leads, not follows."

"You seek to command all my armies?" Leenha nodded. "Why would I give command to such an insolent, brazen—small creature?"

Leenha hissed and spit a steaming wad on the stones. "Sssmall? Turqosi feared, even by mighty Chrysoli."

"You claim the Chrysoli know and fear you?"

"Leenha walked in Chrysoli camp, slaughtered Chrysoli, left untouched, no reprisal."

"This only proves the Chrysoli are weak, not that your Turqosi are strong."

Leenha shrugged again, gave a gesture, and her armies spread out in formation to march. She turned her back on Ogima and stalked to the front of the columns, then she and the armies started to leave.

"Stop!" Ogima called. Leenha lifted her fist to call for a halt. "You are toying with fire. I could destroy you all with a single word."

Leenha turned back to face him and swept her hand toward her armies, suggesting he go ahead and do it, but still Ogima hesitated. She had bet everything on a belief, and it was proving to be right—either he needed her, or his power wasn't as absolute as he pretended. If he could really destroy her armies with a single word, he didn't need any army at all, so the Chalcedi, Jacinthi, and Jasperi were superfluous. Still, he fostered their blind obedience. Leenha was beginning to wonder if Ogima's so-called power was more show than substance. Still, he did command life from death, so she would tolerate him until she learned his secret. Then, she would dethrone him and become Queen. She tossed her head and pulled herself to her full length. "Take offer or not."

Ogima glared at her but didn't strike. Leenha figured her army's presence on the battlefield would offer extra intimidation that might lead the Chrysoli to surrender. Her Turqosi brought large numbers and were skilled fighters. Is that really what Ogima wanted, to avoid a fight? It made sense if his power was more smoke and trickery than truth.

A strange, low hum vibrated Leenha's earholes. The noise was coming from a great distance. When, she glanced back to Ogima, she noticed he didn't seem to hear the sound. Strange. Leenha listened. The hum was slowly but steadily increasing in volume. So, whatever was causing the noise was moving toward their location. Depending on the source, Leenha thought she might use this new occurrence to her advantage, so she stepped back before the altar.

"Ogima, something comes." She pointed toward the southwest. "What? What are you saying?"

Leenha pointed to her earholes. "Hearing. Something comes. From Topazi desert." The hum had taken on a whirring quality like funnel winds. Was it another storm?

"I hear nothing."

Leenha sneered, pointing again to her earholes. Ogima lifted his hand to render punishment for her insolence but stopped in mid-gesture. Did he finally hear the noise? Leenha turned and squinted toward the horizon, which appeared to be darkening when it should be reflecting the sky light's rising. Another storm, then.

She gestured to her armies, who darted across the open field, back toward the tumble of rocks they had used as their hide. Leenha scurried behind them, glancing back twice to make sure Ogima wasn't sending Chalcedi after them. He seemed preoccupied with the gathering storm on the horizon, so she leapt into the rocks and gestured for her armies to find cover. The Turqosi disappeared from sight, all but Leenha, who remained in a position to observe Ogima's response to the approaching storm.

At first, he did nothing. The roiling clouds looked almost like the thick, heavy smoke from burning wet logs. Leenha had never seen a storm like this one. It seemed to grow as it progressed, overwhelming the horizon and blotting out the sky. Now, the whirring sounded like buzzing, as if her head was stuck inside a honey hive, but this buzzing was sharper, an almost metallic clicking, like an Amthysti mechanistic. Odd.

As the clouds came nearer, Leenha thought she could make out shapes moving within the clouds. Brief glimpses of red and gold glittered within the charcoal grey mass. The strange shapes seemed to tumble around and over each other, like piranha fighting over a morsel of food. The mass gobbled up ground until it reached the edge of the encampment. Mere beats later, Leenha could no longer see the camp, and the clouds were swirling toward her position. From within the churning mass, she heard screams.

CHAPTER THIRTY-TWO

The Jacinthi

Kwania and Miakoda pored over their figures and calculations. Based on the rate of change, the mass and frequency of explosions, and the measured alterations in the sky light's size over cycles, they were attempting to predict how many cycles were left before the final explosion obliterated their world. The numbers didn't look good.

Kwania was gratified Kola had freed all the slaves who wanted to leave the compound, but her joy was short-lived as she realized those slaves faced starvation even sooner than the Chrysoli. She pulled out the inventory Kola had provided of food in storage and ran a quick calculation of amount of food per individual under the dome. If each creature was allotted the bare minimum amount of food for continued survival, she estimated no more than 20 cycles before they ran out, probably closer to 15, given the stronger and more powerful Chrysoli would likely demand more food than the minimums. She supposed the good news in all this disaster was they would probably starve to death before the sky light's explosion burned them to cinders.

Miakoda glanced up at Kwania. "It will happen soon?"

Kwania hunched over her figures. "Well, we might starve before it explodes."

"Surely, Master Kola will find a solution for our food shortage."

Kwania looked through the scope at the rising sky light's edges. Her measurements were more difficult now, with the thick clouds obscuring the sky, but she was able to use other instruments to, in

243

essence, 'see' through the clouds to take her measurements. She moved the scope to scan along the horizon and saw a crowd of figures moving on the plains just beyond the dome. At first, she thought they were the last slaves leaving, but she noted the group was moving toward the dome, not away. She adjusted the scope to focus on the crowd, recognizing Jasperi, Emraldi...she stopped the scope on the Emraldi. She recognized her—it was Aleshanee! And Amadah was walking next to her. She thought she'd never see them again.

Kwania jumped up, flew down to the first level, and bolted from the science building, then took off for the front entrance. On the way, she spotted Kola walking across the compound, so she fluttered near him. "A group of creatures approaches the dome."

"Slaves returning?"

"I recognize the two leading the group as friends from before I was captured. They do not pose a threat or danger to the Chrysoli."

"Do they need food? If so, they pose a threat."

"Allow me to meet them at the entrance and ascertain their purpose." But Kola was in no mood for discussion. He waved her away and bounded toward the dome's entrance, calling for Lonan and the other warriors to flank him.

Kwania flew up through one of the open holes in the dome, determined to meet this group before they were confronted by the Chrysoli leader. When she rose above the dome, she saw Jacinthi and Chalcedi standing with the group. Could it be Angeni? Her heart leapt in her chest. How she longed to see her clan again.

Her hope spurred her forward, and as she approached, she thought she recognized Meda. And was that Cholena next to her? She pounded her wings and cried out, "It is Kwania! Kwania!"

At first, she received no response, but after repeating her call, she heard a faint voice. "Kwania, it's Meda."

"Angeni? Kacina?" No one replied. Meda was near where Amadah and Aleshanee were standing, so Kwania dove down and landed before them.

"Kwania!" Meda embraced her. "I cannot believe it is you. How did you come to be here?"

"It is a long story for another cycle. Why do you come to the Chrysoli lands?"

"We have a request for the Chrysoli." Meda stepped aside and pointed to Aleshanee. "Allow them to explain. Do you remember Aleshanee?"

"Welcome, Aleshanee. Amadah." Kwania took Aleshanee's hands in her own. "I have missed you all so very much."

"I'm glad you're here. You must be the one our friends foretold would help us lead the Chrysoli to the light. We have come to ask the Chrysoli to join with us. A terrible war is coming, and it will happen on these plains. If we don't win, the world will be destroyed."

"I fear the world is going to be destroyed regardless of the outcome of a battle. I have been studying the sky light at length. It is dying."

"We know."

"You do? How?"

"Our friends told us."

Kwania drew back. "Your friends. You still speak of such nonsense as invisible creatures talking to you? The Chrysoli are not the type to humor such fantasies, believe me."

Meda stepped forward. "It is true, Kwania. So many things we have seen, so many things you do not know because you have not seen. But you do know me. You know I speak truth."

"Where is Angeni?" Kwania asked.

Meda grimaced. "Angeni..."

"Where is she?"

"She's been deceived and follows the Dark Lord." Aleshanee blew out her breath. "We don't have cycles to explain and argue this. We need to meet with the Chrysoli, for the Dark Lord is coming, and he will be here soon. The Chrysoli must choose a side. You must help them to choose ours."

"To convince them I must understand, and I have many questions. Why is there going to be a war? Who is this Dark Lord and why would Angeni follow him? She must have a good reason. Why do you want the Chrysoli to..."?

"Your questions will have to wait," Aleshanee interrupted. "Can you take us to the Chrysoli or should we go alone?"

"Kola, the Chrysoli leader, is coming. He plans to stop you from entering the dome. You must understand, they are experiencing a severe food shortage. He assumes you are coming to take their meager food supplies."

"We don't want their food."

"Be sure to tell him that."

The many creatures standing behind Aleshanee, most of which Kwania recognized as escaped or freed slaves, were shifting, restless or fearful at the mention of Kola's name. Kola had been the nemesis for many of the slaves, and they were familiar with his short temper.

"Let's leave before he comes," one of the Emraldi said.

"We must offer them the chance to join us."

"As one we are strong," Amadah said. "It is the way."

The dome's gate opened, and Kola and his guards emerged, teeth bared. "You are standing on Chrysoli land. You must leave."

A large group of Topazi, who were huddled around a fire beyond the mass of slaves, walked forward and collected behind Amadah in a defensive formation. "You must be Kola, the leader of the Chrysoli. I am Amadah, of the Jasperi. Kwania and I are dear friends."

"How nice for you." Kola growled and bared his teeth.

"May I introduce you to the others in our group. This is Aleshanee, of the Emraldi, and..."

"Tell your creatures to get off our land."

Aleshanee stepped forward. "We don't want your food. We want to warn you of a coming danger to the Chrysoli and offer for you to join with us against the danger."

"If you won't leave on your own, we will assist you."

"Please listen. War is coming to your lands—not at our hands but at the hands of a Dark Lord, a powerful entity who not only wants your food, he wants your land. He'll appear to have great power, but his power is false. He'll present himself as a friend. He'll act as if you have a choice. But if you choose to reject him as you're doing with us now, he will destroy you and take what he wants. Your better option is to join

246

with us and follow the ways of the light. We must defeat the Dark Lord to be able to complete a mission we've been on for many cycles, one that will save this world from destruction."

Kola looked at Kwania, questioning her with his eyes. "I do not know."

"What destruction?" Kola asked Aleshanee.

Meda's eyes shifted from Kwania to Kola. "Kwania has told you of the sky light dying." She said it as a fact, not a question, and Kola nodded. "We also have been told the sky light is dying, and we have been given a solution."

"A solution?" Kwania shook her head. "That is impossible!"

"Kwania said nothing can be done." Kola snarled. "You think me a fool?"

Meda raised her palms to Kola. "Kwania does not know what we have learned. The Forever, the creator of the world, has given us a weapon to use to stop the sky light from dying. But the Dark Lord Aleshanee mentioned is trying to steal the weapon from us."

"Why would this so-called Dark Lord want to block the solution to the world's destruction? That makes no sense."

"He is quite mad; however, I believe his desire is a larger conquest."

"I don't understand."

"It's too complicated to explain right now, and we don't have the beats to do it." Aleshanee fluttered her little wings and got in Kola's face. "Your choice is this—stand with us against the Dark Lord and save the world, or submit to the Dark Lord's control and die, whether with the explosion of the sky light or at his hand. Which do you choose?"

"I've only heard one side of this tale. I would hear this Dark Lord's side of things before I choose my side." Kola tossed his mane with typical Chrysoli arrogance.

"And by then it will be too late." Aleshanee cocked her head and stared at the sky for a few beats. "Kola, do you value the testimony of witnesses?"

Kola paced, his head whipping from side to side with hackles raised. "We consider witnesses, as long as they are trusted and credible." A rumble rose from deep in his chest.

"You have the testimony Kwania provided about the sky light dying. You hear the same testimony from her friends. Is testimony from two sources credible?"

"Perhaps."

"Would you consider Kwania trustworthy?"

"Perhaps."

"Then her friends are also trustworthy, as they speak the same testimony. They also testify about the Dark One's desire to thwart their task which will save this world from the dying sky light. Is this testimony also credible and trustworthy?"

"I don't know."

Aleshanee looked toward the sky again, and after several beats of silence, her eyes widened, then her mouth set in a grim line. "And I testify once more to you. Something is coming you have never witnessed. It comes before the Dark One arrives. First, a thundering sound and a cloud as smoke rising on the plains from the southwest, then you will know agony. I warn you now, so that you may know my testimony is true, and your 'perhaps' may become 'yes.'"

"Is that a threat?" Kola growled in his throat.

"I make a report to you of events which have not yet transpired, and when my report proves accurate, you will have reason to trust my words and the words of my friends."

"How do you know what is to come?" Kola barked at Aleshanee.

"One of the beings of light who warned us of the sky light dying told me. She is helping us with our quest to save this world from destruction."

"I see no being."

"You can't see them, but we hear them. They are our friends."

"It's a trick."

Kwania leaned close to Kola. "I have heard them speak of these 'friends' before. It is no trick. If they have a method for halting the sky light's destruction..."

"How do I know this isn't some elaborate scheme on their part to get inside the dome and take over our food and land? How do I know they don't intend to destroy us?"

"Look at them, Kola. Most are the slaves you used to command. They are weak with hunger and fatigue, and many are wounded. Do you believe these slaves would return and risk being placed back into slavery without a reason to do so much more pressing than a few cycles worth of food?"

"The Dark Lord is a real threat to you," Cholena said. "I've seen his power. We are no threat. We only offer you the choice."

Kola recognized Cholena as one of the slaves who worked with Kwania on the rebellion. "You don't return for revenge?"

"None of the slaves desire revenge. We want you to join with us."

In the distance, Kwania saw what appeared to be a group of Jasperi running toward them. They were screaming. "Get inside the dome! Quickly! Get inside the dome!"

"Who is this? What are they bellowing about?" Kola grumbled.

"They are former slaves who remained behind because they feared returning to this place," Meda replied, "but apparently they fear something else more."

"What is it?" Amadah called.

"A terrible storm! Run!"

"Listen!" Aleshanee urged. As the group silenced, barely audible in the distance, they heard a low hum, growing and building to a droning roll, like a continuous thunder. Aleshanee whipped around and walked up to Kola. "This is what our friend warned us would come. Listen!"

Kwania spotted something against the horizon. "Look! What is that? Is it the Dark Lord coming?" The horizon was swallowed in a monstrous dark cloud, boiling up from the distant plains and gobbling up ground. "That is no regular storm. I see no sparks causing the rolling thunder."

The Jasperi continued to bellow warnings. The Chrysoli guards looked to Kola, stamping one paw then another as if demanding an answer. Yet, Kola didn't move or speak. He gaped at the growing cloud, eyes wide, panting as if he had run down a jackal.

Kwania poked Kola's shoulder. "We should go inside."

Finally, Kola barked, "Go." The guards scampered back to the dome, but when the group of slaves followed, he turned back and shouted, "Not you!"

"You leave them to their fate in this unknown horror?" Kwania gasped. "What kind of creature are you?"

"Get inside." Kola shoved Kwania.

"No! I remain outside with my friends."

Kola's jowl worked, the fur on his back rippling like lake water during a storm. He burst out, "Fine!" then followed his guards inside the dome and slammed the door behind him.

Kwania looked to her friends with sorrow etching her face. "I am so sorry. I wish I could be more help, but I do not carry much weight with Kola, it seems, despite the help I have given."

Aleshanee looked toward the approaching storm. "If we can't shelter in the dome, perhaps we could find some other way to cover ourselves."

"You are sheltered," Luxor whispered. "Light is your covering."

Aleshanee smiled. "Gather close around the fire." She motioned for the late-arriving Jasperi to join them. "Our friends will be our shelter in the storm."

CHAPTER THIRTY-THREE

The Chrysoli

Kola bounded across the compound, determined to make it to his chambers before the storm hit. "Get inside! Get inside!" The thunderous sound vibrated what was left of the dome, and fragmented pieces still hanging on after the storm of ice clattered to the ground around the Chrysoli as they bolted toward their buildings. The already gloomy sky darkened to black, and the whirring grew so loud, many Chrysoli fell to the ground and covered their ears with their paws, their howling adding to the din.

"*What kind of creature are you?*" Kwania's accusation rang in Kola's ears. Despite himself, he had come to care for Kwania like one cares for a pet. Still, he just left her out in this storm. "*What kind of creature are you?*"

He stopped in his tracks, moaned, slapped himself in the head, and turned back toward the dome entrance, but before he took a step, he saw the smoke tumbling into the dome and spreading in waves across the compound. Within the smoke, Kola made out shapes. They looked like little creatures, even seeming to have eyes. But the many eyes appeared to be part of the cloud. Kola couldn't make any sense of what he saw, until the cloud enveloped him, and he was set on fire. Countless tiny knives jabbed into his hide, inside his mouth and ears, over every metric of his sarkikos. He tried to scream, but his throat clogged with the living smoke, and his insides burned like his coat.

Kola gagged and coughed and spit, shaking his head wildly, but nothing worked. With every breath, more of the smoke entered. He fell

251

to the ground and rolled in the bare dirt, providing a beat of relief for his back, but his belly was aflame, so he flopped over to scrub his chest only to have his back light up with intense, unbearable pain.

Kola was vaguely aware of the howls around him. Somewhere in the recesses of his brain, he thought he ought to try to get inside a building, but he felt paralyzed. All he could manage was flopping like a fish out of water, gasping for air.

He heard more screeches and screams as a wave of Chrysoli poured from the science building, coated as if someone had smeared them with river bottom mud. Their skin crawled across their frame. They tore at it with their claws, beat against it with their paws, and bellowed as the pain caused by their own efforts to bring relief exacerbated the stinging pain caused by the smoke. Kola believed if he could shed his hide, his torment would stop, and only a flicker of rationality kept him from trying to do just that.

Belly against the ground, he dragged himself toward the main hall and his chambers, but just as he neared the steps, Leoti tumbled through the doors, squealing and mewling like a newborn. She looked like a formless, writhing black mass, with only her wild eyes left visible. "Kola!" Her scream was choked off. She clawed at her throat, then flung herself to the ground, much as Kola had done, thrashing and beating herself, until she finally started tearing at her own hide.

"Stop!" Kola coughed. "Stop!" But Leoti's piercing howls drowned his words, and she continued to lash herself until blood pooled in the dirt beneath her twisting sarkikos.

In some disconnected place in his mind, Kola realized that no place was safe from the smoke. The Chrysoli inside the buildings were suffering the same as those on the grounds of the compound. He also had a vague recollection of hearing a warning about this horror coming, but he strained to hold a coherent thought, as the flaming needles continued to stab, dashing rationality apart like shattering glass.

His fuzzy awareness that Leoti's screams had stopped prompted him to glance her way. She appeared unconscious. Unconsciousness could provide relief. Relief. Kola bashed his head against the ground, over and over, but without success. With his last vestiges of strength, he pulled himself to the steps, lifted his head, and pounded against the edge, and everything faded to grey.

CHAPTER THIRTY-FOUR

The Dark Lord

Skia Skotos watched his pathetic followers swallowed up by the swarming acridids from a vantage point well above the cloud. A seemingly endless tide of the pests flowed from what was left of the Topazi desert, consuming all in its wake, but Skia Skotos simply deposited his borrowed sarkikos on the altar and took to the air. He found their screams disgusting and contemplated putting them out of his misery but reconsidered when he realized he could turn the crisis into an opportunity. When the tail of the swarm approached, he could return to Ogima's sarkikos, make a show of commanding the swarm, and appear to cause it to stop, further solidifying his power in their eyes, and their dependence on him.

He enjoyed another consolation in this delay in his plans—he imagined the two witnesses and their group afflicted by the acridids. He would like to have witnessed their suffering, but he was loath to leave his followers untended, not knowing how they would respond to this onslaught. Their misery seemed quite complete. If they started killing themselves or each other he would need to step in, not wanting to lose any additional warm sarkikos from his army.

While he wallowed in his revulsion about his followers, he marveled at the skill with which the Turqosi anticipated and seemed to avoid the swarm. The acridids could worm their way into the smallest cracks, but the Turqosi somehow positioned themselves within the rocks in such a way, they filled the space with their own sarkikos and blocked the bulk of the swarm from reaching them. It appeared they could flatten and elongate their sarkikos into any shape they wished. Such a skill could be extremely valuable. In addition, compared with the madness of his followers, the Turqosi's lack of overt reaction to the acridids that did manage to bite them was impressive.

Leenha's arrogance and disrespect could not be tolerated. That much was certain. But he was beginning to wonder if there was a way to use the supercilious Leenha, and the skill and large numbers of her armies. If what she said was true, and they had attacked the Chrysoli and escaped unharmed, she could be a valuable asset if the Chrysoli balked at acquiescing to his control. The Turqosi could sneak into the Chrysoli camp and wreak havoc before the Chrysoli could prepare a response, then Skia Skotos and his Chalcedi would descend and finish the job.

As his followers became wild things, tossing themselves about in a frenzied attempt to remove the acridids, Skia Skotos considered ways he could accept Leenha's troops without losing face amongst his followers or risking an overthrow attempt by her at some point in the future. Perhaps she would accept a public humiliation if she knew he would then place her in an honored position. If not, he could kill Leenha and take over control of her troops. He just hated to lose her leadership and strategic skills unless it was absolutely necessary.

Bored with the endless wails of his followers, Skia Skotos indulged in his favorite fantasy. The Second World plunged into an eternal darkness. The cursed child and the cursed light ones rally to rescue the Divinethos' most beloved creatures, gathering the Second World back to the First World, only to find that he, Skia Skotos, had planned on this response all along. In fact, he had counted on it.

Restored to his rightful place on the First World and having already tricked the many species on the Second World into following him, he would rally his minions and followers to a final war against the Divinethos, to, once and for all, claim the throne. One by one, the cursed light ones would perish at the hands of his minions, and the brokenhearted child would diminish and fade to nothing. Then, Skia Skotos would slaughter the Divinethos' creatures on the altar before his throne.

Skia Skotos cackled at his imagined sight of the Divinethos feeling the agony of total loss of everything. Yes, the Divinethos would finally feel what he felt when he was thrown onto the Second World like so much garbage, without hope of return. He relished the feeling for many beats before he finished his fantasy, approaching the throne and choking all light from the Divinethos with his own hands. He saw himself turning, with a regal flair for the dramatic, taking the crown from the child's head and ensconcing himself upon the Forever throne, to reign and rule with absolute power and a fist of iron. And because it was the First World he now ruled, he could go back to the beginning and change the course of the Tempor, making it so that he, Skia Skotos, was, had always been, and would always be on the Forever throne, never having been exiled to the Second World, never having met the cursed child, and never having his power questioned for all eternity.

Enthralled by his own imaginings, Skia Skotos almost missed the diminishing size of the acridid swarm. The sky light was descending as the last wave of acridids reached his encampment. Skia Skotos flew down and raised Ogima's sarkikos into the air. Shaking the acridids off the corpse, he bellowed, "Hear me, you cursed creatures, tormenters of my followers, you shall release my chosen ones and return from whence you came!" He shot some sparks into the air for effect. As the acridids moved on, the fools groveled on the ground before him, praising and thanking him for their freedom from the terrible stinging swarm, just as he expected.

"Angeni, command the Chalcedi to build another fire to celebrate, and pronounce this the Cycle of Relief, for I have relieved you from eternal suffering. Keep record of these cycles, for every turn, we shall celebrate the Cycle of Rising and the Cycle of Relief with commemoration and worship that is my due."

"Yes, mighty Lord, oh Great One, I praise you for your mercy. Your greatness will be forever and ever. Your voice is like a thousand thunders. You raise a hand and the creatures of the world obey. Oh, Mighty One, ruler of all, we adore you."

Skia Skotos was tiring of Angeni's obsequious drivel, so he decided to call Leenha back for a private meeting.

258

Chapter Thirty-Five

The Jasperi

Amadah opened her eyes as the thunderous whirring pounding against the invisible shield around her group abated, and the living dark cloud moved on. After such a deafening roar, the silence in the heavy, frigid air felt oppressive.

Sewati kicked a dead insect-like creature with his claw. "Acridids. From Topazi desert. Bad sting."

Amadah's hands were stiff with cold, and as she tried to unclench her fists, she imagined Fala, arms stretched tight above his head, hanging from the metal pole, covered with stinging acridids, heat draining from his sarkikos like blood pouring from an open wound, his mouth slack and eyes drooping as he slid into unconsciousness. He wouldn't survive these conditions, even if Ogima spared him more torture. Her chest clenched like her frozen fingers, for in her heart, Amadah knew Fala was dead. She could sense it.

She drew back from her huddled group, lifting her head to the darkened sky. Was Fala now on his way to the First World? She had only vague impressions left of her journey to the First World after the Dark Lord killed her, but the bits and pieces she still retained held an aura of peace. Was the First World only for a chosen few? Enla seemed certain Yiska lived on the First World. Aleshanee also seemed sure the First World waited for them all. Amadah felt she could almost bear Fala's loss if she knew she would rejoin him on the First World.

259

But what if he wasn't there? Would she prefer finality to an eternity without him? She decided, rather than face his eternal loss, to believe she would see him at the rejoining. It made her all the more determined to see their task completed as quickly as possible.

She looked around to inspect the damage left in the wake of the living dark cloud, but the sky light had disappeared behind the horizon, and the darkness beyond their dying fire was as thick as the air. The screaming inside the dome had stopped. Nothing moved. It was as if the living cloud had frozen the world in place.

"I must go see to the Chrysoli," Kwania whispered, as if speaking aloud might recall the storm.

"Do you think they're all dead?" Kilchi matched Kwania's soft tone.

"I do not know what harm the creatures in the cloud cause. I have never seen such creatures before. Since we were protected from them, I cannot know their impact. But the screaming we heard indicates great pain at the very least. I must see if they need help."

"They wouldn't let us into the dome. Why would you help them now?" one of the Jasperi slaves asked.

"We do what is right, even when others do wrong." Amadah looked at the Topazi surrounding her like a shield.. "It is the way."

"We'll go with you," Aleshanee said to Kwania. "We might not be trained as medichi, but we can help."

"You go ahead, if you want, but we're staying out here where it's safe," the Jasperi slave said.

Amadah and Kwania crept to the dome's door and tried to push it open, but it wouldn't budge. "I will fly over the dome and enter through the damaged area, then I will unlock the door so you may enter."

Kwania took off, as Amadah turned to the rest of her group. "I don't hear any movement inside. I think it is safe for us to enter. Kwania is going to open the door from the inside."

Kilchi, Misa, Enla, Cholena, Chevei, Aleshanee, and the Topazi slaves collected around Amadah, while the rest of the slaves remained huddled together in the darkness, shivering. Soon the heavy door creaked on its hinges, and Kwania beckoned the group to enter. Dim light pooled from open doorways of the buildings scattered across the compound. Chrysoli sarkikos lay strewn across the ground, but Amadah couldn't tell if they were living or dead. "Seri, Sewati, get the Topazi inside one of the buildings where there is warmth." They scurried across the compound to the first lighted building, a large one with high windows.

Kwania hurried from one Chrysoli to another, checking for signs of life. Aleshanee fluttered above her. "Are they dead?"

"They appear to be alive but unconscious." Kwania continued her examinations. "Check for blood, for many appear to have self-inflicted wounds which may be life-threatening. Call to me if you find a severe wound so I may tend it."

The group spread out across the compound, checking each Chrysoli for blood or obvious open wounds. Kilchi waved his paw and pointed to a Chrysoli lying just beyond the entrance to a residential building. "Here!"

"I found one!" Enla yelled.

"Over here!" Cholena called.

Amadah called Kwania to tend a gruesome set of wounds on a female Chrysoli. "It's like they were clawing off their own skin. What kind of horror would make someone do that?"

Some of the Chrysoli were beginning to stir as Kwania scurried around, binding wounds. The Chrysoli who were struggling to stand appeared disoriented and traumatized, shaking and weeping as they wandered aimlessly about the compound, some reaching down to help others to their feet, but most just staggering blindly, their eyes glazed.

"Kola!" Kwania rushed to the steps of the largest building on the compound. Amadah knew Kola was the leader of the Chrysoli who met them on the plains and refused them entry. Kwania still seemed deeply moved as she tended him.

Kilchi bounded up the same steps to check another Chrysoli lying there, a female who appeared gravely wounded. "Kwania, this one is bad."

261

"Stay with Kola. He has a severe head injury and will be disoriented if and when he awakens." Kwania came to the female's side. "Oh, my. Can someone help me lift her?" Chevei came forward, hefted the Chrysoli female on his back, and carried her where Kwania pointed, into the same building where the Topazi sought refuge from the cold.

"Amadah, I'm afraid the Chrysoli are not going to be able to make their choice in this state," Aleshanee whispered.

"Perhaps the Dark Lord suffered the same experience. Certainly, he didn't have our friends helping him or his followers. Maybe that will buy the Chrysoli a cycle or two."

"The Dark Lord won't be patient."

"I know."

"We need to get the Chrysoli inside. It's too cold for them to be wandering around out here."

"You direct the ones who are up and walking to go to their homes," Amadah said. "We'll help the others."

Amadah, Misa, and Meda helped the Chrysoli who couldn't walk on their own toward the building where Chevei and Kwania had taken the female. Those who were still unconscious, Enla and Kilchi carried one by one into the building. Inside, Kwania was scrambling from table to table and cot to cot, trying to stop bleeding and sew up the worst of the open wounds, but it was clear she was losing the battle.

"How can we help?" Amadah asked.

"Can you sew?"

"Yes, I know how."

"Here." Kwania shoved a thin needle and some thread into Amadah's hands. "You take some of the less severe ones."

Amadah busied herself sewing up cuts and gashes. The task was repetitive, so her mind was free to roam, back to the open field where her attempt to free Fala failed. She ran the story over and over in her mind, forward and back again, seeking the one thing she didn't think to do or try that would've saved Fala. Why hadn't she remained with him? At least he wouldn't have been alone when he died.

"And you would be dead, too," Na'ro whispered.

"We would be together then."

262

"And the world destroyed and beyond hope."

Amadah paused for a few long and agonizing beats, then asked the question burning in her heart. "Is Fala on the First World?"

"Kindred took Fala's hand. Those who touch Kindred journey to the First World."

Amadah, unaware she had been holding her breath, exhaled and closed her eyes. "Thank you, Kindred."

"The others need you to lead them to complete your path," Eleutheri whispered. "The sphere must open the way for the rejoining."

"Look around you," Na'ro added. "These many creatures, and many who remain beyond the dome, will all perish into nothingness if the sky light ends before the rejoining. They do not know Kindred and will not take her hand."

"Not everyone travels to the First World?"

"Lead them," Eleutheri replied. "They will follow you."

"I'm not strong enough on my own."

"You are never on your own."

"But without Fala..."

"Fala stands with you."

"He's here?" But she heard no whispered response. So, as she sewed up the wounded Chrysoli's hides, Amadah whispered, "He's with me. He's still with me."

The beats marched by in an endless line of bloody sarkikos. Kwania and Amadah worked throughout the sky fall and into the sky light rising mending the Chrysoli. The others took turns sleeping for brief periods, curled up in corners or under the tables where the Chrysoli lay, unconscious. Those still awake helped move the next Chrysoli onto the gurneys for mending, and the process continued through the next cycle.

Kola awakened mid-cycle, but as Kwania predicted, he was sluggish and disoriented, and she had to assign Sewati to keep him awake, concerned if he lapsed back into unconsciousness, he might not revive.

As sky fall approached, Kwania took Amadah aside. "I have another concern. Infection."

"Infection?"

"When a wound festers. Festering wounds can kill a creature as quickly as the wound itself."

"What can we do?"

"I do not have what I need here to prevent infection. On the high mountain, we had medichinals, unguents, preventatives against infection, but the Chrysoli do not believe in healing sciences. They send their wounded and sick to the plains to die alone."

To die alone, like Fala. Amadah gulped but kept her tongue. "What does it look like if it festers?"

"The wound will appear red and filled with pus, a yellow-green ooze. All we can do is clean out the wound as well as we can, then hope they are strong enough to overcome the infection."

"Should I start cleaning the wounds?"

"If you would, yes. Ask Aleshanee and Misa to help you. Then, you need to rest."

"You need sleep, too. You won't be any good for anyone if you collapse from exhaustion."

Kwania sighed. "I will rest when I am able."

"Kwania," Kola croaked. "Kwania, come here."

Amadah walked with Kwania to speak with Kola. Perhaps he would be receptive to their pleas now that he had experienced the works of the darkness.

"Yes, Kola. Do you need something?"

"How fares my pride?"

"Most are recovering. Some still need supervision of their wounds to ensure recovery."

"Leoti?"

"Leoti remains unconscious. She lost much blood, but I have sewn her wounds closed, so I am hopeful."

Kola closed his eyes and sighed; his brow rippled with the effort of concentration. "What was it the Emraldi said?"

Amadah leaned close to Kola. "She warned you about the terrible cloud, then she told you of the coming of the Dark Lord. Do you remember?"

"The cloud." Kola shivered. "I remember the cloud with eyes."

"We need to talk about the Dark Lord. Do you remember her telling you he is coming to destroy you?"

Kola groaned. "We aren't in any state to defend ourselves from anyone."

"We're hoping the Dark Lord's followers suffered from the cloud, too, and it will delay his coming."

"You're hoping?"

"Yes, we don't know for certain."

"Can't the invisible light being tell you?"

"They've not said anything yet. Will you stand with us when he does come?"

Kola groaned again. "Don't bother me with your problems with this Dark Lord. They aren't my problems, and I have enough of my own."

"The Dark Lord will be your problem when he comes to invade the dome and take over your lands."

"Sounds to me like if we join him, we'd be in better shape than if we fight him."

"Maybe, at least until the sky light dies, then you'll all be dead."

"Why don't you surrender to him, too? Give him whatever it is he wants. Then maybe he'll leave you alone."

Amadah sighed. "You don't understand his ways. You can't work with this being. You fight him or you're destroyed by him."

"If we join with you against him, we're destroyed by him anyway. Leave me alone. I'm tired." Kola turned on his side, his back to Kwania and Amadah.

"The cycle is coming, too soon, when you must decide," Kwania warned. "You cannot put off this choice forever, for not choosing is making a choice. The sky light continues to deteriorate and expand. It will not be long before the flames reach our world and consume it. If Amadah and her clan can stop it, we must help them."

"You help them if you must. Just let me be." With a heavy sigh, Kola covered his head with his paw.

"You can't hide from what's coming," Amadah warned. "Remember what the invisible light being said? She was right about the cloud."

Kola growled deep in his throat. "I said, leave me be."

Kwania took Amadah's arm. "Do as he asks. The Chrysoli grow more obstinate when pushed."

"They are running out of beats."

"I know." Kwania pointed to the grey sky, visible through slats high on the walls. "At the rate the sky light is expanding, it may explode before the Dark Lord arrives."

"Then all is lost. But I don't believe that. I can't." Amadah shook her head as if she was awakening from a long sleep. "Our friends wouldn't tell us to hope if there was none."

"All we can do is care for the wounded and hope our care wins us favor with Kola, although I have not seen them appreciate medichi in my past dealings with them."

"I'll call the others and begin cleaning the wounds."

The somber mood in the compound added to the cold, wet heaviness of the air. Many of the Chrysoli who made it to their homes the prior sky fall were out now, walking the compound and looking for answers. Amadah called Aleshanee away from her conversation with a small group of Chrysoli to help with cleaning the wounds. "We must be preparing for the Dark Lord. I've been trying to recruit these Chrysoli to our side."

"I don't think they'll do anything without their leader's direction, and Kola continues to resist."

Aleshanee moaned. "We'll need to leave soon if we want to escape the Dark Lord's detection."

"I know. Kola still won't listen."

"What is it going to take?" Aleshanee cried.

As if in response, Kwania called from the door of the science building. "The wounds are beginning to fester! Hurry! The infection is setting in."

Amadah, followed by Aleshanee, raced across the compound to join Kwania. She handed them cloths and a white, harsh-smelling substance, and told them to coat the wounds with the liquid. When Amadah dabbed the substance on a wound, the Chrysoli howled and snatched her limb out of Amadah's reach. "Stop! It hurts!"

"I have to do this. Your wound is festering. It will kill you if we don't treat it."

"Send me to the plains!" the Chrysoli cried. "It hurts!"

"For such large and apparently strong creatures, you are very weak-willed" Amadah couldn't believe how they were acting.

"They have no experience with suffering," Eleutheri whispered. "Their strength of sarkikos matters little when they have no resilience, forged in the fires of pain and strife."

Amadah sighed. "The Chrysoli leader still won't commit, despite hearing our warning and seeing what happened."

"He hardens his heart to protect himself," Eleutheri replied. "You must prepare to stand against the Dark Lord with only the sphere bearers."

"Only the few of us? What of the slaves? The Chrysoli? Will they take the side of the Dark Lord?"

The moans of the Chrysoli grew louder. Kwania ran up to Amadah, frantic. "We are losing the battle with some of them. Their fevers are spiking."

Amadah and Aleshanee raced around the room, soaking wounds in the white substance amidst screams and howls of protest. Soon, a noxious cloud hung over the sick room, and Amadah felt dizzy from the fumes. Aleshanee was forced to leave, vomiting as she reached the exit. Amadah joined her a few beats later, gasping in gulps of fresh air.

Aleshanee groaned, holding her stomach. "I don't think they're going to make it."

"If they die without making a choice..." Amadah began.

"They must!"

"Our friends told me we'll need to stand against the Dark Lord without them."

"Really?"

"And without the slaves. She seemed to be saying the slaves might also abandon us."

"Why did we come here, then? Why not send us to the Saphiri straightaway?"

"We had to give them the chance to make the right choice. But maybe that's what we should do now—go to Misa's clan."

Aleshanee frowned. "I don't understand. Our friends told us to come here. They said they saw all the possible paths, and only one leads to success. But it looks like their plan failed. Didn't they know what was going to happen?"

"I don't know. Maybe our friends don't know for sure what others will choose. Maybe they only know the choices for us to make, the choices for our right path."

"Have we failed?"

"It didn't sound like it. She said I'm to lead the group and finish the path. She said the sphere has to be placed on the high mountain, so there must be some way for us to stand against the Dark Lord without the Chrysoli or the slaves."

"Another way?"

"There must be. But what is it? Where am I to lead?"

Phosi's voice rang in her heart. "The two witnesses will stand before the Prophet and the Dark Lord. When you speak, your words will be like fire in their ears. The sky will be like ash, and the waters will disappear before the Dark Lord arrives with his armies. At that moment, when all appears lost, all will see."

"All will see? See what?" Amadah asked.

A flash of brilliant light split the sky, like a diving skimmer picking suplei from the waters, until it fell to the ground and burst into flames somewhere near the river where the slaves were once camped. The ground and dome shook from the violence of the impact, bringing Kwania, Seri, and Sewati to the door. "What was that?" Kwania cried.

Amadah pointed to the billowing flames shooting into the air, but Kwania was looking up. Thin streaks of light streamed toward the ground, paving paths across the sky, and everywhere they landed, fires burned. Kwania's eyes widened. "Another ejection from the sky light. This one split into smaller fragments in the sky."

Streams of light continued to fall, some landing on what remained of the dome, some landing inside it and catching the remnant of pummeled crops on fire. Amadah and Aleshanee ducked inside the doorway to escape the falling fireballs. Kwania glanced at them, her face etched with concern. "The disintegration of the sky light is escalating, as I feared. We are on shortening cycles."

Amadah called her new Topazi friends over. "Seri, Sewati, will you go to the slaves and try to convince them to enter the dome? I fear for their safety on the plains."

"Chrysoli no more threat," Seri said.

"Weak. Soft. No bones," Sewati agreed.

"Slaves come," Seri promised.

"Bring them to that building." Amadah pointed to a large structure adjacent to the science building. "They will have plenty of room, and it looks sturdy." Seri gave a single nod, and the two Topazi lowered to the ground and raced across the compound toward the dome entrance.

Another flash lit up the entire sky, but this one didn't fall to the ground. Instead, the fire skipped through the air, burning in the atmosphere. For Amadah, it was like watching the Whisperer's prophesies come to life. "The sky will be like ash...Kwania, where do the Chrysoli store water?"

"They have several deep wells on the plains beyond the dome. They pump the water for the compound in from the wells."

"My friend said the waters will disappear. Please tell me they keep water stored for dry seasons."

"I will ask Kola."

A burning fragment landed on the roof of a nearby building, one of the personal residences, and soon the building was engulfed. Some of the Chrysoli made a few feeble attempts to douse the flames, but it was too late. The residence collapsed a few beats later.

As burning fragments continued to fall and the compound burned, the Chrysoli disintegrated into chaos, scrambling without any clear direction, grabbing handfuls of food from their residences, some even running from the dome out onto the plains. Chevei and Meda took to the air, calling for calm, but no one heard them amidst the pandemonium, so they landed where Amadah stood with Aleshanee in the doorway of the science building, watching the Chrysoli scatter like antlings on a disturbed mound.

"Our friends say the Chrysoli have never known suffering, so they don't know how to handle such things." Amadah watched the Chrysoli scrambling for a beat, then lowered her head.

Meda's expression was grim. "One of the consequences of owning slaves. They passed their hardship on to others and in so doing failed to learn the lessons of their experiences. They knew power but not strength."

Amadah tilted her head, then nodded. "I hadn't thought of that, but you're right. The slaves did all their work and handled all their struggles. They never developed any inner strength or resiliency. Plus, Kwania said the Chrysoli don't treat disease—they just send the sick out onto the plains to die."

"How horrible!"

Aleshanee's soft features scrunched into a ball of fury. "Amadah, let's leave this awful place and go to the Saphiri. They will stand with us—I know they will."

"What about the slaves?" Meda asked.

"I sent Seri and Sewati to bring them into the dome. We'll ask them to come, but I don't think they will. I imagine they're terrified."

Kwania returned to stand with the group in the doorway. "I asked Kola about the water supply. He says they have a tank filled with water in the building where they store their food, but I do not know how long the supply will last."

Amadah nodded. "Chevei, would you go find everyone and tell them to meet us here?" As Chevei left in search of their group, Amadah turned to Kwania. "We're leaving to bring the Saphiri to our cause, and we want you to come with us."

"I cannot."

"These creatures are weak, hopeless beings who want to give up and die. You could be of more service with us."

"All you said may be true, but I am still needed here, and I cannot walk away from my post."

Amadah sighed, shaking her head. "We'll fly to the Beryli Sea, where Misa can speak to her clan. We have special water that will give them legs like Misa, so they can leave the water and stand with us when we meet the Dark Lord and his Prophet on the plains."

""I will remain here and do my best to heal the Chrysoli's festering wounds," Kwania said.

"Please, Kwania, reconsider. Come with us."

Kwania shook her head. "I will continue to try to convince them to stand with you, and when you return, I will be here."

"Do you stand with us, even if the Chrysoli refuse?"

"I stand with you."

Amadah embraced Kwania. "Then, until we return, my friend. Be safe."

"And you as well."

Soon, the rest of their group gathered around Amadah. "Aleshanee and I have decided we will go forward to the Saphiri and see if they choose to stand against the Dark Lord. The Chrysoli refuse to stand with us, at least they say so now, so it won't do any good to remain here."

Kilchi looked around the destroyed, burning compound filled with panicked Chrysoli and the smoke-clogged sky. "You're right, there's nothing here for us."

"Seeing my father once again for me is joyful," Misa shared.

Aleshanee took Misa's hand. "We'll need you to swim to your clan and plead our case. It's important they join us."

"Having logic and good sense is my father and my clan, able to see reason."

"I'm sure Towila will join us," Kilchi echoed.

Amadah spied Seri and Sewati crossing the compound with the herd of slaves in tow. "Let's invite the slaves to come with us, but if they choose to remain here, we have to make sure they remain on our side."

She met the slaves at the doorway of their new temporary housing. "We're glad you came with the Topazi. We were worried you weren't safe."

"The fires outside the dome are horrible, much worse than inside," one of the Emraldi said. "At least inside we have a covering over us to protect us from some of the falling fire. The Topazi said we had nothing to fear from the Chrysoli anymore."

"That's true. And we're glad you're safe. Our group is leaving now to find the Saphiri and ask them to join with us. Will you go with us on this journey?"

"Why would we go?" a Jacinthi asked.

"Well, to remain together as a group. Strength in numbers," Kilchi replied.

Misa nodded. "Helping show my kind our unity and determination."

"It's dangerous out there, and scary," an Emraldi whimpered. "Is it a long journey?"

"We will go all the way to the Beryli Sea."

"No water," Sewati protested.

"You won't have to get in the water," Amadah reassured the Topazi. "Only Misa."

"Long way. Too cold," Seri said.

"Topazi stay," Sewati agreed.

Kilchi whispered to Amadah. "They're right. I'm afraid the Beryli Sea is too far away for them to make it in the cold unless we can fly them."

"The Jasperi will not go."

"It seems more prudent to remain here than to attempt a long journey under these conditions. Neither will the Jacinthi accompany you." The rest of the slaves mumbled their agreement.

"Will you remain in the Chrysoli compound?" Meda asked.

"As long as the Chrysoli leave us in peace, yes," the Jacinthi answered.

"Help Kwania," Seri replied.

"Useful," Sewati agreed.

"We'll return for you, I promise," Amadah said. "When we return, will you stand with us and with Kwania?"

"Topazi stand with Amadah."

Amadah clasped Seri's and Sewati's arms, and they lowered their heads, which she knew was a gesture of Topazi honor.

For a moment, the image of Fala, left alone to die, flashed across her vision. Amadah swallowed and closed her eyes, forcing the image away. She wasn't leaving these Topazi to die. Not again. It wasn't the same. They were choosing to stay here, where they'd be safe until she returned. It was best. And she would come back for them, as she promised.

"The rest of you? Will you stand with us against the Dark Lord?" Aleshanee asked. The slaves mumbled among themselves, but no one responded.

"Do you not remember how we stood on the plains and the light shielded us from the swarming cloud? Do you not remember hearing the screams of the Chrysoli who were not protected?" Meda asked. "The Dark Lord brings with him terrible destruction, like the cloud. Would you choose to leave the protection of the Forever and walk with the one who would bring such horror onto the world?"

Their silence broke Amadah's already tortured heart. "The Dark Lord comes with promises of great things—endless food supplies, protection, riches, and power. Don't listen to him. Don't believe him. Whatever he says to you, he will not do it."

The slaves nodded, but still, only the Topazi promised their support.

"We'll be back. Remember what you've seen, and remember our promise, always." Amadah and rest of the sphere bearers took their leave of the slaves.

"Topazi remember," Sewati replied.

"Always," Seri echoed.

Amadah flinched as an overwhelming feeling of guilt washed over her. Was she leaving the Topazi to a horrible fate? She knew the Dark Lord was coming to the Chrysoli compound. And here she was, abandoning them like doelani before jackals. "Like Fala," she murmured under her breath. "Just like Fala."

"As before, fliers carry walkers," Aleshanee said. "We go with all speed to the Beryli Sea to find the Saphiri."

Amadah moved a few steps away from the group and looked to the sky. "Am I doing the right thing?" Somewhere, in the deep recesses of her heart, she thought she heard, "We are bound."

She closed her eyes and whispered, "Forever."

Chapter Thirty-Six

The Saphiri

Towila plowed through the deep waters, searching for any signs of food for his clan. All the suplei were gone. The strange storms and weather had forced the suplei and any other sea creatures inhabiting the shallows out to the open sea. Towila had negotiated with two Jasperi living on the shore to bring his clan land food in exchange for sharing their suplei, but now that the suplei were gone, he had nothing to trade, and the Jasperi were refusing to share. He waited too long to act, and his best hunters were too weak from hunger to brave the tides, so Towila was forced to leave the clan behind to seek food in the deep waters on his own. So far, even the deepest waters appeared barren.

Soon, Towila knew, he would be forced to return, for he was swimming on the last of his strength. He couldn't bear to return with nothing, but nothing could be found. His desperation led him to take greater and greater risks, diving deeper, remaining under longer, going farther from shore. It was looking more and more like his clan was going to be forced to leave the Beryli Sea for different waters, but where and how? Without food, they were all too weak for a long journey in deep waters to a far-away ocean, with no guarantee of finding sea creatures there.

A faint coo reached Towila's ears. The call was too distant to make out the message, but it was clearly from one of his clan so Towila turned for the shallows. As he approached, he almost imagined he heard his daughter's name in the coo. Misa. Misa. No, it was impossible. She was long gone with her Carneli mate. Surely, after all

275

these cycles, she wouldn't show herself here. Bile rose in Towila's throat as he pummeled his tail against the waves. He would never forgive the Carneli for stealing his daughter from him, nor would he forgive his daughter for leaving.

There it was again—Misa. Did he hear correctly? Misa had returned? Towila quickened his pace and was soon entering the shallows. He lifted his head to search the water for any sign of her deep blue hair and—wait, he saw a glimmer of cerulean in a swish of motion, but the movement was on the shore, so it couldn't be his Misa.

"Misa?"

"Papa!" He recognized her voice. It was Misa. But where was she?

"Misa, where?"

"Here, Papa!" Again, a flash of blue and a waving hand from the shore pulled Towila up short. He bounced along in the crests and troughs, his mouth agape. He knew he couldn't be seeing what he thought he was seeing—Misa standing on land, surrounded by other types of creatures. A shiver rolled from his neck down his arms, raising pinpricks across his skin. What had the Carneli done to her? He couldn't manage a reply to her call but swam slowly to the shoreline. Misa splashed out into the waves, her arms flailing, screaming, "Papa! Papa!"

It was true. His Misa was standing on legs like a land creature. Towila's shock turned to fury. Still, his voice betrayed him. Misa wrapped her arms around his neck, crying. "Oh, Papa! Seeing you so long after is joy! Missing you very much!" Towila's soundless glare and limp arms pulled Misa out of her embrace. "Papa?"

"Having done a great abomination is your greeting?"

"Papa, no! Watch!" Misa took the cask of living water from her pack, took a sip, and collapsed into the water, her silvery blue fin just below the surface.

"What is this? What magic?"

"Being no magic, a gift! Giving the same gift to all Saphiri is making survival possible."

"Survival you call this? A gift is it to lose your very nature?"

"Papa, yes a gift. Finding food, shelter, coming with Misa and our friends is possible because of this gift. Not losing, gaining."

Towila gave a fierce shake of his head and turned away.

"Papa! Leaving not is what I desire. Seeing you is an even greater gift."

Towila couldn't help himself. His heart softened at Misa's words. He did love her so dearly. He glanced back over his shoulder. "Remaining with your kind, in your true nature?"

"Being able to remain in the water is no Saphiri's fate, Papa."

"The oceans are dying, Towila," Amadah said. "In fact, the world is dying, because our sky light is dying."

"Having a way for stopping the end is our group, a sphere of light. Remembering the Light, Papa? Coming from the Light is the gift, to save us."

"Saying the Light takes your fins?"

"Giving legs instead, for cycles' need," Misa explained.

The other Saphiri, who had been ogling Misa from afar like she was some kind of aberration, approached her. "Misa?" Her friend, Leytia, reached out and touched her tentatively. Misa embraced her friend, who smiled and relaxed into her hold. "Happiness to see you."

"We must prepare to leave," Aleshanee said. "We have living water for all Saphiri to drink, and fruit to strengthen you again."

At the mention of food, all the Saphiri except Towila pushed themselves onto the sand and clamored for the fruit. "Stop!" Towila shouted. "No one eats or drinks!"

"Towila." Kantila sighed and shook his head. "Starving is your clan."

"Allow us to eat and drink," Leytia begged.

"Try the fruit, Papa. Seeing then its power." Misa proffered a small piece of the fruit. "Trust me."

Towila didn't have the heart to let his beloved daughter believe he had lost trust, a foundation of everything the Saphiri believed, for without trust, they were nothing to each other. He wouldn't say that in word or deed, so he accepted the piece of fruit and ate it. As he swallowed, his sarkikos shook, pulses of energy radiating from his core.

Rather than feeling like an ancient, dying sea creature, he felt new and vibrant, strong again and ready for anything. Looking at his clanmates, he nodded. Enla, Cholena, Meda, and Chevei handed out small pieces of the fruit to all.

"Having more may we?" Kantila asked. "So hungry are we."

"I'm sorry, we must preserve some in case one of us gets injured, and we have so little left," Aleshanee replied. "But as soon as you leave the water, we'll search for food for you on land."

"Leaving the water is not for Saphiri," Towila decreed.

"Papa..."

"No! Without discussion."

"Discussing is the Saphiri way, not commanding." Kantila raised his head high, a challenge to Towila's authority.

With a thrust of his tailfin, Towila raised out of the water to tower above the rest of his kind. "Leaving the Saphiri way is leaving the water." His declaration brooked no argument.

Farther out from where the Saphiri congregated, the water churned as if a cyclone spun the waves like a youngling's spinner. The Saphiri withdrew higher on the shore, some even lifting their tails from the agitated sea, while others clutched each other in viselike grips. A ball of fire plummeted toward the center of the swirling water. More fireballs arced through the air and landed in the water. Steam from the water rose in plumes of color, reds and yellows and greens and blues.

Thunder rumbled over the sea, and sparks flashed from the dark grey clouds to the water. Fireballs streaked across the sky and pounded into the churning waves.

"Quickly!" Misa restored her legs, stepped from the water, and reached out her hand. "Get out and take the living water! Hurry now!" The Saphiri opened their mouths to receive drops of the water from Aleshanee, Amadah, and Misa, but Towila remained in the water.

"Being stubborn are you, pointless and irrational." Misa balled her hands into fists and shook one at Towila. "Stop it! Burning is the water as will you."

"Not possible is water burning with fire." Towila turned his back again, his nose in the air.

278

"Look and see."

Beneath the dark clouds, where the fire poured into the water, orange-red flames spread out across the surface, making the sea look more like a flaming forest than an ocean.

"Receding are the waters!" Leytia cried. "Look!" The shallows were becoming mud pools, and the water was retreating from the shore, but as the waters withdrew, one by one the Saphiri stood on new legs. Some cried out, some laughed, and some stared in awe. And still, Towila remained in the water, retreating farther from the shore in search of enough water for swimming.

"I'll go get him and carry him out," Kilchi offered to Misa.

"Never!" Towila shouted.

Misa wept. "Forgiving you never if you do. Choosing is sacred to Saphiri. Live or die, wrong it is to remove his freedom to choose."

"Better you're mad than he's dead." Kilchi marched out onto the muddy sand. "I'm coming for you, Towila. You're coming with your daughter, one way or another. I won't see her hurt again like she was when you refused to come with her before."

"Kilchi, do not!"

Towila pointed to Misa. "Hurting her are you."

"You might as well come out on your own. Either way, you're coming out."

The fire skipped across the surface and spread quickly. Kilchi loped across the mud then splashed through the shallows that remained, but when he reached Towila, the Saphiri grappled him around the neck. "You! Your fault is this!"

"Let—go..." Kilchi shook, trying to dislodge Towila's arms.

"Stealing my daughter from me." Towila tightened his grip.

Kilchi bucked wildly, and Towila tumbled backwards into the waves. With a vicious snap of his teeth, Kilchi bit down on Towila's arm and dragged him through the shallows and across the sand. Towila's howls were echoed by Misa's screams, but the heat from the flame was scorching Kilchi's fur and Towila's skin, so Kilchi paid no attention to Towila's cries of pain. He deposited Towila on the rocks before Misa's feet. Before Towila could protest further, she dripped living water into his mouth. Towila watched, his eyes a mixture of rage, pain, and fear, as his fins transformed into legs. Once the change was complete, Towila remained prone on the rocks, refusing to rise or use his legs.

"Ashamed of you am I," Misa hissed in Towila's ear. "Humiliating yourself before the clan." She turned to Kilchi and folded her arms. "And you! Speak to me no more! An abomination, what you have done, a violation of a sacred tenet."

"Misa, I—I'm sorry, I just wanted..."

Misa turned her back on Kilchi and leaned down to her father again. "Rise now and redeem yourself."

Towila turned his face away from his daughter, pining for the disappearing sea.

"Would you really rather die than change?" Kilchi asked, but Towila wouldn't acknowledge him.

"We will carry him if we must." Cholena patted Misa's arm.

"Let us leave this place," Meda urged. "The breath of death sours the air."

"Help the Saphiri." Amadah directed the others to lift the Saphiri and assist with their balance as they tried out their legs. "They'll need some beats to get used to walking. Then, when they're ready, we'll go."

As the Saphiri stumbled around on the rocky shore, trying to get their land legs, Towila spotted the two young Jasperi who had traded for sea food, hiding in the brush down the beach. He stole a glance at his daughter, but she didn't see them. Should he tell her about them? He sat up and looked straight at them, hoping they would recognize he spotted them and come out of hiding, but instead, they shrunk back deeper into the thick growth along the edge of the beach. If they didn't want to be seen, Towila decided he wouldn't bother revealing their presence to Misa. As far as he was concerned, they could survive, or not, on their own.

"Stand, Papa." Misa held out her hand. "Seeing not so bad is walking and coming back to the sea when the sea returns is possible."

Kantila walked haltingly to Towila's side. "Letting me help you."

Towila gave a dismissive wave. "Leave me alone."

"Coming with us, Papa. Leaving you alone is not an option."

Towila huffed his frustration, but he pushed himself up off the rocks until he balanced on wobbling legs. "Satisfied are you?"

Misa smothered him in her embrace, and once again, Towila's heart softened. He could deny his daughter nothing. In his mind, the image of his mate rose unbidden, and his chest tightened. She looked very much like Misa. Memories of the three of them frolicking in the open waters, dancing through the waves, and lying cuddled in the shallows flashed across his vision. He rarely thought of his mate anymore, but seeing Misa rekindled his connection, and his love began to thaw his heart. They had been so happy before the attack. During those cycles, he saw the Light all around him. Now, he only saw darkness.

As if cued by his thoughts, Misa opened her arms before her friends. "Listen! Remembering again the true Light, opening your hearts to hold the Forever once more is necessary. Holding the memory is no one in this generation. Without memory, wisdom is lost." The ring of her final words echoed amongst the rocks down the shore, then all fell silent.

Finally, Aleshanee's small voice broke the hush over the group. "The smallest taste of the beauty of the First World can be known in the faint glimmers we've seen on our world—the colors on the horizon as the sky light falls; the dancing lights in a waterfall; the majesty of the high mountain; the delicate wings of a flutterby with their many intricate shapes and colors." She stopped and looked around at the disappearing sea, the blackened fingers of burned trees poking the air, and grey smoke obscuring the rose color of the sky. "It is hard to see those glimmers now. All around we see destruction and death, and more is to come. But you all must remember and return to the Forever and the Great Love. You must. Or we are lost."

"I know this won't make sense to you, but we have a great task to accomplish," Amadah explained. "We must open the way for our world to rejoin the First World. As Misa told you, we have a way to do this thing, a sphere that will open the portal, but other forces oppose us, a Dark Lord who seeks to kill us, particularly Aleshanee and me."

281

"Destroying you two why?" Towila asked.

"We are the witnesses who have seen the First World and can testify to the truth."

"We must get the sphere to the high mountain before the sky light dies. The Dark Lord stands between us and the mountain, so we are going now to stand against the Dark Lord on the open fields of the plains, as has been foretold to us." Amadah raised her brows and pressed her lips together. "They have a large army. We have only each other. Our victory seems impossible."

"One thing is certain—should we stand without the Forever and the Great Love, we will fall." Aleshanee closed her eyes and hummed a few mournful notes.

"Will you stand with us?" Amadah looked into the eyes of each of the Saphiri standing before her.

"Keeping safe my clan is my only priority," Towila murmured. "Seeming a fool's errand is this you describe."

"Perhaps it is." Amadah sighed. "But it is our only hope."

CHAPTER THIRTY-SEVEN

The Turqosi

Leenha positioned herself next to Ogima's altar, her armies arrayed in a fan formation around her. She wanted to make it clear to all the Chalcedi and to the Jacinthi prophet who was second in command. Angeni's glare let her know her message was received.

"You have had ample cycles to recover from your torment from the acridids." Ogima flipped his hand dismissively. "I grow weary of waiting because of your weakness. Look at Leenha and her armies. They have never faltered, even during the swarm. Their strength is undeniable. You Chalcedi, on the other hand, have been whimpering, blubbering masses, demanding oblivion rather than dealing with your pain. And you Jacinthi and Jasperi continue to be useless to me."

"Surely not I, Lord," Angeni cried.

Ogima's red eyes sparked toward Angeni. "Did you stand during the swarm, or did you scream and wail like a newborn and flail around like a serpentus in hot ash? Tell me!"

"The pain was excruciating, Great One. I—I could not bear it. Just as you said."

Ogima smirked, satisfied. "Yet, Leenha and her kind uttered no sound, and after I destroyed the swarm, they stood, uninjured and ready to fight for me. Perhaps Leenha should wear the robes of my prophet."

"Please, Lord, no! Allow Leenha to serve as the general of your armies, where she is best equipped, yes, but do not take from me my title of Prophet. Does Leenha see into the future? Can she speak what will come, as I do?"

283

Ogima turned to Leenha. "Do you see the future?"

Leenha hissed and spat a sizzling stream of venom on the ground. "Prophesy victory."

"There, you see, Angeni? She is also a prophet."

Angeni crawled forward and groveled at Ogima's feet. "I would die for you, my Lord. I have given you my all. What else must I do for you to allow me to remain at your side?"

"Stop sniveling. You will be beside me when we go to the Chrysoli. You shall convince them to join my cause. But on the battlefield, Leenha will be by my side."

"I thought I was your general." Chatan pouted and folded his arms.

"Silence! Prove your worth on the field of battle, and I will reward you. Or die in my service. Otherwise, I will kill you myself."

Leenha spread her colorful cowl and shot a coy glance toward Ogima. "Ssserve Ogima."

"A creature of few words. Finally."

Angeni stood before Ogima, straightening her feathers and puffing her chest, probably trying to look important. "Will we go to the Chrysoli now, Lord?"

Leenha's eyes narrowed. Angeni sought to position herself as useful in Ogima's eyes as quickly as possible, a cunning move on her part, but Leenha had other plans. "Sssend Turqosi to Chrysoli as ssspies, sssaboteurs. Turqosi prepare attack. Weaken Chrysoli."

"Ahhh, I see. You would set up your armies within the Chrysoli compound, taint their water, poison their food, and ready them for the slaughter should they refuse to join with me. Excellent idea." Ogima clapped his hands. "So be it. Go, Leenha. Go to the Chrysoli compound with haste. Establish positions in hiding within the compound. Do what damage you can. I will signal you to attack when I am ready."

"Sssignal?"

"You will know it when you see it."

Leenha gestured to her armies, who moved like a single organism in a rippling wave across the fields. Leenha brought up the rear, keeping a watchful eye on her clan while making sure none of the Chalcedi followed with malicious intent, or Angeni came after her to kill her.

The Turqosi crossed the barren, rolling hills without stopping for rest and reached the outskirts of the Chrysoli plains before sky fall. It was perfect, Leenha thought. They would enter the compound under the cover of darkness and establish positions while the Chrysoli slept in their buildings. Leenha would never understand why creatures built huge structures. It seemed a massive waste of resources and energy to her, but these same structures provided her armies with wonderful cover, and she was happy to use them for her purposes.

Leenha scouted the compound, finding the door, usually sealed shut and bolted, cracked open. How odd. Why would the Chrysoli's defenses be so slack? Did they suffer under the swarm as well? If true, this was information Ogima needed to know. She believed it was worth the risk to find out, so she slid into the compound alone.

The grounds were battered and empty. Leenha assumed the Chrysoli were housed in their structures, so she skittered to a window and peaked in to find a group of mixed species she recognized. So, the slaves had returned to their masters. Interesting.

She moved to the next building and peered in the window. Chrysoli were stretched out on cots, being tended by some slaves. So, the swarm had hit the compound, and they were still recovering. The Chrysoli in a weakened state was excellent news to send to Ogima.

Leenha risked a scamper across the compound to the largest building, sidled up to the side of it, and looked in the only window she could reach. A small group of Chrysoli males clustered before a dais where a larger Chrysoli paced and talked. He must be their leader. Leenha wished she could hear what he was saying, but she wasn't willing to risk capture at this juncture, so she withdrew and made her way back to the compound's entrance.

Clicking her tongue against the roof of her mouth, she called her generals to her side. Darkness had fallen over the compound, so Leenha felt certain they could get inside undetected. Her quick gestures sent groups of two sliding through the doorway and establishing positions within the compound, each group with instructions for sabotage. Leenha took Lise aside and gestured the Chrysoli's present state, then sent her back to Ogima with a few of her Turqosi warriors to make a report. Leenha's final gesture let Lise know they were to return as soon as her report was made and rejoin the army.

Once the army was inside and set up, Leenha slithered up to the large building housing the leader. She was determined to hear what he was planning, so she crawled up the side of the building to an open vent cut out of the stone. Using her claws to cling to the edge of the opening, she laid her head against the stone and listened for the vibrations of voices within.

"Leoti will be enraged when she recovers fully," one of the voices hummed.

"Leoti will do as I say." Leenha assumed it was the voice of the leader.

"You are housing and feeding slaves on our compound who are serving no purpose. Using our food. Giving them our shelter. Why?"

"They were promised safety."

"Promised by whom?"

"Never mind. I will not send them back out onto the plains to starve to death."

"Have you completely forgotten our ways? You have Chrysoli who should already be out on the plains to die being tended by slaves and medichi—a waste of resources. You have slaves who aren't working eating and drinking our very limited food and water supplies—a waste of resources."

Limited water and food supplies. Leenha's tongue flitted across her lips.

"Have you ever thought we waste resources when we send our own out to the plains to die? Perhaps creatures are more important resources than you credit."

"You speak the words of the slave Kwania, not the words of the Chrysoli leader. Who leads the Chrysoli? Kola or Kwania?"

The leader, Kola, growled in his throat. "Be careful what you speak aloud."

"I speak what all are thinking and what Leoti will surely say."

"I have decided, and there will be no more discussion. We must look to securing the compound again. We must find a way to repair the dome and shore up our defenses, for we have been told an army is coming against us."

"Who says an army comes? I see no army."

"Those from the outside who spoke of the army have seen the army. We must meet with the leader of this army from a position of strength."

"Why?"

"If we appear to surrender, they will dominate or destroy us. The masters become the slaves. I will not see this happen. If we present strength, the leader will ask us to join him and fight on his side, seeing us as useful to strengthen his army against the other group. That way, we serve a purpose for him, and he doesn't destroy us."

"Won't we still be his slaves, fighting under his rule? I think not."

"We may not have a choice."

"If we remain inside our dome, and they are outside, we never have to meet with him at all. Just refuse them entry."

"He doesn't sound like the type to walk by us and leave us alone."

"Kola, we have little food, little water; many of our kind are injured and sick. How are you going to convince this creature we have something to offer?"

"We must give the impression of strength, as I said. That's why we must repair our dome and send our strongest out under a flag of truce to meet with him before he attacks."

But Leenha would make sure Ogima knew the Chrysoli were weak and vulnerable.

"And you plan on offering to take his side in battle?"

"I will give the impression of disinterest and let him believe we are strong enough to resist him. I will also let him know I have received an offer to join with another army and ask why I should join his instead."

"That's risky."

"Yes, but it also gives the appearance of strength, as if I am negotiating the best deal for the Chrysoli, which assumes I have a position from which to negotiate. I will see if, by chance, he decides he would rather we not take part in the battle at all instead of taking the other side. I will offer to remain neutral, as long as he leaves us alone."

Leenha had what she needed. As she thought, the Chrysoli were ripe for picking. Now, she would be able to tell Ogima their plans. She would deliver the Chrysoli into Ogima's arms, and Ogima would reward her. Perhaps he would share some of his magic.

Leenha slid down the wall, landing on all fours, then scurried behind the structures and through the heavy door. She would wait there for Ogima's arrival.

Lise and her warriors returned first, reporting Ogima was coming behind them. Leenha sent Lise inside the compound to tell her armies to ready themselves. At the sky light's rising, Leenha saw the clot of Chalcedi and Jacinthi flyers above swirls of dust, which she assumed Ogima's caravan stirred. She crept from the shadows and crossed the plain toward the plumes.

From his perch atop a palanquin carried by four Chalcedi, Ogima looked pale and discolored. Strange. Angeni toiled beside the litter, her scarlet robe coated with dust and filth and her hair looking more grey-brown than white.

"Ogima," Leenha hailed. "Report."

"Speak."

"Chrysoli liars trick Ogima. Make think stronger but are weak. Pretend fight Ogima but want no fight."

"Is that so? Hmmmm."

"Divided."

"Divided? In what way?"

"Over slaves."

"Interesting. So, if their leader decides to refuse me, I can use those who oppose the leader to take my side and overthrow him."

Leenha nodded. "Ssslaves there."

"There, meaning in the compound again?"

Leenha nodded.

"Some of the Chrysoli want the slaves gone? Or do they want to enslave them to their will?"

"Gone."

"I see."

"Turqosi ruin water, food. Nothing left."

"Excellent."

"Leader weak."

Ogima nodded. "Well done, Leenha. Are your troops positioned inside the compound?"

Leenha nodded again, spreading her webbed fingers to indicate the armies were stationed throughout.

Ogima's smile looked odd to Leenha, crooked and loose, like skin on an aging Turqosi, with cavernous lines on his face. Leenha was beginning to wonder if Ogima's magic for bringing life from death was limited.

"Angeni, you will approach the Chrysoli to negotiate with their leader. Give all appearances of cooperation. Make it seem we want their support. Share your prophetic vision of the future. Be sure you mention unlimited food—that should get their attention. We will have the Chrysoli before the sky light's apex. And if not,"—he looked at Leenha—"your troops will destroy them."

The army stopped before the Chrysoli door, the other Chalcedi and Jacinthi landing behind Ogima's litter to stand with the Jasperi and Turqosi. Angeni marched forward and pounded on the wall. "The Great Lord Ogima has come to give audience to the ruler of the Chrysoli. May I enter and bring your leader before our Lord?" She turned to Ogima. "The door is ajar. We could walk in, and I doubt they would resist."

"I prefer to enter by invitation."

Angeni pounded on the wall again. "Chrysoli leader, I am Angeni, the Lord Ogima's true Prophet. May I enter and speak with you?"

Through the cracked door, Angeni spied Chrysoli bolting across the compound, some hurrying into what appeared to be residences, others running toward two larger buildings on the far side of the compound beyond the fields.

"I do not like to be kept waiting." Ogima's voice took on an edge.

"It appears the Chrysoli are going to their leader for instruction, my Lord. I believe if we are patient, he will come."

"If he delays much longer, I will simply take what I want."

"Yes, my Lord. I see someone coming now from across the compound, accompanied by what appears to be guards." She looked at Ogima. "He is their leader, Lord. I am sure of it."

Soon, the door swung wide and a group of Chrysoli stepped out onto the plains. "I am Kola, the leader of the Chrysoli. Who seeks audience with me?"

Angeni clucked. "Oh, no, Master Kola, we offer audience to you with the Great Lord Most High, Lord Ogima. I am Angeni, the Lord's Prophet. I speak to you on his behalf."

"Can he not speak for himself?"

"He asks that I assess whether you are worthy of his attention. As his Prophet, I will tell you now of his greatness and the works of his hands. The Jacinthi were starving and in desperate need, until the Lord came. We have feasted since. Wicked, horrid creatures attacked our camp, striking down Lord Ogima with a sword, but in his mighty power, he brought life back to his sarkikos and now stands before you. The swarm cloud of acridids attacked our camp, but the Lord Ogima sent them away with a wave of his hand. His power exceeds all known powers. His greatness dwarfs the greatest of creatures, even Chrysoli who are known for their strength and their domination of the land and slaves they possess.

"We offer your compound unlimited food, protection from invading forces, and help with reconstruction." Angeni pointed to the broken dome. "I believe you might need such help. The Lord Ogima also offers his healing powers for your sick or injured. In exchange, you will help us fulfill the wondrous prophecy, given to me by a power from another world, which states all creatures will come to the high mountain and live together in peace. This is the dream of our Great Lord. Peace and prosperity for all. If you swear allegiance to our Lord and bow before him and agree to fight on our side in the war against those who oppose us, we will give you these things."

"We heard quite a different tale," Kola said.

"Those who speak ill of our Lord are those who ruthlessly attacked our camp, unprovoked and without cause, and struck down our Lord. They do not seek peace. Their hatred is boundless and will destroy us all."

"According to these ruthless creatures, you will destroy everything. Who am I to believe? Perhaps it is best the Chrysoli remain neutral in this war." Kola made a gesture as if to reenter the compound.

"Stop!" Angeni screeched, then lifted her hands and patted the air. "Please. Hear us. We desire you to be a part of the great unity of all creatures. We want your help to see it come to pass."

"Why should I believe your story over the story of the other side?"

"What did they offer you? Did they offer to provide food? Assistance? Protection?"

Kola paced before Angeni. "They offered to save the world from destruction."

Angeni threw back her head and laughed. "Those creatures cannot save themselves, much less the world. Do you not see? If we all stand together, united and strong, we can overcome any obstacle."

"Even the death of the sky light?"

"If anyone can spare us from the sky light's end, it will be the Great Lord Ogima. He has power beyond your imagining, even power over life and death. What do those others have?"

"They claim they have a weapon."

"Did you see this so-called weapon?"

"No."

"Because there is no weapon. They come to you empty-handed with stories. We come to you with a living God and food for your pride. Do you want to know how to choose who to believe? Trust your own eyes." Angeni swept her hand around, and the Chalcedi brought forth baskets brimming with meat, and smoldering bowls emitting a sickly-sweet aroma. Ogima waved his hand, and the smoke from the bowls wafted over the Chrysoli guards. Soon, their tongues lolled from their mouths, their saliva dripping, leaving round indentations in the dirt.

"We're starving," one of the guards moaned, licking his snout.

Kola snarled and nipped the guards hide. Turning back to Angeni, he said, "You weave a nice story. I also saw the other group rush to our aid after the stinging cloud, and they didn't ask us to bow down to them. They didn't demand we follow them. They offered their help freely. You bargain for our support with food and whatever that awful smell is, but you demand we serve. The Chrysoli serve no one."

"All serve one side or the other, whether they are aware of it or not."

"And what will you do if I say the Chrysoli will choose neutrality in this war?"

"You cannot remain neutral." Ogima's voice vibrated the air.

"Why is that?" Kola boldly approached Ogima's palanquin.

Angeni stepped between Kola and Ogima. "This war determines the fate of this world. Any creature who is a part of this world must choose, for good or ill."

"I was once told not choosing is making a choice." Kola tossed his head. "I choose not to choose a side. Take your food away." Kola turned tail and stalked back toward the compound.

"No!" one of his guards whined.

"We want the food!"

"We need food!"

Kola glared at his guards, who fell silent under his gaze, then followed as Kola entered the door. It slammed behind them, and the lock slid into place with a loud clank.

Ogima stared down Angeni, who cowered before him. "You failed me." His voice was ominous, implying threat.

"Kill? Or starve them out?" Leenha asked, inserting herself between Ogima and Angeni.

"No, Lord Ogima, do not attack and destroy them," Angeni begged, although Leenha wasn't sure if her pleas were to save the Chrysoli or to save her own feathers. "I am certain I can convince them.

Kola's mind has been perverted by the lies of our enemies. Allow me to enter their compound and meet with their elder council, if they have one. Someone will listen to reason!"

Ogima hesitated, looking from Leenha to Angeni. Finally, he spoke. "One chance. I will allow you one more chance. If you convince them to join us, you will have them come to me and fall before me in worship. In this way, they will demonstrate their loyalty. If they will not, I will know they are false, and I will release Leenha's armies to do as they will."

"They will bow before you, Lord, this I swear by your great name."

"So be it. Go now and see it done."

CHAPTER THIRTY-EIGHT

The Chrysoli

Leoti stretched her weakened muscles and flexed her paws.

She was ready to leave the stench of the medichi behind, but that know-it-all slave, Kwania, kept telling her she wasn't healed and set a Topazi as her guard to keep her in her cot. Well, she would just see about that. Arching her back and ruffling her fur, Leoti dropped to the floor. The moment of dizziness passed, and as she thought, she was able to walk with minimal difficulty.

"Stubborn. Head of stone." The Topazi moved to guide her back to her cot.

"Keep your claws off me, slave. I'm leaving, and no one is going to keep me in this death swamp for another beat. Do you understand me?" Leoti popped her claws and ticked them against the stone floor. Rather than fight, the Topazi shrugged and went to find Kwania.

She was indeed weaker than she had ever been, but she knew the remedy. If she had been moving these many cycles instead of lying about like a blob of Turqosi spit, she wouldn't be so fragile now. Movement was her answer, so she limped through the door and out onto the compound. Just being outside helped her spirits, although the air was different than she remembered it—thick and wet like fog off the river, with an odor that reminded her of rotting things. What had been happening while she lay wasting away in the medichi?

Across the compound, she spotted Lonan. He would tell her the news. She started toward him, but quickly realized he would be out of sight before she came close, so she called out to him. "Lonan!"

He turned and brightened when he recognized her. "Leoti! You're better!" He bounded to her side and nuzzled her.

"I will be soon." She winced. "Careful, some of my wounds are not fully healed. Tell me what I've missed."

Lonan lowered his head, his thick brow furrowed and a growl rumbling in his chest. "Kola has abandoned our ways. He allowed the slaves to return to the compound and commandeer a building as their own, without any expectation of labor. He was even feeding them, and with so little food and water left."

Leoti's eyes widened.

"That's not all. After the stinging cloud came, and everything was chaos, visitors came into the compound uninvited and kept Kola from sending the injured to the plains. Then, they left without a word, and another army showed up at our door. They didn't attack. They offered us food and protection. And get this—Kola refused it all. Our pride is starving, and he refused their offer of food."

"Could it have been a ploy to gain entrance to the compound?"

"I was there, Leoti. I saw the food. They had baskets of it—meat, too."

"Why would Kola do such a thing?"

"He said accepting the food would make us servants to this other army's master—a strange creature, but according to his servant, he has great power. Jacinthi, Turqosi, Chalcedi, and Jasperi all serve this master. Apparently, he was struck down by a sword and came back to life. Then, he saved his army from the stinging swarm. They say he has healing powers. I don't know. All I know is he offered us food, and Kola sent him away."

"Fool!" Leoti growled deep in her throat. "He could've taken the food, then killed the army's master, taken over his army, and used it to conquer the first group and make them our slaves."

"And that's not all of it. Somehow, the water has been tainted and is undrinkable, and our meager food supplies are destroyed. It's Kola's fault. He turned down the army's offer of food, and now we have nothing."

"You're right, Lonan. Kola has abandoned the Chrysoli's ways and become a wobbly-legged, tail-dragging weakling."

"I told them all you'd be upset when you found out."

"I won't stand for it. You will issue a challenge and tell your warriors to stand beside you. In his current state, Kola will likely resign without a fight, and you will take his place." She purred, smiling. "And I will be your mate."

"For you, anything."

"Then we will have our meat and our slaves—and our way of life back again. I will go to Kola to distract him while you collect your warriors for the challenge. Come to him when you are ready. Kola will not suspect that I am taking your side in this challenge, and when I do, he will back down."

"You will have your way of life back, I promise you."

Leoti rubbed her neck against Lonan's mane. "Go, my love."

As Lonan loped toward the barracks, Leoti walked gingerly to the great hall. Her last experience of this place was when she ripped her own skin from her bones to try and stop the unbearable stinging torment. She shivered as she made her way up the steps, down the hallway, and into the oval chamber. She found Kola, reclining on his settee, staring off into space like the brainless fool he was.

"Kola, I've returned."

Kola startled, sat up, and gawked at her like she was a revivified spirit coming to suck his marrow from his bones. "Leoti, are you fully recovered?"

"I am on the mend. You?"

"I just had a head bump. Nothing of concern."

"The compound looks—how can I put this? Desolate? Devastated? Destroyed?"

"Much has happened, and none of it is good for us."

"What do you mean, it isn't good for us?"

"Everything is gone—our crops, our water supply, all of it. We have nothing."

"What happened to our wells on the plains?"

"They dried up. The world is falling apart, Leoti. Kwania says..."

"Kwania says? Why do we care what a slave says?"

"She is a great scientist of the Jacinthi clan. She knows things we don't know."

"So she claims."

"She has proven herself fourfold." Kola gestured toward Leoti. "She saved your life."

"And kept me locked up in the medichi for cycles and cycles."

"I'm sure it was for your own good."

"Because Kwania knows best, is that it?"

Kola waved his paw dismissively. "All I know is everything she told me is coming to pass. The sky light vomits out fire and burns up the air above us and dries up all the water. Then, the stinging cloud came. Now, Kwania and her friends say the world is coming to an end."

"Kola." Leoti spoke as if she were speaking to a small cub. "Did it not cross your mind Kwania foretold these things because she was causing them? Of course, she knew what was coming. She probably sent for the stinging beasts! Her slave friends probably poisoned our water and destroyed what little food we had. And you played right into her hands by allowing the slaves to return and lay claim to a home within the compound. What were you thinking?"

"Everything was so chaotic when the stinging cloud came through, I couldn't—I didn't stop any of it. The slaves acted like they came to help, and some did help in the medichi. Once they were here, I didn't want to ask—tell them to leave. They have nowhere else to go."

"So, we are left without any resources." Leoti glared at Kola, her eyes narrowed and her lips curved in a sneer.

"It matters little. We will all be dead soon anyway. What is a couple of cycles more or less?"

"And you say this because Kwania said..."

"Look around you!" Kola interrupted. "You can see with your own eyes."

"I hear you turned down food."

Kola lifted one side of his mouth back from his teeth. "Have you come to question my decisions? Or do you seek to challenge me?"

298

"Kola!" Leoti feigned shock. "I would never challenge you. You are to be my mate."

Satisfied, Kola reclined again. "We received a visit from a group—no, more like an army, but what an odd array—Jasperi and Jacinthi, Chalcedi and even Turqosi, and one Amthysti who was their leader. Listen to this. He supposedly was stabbed to death with a sword but brought himself back to life. Honestly, he looked more dead than alive to me."

"And this army had food."

"They offered to give it to us, on the condition we bow down and worship their leader. A Chrysoli, bowing to an Amthysti? Ridiculous."

Leoti slid beside Kola on the couch. "You could've taken his food and slashed his throat for his trouble."

Kola stroked Leoti's fur. "He had greater numbers protecting him, and some of my strongest warriors were still on the mend from the stinging cloud attack. Better to keep him outside the dome."

"Do I hear correctly? The mighty Kola sees a few Jacinthi philosophers, some Chalcedi imbeciles, a couple of Jasperi, and a few little Turqosi purwiggies, and he trembles with fear?"

"Wisdom is not fear."

"You and Lonan and two other warriors could've killed them all without any help from any other Chrysoli. The question is, why didn't you?"

"I wasn't altogether sure we could. The Chalcedi are many, and the Turqosi are small, yes, but very dangerous."

Leoti chuckled. "I never thought I would see the cycle when Kola backed down from a croaker embryo or a flapper."

Kola growled in his throat. "You may be my promised mate, but I won't allow you to speak to me that way. That's enough."

"Yes, Kola."

"I know what I'm doing."

"Yes, Kola."

A messenger entered the chamber. "Kola, you have a request from a Jacinthi named Angeni to speak before you. She states she comes alone and will stand in your chamber, if you will permit her to enter."

"Oh, this should be fun!" Leoti whispered.

Kola gaped at Leoti. "You would give her audience?"

"Why not? We can toy with her for a while, then if she displeases me, you can slash her to ribbons for me for sport and send her back to her master as a coat for him to wear."

Kola studied the floor for a few beats. "Tell her I will see her."

Lonan and several of his fellow warriors strode into the chambers, passing the messenger as she exited. "Kola, we would speak with you."

"I'm afraid it will have to wait. I have another who requested an audience, and she takes priority, given our situation."

Lonan bowed up, but Leoti melted off the couch and oozed up to Lonan. "You won't mind if Lonan and his friends stay in chamber to hear the Jacinthi, right, Kola? I'm sure they will be very interested to hear what this Angeni has to say."

As Leoti hoped, Lonan's eyes widened a bit at the mention of Angeni's name. He gave the slightest nod, letting Leoti know he got the message—let Kola hang himself during the meeting with Angeni, accuse him of betraying the Chrysoli, and demand he step down as leader.

"I don't mind, if they remain silent and do not interrupt."

"Oh, I'm sure Lonan and the others will be as silent as the Chrysoli burial plain. Won't you, Lonan?"

"Not a word."

"Now, then, that works well. As soon as your meeting is finished with this Angeni creature, you can have your meeting with Lonan." Leoti returned to the settee and stretched out beside Kola. "My sweet, when shall we have our official ceremony?"

Kola sighed. "I find it difficult to think about a frivolous ceremony in the midst of this crisis for our pride. We must work together instead to secure a future for us all."

Leoti puffed her cheeks and frowned. "Do you find me so undesirable?"

"It isn't about you, Leoti. Our circumstances demand such formalities must wait until the pride is stable."

"As you wish." Leoti pouted, swatting him with her tail. She looked beyond Kola, and her eyes gleamed at Lonan, whose eyes danced in response.

The messenger reentered and announced, "Angeni, the Jacinthi, follower of Lord Ogima." She stepped out as Angeni swept into the room. She was clothed in bright red robes with twisted gold braids through her silvery-white hair. Kola stood as she approached the platform.

"Welcome, Angeni. Would you sit?" Kola swept his paw toward a pair of chairs positioned beside the platform.

"Thank you, I prefer to stand."

Behind Angeni, the door to the chamber burst open. "Angeni? Angeni, is that you?" Kwania dashed into the room. "It is you! I thought I saw you walking across the compound. Oh, Angeni, it is so good to see you again!"

"Kwania! What a surprise!" Angeni opened her arms wide, and Kwania fell into her embrace.

"You know this creature?" Kola asked.

"Angeni is my leader from the high mountain. I have not seen her since I was captured by the Turqosi and sold as a slave."

"The Turqosi?" Angeni gasped. "You are a slave?"

"You follow her?" Kola asked.

"I—I did, yes."

"And now?"

Kwania turned to Angeni. "I hear disturbing things. Meda says you have changed."

"What foolishness! I have not changed. I remain Angeni."

"Why do you seek audience with Master Kola?" Leoti asked Angeni.

Angeni pushed Kwania behind her and turned to Kola. "I come to plead with you, to beg you to receive what the Great Lord Ogima offers you from the generosity of his spirit."

"What does this Ogima offer the Chrysoli?" Leoti's lips lifted to bare her fangs.

Kola placed his paw on Leoti's shoulder. "I'm aware of Ogima's offer, and his demand. If he would like to feed my pride, I welcome his help, but without the requirement of subservience. The Chrysoli do not bow to other creatures. The Chrysoli do not serve at anyone's whim."

Kwania pulled Angeni's arm. "Angeni, you cannot mean you follow Ogima, the betrayer?"

Angeni swung around, her eyes blazing. "He is no betrayer! He is our salvation!"

"He set the device to destroy the world. Do you not remember?"

Angeni shook her head. "No. No, that was the Chalcedi. They forced Lord Ogima against his will..."

"He *leads* the Chalcedi!" Kwania cried.

"The Chalcedi follow the Great Lord now, having seen the error of their ways."

"You do not believe what you are saying. You cannot." Kwania moaned. "My dear, dear friend, come back to reason."

"What do you know?" Angeni's face contorted with rage, her eyes bulging. "You have always been a simpering fool." Kwania's wide eyes brimmed before she turned away and covered her face.

Kola stepped down from the platform. "You'll not insult my scientist in my chambers. You will leave. Now."

"Kola, what are you saying? You would be rude to our guest over the hurt feelings of a slave?" Leoti almost shook with excitement. This exchange couldn't have gone better if she'd scripted it.

"Our guest is the one being rude. Angeni, I will not bow down to your petty lord, and I will not accept his so-called gifts, for they come at an unbearable price."

Angeni tossed her head. "The Great Lord Ogima is the Lord of all! I have given him my guarantee that you will see reason, and I will not disappoint him, for you will bow down to the Great Lord, either by choice or by force." Angeni stepped forward and pressed her beak against Kola's snout. "Now, you will listen to me, you arrogant, impudent milksop. You dare to speak of our Lord in this way again, and I will pull your guts out through your nose."

Kwania spun around, her beak open, gaping at Angeni. "Angeni! Kola, this is not the Angeni I followed on the high mountain. I do not know who she is, but she is not my Angeni. Just as Meda warned, she has turned, and her heart has grown cold."

"Lonan, remove this creature from my chamber," Kola commanded.

Lonan stepped forward, but instead of grabbing Angeni, he stood beside her, facing Kola. "I will not."

Kola growled and tossed his mane. "Do you challenge me?"

"I do." The other warriors stepped forward and flanked Lonan, indicating their support.

"You would grovel before this creature's lord and submit to his control?"

"We would accept his offer of food and protection, for the good of the pride," Lonan replied.

Leoti slid from the couch and moved to Lonan's side. "I choose Lonan to be my mate." She emphasized her choice with a lick of Lonan's muzzle. "I desire someone strong and powerful, not you, a weak-willed and short-sighted failure who has abandoned Chrysoli ways and invited slaves to live as freed creatures on Chrysoli lands."

"Kola, what is happening?" Kwania glanced from Leoti to Angeni, whose lifted head bore a self-satisfied smirk.

Kola gathered himself to pounce, his growl reverberating off the chamber walls. After several tense beats, with Lonan and the warriors bearing their fangs and snarling, Leoti roared. "Attack!"

Lonan leapt at Kola, but he dodged the attack and bounded toward the exit. "Stop him!" Leoti shrieked.

Several warriors jumped Kola and pinned him down. With a flap of her wings, Kwania dove into the pile, pecking and ripping the warriors' hides with her talons. Lonan bolted toward Kwania, and with one vicious swipe of his paw, he slung her against the wall, where she crumpled to the floor in a heap of feathers.

Leoti sashayed around the pile, whooping. "Bind them both and take them to the quarters occupied by the slaves. Then barricade the door and leave them there to starve."

Kola, gripped by the warriors, shot Leoti a black look. "I hope you are pleased with what you have chosen and what you will reap in return."

As the warriors marched Kola and Kwania down the hall, Leoti turned to Lonan. "Go quickly and call all Chrysoli to the center of the compound, including those still in the medichi. Any who are not well enough to come out will be taken to the plains. Once we gather, Angeni will bring Ogima before you to give you the food."

Angeni lifted her hand. "You misunderstood. The Great Lord Ogima does not come when summoned. You will come before him, out on the plains. There, you will bow before him, and then you will receive food as he deems fit."

Leoti's fur ruffled along her neck and shoulders. "Why should we go onto the plains? Let him come to us if he desires our allegiance."

"You will come before him, along with the rest of your pride, and you will bring an offering demonstrating your veneration of the Lord. Unless you prefer he raze your compound to the ground and destroy you all?"

Lonan cut his eyes toward Leoti, then addressed Angeni. "We will meet Ogima as you wish. Allow us a cycle to prepare."

"Very well. I will inform Lord Ogima of your decision." With that, Angeni strutted from the chamber.

Lonan paced before Leoti. "What now?

"Now, you do as I instructed. When we go before him, we make a show of submission, we take his food. Then, we kill them all."

Chapter Thirty-Nine

The Topazi

Seri spotted Lonan striding across the compound toward the medichi unit where she was working with Sewati, caring for the injured. For reasons she didn't comprehend, a warning resounded in her chest. "Sewati." Sewati looked up from his labor. Seri pointed toward the door to the approaching Chrysoli. "Trouble."

Without a word, Sewati slithered through the tables and cots holding the wounded Chrysoli toward the back of the room, Seri on his heels. They dove behind a large storage container just as Lonan flung open the door.

"Everyone out onto the compound. We have visitors coming. If you aren't strong enough to stand with your pride, you will be escorted to the burial plains."

"Kola told us we could recover here. Where is he?"

"Kola is no longer the Chrysoli leader. I am. Kola is locked away with his friends, the slaves, in the slave quarters, and there he will remain until judgment is passed. We return now to the ways of the Chrysoli. You contribute to the pride, or you die on the plains."

One by one, the injured Chrysoli slowly dropped from their cots and dragged themselves to the exit. Some couldn't move from their beds, and some didn't make it to the exit before collapsing. From the doorway, Lonan gestured for other Chrysoli to come and collect the wounded who couldn't make it to the compound and take them out to the plains. They were too weak to resist.

Once the unit was silent, Seri hissed. "Savages."

Sewati nodded. "Stone heart."

"Murderers."

"Kwania with Kola?"

Seri shrugged. "Find Kola, find out."

Sewati thrust his snout toward the rear entrance, and the two Topazi slipped quietly from the building. They hugged the back of buildings and hid in clumps of brush when Chrysoli came into sight, making their way to the building where the slaves had taken up residence. Many Chrysoli were congregating on the compound nearby, so Seri pointed to the building's crawlspace, and she and Sewati squirmed in and settled down to wait.

CHAPTER FORTY

The Jasperi

Amadah trudged alone behind the Saphiri, who walked slowly as they struggled to adjust to their new legs and the implications of their journey. Towila remained adamant—his clan would not fight in a futile war. Misa walked beside her father, a continuous stream of reasoning in his ear, but his face remained grim and resolute. Amadah's sense of urgency grew as the cycle wore on with little progress toward their goal, but if she pushed too hard, Towila could plop down and refuse to go any further, so she held her tongue.

Hold in your tongue. That was what Fala used to say when someone spoke something untoward. How Amadah wished she could hear his voice again, even a single word. How she longed for the comfort of his arms, the strength of his presence, the wisdom of his insights. He would know exactly what to say to Towila, and Amadah knew Towila would heed Fala's words, if he was here. But he wasn't.

She shook her head. If she allowed herself to dwell on those thoughts, she would break down again, and the fragile group couldn't withstand her collapse. Yet, her mind wandered once more into memory, where she was running up to Fala to embrace him when he returned from the cave. Fala risked himself to cover her when the Chalcedi attacked. Fala, bloodied and hanging—no, she couldn't go there.

"Resting is needed," Towila announced.

Amadah groaned and rolled her eyes. "We've not walked a half cycle yet, and you want to rest again?"

307

Towila tossed his head, indignant. "Responding to the needs of my clan is my only goal. Caring about your task or your fight I do not. I will not."

Misa sighed. "Papa, please..."

"It's fine, Misa. We'll rest."

The Saphiri sank to the ground, apparently appreciative of the break from walking. Amadah heard their murmurs and grumbling, and she knew she was losing her tenuous hold on keeping the group together. She glanced at each of the members of her group who survived the challenges in the cave—Enla, Kilchi, Aleshanee, Chevei, and Misa—but she couldn't bring herself to ask any of them for advice. For someone who had been a loner most of her life, she had never felt so abjectly alone. The weight on her shoulders reminded her of being buried in the suffocating sand of the Topazi desert before Fala dug her out and rescued her. How could she bear the burden alone?

"You are not alone," Na'ro whispered.

"Then tell me what to do."

"You know what you must do."

"Rrrrruh!" Amadah flailed her clenched fists and bolted from the group, hot tears on her face.

Aleshanee approached her after several beats, but she didn't speak. Gradually, the flow of tears subsided and all that was left was an aching, black emptiness.

"I wish you had a clearer memory of the First World." Aleshanee smiled. "If I close my eyes, I can see the pristine green fields, the sky so white you must squint your eyes against the dazzling gleam of it, the fresh breeze like a cleansing balm in your lungs, the sparkling cool water like blue crystal. Oh, and the explosive joy of standing within the Forever." Her eyes brimmed with tears.

"Flashes."

"Hmmm?"

"That's all I have. Flashes, like bolts from the air across my vision. I can capture the feeling for just a beat, then it skitters away like a hopper into a hole."

308

Aleshanee dug her toe into the dirt. "If we can't get the Saphiri to move along, we're going to have to leave them behind."

"I know."

"Misa will be devastated."

"She may choose to remain with her kind. You know that. It would be better if Towila was the one to choose to stop, then at least she wouldn't blame us."

"How will they survive?"

Amadah rubbed her face with both hands. "I don't have any idea."

"I feel it in my heart, the cycles are running out. If we don't get the sphere to the mountain soon..."

"It will be too late."

"Yes."

"We have to try to motivate them to move. They don't seem to grasp what we're telling them."

"Misa says the Saphiri have never really experienced drastic change. Their lives are simple and much the same cycle by cycle. So, they don't know how to adapt."

"They need to learn on the run."

Aleshanee giggled. "I wish they *could* run."

Amadah gave a half-smile and shook her head. "Well, let's go and see if we at least can get them to walk."

When they returned to the group, they found Misa standing before the reclining Saphiri, pounding a fist in her hand and shouting. The rest of Amadah's group huddled together like doelani who just heard a leopard's growl. The strange scene, so unlike Misa, brought Amadah up short. "What in the world?"

Aleshanee ran up to Misa, and Amadah followed close behind her. "What's wrong?"

Misa turned to her friends, and Amadah saw wet streaks on her blue face. "Threatening to remain here are my clan. Tired they say they are, thirsty and hungry, and refusing to continue."

"How hungry and thirsty do you think you'll be after you sit here for the rest of your cycles?" Amadah retorted. "You make no sense!"

Aleshanee pulled Amadah aside and whispered, "I think they're in shock. The transition out of the water was more than they could handle."

"Misa managed it."

"Misa had Kilchi's help."

Amadah threw up her hands. "We're trying to help them! They won't let us!"

Aleshanee stroked Amadah's arm. "Think how you would've felt if you didn't have Fala to help you along the way." She pointed to the despondent Saphiri. "They don't know us or trust us, so our support has little meaning. They just feel pressure from us."

"They trust Misa."

"Yes, and she's trying, but they're struggling to make sense of everything we've said, on top of trying to get used to being out of the water. It's a lot for anyone."

Amadah's frustration and sense of urgency wrestled with her compassion for dominance. Her anger won. "Fine, then, let them stay here!" She stormed over to the rest of her group. "Collect your things. We're leaving."

"Amadah..." Misa groaned, anguish etched on her face.

"We have to move. So, they come with us, or they stay here. It is up to them."

"Papa, begging you, please..."

"Knowing my mind, daughter. Having no interest in continuing."

"Surviving how?" Misa asked. "Going where? Gone is the sea. Tainted are the ocean waters of our home. Where?"

"Choosing death over life as it is for us now." Towila dropped his head to his chest.

"Choosing death, Papa? For all Saphiri? Considering your daughter at all in this choice?"

Amadah took Misa's hand. "Let's go."

"No!" Misa shook off Amadah's hold. "Irrational is your choosing! Kantila? Leytia? Choosing also death?"

Her question hung over the group like a death knell. No one responded. After a few beats, Amadah pulled the last of the living tree fruit from her bag. "Here, Misa. Give them this. It will sustain them for a cycle or two if they use it wisely."

"Wasting it on those who choose death," Misa snapped. "Keep it, for needing it we may, to complete our task."

Amadah decided to give it one last try. "Listen to me, Saphiri friends. If you can hold on for just a while longer, we will find food and water when we reach the Chrysoli compound. We have friends there, friends who will take us in and feed us and give us places to rest."

"Running into your enemy is more likely." Towila's mutter solicited fearful murmurs from the Saphiri.

"We may. But the longer we tarry, the more likely it becomes. If we move now, one final push to the goal, we will find food and water and shelter, and you may rest and recover. Please."

"Towila?" Kantila asked.

"Knowing my mind," was Towila's last word.

Misa cried out, grabbed her father in a fierce embrace, then turned without a word and walked to the rest of her group. "Leaving now." Her words sounded like they choked her.

Chevei leaned close to Kilchi and whispered in his ear. "If the Saphiri remain behind, we can fly again, which gets us back to the Chrysoli quicker."

"Let's get going, then, before Misa changes her mind," Kilchi murmured.

Cholena, Meda, and Chevei picked up their passengers as before, and with one last look at what was left of the Saphiri clan, Amadah waved her hand. "Fly."

As Chevei stated, the flight went much faster than walking, and they were within sight of the plains before sky fall.

Kilchi, whose eyes were the best of the group, called out. "I see something out on the plains. I guess it could be the slaves, if the Chrysoli kicked them out of the dome, but I'm afraid it's Ogima, already encamped before the dome."

Aleshanee moaned. "We're too late."

"Not necessarily," Amadah replied. "But let's land here, where we can hide in the brush, and stay until the sky light rises. We can make our plans, rest, and prepare, for I believe tomorrow will be the cycle we face our enemy."

Chapter Forty-One

The Jasperi

Kai and Alatha watched the exchange between Amadah and the Saphiri from among the blackened branches of a tree, long dead, some distance away from the group. As Amadah climbed onto a large flying creature, Kai pressed his mouth to Alatha's ear. "She said there's food where they're going."

"And water and shelter."

"Let's follow."

They slid down the trunk, skirted the lounging Saphiri, and scurried through the undergrowth, trying to keep the flyers in sight as long as possible.

"They're getting away from us!" Alatha cried.

Kai gauged the position of the sky light in relation to their flight path. "We keep going this direction, then. They'll take the shortest path to their destination. They said they're in a hurry."

"Kai, what are we walking into?"

"I don't know. The Saphiri mentioned war and enemies. Typical Amadah, making enemies everywhere she goes. No wonder the Saphiri didn't want to come with them."

"I don't want to fight."

"Don't worry. I have no intention of fighting in Amadah's war or taking her side against any enemy. She killed Sani, and it's Amadah's fault Alana is dead."

"Will we fight for her enemy, then?"

"Maybe not fight, but we can give him information. If he gives us food."

CHAPTER FORTY-TWO

The Chrysoli

Kola paced before the barred door, a continuous growl vibrating in his throat. The sky light was falling, and the power to their building had been cut, so he knew their chance to intervene before the Chrysoli became subservient to Ogima was almost over.

When Kola and Kwania were thrown through the door and the door was barricaded, the slaves removed Kola's and Kwania's bonds, but they were filled with questions. Why was Kola restrained? Why did the Chrysoli lock the doors? What had Kwania done wrong? If Kola was no longer Master, who took his place? Why was Kola challenged? Why did the Chrysoli want to serve Ogima? When it became apparent the Chrysoli were locking them all inside for good, the slaves became surly and irritable, blaming Kola, who they said had assured their safety when they reentered the compound.

Receiving no further help from the slaves, Kola tackled the door while Kwania tried to exit through the window slats and out the back of the building. They both failed. Kwania now perched up in the corner by the window slat, watching as the Chrysoli gathered around Lonan and Leoti in the center of the compound.

"What do you hear?" Kola asked again.

"Lonan spoke about taking over for you, but it is Leoti who actually leads this meeting. She is talking about returning to the Chrysoli way of life—more like 'way of death' in my opinion—and the changes that will be implemented as a result."

Kola grimaced. "What else?"

"Now, she speaks of Ogima and his offer of food and something about a gift for Ogima to show their loyalty."

Kola resumed his fruitless march.

"You realize you are wasting energy," Kwania pointed out.

Kola paused to glare at the Jacinthi, then continued his pacing.

Kwania snapped her beak. "We are out of options. Without implements to use, we must wait until the door is opened from without."

"We have no food and no water. How long do they think we're going to last in here?" one of the slaves barked.

"I do not think they care." Kwania perked up. "Wait, this is interesting. Leoti is outlining a plan to turn the tide against Ogima. Apparently, Lonan and the Chrysoli warriors plan to kill Ogima once they have the offered food. Leoti wants to take over Ogima's army."

"Fools! I suppose she believes the Chalcedi and Turqosi will simply move out of the way and let them slash Ogima's throat?"

"She did not specify."

"This will be the end of the Chrysoli. Ogima will wipe them out without a second thought."

Kwania listened for a few more beats. "Leoti is assigning tasks now, where everyone will stand, who will make the gift for Ogima. Angeni will come to lead everyone out onto the plains to bow to Ogima at sky light's rising, so everyone is to be in position near the dome entrance before first sky light."

Kola pounded the door in frustration. "We have to do something, before it's too late!"

"And what would that be?"

"Yell out to the Chrysoli and tell them I said not to follow Lonan and Leoti. Tell them I said don't listen to them because if they do, they will die tomorrow."

Kwania tilted her head. "And why do you think they will listen to me, a slave and a prisoner?"

"Tell them you speak for me!"

"I am not certain they will believe me, but beyond that, you have no voice. You, too, are a prisoner, and no longer Master."

Kola grunted and flopped to the stone floor. "Then it's already too late."

"The crowd is dispersing, going to their residences it appears, except for a few. I believe those are the ones responsible for creating the gift for Ogima." Kwania fluttered down from her perch to sit beside Kola. "One positive note."

"What's that?"

"We will be in here tomorrow and not on the plains when Ogima and his armies slaughter the entire Chrysoli species."

Kola closed his eyes and leaned his head back against the door.

The sky light disappeared a few beats later, plunging the room into total darkness. Kola couldn't see his own paw, much less Kwania or any of the slaves. A deafening silence descended over the room, the kind where the whirl of unspoken thoughts and feelings thickened the air louder than the droning of an Amthysti mechanistic. In that awful silence, Kola heard a scraping sound.

"Do you hear that?" he whispered to Kwania.

More scrapes and scratching noises, then, "Psssst."

"Who's making that noise?"

"Psssst. Here."

"The noise is coming from up there," Kwania said, pointing to the back wall.

"Seri."

"Seri!" Kwania leapt into the air and flew to the window slit on the back of the building.

"Seri opens back door. Leave. Quick."

"Everyone!" Kwania called. "We are being rescued. Seri is opening the back door. Get up! We have to leave quickly."

Kola bounded across the stone floor, running into the slaves fumbling to pick up their meager belongings. "Leave your things. Hurry!" He arrived at the back door just after Kwania landed. He heard bolts slide back and the latch turn, then the door creaked open.

"Come. Follow Sewati."

"Across field to brush." Sewati slithered across the field.

"Run," Seri insisted, pulling Kola's mane to hurry him out the door.

Kola crouched low to the ground, as if he were hunting game, and rushed to follow Sewati. The tiny bit of light reflecting from the Chrysoli compound was swallowed up quickly in the darkness, and Kola soon lost sight of the Topazi, but he kept running until he reached some dense undergrowth planted near the edges of the dome to hide the compound from prying eyes.

Someone touched his shoulder. "Must move. Go toward entrance." Sewati shoved Kola in the right direction before circling back.

The lights near the entrance were in sight when Kola nestled into some thick bushes to wait for the rest to catch up. He heard movement nearby and grabbed a handful of feathers as they passed. It was Kwania.

"Stay here. We're in the darkness but within easy reach of the exit. And here we can watch when the Chrysoli line up to leave for the meeting with Ogima."

Kwania turned and whispered instructions to the rest of the slaves as Seri and Sewati slipped in next to Kola. "All hidden," Seri reported.

"Still. Quiet," Sewati added.

"All Chrysoli are meeting here before sky light's rising. They plan to go before Ogima and bow to him."

Seri hissed. "Fools."

"I know, but I don't know how to stop them."

"Too many to fight," Sewati said.

"Yes. Lonan has the allegiance of all the warriors."

"Slip out after they leave," Seri suggested.

"What of my pride? Do I just leave them to their fate at Ogima's hands?"

"Wait. See." Sewati settled deeper into the brush.

Seri nodded. "Circumstance may change. Nothing sure. Yet."

318

CHAPTER FORTY-THREE

The Dark Lord

Skia Skotos' whole being burned like he was draped with an acidic slime. He couldn't wait to shed the decaying sarkikos that was once Ogima. As it was, it was getting more difficult to cover the smells and discoloration of rot. He would need to find an alternative, and soon.

He was also irritated with Angeni, who was yet to produce the promised Chrysoli surrender. He considered indiscriminate destruction to relieve the roiling fire within him but thought better of it until he was certain of the Chrysoli response. Instead, he might just fry Angeni for sport.

The dome's creaking door gave Angeni a temporary reprieve. She marched from the dome, followed by the Chrysoli, who were led out by a large male and slinking female. The Turqosi armies followed the Chrysoli as they exited the dome and approached Skia Skotos en masse. In the center of the pack, two Chrysoli carried what appeared to be a huge stone of mottled grey streaked with brown. Skia Skotos supposed this chunk of rock was meant to honor him, but he was insulted by its plain ugliness.

Angeni stepped forward and greeted the two leaders. "Great Lord Ogima," she intoned, turning to face him, "May I introduce Master Lonan of the Chalcedi and Mistress Leoti, his mate."

Skia Skotos contorted the festering face into a semblance of a smile. "Welcome, welcome. I am gratified you honored me by accepting my offer of food and protection. I am sure we will develop mutually beneficial collaboration for many cycles to come."

319

Leoti, the female, waved forward the two Chrysoli lugging the monstrosity. With a thunk, they dropped the stone at Skia Skotos' feet. "Lord Ogima, we present this valuable offering to you, a sign of our allegiance and honor, and a promise of our ongoing support." Leoti tilted her head, fluttered her lashes, and ruffled the fur along her back.

"How nice. Now, let us get down to business. Prostrate yourselves before me..."

"Wait! You've not seen it yet!" Leoti interrupted.

"I beg your pardon?" Skia Skotos seethed. He could not abide interruption.

A Chrysoli came forward with a sledge. Leenha gave a quick gesture, and several Turqosi rushed to surround the offending Chrysoli, but Leoti groveled before Ogima. "He only seeks to prepare your gift."

Skia Skotos waved the Turqosi away, and Lonan and Leoti stepped back as the Chrysoli hefted the sledge overhead, swung it in a giant arc, and brought it crashing down on the stone. With a loud crack, the stone split in two, revealing within what looked like a crystal garden. Trigonal spires of purple bristled out of the inner wall of the stone, some large like castle turrets, some thinner like tiny purple icicles, some small and rounded like stones in a rushing stream. In effect, the inner world of the rock was a crystalline city.

"We are aware amthyst is the sacred gem for your clan. It is said to have healing powers. We understand you, also, have healing powers. So, we brought you the largest amthyst we own to honor you." Lonan bowed, his snout touching the ground.

Skia Skotos gawked, mesmerized by the sparkling purple gemstones, and the seed of an idea began to sprout in his mind. Recovering, he forced a smile. "How very thoughtful of you! Yes, very meaningful indeed."

"We're so glad you're pleased."

"Now, if you and your subjects would swear fealty and bow before me, I will accept your vow of service."

Lonan and Leoti lowered their heads, and the remaining Chrysoli followed their example. Lonan spoke for the pride. "We swear our allegiance to you, exemplified in our gift of sacred gems."

"And your service?"

"We serve at your pleasure."

"I accept your vow of service and your fealty. Rise, my subjects."

Angeni embraced Lonan and Leoti. The Chalcedi whooped and gibbered. The Jacinthi and Jasperi rushed up and congratulated the Chrysoli. All the racket irritated Skia Skotos, so he raised his arms to silence them. As the noise subsided, another sound, very familiar to him, found its way to Skia Skotos' ears, a shrill, piercing tone like the tinkling of too many bells. The hated light ones were here! He turned.

Walking out onto the open field, he saw the two witnesses, flanked by their entourage. The cursed light ones flocked around the group, covering them with brilliant beams that seared his eyes. He sent out the call for the Dark Ones to appear at his side.

"Ogima. Come out and meet with us, or prepare to stand against us," the little Emraldi, Aleshanee, sang.

Skia Skotos couldn't decide if this display was comical or pathetic or insulting, so he settled on a derisive cackle. "Do you come to be slaughtered or to follow me?"

The Chalcedi and Turqosi rushed forward to form a blockade before Skia Skotos' litter. Out of the corner of his eye, Skia Skotos spied a horde of creatures dashing along the edge of the field toward the witnesses. One of them was Kola, the former Chrysoli leader. So, these were the slaves from the compound. He pointed to the runners. "Turqosi! Stop them!"

A unit of the Turqosi army, positioned to defend Skia Skotos, scurried after the slaves, but they didn't react quickly enough. Luxor, one of the most despised Bellator, raised her sword, and a shaft of light cut through the air between the Turqosi and the escaping slaves, barring the Turqosi's path. One Turqosi touched the edge of the light, squealed, and fell to the ground, dead. At a gesture from Leenha, the Turqosi withdrew from the killing light and moved to flanking positions some distance from the witnesses. Skia Skotos howled in frustration as the escaping slaves passed by the witnesses and ran across the open plains and into the scrub brush beyond; all except two Topazi, who veered right and took a protective position in front of the Jasperi, Amadah, and Kola and a Jacinthi, who shielded Aleshanee.

The group tramped closer. When they stopped, Amadah and Aleshanee stepped forward. Light from the hands of the 'Ro bathed over them and pooled around their feet.

Aleshanee spoke first. "We stand for the Forever."

"We bring truth and light. We come to testify about the First World." Was that hesitation Skia Skotos heard in the Jasperi's voice? Having doubts, was she?

Skia Skotos chuckled. This confrontation amounted to an annoying distraction, nothing more. "Your Forever must be a fool, to send such woefully inadequate representatives. Or is your Forever just weak, like you?"

Aleshanee took another step toward Skia Skotos. "Listen, all who follow the Dark One. This world is coming to its end. The sky light is dying. We have one hope—one chance. The Forever has given us a way to open a portal to the First World, so all on this world may be saved. The one you call Ogima seeks to stop us. He killed our friends and tried to steal the sphere which opens the portal. He is willing to destroy you all to have what he wants."

"You talk crazy! Ogima protects us. You try to trick us," Chatan cawed.

"You've seen the signs of this destruction: the ball of fire from the sky, the earthquakes, the ice, the horrible storms, the burning of the air, changes in weather, the acridid swarm, the water drying up. What more do you need to see?" Amadah asked.

"Enough of this." Skia Skotos leaned down to whisper in Angeni's ear. "They know their weakness and tremble with their doubt and fear. Send your Jacinthi and Jasperi to treat with the two witnesses. See if they are able to reason with them."

Angeni called Hanai to her. "Hanai, take Catori, Nadie, Kacina, and Sonta and speak with Amadah and Aleshanee. Convince them of the futility of their position. Have Catori talk to Chevei—they were once close. I am certain Catori can convince Chevei to see reason. Ask Sonta to speak to Amadah, for she respects Sonta and may heed his plea.

Kacina may be the best to reach out to Aleshanee. Meda is with them. Nadie is the one to speak with her, for they are dear friends. Surely, Meda will not reject Nadie. Go, Hanai. Make them see."

"I will, Angeni." Hanai collected the other Jacinthi and Jasperi and began their slow trek across the plain. Hanai lifted his hands as if in surrender. "We come only to talk. Will you speak with us?"

"Nothing you could say would ever change our minds," Amadah replied.

"We would only like the chance to tell you of our experience with the Lord Ogima."

"I am well acquainted with experiences with Ogima," Meda snapped. "I also know you are blinded to his lies."

Nadie moved forward, wringing her hands before her. "Meda, my friend, I do not know what you were told or what you believe you experienced, but you have not seen the miraculous power I have seen. Lord Ogima brings life from death. How can power over death be something to fear?"

Meda sighed. "You simply cannot see. He has blinded you."

"I am not blind. Will you not consider the possibility you are the one who has been blinded?"

"I know what I know, Nadie."

"As do I."

Meda reached out and touched Nadie's arm. "What do you know, Nadie? Do you know what the food consists of which you have been consuming so willingly? Do you know of the many living creatures Ogima has killed? Do you know the effects of the substances he has you breathe and consume? Do you understand his plans for this world?"

Nadie shook her head. "I am saddened to find you so resolute. It will be your undoing."

"What kind of creature destroys another just for disagreeing with him? Can you answer?"

"Lord Ogima does not destroy unless he has no other choice. Those who seek his life deserve death," Hanai interjected.

"I didn't seek his life. Yet, he planned to kill me, if my friends hadn't rescued me," Cholena said.

323

Aleshanee lifted her hand. "We do not seek his life. We only seek to be allowed to finish our task. Yet, he threatens to destroy us."

Catori gestured toward Chevei. "You are a creature of logic and knowledge. I cannot believe you stand on the side of delusion over the side of reason."

"Reason without insight almost cost me everything. I stood face to face with my worst fear, and no amount of reason could conquer it. Only faith and trust could overcome the power of my fear."

"Lord Ogima takes away our fear."

"Does he? Or does he use fear to control you?"

Amadah blew out a breath. "Why do you stand before us? What's your aim here?"

"We just want to talk," Sonta replied. "We don't understand what you have against the Lord Ogima."

"Sonta, you of all creatures! I can't believe you've fallen for his tricks."

"It's simple. We were starving. He fed us. We had no home. He gave us a home. He saved us."

"He didn't save you, he manipulated you and enslaved you. Sonta, you were one of my only friends. Please listen to me!"

"Amadah, you've always been the one against. You were against Sani, against the elders, against the Jasperi way of life, against being restricted to the forest, against isolation from other species, against the rules and order of our lives. Now, you are against Lord Ogima. Everyone, listen to me. You follow someone who stands against Lord Ogima just because she always stands against everything."

"They don't follow me, Sonta. They follow the Forever."

"There never has been any way to reason with you." Sonta turned to walk back to Skia Skotos.

"Wait, Sonta. Please, don't go back to him. Please!" Sonta threw up a dismissive wave but didn't turn back.

Kacina spoke to Aleshanee. "I have always been impressed with your insights and your special knowledge. You were always so interested in the writings of our ancient texts. If I could show you how the ancient texts predict Lord Ogima's arrival and his victory, would you heed me?"

324

"Have a care, dear one," Veritor whispered. "She perverts the ancient texts toward her desire."

Aleshanee nodded. "Would you hear the story of our experience in the cave where we discovered the sphere and tasted living water and fruit from the tree of life? We can exchange stories."

Kacina gaped. "Tree of life? Living water?"

"We have seen both."

Pseudos materialized beside Kacina. "If you listen to her, your mind will be twisted, and you will lose your ability to comprehend the ancient texts. She pulls phrases you have told her from the texts to use them against you."

"Silence, scum!" Luxor shot a blast of light into Pseudos' chest. She yowled and disappeared.

"The Lord Ogima fulfills what is prophesied in the ancient texts of one who comes to save all from destruction," Kacina reasserted. "He will also fulfill Angeni's prophecy of all species collecting together on the high mountain. I will not listen to your false story. I pity you." Kacina walked away to join Sonta.

"If none of you will listen to reason, then heed my warning." Hanai pointed his finger at the group. "The Lord Ogima will not allow you to threaten his good work or his plans to fulfill Angeni's prophecy. If you leave him no choice, he will destroy you all."

"So be it," Amadah replied.

Nadie shot one more pleading look toward Meda, then she, Catori, and Hanai strode away and returned to Angeni. "We were unsuccessful."

"I gave those ungrateful wretches every opportunity to turn from their destructive ways," Skia Skotos snarled. "But my patience is exhausted. Chalcedi, to the air! Turqosi, attack!" Leenha waved her arm, and the flanking Turqosi swarmed toward the group. The Chalcedi took flight above them, while Leenha led the rest of her army in a frontal assault.

Before the Turqosi reached Amadah and Aleshanee, Skia Skotos felt a strange pull on the back of Ogima's sarkikos, then a terrible ripping as Ogima's neck was laid open by Lonan's claws. The muscles in Ogima's sarkikos had deteriorated so much, the head lurched back, wobbled, fell with a thud, and rolled off the litter. Skia Skotos vaulted from the sarkikos, which crumpled to the ground.

Angeni screamed. The Turqosi stopped in their tracks at the same moment Lonan roared for the Chrysoli to attack. Skia Skotos watched from above as the Chrysoli bounded across the field and jumped the Turqosi from behind, rolling them up like an ocean wave washing across the sand. The Chalcedi dove into the Chrysoli, grasping them in their talons by the back, the mane, or the throat and hurling them off the Turqosi.

Teeth tore into flesh. Feathers flew. The Turqosi spit wads of venom into the Chrysoli's faces, while the Chrysoli ripped into them with claw and fang and battered the Chalcedi with their paws. The field became a churning, writhing mass of interlocking sarkikos, soon obscured by clouds of rising dust.

"My pride!" Kola roared and dashed toward the fray.

Kwania grabbed for his mane, crying, "Wait!" but Kola pulled away and rushed toward the nearest Chalcedi, who was tearing the back of a Chrysoli with his talons.

Skia Skotos yelled for his Dark Ones. "Take to the field of battle! Embolden my armies in the fight!" Thanatos led the Dark Ones onto the field, but the Bellator Warriors rose and soared over the mass of creatures below, meeting the Dark Ones in mid-air.

"You shall not interfere!" Impetor commanded, Paxor and Munior by her side.

"Out of the way!" screeched Thymos.

Luxor whirled her gleaming sword in an arc, spraying the Dark Ones with a shower of light. They shrieked and dodged but kept coming. Impetor butted shields with the raging Thymos, while Paxor chased Hedraios. Hedraios called, "You will never catch me. You might as well go skulk back to the 'Ro for some hand-patting."

But Paxor laughed. "Your lies will not work on me, fiend." He chased the Dark One in ever-decreasing circles until he had Hedraios in a chokehold.

Parator grappled Nothrotos for a few beats, but the Dark One broke away and scuttled back to Skia Skotos, her tail between her legs, only to be beaten for her retreat.

Munior locked swords with Zelos, bellowing, "The end of your cycles has come."

"I have had more pleasure in my cycles on this world than you have known in your entire existence." Zelos laughed. "If I end this cycle, my life will still be greater than yours can ever be!" Munior slashed Zelos' face, and she screamed in agony, then redoubled her attack. Parator dove to Munior's side, and their two swords backed Zelos down to the ground, where they pressed her flat on her back and held her.

Luxor howled, "Perish, evildoers!" and rushed a whole group of Dark Ones. Ademoneos cried, "We cannot prevail!" and scampered away, but the other Dark Ones met the charge, and their sparks rebounded off the Light One's sword. Luxor's sword was swift and true, and after she parried another flurry of bolts from the Dark Ones, she fired beam after beam, until the smell of burning filled the air.

Veritor charged Thanatos, and the two mightiest warriors of their respective kinds pummeled sword against sword, showering sparks and rays of light over the battlefield. They rose in a swirling spiral of bolts and beams. The clangor of metal on metal reverberated over the plains.

"Do you need aid?" Luxor called, while hacking away at the Dark Ones surrounding her.

"I have him," Veritor replied. His voice was as calm as if he were reciting a poem from the ancient texts.

"Take down the wretch!"

Admonitor, who made quick work of Phobos, called out to Veritor. "Where is the one with no name?"

"He circles above my ward. Keep him away from her, lest he try to inhabit her!"

Eleutheri left the Whisperers guarding Amadah and Aleshanee and joined Admonitor, who hurried to Angeni's side. Angeni knelt beside Ogima's headless sarkikos and wept. Hanai and the rest of the

327

Jacinthi huddled around her, some shedding their own tears. They tried to comfort her, but she would not be consoled. Skia Skotos was somewhat pleased to see their grief, until the hated light ones arrived and blocked her from his view. He was tempted to do something about their interference, but he had to pay close attention to the battle waging on the field. His troops were destroying each other. So far, his prophet had done nothing to stop it, nor did the Jasperi or Jacinthi join in the fight against the Chrysoli traitors. He might need to devise some other way to intervene.

Before long, tattered and bloody creatures started stumbling away from the fight. Chatan, severely wounded, limped back to Angeni, unable to fly. Lonan staggered out of the knot of entangled creatures, his throat gushing blood. Dead sarkikos piled higher and higher in the center of the field.

Leenha tried to reorganize her armies into a double pincer attack, but the noise of the battle and screams of the wounded drowned out her command, and no one could see her signal through the dense cloud of dust. All she did was draw attention to her position, and before she could flee, she was swamped under a group of Chrysoli warriors, spitting, clawing, and fighting for her life.

Still, they fought, Chalcedi against Chrysoli, Chrysoli against Turqosi, Dark Ones against Light. Beyond the melee, the two witnesses stood watching, quiet and still, surrounded by their friends and the light of the 'Ro and Metanoi Whisperers.

"Admonitor, Impetor needs your help!" Veritor commanded.

Admonitor raced back to the battle, leaving Eleutheri to protect Angeni from being inhabited by Skia Skotos. But Eleutheri alone was no match for Skia Skotos, who swept down to Angeni. "Fear not, I am still here."

"Oh, my Lord." She moaned, holding her head as if she feared it might fall off like Ogima's.

"I need you to do something for me. Once I get the attention of the masses, I need you to call them forth to stand before the amthyst stone and watch a miracle. Then, you go to the stone, lean close to it, and speak into it."

"What shall I speak, my Lord?"

"It does not...never mind. Say, 'I call you forth. Come now to life.'"

"Come to life?"

"Just do it."

"Yes, Lord."

Eleutheri fled before Skia Skotos could turn against her and returned to the Metanoi and 'Ro. "The nameless one plots a terrible deception."

"Can we stop him?" Elegosi asked.

"I believe it is too late."

Skia Skotos rose high into the air, almost to the edge of the low-hanging grey clouds. On his command, the Dark Ones broke off contact with the Whisperers and established a wall before Skia Skotos. He spread his arms and shot bolts and sparks from the ends of his fingers. Jagged streaks cut through the sky toward the wrestling throngs below, some shattering the ground and others singeing the fur of the opposing force. The display continued until a few Chrysoli suffered a direct hit and burst into flames, and the combatants fell away from each other to stare and tremble below the ominous sky.

Kola hobbled to Kwania, who helped him the rest of the way back to their group. "Even the elements rage against this battle. We can't win!"

"I think the Dark Lord is the one raging." Kwania pointed to Ogima's prone, headless sarkikos. "Look there. Ogima is no more."

Kola stared, his face a war of emotions from fear to disbelief to joy. "Is it over?"

"I don't think so," Amadah's tone was ominous.

Skia Skotos whispered to Angeni. "Now!"

"The Great Lord Ogima calls you forth to witness the miraculous work of his mighty hands!" Angeni cried. Skia Skotos punctuated her command with a flurry of sparks that hit behind the clustered fighters, urging them forward. "Come now, those who love our Lord and those who would reject him and see what our wondrous Lord can do!" She watched as the spellbound fighters shuffled forward and gestured for Amadah and Aleshanee to bring their group, but the witnesses didn't move. She directed the armies to stand before the amthyst crystals. Once everyone was assembled, she moved regally to the crystals, spread her arms and wings, and leaned toward the stone. "I call you forth. Come now to life."

A broad, sizzling bolt of white light split the sky and struck the purple crystals. As the crystals became molten and pooled in the space between the split rocks, Skia Skotos darted down to the stone and, using his sparks, slowly stretched the molten material up, shaping it as it expanded until he formed it into a crystalline figure resembling the shape of an Amthysti sarkikos.

"Witness the great miracle!" Angeni cried. "The crystal lives!"

Skia Skotos melded into the newly formed crystal and spoke, his voice echoing like clashing cymbals. "Those who would destroy my magnificence, see the futility of their attack. I cannot be destroyed by mere creatures, for I am above all. Fear me now or perish!"

"Another trick!" Aleshanee yelled. "There is only one who is above all, the one who made all things, the creating one, the first before all, the one worthy of all glory and honor and praise. The Forever!"

"*I am the forever*!" Skia Skotos' voice reverberated through the air.

The cowering masses fell to the ground before the shimmering crystal statue, leaving Amadah, Aleshanee, and their little group of friends standing alone.

This ploy was perfect. The statue remained upright without Skia Skotos holding it erect, so he was free to come and go as he pleased while still maintaining the illusion of corporeal substance. His followers would be even more servile and obeisant since he had made the crystal come alive before their eyes.

"I will be known as Ogima no longer! You will call me Skia Skotos, for I am a God, the God of darkness and shadow. I have the power of life and death, and death obeys me. You shall have no other gods but me!"

"Oh yes, mighty Lord, the one true forever. Skia Skotos is your name, the God of darkness and shadow. Our Lord and our God, we honor you. We tremble before your might and your beauty. No one is like you." Angeni chanted like one in a trance, rocking back and forth with her arms across her chest.

"Because of the abomination of your transgressions against me, you shall bring before me an offering. I demand an offering of beauty, of power, a worthy sacrifice to my Great Name."

"Who shall we bring, oh Great Lord? Who is worthy of such honor as to be chosen by you?" Angeni wailed.

"Bring me Leoti of the Chrysoli!"

Leoti screamed and stood to flee, but the Chalcedi grabbed her and dragged her to the foot of the living stone. A silver bolt shot from the place on the statue where a mouth might have been and struck Leoti. The Chalcedi were blown back by the force of the strike. Leoti stiffened, and the sizzling silver thread wrapped around and around her while she tremored in place, until she fell to the ground, immobilized.

Skia Skotos licked his lips. The last flesh he had consumed was on the high mountain. Since then, nothing, and he was famished. "Your transgressions are great, my little harlot. You claim loyalty to Kola while you plot against him with Lonan, then you claim loyalty to me while you plot against me and send your mate to destroy me. For that, I will consume you."

Skia Skotos exited the crystal and enveloped Leoti's sarkikos. For a brief moment, a flickering, translucent image of Skia Skotos' true appearance could be seen, but no one bowing before the crystal had been watching the unfolding horror, instead burying their faces in the dirt. Only the witnesses and their friends saw his hideous visage. Then, he melded into her flesh and consumed her from the inside out. Only the witnesses saw him consume Leoti's flesh while she still lived, but everyone heard the terror and pain in her shrieks before her echoes faded to silence.

"*You* are the abomination," Amadah yelled across the plain.

Skia Skotos cackled and rose into the air once more, leaving a pile of steaming bones in his wake. With a wave of his hands, he projected bizarre, kaleidoscopic colors across the terrified throng, and entranced them. Ademoneos whispered to two of the Chalcedi, who

331

shuffled to Ogima's palanquin and lit smoking pots until a sweet-smelling mist floated across the crowd, mingling with the strange spinning colors.

"Turn away," Veritor warned. "Do not breathe the foul air." The sphere bearers turned their faces away.

Only beats later, Skia Skotos' followers stopped cowering. Their sluggish movements and glassy eyes let Skia Skotos know they were ready to be controlled. They wandered without purpose or direction, stupefied, mumbling nonsense to themselves, some of them even grabbing at the air as if they were trying to catch something that wasn't there.

Skia Skotos floated low over the throng, They became weirdly agitated, but their eyes remained vacant, devoid of independent thought. "Chalcedi! Turqosi! Jacinthi! Jasperi! Chrysoli! I call on you now! Fight for your God! Fight against the usurpers, the liars, all those who stand against me! Destroy them all!"

Angeni pointed across the field. "There they stand! The usurpers! The liars! Those who claim the dread God of darkness and shadow is not the forever! Kill them! Kill them all!"

Chalcedi, Turqosi, Chrysoli, Jacinthi, and Jasperi turned as one to face the sphere bearers. For effect, Skia Skotos shot some jagged bolts over the heads of his shuffling, stupefied horde. His armies started growling, chanting nonsensical phrases, and screaming. The cacophony was deafening. Skia Skotos saw Amadah close her eyes and assumed she was accepting her fate.

Beyond Amadah's group, movement ruffled the bushes. From within the underbrush, a mass of blue creatures waving sticks and rocks dashed onto the plains and raced to join Amadah's group. Saphiri! But they walked upright.

"Papa!" Misa opened her arms to embrace him.

A squad of Turqosi peeled off from the combined armies to ambush the approaching Saphiri, but Luxor rose again and blocked their path with a broad beam of light. The Turqosi were so stupefied, they walked directly into the beam and perished.

Behind the Saphiri, the slaves who escaped from the dome returned and ran to Kwania and Kola, who greeted them with joy. Kola positioned them in lines behind the main group. "Stay here. Don't stray beyond the circle of light."

Aleshanee raised her hands in the air and sang:

"Salvation belongs to the Great Love.
For judgment comes, swift and true,
Avenging the blood of the servants.
We will rejoice, give thanks and praise,
For the Great Love reigns forever.
Give glory to the Great Love who brings
White, clean adornment for us.
The Great Love has made us holy,
Righteous, fearless, and true.
The cycle has come for victory!
Blessed are those who stand with the Forever.
Blessed are those invited to the Great Love's feast."

The heavy clouds parted, the sky split open, and a swath of brilliant light shot from the aperture. Down through the clouds, as if riding on the beam of light, a colossal beast descended, its white face like that of a leopard, with curved fangs so large they protruded from its mouth on top and bottom. It boasted massive, paddle-shaped horns tipped with a row of spikes near their ends. Its shoulders were broad, muscles rippling beneath the luxurious white fur, and expansive wings billowed out from its sides with each individual feather larger than the largest Turqosi. Astride its back sat a figure consumed in white flames.

"Kindred!" Amadah and Aleshanee cried in unison.

The beast's thick, prehensile tail whipped back and forth with agitation as it opened its mouth to omit a thunderous roar that cracked open the ground under the feet of the shuffling horde. They scrambled away from the gash opening beneath them and scattered to either side.

Skia Skotos growled under his breath. "Thanatos, Thymos—lead the Dark Ones against this apparition."

"Yes, my Lord."

333

"Lord, what weapon do we have against this apparition?" Phobos quavered.

"Go!"

As the Dark Ones sped across the field, the Whisperers ascended to meet Kindred in the air. A band of light arced across the plains, blocking the advancing Dark Ones, as the beast carried Kindred, surrounded by the hated Whisperers, to stand before the two witnesses and their ragtag followers.

Kindred wore a pearlescent crown which reflected her fire in shimmering fluctuations of color. In her hand, she carried a curved blade akin to something an Emraldi might use to harvest grain for their bread, but hers was longer than the beast on which she rode. The strange sword was also ablaze.

"I have returned to you now, at the cycle of annihilation, to separate those who will embrace the Great Love and the Forever from those who choose the ways of darkness."

Skia Skotos descended to hover poised above his followers. His Dark Ones took protective positions around him, their hideous faces contorted with rage, their claws and teeth bared. Skia Skotos' eyes burned red, as he raised his palms toward the sky, two balls of sizzling, writhing sparks growing in his hands. "I do not fear you, Kindra." He punctuated the use of her world-name by exaggerating the 'ra.' "What power could a mere child hold against the great God of darkness and shadow?"

"Phaini." Kindred used his former Metanoi name in response. Her voice was soft, almost kind, but filled with sorrow. "Relinquish your hold on these creatures, for the cycle of your end is upon you. Do not carry them into the darkness with you."

Skia Skotos cackled. "Phaini is long ended. Skia Skotos will live forever. It is you who has come to her end." He hurled a blue-white ball of sparks at Kindred's beast, but the white beast opened its cavernous mouth, inhaled, and blew a stream of fire like lava from an erupting mountaintop of old, blasting the ball into sizzling embers. Skia Skotos' followers covered their heads and fled from the hot fire raining down on them.

Kola rushed forward. "Great Lady, do not destroy my pride. Let me speak to them. Lonan and Leoti are gone. I'm sure they'll listen to me now."

"Have a care, Kola. Would you not clean your own fur before attempting to clean your mate's?"

"My fur is clean."

"You have shaken out your mane and cleaned your coat with your tongue, but the hard work of cleansing inside you has not yet begun."

"I don't understand."

"The motives inside your heart are what defile you—rage, revenge, hatred—these remain to be cleansed."

"How can I stop the hatred I feel for the destruction wrought against my pride? You ask the impossible."

"Many have walked through the fire of cleansing and touched the First World, but you have yet to see. Your cycle will come."

"Before this is over, Kola will be mine!" Skia Skotos proclaimed.

"Silence, scum, or feel the sting of my sword!" Luxor shouted.

"Oh, Phaini, how deep in the pit you have fallen." Kindred sighed. "You who have chosen the name of a god, and therefore have no name, as desolate as your title."

Angeni bellowed like an angry banask, pumped her wings to ascend, and shook her fists at Kindred. "You will not desecrate the glory of the God of darkness and shadow with your lies, not while I still live."

Veritor, his heart in anguish, approached his ward. "The cycle of choice is upon you, Angeni. Examine your heart if you can find it once more. Remember what you once knew." He saw no sign of recognition on Angeni's face, no indication she heard his whispers. She was truly lost.

"I shall wait no longer." Kindred raised her curved sword. "Those who wish to follow us may join us on our march to the high mountain. Those who choose the way of darkness may remain here. Know what you are choosing. This world will soon end in cleansing fire."

335

"No one moves." Angeni's screech was deafening as she descended before the throng of Skia Skotos' armies. "The dread God of darkness and shadow will destroy any who leave to follow her and her beast to the high mountain. Which do you most fear? The empty words of promised destruction with no evidence? Or Skia Skotos, your Lord and God, whose powers you have seen demonstrated over and over again, he who reigns over death?"

The silence from his armies was deafening for Skia Skotos. The hated child was fomenting doubt in his followers, and he couldn't stomach it. He would not have it! To remind them of his power, he descended into the crystal statue in a flurry of sparks and spoke from its depths. "Who brought life to the lifeless? Who brought himself back from a mortal wound?"

"The answer is Kindred," Amadah cried. "Angeni, you were there. You saw. For three cycles, Aleshanee and I were dead. Kindred raised us to life. Kindred, who died herself to save us and then came back to us. Kindred, who sits before you, was dead and now lives."

"It is true! We are both witnesses to the First World and the Forever and the power of the Great Love!" Aleshanee proclaimed.

Angeni squawked and fluttered her wings to rise higher above Skia Skotos' armies. "Who protected you from the deadly swarm?"

"Our friends protected us, and we suffered no harm. But those who followed the Dark Lord suffered greatly."

"As did the Chrysoli," Kwania added.

"Do not listen to these liars!" Angeni flew over the crowd, pointing to the crystal statue. "Kindred shows you nothing! Look to your God who reforms material substance and brings it to life before your eyes! See his mighty power. He has power over death!"

"Kindred is the power of life!" Amadah replied.

Aleshanee raised her hands in the air. "She is love!"

"She is nothing!" Angeni screamed.

Kindred lifted her hand to call for silence. "All must choose."

The armies milled about and started to congregate with their own kind. Soon, they were huddled together by species, muttering amongst themselves. The Chrysoli were the first to respond.

Kasa, one of Lonan's warriors, stepped forward. "Chrysoli follow no one."

Miakoda joined Kasa. "We will return to the dome and live what is left of our lives in peace."

"No! Not choosing is still a choice!" Kola cried.

The Chrysoli turned toward their dome.

Kwania called out. "Miakoda, wait! My friend, do not go!"

Skia Skotos shot long, blue bolts across their path. "You dare defy your God?"

"We refuse any god!" Kasa replied. "We follow our own way."

"Then you will die."

With a cry, Kindred commanded the great white beast. "Destroy the crystal." The beast roared and exhaled another stream of fire. The fire enveloped the statue like something sentient, swirling around and around it until the crystal once again started to sag and melt into a purplish pool.

Skia Skotos vaulted into the air as the fire hit. Kindred spurred the beast forward. It crossed the distance in three bounds, then Kindred leapt from its back. "You will not kill these creatures."

"You cannot stop me!" Skia Skotos raised his hand to deliver a shower of sparks, but Kindred jumped between him and the fleeing Chrysoli and swept her flaming curved sword, catching and deflecting his attack. Skia Skotos howled in frustration.

Kindred reached down and picked up the silver thread Skia Skotos used to bind Leoti, lifting it by the end of her sword. "With your own weapon, I bind you," she cried, hurling the thread at Skia Skotos. He screamed as the cord wrapped around and around him, as it had done to Leoti. Before their eyes, Skia Skotos' true form became visible to all as he plummeted to the ground, bound head to foot. His deformed features bore only a vague resemblance to any creature known on their world. He had wings, but rather than feathered, they were leathery and black. Where his face should've been, the skin was sunken as if it had turned in on itself, leaving only sepulchral caverns and folds of leather. His eyes, blazing red, gleamed from within his tortured visage like two tiny sky lights in a vast back sky.

337

The thread cut into what would've been his mouth, so all he could utter was a grunt or a throaty, high-pitched growl. Seeing him so disabled, his armies started to squirm and shuffle their feet.

"You are all free to choose. Choose wisely." Kindred remounted her beast and turned its head toward the west and the high mountain.

Kola stepped toward Kindred. "I choose to stay with my kind. I must convince them their refusal to join you is folly, and they must choose to come to the mountain. They need my leadership."

"Kola, do not remain here," Kwania pleaded. "What will you do if your pride refuses to leave the dome?"

"I have to convince them otherwise. I have to try."

"But..."

"I'll join you before it's too late," Kola promised.

Kwania wrapped her arms around his neck and buried her face in his thick mane. "Please, do not wait too long." Kola nodded and stalked to his pride, who congregated at the dome entrance, and led them inside the dome.

Kindred raised her hand. "Come, my friends. We must make all haste to the high mountain." The great beast marched across the plain, followed by Amadah, flanked by Seri and Sewati, and Aleshanee, who clutched Enla's paw. Meda, Cholena, and Chevei took off and flew above the group. Misa walked beside Towila, who led the rest of the Saphiri. Kwania and Kilchi walked with the slaves. The Whisperers flew above the procession, their wary eyes on the Dark Ones.

Angeni grabbed the silver cord in her talons and yanked it with a loud cry, but the cord held fast. "Help me!" she commanded the Chalcedi. They, too, gathered around Skia Skotos, pulling and ripping at the silver thread, but no one could break it or loosen its grip. Leenha tried her spit, but Skia Skotos shrieked as the venom hit his skin, so Leenha backed out of Angeni's reach, turned, and with a signal to what remained of her armies, she fled.

"Use your sparks to burn it away, Great Lord," Angeni suggested, but Skia Skotos' only glared at her. "Can you leave this form and take another?"

Skia Skotos writhed in his bonds, but the binding stuck him in the limited, physical form like Tempor trapped this world. His rage became a spreading conflagration, until he thought it would consume his being and transform him into an inferno of fury. Still, the thread wouldn't budge.

One by one, Skia Skotos' remaining followers wandered away, until only Angeni remained by his side.

CHAPTER FORTY-FOUR

The Jasperi

Amadah was aware of an encroaching melancholy pushing away her urgency to collect the sphere and transport it to the high mountain. Yet, she was also cognizant of her deep desire to join Fala on the First World. Now that the battle was over, she had too much space to think. And to feel. Did she doubt he would be there, and she would see him? On some level, did she believe she would be left here without hope? Aleshanee's reassurances did little to assuage her sadness.

Seri and Sewati, very Topazi-like, walked in silence. She was oddly comforted by their presence, though, feeling a sense of familiarity in having a big reptilian creature beside her. Still, they were not Fala, and she felt herself waning in the face of the loss of his supportive strength.

Kindred called for a halt. She hopped down from her beast and motioned for everyone to gather around her. "Now, we must divide our group. Amadah, Aleshanee, and those who retrieved the sphere from the cave will turn here and go to collect the sphere, while the rest of us will proceed to the high mountain."

"Why must we separate? It seems wiser for us to remain together." Kwania looked anxiously from Amadah and Aleshanee to Kindred.

"We must precede Skia Skotos and his forces to the high mountain to protect the altar, for if he arrives before we do and destroys the altar on which the sphere must rest, all is lost. Those who carry the sphere have their own journey to make, one only they can complete. Our task is a different one."

"Topazi with Amadah," Seri said.

"No, I am afraid you will not be able to accompany Amadah on this leg of her journey."

"Topazi go," Sewati argued.

"You are as loyal and as headstrong as Fala." Kindred smiled, but her smile was tinged with sadness. "Still, you cannot go with Amadah. She will rejoin us at the high mountain once she retrieves the sphere."

Amadah touched Seri's shoulder. "All is well, friends. You will see me again. Kindred needs brave warriors like you beside her to stop the Dark Lord."

"Who protects?"

"My friends and I have protected each other for many cycles now." Amadah circled her finger toward those who retrieved the sphere with her. "We are bound. I'll be fine." If she were honest, she would miss her new friends and wished they could go with her, but she trusted Kindred. So, she accepted another insult to her heart. What was one more on top of so many?

Kindred embraced Aleshanee, then Amadah. "Your group is diminished, but this task is yours to complete. You must be strong."

Amadah wasn't feeling very strong, but she nodded and gave Kindred a wan smile.

"We will be at the base of the mountain. Approach quietly from places of hiding and observe before you let your presence be known." Kindred clasped their hands.

"I thought the danger had passed with the victory on the plains. Isn't Skia Skotos bound?" Aleshanee asked.

"Do not underestimate the Dark Lord or his minions."

"But you bound him."

"The binding is of his making so it will not last long." Kindred gazed back in the direction from which they came. "We are not done with him or his armies. But do not worry." She looked pointedly at

Amadah. "I promised Fala I would deal with him once and for all. And I will."

Tears sprang unbidden to Amadah's eyes. She nodded once, then bowed her head.

"Go now. Be on your guard. Remain hidden from prying eyes. Once you have the sphere, make haste. The sky light has few cycles left to it before it is no more, and the sphere must be placed before it ends."

Kindred turned and mounted her giant beast. "Farewell, dear ones. The light of the Forever walks with you."

Misa embraced her father. "Be careful," Towila whispered into her hair.

"Let's go. The sooner we begin, the sooner we are done." Amadah clasped Seri's clawed hands, then Sewati's, then she hugged Kwania, Cholena, and Meda. "I wish we could all stay together."

Aleshanee crooked her arm through Enla's thick, furry one. "We're on our way!"

Amadah took the lead, followed by Aleshanee and Enla, Misa, Kilchi, and Chevei flying overhead.

Kilchi drifted closer to Misa. "Misa, my love. Will you ever forgive me?"

Amadah spied Misa's pained expression when she glanced at Kilchi. Misa lowered her eyes. "So great is your offense."

"I—I was only trying to spare you the pain of losing your father again."

"At the expense of his sacred freedom. With violence."

Kilchi huffed. "I don't understand you. Towila would've burned to death in the water if not for me. But now, he's alive and with Kindred. How is that not a good thing?"

"Understanding not the grave nature of removing freedom?" Misa sighed. "Glad am I Papa lives. But forgiving your transgression? Who is to say violence toward me would not come?"

"Please, Misa. Don't abandon me. Not now. Not for saving your father's life. If I had to do it over, I'd still do the same. For your sake."

Misa walked, silent and remote, for many beats. Finally, she faced Kilchi. "Finding my love for you again amid such severe violation is difficult. But believing I can rediscover it."

"Will you forgive me?"

"For the sake of my living father and our love."

Kilchi bowed his head and nuzzled her hand.

They made it to the rock-strewn hills as Kindred and the rest of the clan disappeared from sight.

Chevei landed by Amadah. "Kindred said we should remain hidden. It may be better for me to fly up in the clouds, but you will not be able to see me if I do."

"What if Chalcedi come looking for us?" Enla asked. "Wouldn't it be better if you walked with us?"

Chevei looked to Amadah, his face broaching the question.

"I don't know." Amadah didn't feel like she could decide to take another step, much less the fate of their group. "I'm not sure what we need to be looking out for—the Chalcedi? Angeni and the Jacinthi? The Dark Ones? The Dark Lord?"

"All of the above?" Chevei suggested.

"Then, I guess since they have fliers, we need to go to ground, as Fala used to say."

"Is anyone else worried about us being able to lift the sphere?" Kilchi asked. "We can't roll it through the fallen rocks, so picking it up is our only option. Can we do it with only six of us?"

"Six who are not the strongest members of our group who carried it before," Aleshanee added.

"Kindred wouldn't have sent us if the task was impossible." Amadah tried to sound more confident than she felt. "We'll figure it out."

"Enla, you marked the place where we hid the sphere. Do you think you can find it again?"

"I can. I know the marks I made."

"Then, let's hurry and find it. I'm ready to be done with this whole thing." Amadah's slow inhale hitched, as if the act of breathing was too much effort.

As they climbed over and through the rockslides, Enla moved up beside Amadah. "What's wrong?"

"I'm just tired."

"That's not all."

"I miss Fala. My heart feels like it's been sucked into a void, but it—hurts, even though it feels—gone—empty—I don't know, I can't describe it. I just know I'm done with it all."

"Do you still have hope?"

Amadah smiled wistfully, remembering how Enla and Yiska used to talk about hope, and how they kept their little band hoping even when everything felt impossible. "I might have a thin thread of it left, but it's hard to find these cycles."

"I have great hope I will see Yiska again. And you will see Fala, too. I know it!"

Amadah couldn't muster another smile for Enla, although she found her hopeful assurance heartwarming. Wherever her heart had gone.

As if responding to her thoughts, Spa'ro whispered, "Would you like to hear a story while we travel?"

"I love stories!" Aleshanee crooned.

"Many, many cycles ago, or perhaps many, many cycles in the future, on another world somewhat like this one but also very different, a creature was preparing a huge feast. He was soon to be bound forever to a beautiful bound mate."

"Was she very beautiful?" Aleshanee asked.

"She was indeed, in heart and spirit and aspect. However, the bound mate did not know the cycle of the creature's coming."

"Why?"

"He had preparations to make. He wanted everything to be perfect for his bound mate, and his work took him much longer than she expected. She grew weary of waiting, and sad. She decided his delay was because she was not good enough for his love, and if she performed for him, and her performance was good enough, he would come for her. So, she danced and sang and tried to do everything perfectly, but still he did not come.

"Then she despaired and began to doubt if he was coming at all. She began to tell stories to herself, stories where her bound mate's promise to come for her was really more of a wish he had and not a promise, where his love for her was more of a general love for all things like trees and mountains and sky, and nothing special for her. At one point, she told herself he was dead. Then, she told herself he never existed, and she started to bind herself to other things, things of their world. Soon, she did not remember him at all."

"Did she love the creature?"

"Perhaps she did once, as best she could, but she did not really understand love, for the creature had yet to show her all about the true nature of his love and what it means to be bound. The creature was so very sad when he came for her and found she did not remember him, and she was bound to so many other things. But he asked her to be bound to him anyway.

"The bound mate was angry when she saw him. She said he was late in coming and rejected him straightaway."

"What did he do?"

"He loved her still, so he made a great sacrifice to show her the true nature of love and what it means to be bound. After the sacrifice, he invited her to his great feast."

"Did she go to the great feast?"

"We will see."

Aleshanee pouted. "I like stories with a happy ending. I can't tell if that story is happy or sad. It sounds very sad, but if she goes to the feast, then it's not."

"Very true."

"Tell a different story—a happy one."

Spa'ro tittered. "Very well, dear one. I will tell you a story of an Emraldi. This Emraldi carried seeds to be planted in a sack she carried over her shoulder. But, she was easily distracted, as Emraldi can be. She chased flutterbys and picked flowers and skipped along the path. What she did not know was her sack had a hole in it. The seeds scattered, some along the path, some amongst the thick grass of the field, some in

346

the rock gardens where the flowers were tended. When she arrived at the plowed fields and pulled out her sack, she saw what had happened.

"She quickly planted what was left of her seeds in the plowed ground, then rushed back to the path to try to find her lost seeds. But those seeds were gone, having been blown away by the wind or eaten by the wild creatures. She looked far and wide, but she could not find her seeds. Then, she hurried to the grassy fields, but the grass was so thick, she could not see the seeds anywhere. She tried to press the tall grass down to see the dirt, but the seeds were caught up in the grass and hidden from her. She pawed through the grass for cycles and cycles, but still she found no seeds.

"Finally, she ran to the rock garden. She was thrilled to find a few of the seeds had taken root and were straining to push through the rocks toward the sky light, but she could not pull them out to replant them without damaging the roots, and she could not leave them for they would not have enough water to sustain their growth. Soon, as she feared, those plants withered and died."

"You said this was a happy story!" Aleshanee complained.

Spa'ro laughed. "So, the Emraldi returned to the plowed field, and there, to her great joy, she saw all her seeds had taken good root and were growing. So, she tended those seeds, watered them, weeded them, and produced a great crop, enough to feed all Emraldi for the season."

"Harvested by one, shared by all," Aleshanee declared.

"Yes, dear one. The Emraldi knew seeds, well-tended, will bear fruit for the feeding of the whole clan."

"I like that story!" Aleshanee said.

After a few beats of silence, Amadah whispered. "Your story of the bound mates. That story was really a story about our world and the Forever, wasn't it?" But Spa'ro didn't answer.

The group had walked in silence for many beats when Enla cried out. "I think I see my markings!" She scurried up the hillside, disappearing behind fallen rocks and dirt from landslides. Finally, they saw her waving her arms overhead.

Kilchi, the most agile of the group, scampered over the rocks toward Enla. Amadah was not aware of her anxiety about the sphere until Kilchi disappeared into the rocks, then she realized the knot in her stomach was turning into a chokehold on her throat. What would they do if the Dark Lord had discovered their hiding place and stolen the sphere? How could they ever find it again?

Soon, they heard Kilchi's howl. They had found the sphere! Amadah closed her eyes and breathed again.

Chevei risked flying up over the hillside to where Kilchi and Enla were standing, while Amadah, Aleshanee, and Misa climbed over the rocks to the well-hidden cave mouth behind a boulder. Kilchi, Enla, and Chevei had already rolled the sphere to the mouth of the cave when they arrived.

"Let's lift it and see if we can do this." Kilchi put his shoulder into the sphere.

For some reason, the sphere didn't seem quite as heavy as it did when they first found it. They were able to lift it and carried it as one across the rocks to the valley. There, they hugged the base of the hill, walking in shadow on the long trek toward the high mountain.

Amadah couldn't stop pondering the story of the bound mates. The story haunted her. It wasn't long before she saw her own despair and doubt mirrored in the story. Hadn't she forgotten the First World? Hadn't she given up hope of seeing the Forever and Fala again?

Her heart sank at the thought of rejecting the love offered by the Forever because she was angry with the Forever for taking Fala to the First World, when he had just been restored to her. No, she decided she wouldn't be the kind of bound mate who gave up because what she desired was delayed. She would hope, like Enla, and wait with excited expectation to see her bound mate and the First World and the Forever again. And when she was invited to the feast, she would be overjoyed to attend.

Chapter Forty-Five

The Jasperi

Kai crouched in the thorny undergrowth and watched as

Turqosi, Chalcedi, Jacinthi, and Jasperi shuffled away from the bound, prone figure and wandered in groups of their own kind across the plains. Some went southeast toward the Chalcedi aerie. Some wandered southwest toward what was once the Jasperi forest. Others went due south as if they were heading toward the river lands and the sea. Still others went northwest toward the hills. Soon, a lone Jacinthi remained. The aged Jacinthi wept and pawed over the bound figure, who writhed on the ground like a serpentus trapped in the hot season's sky light. The Jacinthi couldn't seem to free the creature from the strange gleaming rope binding him.

Alatha crept up behind him and leaned over his shoulder to look at the scene. "Is that the Jacinthi leader, Angeni from the high mountain?"

Recognition dawned, and Kai nodded. "I think so, although she looks much older and—worn down."

"As do we all."

Kai nodded again, wondering how Angeni ended up alone on the plains with the hideous-looking creature before her.

"What is that thing she is tending?" Alatha asked.

Kai shrugged. "Strange looking, isn't he?"

"Hard to tell from here. Perhaps he's injured."

"Disfigured is more like it."

"What're we going to do now?"

"I say let's go talk to Angeni and see if she has food and water. After that, we can always join Sonta and Itai. They went that way." He pointed toward the southwest.

"There's nothing that way."

"I know, but if we catch them, we can all decide together where we want to live. Right now, though, we need food, and Angeni might have supplies. They brought a lot of stuff with them."

"Very well, if you think it's safe."

"What could they do to us? Look at them."

Alatha nodded, and the two of them pushed through the stiff bushes to step onto the open field. Angeni didn't seem to notice them as they approached, so rather than frighten her, Kai called out and waved. "Angeni!" Alatha remained in his shadow.

Angeni appeared startled at first, then she stood and returned Kai's salute. Kai walked to the prone creature, looked at it, then faced Angeni. "My name is Kai, and this is Alatha of the Jasperi. Do you remember us?"

"You were in the Jasperi group who came to the high mountain."

"Yes, we met you there."

"Yet, you did not remain with the group after the confrontation with the Chalcedi."

"Alatha and I have been on our own for many cycles."

"I am sure the Jasperi thought you dead."

"Amadah did." Kai frowned, remembering his final confrontation with Amadah.

Angeni's frown matched his own. "Amadah. Traitorous, lying creature."

Kai smirked. "So, you've met her."

"This was all her doing. My Lord suffers in bondage, all because of Amadah and that little Emraldi."

"Why don't you cut him out?"

"I have tried. I cannot. My talons and beak cannot break the strand."

"Who is he anyway?"

"He is the God of darkness and shadow, the Great Lord Skia Skotos, Lord of all, who holds the power of death in his hands."

"He doesn't look so all-powerful to me."

Angeni bristled. "Take care what you say about my Lord."

Kai shrugged. "Sorry about that. Let me give it a try." He pulled on the strand and was surprised to find it tingled in his hands, like it held an energy of some kind. He tried lifting it, tearing it, and loosening it, but the cord wouldn't budge. "So, it's magic."

"It is the Lord's own power unleashed against him by a most heinous creature, one my Lord will destroy and free our world from her tyranny, as soon as he is released."

"What else did you try?"

"Cutting it does not work, nor does sliding it off his sarkikos. The Turqosi even tried their spit, which burns through anything, but it did not disintegrate the thread."

"Fire?"

"I fear the Lord would be harmed in his present form. The Turqosi spit burned him."

"Well, I guess if the spit from a Turqosi couldn't burn it off, fire probably wouldn't work anyway. How about unwinding it?"

"What?"

"It has to have a beginning and an end, right? What if you unwound it?" Kai fingered up and down the string, looking for an end to it. He even turned Skia Skotos over, even though the creature protested by grunting, growling, and struggling against Kai, and ran his hand down the strand along the back. Finally, he found a place where the thread seemed a bit thicker, like it was wrapped around itself. He pried the place loose and discovered the end of the silver cord.

Angeni squealed and clapped her hands. Kai lifted the struggling Skia Skotos to the standing position and started the laborious process of unwinding the strand, which encircled Skia Skotos so many revolutions, Kai lost count. Although Kai found the cord's end, he couldn't tell if he was making any headway and started to wonder if part of the magic of the strand was that it continued forever. Still, he kept circling and pulling the thread.

"I can see some space between the strands!" Angeni hopped up and down, clearly impatient to see Skia Skotos freed.

"Here." Kai handed the pooled cord to Alatha. "Hold this and collect it as I unwind." Then, he glowered at Skia Skotos. "I'm doing all the work here. Spin."

Skia Skotos scowled at Kai but started spinning. The unwinding went faster as Kai pulled on the cord and Alatha gathered it up in a bundle, until finally, Skia Skotos broke free and vanished, and the few remaining dregs of thread fell, limp, to the ground.

"Where did he go?" Alatha squealed.

"I told you, he is the God of darkness and shadow, most powerful. He can exist in many forms."

"Well, do we at least get a reward for freeing him? We need food, water."

"The Lord Skia Skotos has abundant food which he will most graciously share in gratitude for your efforts in freeing him." Angeni went to the palanquin and rummaged through several bags, producing wrapped meat and a container of water.

Kai grabbed the water and gulped it down before handing the container to Alatha, who drank greedily. Then, he unwrapped the meat, ripped it apart, and gave one piece to Alatha as he stuffed the other piece in his mouth, whole. "Thanks," Kai mumbled through the huge wad of meat.

"Thank you for freeing my Lord and King."

Kai swallowed. "What now for you and your king?"

Angeni's face darkened. "Now, we gather our armies and march to the high mountain to reclaim his throne from the usurpers."

Kai gestured around the plains. "What armies?"

"We will find them, and they will pay for their desertion. Then, they will march against Amadah and Aleshanee and destroy them all."

CHAPTER FORTY-SIX

The Jacinthi

Angeni stopped short and looked around her. She heard her name whispered— "An-gen-ni. An-gennnn-ni"—as if the breeze had come alive and was calling to her.

"I am here, Lord."

"What?" Kai blurted.

"Shhhh, Listen. My Lord calls my name."

Kai and Alatha exchanged glances, but Angeni didn't care. Let them think whatever they wanted. She recognized the voice of her Lord. "Are your wounds healed, my Lord?"

"I need you, Angeni." The breeze wafted around her head, fluttering her feathers and lifting her hair. Coolness settled on her neck like the touch of a hand drenched in cold water.

Angeni closed her eyes. Her chest broadened and a strange feeling like the ones she experienced on the high mountain in the Lord's presence washed over her. She felt floaty, like a loose feather carried on the wind. "Whatever you need, my Lord." Her voice sounded to her as if someone else was speaking.

"Give me form. Allow me to take your sarkikos."

"Hey! Wake up!" Kai shook Angeni gently. "Who are you talking to?"

"The Lord asks me to allow him to take my form." She looked to the sky. "Yes, I agree, Lord. Take me as you will."

Her sarkikos stiffened. A searing heat flooded through her, and her skin felt like it was splitting open. The worst pain she had ever

353

known, worse than she could've imagined possible, stabbed her chest. It was as if her very essence was ripping apart like shredded paper.

An image flashed before her eyes, a memory of a great white being, surrounded by light, who cradled her in his arms and comforted her as she wept in abject grief. She had forgotten. How had she forgotten that feeling of warmth, of peace, of complete rest? Now, the arms around her tore at her, and the terror she felt consumed her until rational thought fled like tiny frightened birds flushed from their nests by jackals. What had she done?

A black cloud that wasn't a cloud but somehow had substance pressed her further and further down toward a pit she wasn't aware was there within her. She reached to grab the edges of the pit with her talons, but she didn't have talons anymore. Now, the black cloud had talons, talons which gashed her flesh and tore off her feathers, sticking her feathers onto the black cloud like a child might glue sticks and rocks on a picture to give it shape and dimension.

Red-hot fire burned the back of her eyes until they shrank and sizzled to nothing. Now, where her eyes had been, she found red pinholes, where she was able to make out indistinct shapes and movement but not really able to see. She realized she was blind to all beauty. The rose sky, the white clouds, the majesty of the high mountain, the intricacy of snowflakes—all lost to her.

She became dimly aware of a voice screaming. Who was in such agony? She couldn't see. She tried to grope for the creature to offer comfort, but she had no hands. As the black cloud, now fully formed, shoved her deep into the pit, she realized it was her voice screaming. The last thing the cloud took as he covered the pit forever was her voice.

CHAPTER FORTY-SEVEN

The Dark Lord

Skia Skotos reveled in his new form. Why hadn't he thought of taking Angeni before now? He fluttered into the air and spun in a circle before diving down before the cowering Jasperi, Kai and Alatha. "I am grateful for your service, Kai of the Jasperi. Serve me, and your rewards will be great."

"Angeni?" Alatha clutched at Kai, trying to squeeze behind him.

"Um, I don't think that's Angeni anymore," Kai muttered.

Skia Skotos fluffed out Angeni's sagging feathers and pressed the lines of age from her face. "I am Angeni and the Lord God Skia Skotos. We are one, as it was always meant to be."

Alatha knelt before Angeni/Skia Skotos, but Kai stood, his arms folded.

"Your great deed in freeing me will be rewarded!"

"Never mind. We don't need anything else from you. We're going to go now. Come on, Alatha." Kai grabbed Alatha's arm and pulled her to standing, then shoved her to start walking in the direction the other Jasperi had gone.

"Halt!" Angeni/Skia Skotos bellowed.

Kai turned to face Angeni/Skia Skotos. "Look, I set you free from the magic cord. Angeni couldn't figure it out, and neither could your armies. I didn't have to do it, but I did. Now, let us be on our way. We just want to live our lives."

"There will be no life as long as the cursed child and the two witnesses live." Skia Skotos' eyes danced as an idea sprang to his mind.

He enjoyed stealing Angeni's intelligence. "Now, the two of you shall be *my* witnesses. You shall tell everyone what you saw—the amazing transformation where Angeni became one with her Lord God. As my witnesses, you will stand with me on the high mountain and testify to my power. Kacina shall read from the ancient texts about the bridegroom coming for the bride, and all shall believe."

Alatha trembled in Kai's arms. Angeni/Skia Skotos knew Alatha was weak and wouldn't resist. Yet, Kai argued. "We just want to join with our Jasperi friends and make a life again, somehow."

"I will give you a life more abundant than you have ever known. Food without limits, Freedom to do whatever you want and have whatever you desire. No more scrounging for berries and nuts. No, you will have it all—riches and honor and power. All yours for the taking if you follow me."

"Kai, please. We'll starve to death on our own," Alatha whispered.

Kai hesitated. "It sounds like you need us. Everyone will think you are just Angeni without us."

"I need no one. I choose to use you."

"Seems like you do."

Skia Skotos shot a spark from his finger and singed Kai's arm. "Take Angeni's advice and have a care what you say."

"Kai..."

"So, if we follow you, you say you'll reward us? Keep us fed?"

"Of course! You will be high in my councils, revered and respected."

Kai sighed. "What would you make us do?"

"Accompany me to reclaim my armies and testify to what you saw. That is all. In exchange, you will be held in esteem by all as the one who rescued the Lord from bitter bondage at the hands of the cursed child. You will have a seat at my left hand."

"Where do we have to go to find your armies?"

"They will not have gone far."

"I saw the Turqosi go toward the river."

"Very well, to the river!" Skia Skotos took to the air.

"Wait, we can't fly!" Alatha cried.

"Then run!" Skia Skotos called down to them, cackling wildly as he relished his new physical wings.

As he expected, the wounded Turqosi had not gone far. He circled high above them, waiting on Kai and Alatha. For they were right—he needed their testimony to convince the Turqosi he was more than just Angeni trying to trick them into fighting for her. He knew Leenha wouldn't follow someone like Angeni, someone she saw as weak and easily controlled, but she had always seemed enticed by his displays of power.

As Kai and Alatha approached, he swooped down and walked with them into the Turqosi camp. A line of Turqosi formed quickly to bar his way. "Leenha! I have returned."

Leenha slid through the line after a few beats, her brow furrowed. "Angeni." She spat a steaming wad at Skia Skotos feet.

"I am Angeni, but I am much more than Angeni. I am one with Skia Skotos, your Lord and your God."

Leenha sneered, as Skia Skotos knew she would. "See Angeni."

"You also saw a crystal statue until I entered it and brought it to life."

"We witnessed it," Kai interjected. "Angeni gave the creature Skia Skotos permission and he—went into her sarkikos."

Leenha cranked her head to the side. "Angeni?"

"Angeni and I are one."

Leenha poked Angeni/Skia Skotos' chest, as if she thought he wasn't real.

"I am willing to forgive your abandonment, after appropriate punishment, and allow you to rejoin my armies."

"No punish."

"You left my side when I was in my greatest need. You broke your vow. Why would I not punish you?"

"Your fault."

With a flap of wings, Skia Skotos rose high above Leenha. His emitted an icy blue aura from the sarkikos, giving it an eerie glow, and made his voice an octave lower than Angeni's usual range. "How dare you say what happened was my fault? You failed in your job to protect me!" He unleashed a flurry of sizzling sparks, raining down on the Turqosi, who howled and scattered beneath him.

"Enough." Leenha bowed her head. "Follow."

"I will consider the appropriate punishment and impose it when I see fit. Now, we go forward to collect the rest of my armies. Kai?"

"The Jasperi shouldn't be too far from here—toward where the forest used to be. The Jacinthi went toward the hills, that way."

"Come. We march and gather the Jasperi and Jacinthi."

They found the Jasperi easily. Sonta and Itai were excited to see Kai and Alatha alive, welcoming them and their incredible tale. Not wanting to try to survive on their own in the desolate wasteland that used to be their forest home, the Jasperi were happy to rejoin Skia Skotos' army.

"Punish," Leenha demanded.

"All will receive their due. This I promise."

The Jacinthi, while just as easy to find, were more reticent.

Hanai spoke for the group. "We would follow you and return with you to the high mountain, Angeni, but we do not desire a fight against the Chrysoli or against Kindred and her beast. None of us saw this magic you claim, and we do not believe the Lord has entered your sarkikos. You do tend toward madness. I believe the loss of the Lord has addled your mind."

"Alatha and I saw it."

"Yet, you offer no evidence beyond your word."

Skia Skotos puffed Angeni's sarkikos to her maximum breadth. "You question my word? You demand evidence?" He threw a massive bolt, blasted Hanai in the chest, and sent him cartwheeling like a Topazi tumbleweed.

The Jacinthi cowered. "We see! We believe you! Angeni could not perform such magic."

"Kacina. You shall read now from the ancient texts, where the bridegroom comes for the bride."

Kacina pulled the bulky manuscript from her pack and fumbled through the pages. "Ah, here it is. 'The bridegroom took many cycles to arrive, and all who were waiting grew tired and fell asleep. Then, the shout rang out, the bridegroom comes! Let us rejoice and be glad, for the bride has made herself ready, and now belongs to the bridegroom. Come and I will show you the bride.'"

"You see? The prophecy is fulfilled. Angeni waited for me while everyone else left my side. She made herself ready and welcomed me to join with her. Now, my witnesses shout I have come, and they show you the bride and bridegroom are one."

The Jacinthi bowed and raised their hands. "We follow only you, Lord!" Kacina shouted.

"We return to the Chrysoli compound. Together, we shall bring the Chrysoli into the fold, or we shall destroy them."

"Lord, what about Hanai?"

"If Hanai cannot walk, carry him or leave him. I care not." Catori lifted Hanai to his feet, but Hanai couldn't walk without support, so Catori and Nadie each took an arm and half-carried Hanai on the march.

CHAPTER FORTY-EIGHT

The Jacinthi

Kwania noticed an odd shift in the sky. The clouds were evaporating, a welcome change after so many cycles in gloom, but the transformation didn't stop there. The light intensified to the point where Kwania could no longer make out the sky light's edges. Waves of heat caused the air between her group and the high mountain to shimmer like a Topazi desert mirage.

Seri tugged on her arm. "Hot."

Sewati leaned close to Kwania. "Sky wrong."

"You are correct, something is amiss." Kwania scurried forward and caught up with the white beast who was leading them "Kindred?"

"I know. We must reach the caves at the base of the high mountain before the heat takes us."

"Is this the explosion? If it is, it will not matter if we are in the caves or in the open—either way, we die."

Kindred's eyes were mournful, her dejected smile heartrending. "Thus begins the end. The cycle of opportunity is closing soon. Should the sphere not reach the altar…"

"What do we do?"

"We trust the Forever. We trust Amadah and Aleshanee. This is all we can do. Now, hurry everyone along. The high mountain is ahead, but we have a long and difficult passage through fire to reach it."

"Kwania, what did Kindred say?" Cholena asked as Kwania returned to the laboring assemblage.

"She said we must hurry. We must reach the mountain quickly."

"Many of the slaves fall behind, exhausted and suffering from the heat."

"I know. We cannot allow them to falter. From this point forward to the end of all things, we will know nothing but suffering. We must be strong if we are to survive."

"I'll speak to them and explain." Cholena fluttered to those lingering behind.

Kwania encouraged the mass of slaves to hurry. "I know it is difficult, and the heat is oppressive, but it will only worsen, so the sooner we reach the high mountain and enter the caves, the better for us all."

"We need water!" one of the slaves cried.

"I know. Perhaps we will find a water source in the caves."

"Topazi carry falling ones," Sewati offered.

"You could manage it?"

Seri pointed toward the sky light. "Heat like desert."

"Everyone, if you see someone near you faltering and unable to continue, call for one of the Topazi. They have offered to help carry any who cannot continue. Now, move at your fastest possible speed."

The slaves picked up the pace, many helping those around them who were struggling to keep up, and the high mountain grew closer.

The air turned white hot. The ground scorched their feet. Soon, Kwania could barely make out the outline of the mountain or the color of the rocks. It was as if the heat was washing out all form and shape and hue and shading from existence. Still, she pressed forward, her head down to protect her eyes from the brilliance of the light and her face from the sky light's penetrating rays.

Kwania walked as someone blind. She shuffled her feet like an aged Jacinthi, with her hands extended before her to prevent bumping into those around her. Despite her attempts at self-protection, she still stumbled over unseen obstacles in her path and slammed into more than one slave who stopped to catch their breath. She felt the air burn like a flame inside her chest with every breath she took.

Finally, Kindred called for a halt. Kwania squinted to see what Kindred was doing but couldn't make out her movements and soon closed her eyes against the stabbing pain. Her head was reeling. She felt like a baked casserole, boiling on the inside, and browned and crusty on the top. Suddenly, the ground spun up and slammed her in the face, squashing her beak into the dirt. What was happening? Where was she?

Through a numbing tingle, she thought she felt hands pawing at her. What were they doing to her? Suddenly, she was flying—no, more like floating, because she couldn't feel her wings. Then, darkness.

364

CHAPTER FORTY-NINE

The Turqosi

Leenha organized the reunited mob and led them on the march back to the dome, while Angeni/Skia Skotos soared overhead. As promised, Kai and Alatha were designated ambassadors and walked with Leenha before the rest of the troops.

Leenha felt the rising heat in her slimy flesh and gestured to Lise and Eteena to ready the armies for quick march. The burning light covering the sky intensified until all of Skia Skotos' troops were walking with their eyes shielded. Soon, the heat was unbearable, and his followers were crying out to him for relief.

"We must find shade," Nadie cried.

Sonta gestured toward the empty fields surrounding them. "There isn't any shade."

"We're going to burn up out here." Kai was forced to carry his companion, who had swooned like the weakling she was. "You have to do something!"

But Skia Skotos did nothing. The heat worsened, and the light blinded them. Leenha gestured for her armies to turn for the river, but Skia Skotos spiraled down from the sky and landed before them. "Leave me again, and you will be dead before you travel a single metric."

"Dead anyway," Leenha hissed. She gestured, and her armies formed a protective circle. They used each other's sarkikos as shields from the awful heat as they scuttled toward the river.

A few Jacinthi took flight for the dome, and everyone else disintegrated into chaos, some fleeing in the same direction as the Jacinthi, others just running blindly as if they could outpace the heat. Skia Skotos howled and dove after the fleeing runners. Leenha gestured for the Turqosi to increase their speed.

Still, the heat escalated. The screams of fleeing creatures pierced the burning air as, one by one, they collapsed onto the barren plains. Leenha risked an upward glance and saw Angeni's sarkikos was beginning to suffer damage, too. Clumps of feathers molted and fell to the ground. She knew if Skia Skotos didn't act soon, he would lose this sarkikos.

She saw Skia Skotos turn, leaving his scattering followers and pressing hard toward the river where Leenha's armies had once camped. Her clan almost missed the river, for all that was left of it was an indentation in the ground coated on the bottom with a layer of thick, black mud, but it was enough. She slid into the mud and coated her sarkikos with it. Blessed relief, but no water to quench her thirst. Lise and Eteena and their troops followed Leenha into the river mud, burrowing in as deep as they could to escape the ravaging heat.

A little farther down river, Leenha saw Skia Skotos imitate the Turqosi, rolling his new sarkikos in the black mud until he looked more like his true form than a Jacinthi. With all her troops accounted for, Leenha burrowed her face into the mud. All she could do now was wait out the terrible heat and hope some of her army survived.

CHAPTER FIFTY

The Chrysoli

Kola felt an odd sense of reexperiencing as he rushed to and fro, ordering his pride to shelter in buildings with underground storage areas where they could escape the horrible heat and blinding light. It was just like earlier when the fires burned the sky. Kwania would explain this phenomenon to him if she were here. But she wasn't, and he was on his own. She warned him the sky light was going to explode. Was this the end?

He could tell the heat was taking its toll on him. Just before he made it to his quarters, a few Jacinthi flyers dove through the shattered dome into the compound.

"Help! Help us!" He could barely hear their feeble cries. He knew if he tried to make it to them and back again, he would likely faint and perhaps die from the heat, so he roared to give them a sound to follow. "This way!" He felt like he called to them through a mouthful of Beryli sand.

The Jacinthi staggered across the compound toward him. A beat later, two more flew in, but they collapsed upon landing. He had no choice—he would have to try to get to them. "Help me get your friends," he called to the approaching Jacinthi, who were quickly fading, but despite their condition, they turned to go to the new arrivals.

The blazing light obliterated Kola's field of vision. All he could do was stumble in their general direction and hope he ran into them. Before he reached them, however, the Jacinthi got to him. He could just make out they carried their friends, so he turned and led them back

367

toward his quarters. When one collapsed, he picked up their load, and another Jacinthi helped the one who fell. Through the haze in his brain, Kola couldn't help but wonder how these noble, caring creatures had fallen in with such a horrible entity as Ogima or Skia Skotos or whatever his name was.

He dragged himself and the Jacinthi hanging over his back up the steps and slung open the double doors. Heaving his burden into the entrance hall, he gave a cursory glance across the compound to see if any Chrysoli remained, while the rest of the Jacinthi stumbled through the doors. Everything looked like a bleached blanket. He couldn't detect any movement, so he stepped in and closed the doors behind him.

The darkness in the entrance hall was complete, but he realized it was only because his eyes had adjusted to the brilliant light outside. "From blindness to blindness."

"Thank you," one of the Jacinthi wheezed.

"We must get below ground, or the heat will overtake us. Follow me."

"Others are coming. If they make it."

"What others?"

"Jacinthi. Jasperi..."

Kola shook his head. "At this point, I can't do anything for them. They'll have to find their own way to shelter."

He led them down a series of stairs, a Jacinthi leaning on each shoulder. In the basement darkness, the cool air was a salve to his burning lungs.

"Do you have water?" one of the Jacinthi asked.

"I'm afraid our water supplies are gone."

"Then we cannot remain here," the Jacinthi said.

"Not long, no. Hopefully, this is just a passing event, like the flames in the sky. Otherwise, I fear we've no hope."

"So, we wait?"

"I don't know what else to do."

The Jacinthi spread across the cool floor of the basement, lying on their backs with their wings unfurled to soothe their blistered flesh.

Kola sat at the door listening in case a Chrysoli or some other creature sought refuge. In his mind, he wrestled with the impossibility of their situation. The combination of burning heat and no water meant zero chance of survival. Even if the sky light retreated again, how would he provide water and food for all his pride plus these strays from Skia Skotos' army? Where could he take them on a destroyed world that would be any better than where they were now?

Kindred and her beast were taking the others to the high mountain. Would there be water there after this terrible blast of heat? Did they have food? And how would the Chrysoli survive the trip across the plains and hills, already weakened and without any resources? Everything in him wanted to just lie down, give up, and wait to die, but he was the pride leader, and all were relying on him for answers.

He had none.

CHAPTER FIFTY-ONE

The Emraldi

Aleshanee faltered under the weight of the sphere. The heat baked her pale skin until it was blistering, and she could barely see the creature next to her for the blazing light. Her wings felt like wet rags draped on her back, but the moisture didn't relieve the burning in her sarkikos. "I—I can't..."

"We—must—keep—going," Chevei puffed.

Aleshanee felt like she was seeing everything through an Emraldi wing or a thick, early morning fog in the valley. The ringing in her ears chased her thoughts away like a startled flock of estrildids. "I'm burning up."

"We all are." Amadah lowered her head against the howling, scorching wind. "We're almost there. We can make it."

"Maybe—we should—find—shelter." Kilchi's panting sounded like claws scraping across glass.

"We can't stop. Must reach the mountain."

"Cannot breathe. So hot the air." Misa groaned.

"We—have to—take cover. Now!" Kilchi growled.

"No! Too long—taking too long," Amadah objected.

"Ama..." Enla wheezed and groaned, then collapsed, and the sphere toppled from their grasp.

"Enla!" Amadah knelt beside the Onyxi. "Her fur is soaked."

Misa slumped to the ground beside her. "Not able."

Kilchi leaned down to check Misa. "She's in trouble. Her breathing is labored. Amadah, we can't stay out in this heat."

371

"Living water." Aleshanee fumbled with the pack on Enla's back.

"No, no, we can't spare it. We may need it on the mountain."

"Fruit."

"It's our last piece!"

"We cannot just sit out here and get baked like bread in an oven." Chevei tried flapping his wings over Enla but all he succeeded in doing was adding to the hot wind.

"Enla, Misa, and Aleshanee are down. We need to find a cave, roll the sphere in there, and wait this out," Kilchi argued.

"We can't afford to wait," Amadah yelled back. "The sphere..."

"What do you propose, then?" Kilchi stood protectively over Misa.

"The mountain is so close. We must press on."

"And what, leave them behind?"

"Stop it!" Aleshanee cried. "Stop—arguing." She thought she heard a sound like whispers on the wind. "Listen."

"Common sense says..."

"Quiet!" Amadah interrupted Chevei. Chevei bristled but snapped shut his beak. "Listen."

"Where is love now?" Chariti whispered. "Where is gentleness? Where is kindness? Where is faithfulness?"

"Remember what brought you this far," Cla'ro added.

"Is it fear that determines your responses, or will you allow love to guide you? One drowns out the other. You cannot listen to both," Chariti whispered.

"Yes, you may try to press on and leave behind those who cannot continue. Or you can look to the needs of your friends. Which do you choose?" Elegosi asked.

"I'm not leaving anyone behind!" Kilchi barked. "If you and Chevei want to try to carry that sphere to the mountain on your own, I wish you the best. I'm going to find us shelter." With Misa draped over his back, Kilchi labored to the base of the hill and sniffed along the edge until he howled, "Over here!"

"Chevei, help me carry Enla." Amadah blew out a deep breath. "Aleshanee, can you make it on your own?"

"Don't know."

"I can manage Enla. You help Aleshanee," Chevei said.

Amadah hefted Aleshanee like cradling a baby, and the battered foursome dragged themselves to the cave entrance that Kilchi discovered. He had already carried Misa out of sight, deep into the darkness. The cave wound down under the hill, perfect for escaping the terrific heat. Soon, Aleshanee saw they had reached an open chamber in the heart of the cave. Luxor was settled near the roof of the chamber with her sword drawn to give the group a little light.

"Let's go get the sphere." Kilchi grabbed Chevei, and the two disappeared back through the tunnel, returning several beats later to roll the sphere into the chamber.

Once everyone was settled and the sphere positioned safely in the center of the chamber, Kilchi looked at Amadah. "You know we're not going anywhere without some way to recover. We at least need to give those suffering a sip of the water."

Amadah sighed. "I guess it doesn't matter now." She pulled the last container from Enla's pack. She dribbled some water into Aleshanee's mouth, then shared the water with Misa and Enla.

"Better," Misa breathed a sigh of relief.

"Still, you need to rest," Kilchi insisted. "Come with me."

Everyone fell into a tense silence. The sphere rested, dormant, next to Aleshanee. Kilchi and Misa settled in a far corner and whispered, holding each other close. Enla slouched over her bowed legs, fingering pebbles. Chevei paced back and forth along the back wall. And Amadah, her eyes closed as if sleeping, leaned against the side wall of the cave, with only the occasional deep sigh letting her fellow travelers know she was still with them.

After what seemed like endless beats of waiting, Enla rolled up on her haunches and stood in her Onyxi way, then lumbered up the incline toward the cave mouth. Several beats later, she returned. "Still burning hot," was all she said.

Aleshanee, feeling much better, fidgeted and squirmed at the delay. She was excruciatingly aware of how long they'd been languishing in the cave. Amadah was right. They had limited beats to get to the mountain, carry the sphere to the top, and place it on the stone altar to open the portal to the First World. And once the sky light exploded, the portal would be forever closed. Aleshanee grunted. "We can't just sit in here forever. What if the sky light has already exploded and everything just gets worse and worse from here on?"

"We're already too late." Amadah's voice was flat and dead, devoid of hope.

Aleshanee tilted her head. "But I don't think our friends would be so serene if this was just a place for us to curl up and die."

Enla wrung her paws. "Kindred and the others are waiting on us at the high mountain. They can't survive out in this heat either. Are we too late?"

Aleshanee shook her head. "I won't believe it. I can't. Kindred will protect them and lead them through the caves to the top, like Nikani was going to do for us. We'll have to find a way, too."

"If we can ever make it there." Enla groaned.

"Unless my senses are really off, it should be near sky fall," Kilchi said.

"Maybe sky fall will bring relief from the heat."

Enla shrugged. "It was still full-on bright when I was up there. I'll go check again." In a few beats, Aleshanee heard her voice, faint but clear. "I think it might be getting a little better."

Aleshanee was up like a shot. "Let's go!"

Chevei, Kilchi, and Misa moved to the sphere, but Amadah's eyes remained closed, and she didn't move from the wall. "Come on, Amadah."

"What's the point?"

"Enla said things were a bit better."

"We'll drag the sphere all the way up there and kill ourselves trying to make it, just to fail. It was over when you collapsed."

Aleshanee vacillated between hurt feelings and exasperation. "You act like I did that on purpose. And by the way, since when are you so fatalistic? You've always charged ahead, no matter the consequences."

"And look where it's gotten us."

"What do you mean? We're almost to the high mountain. We're so close to finishing our task now."

"Fala, Yiska, Nikani—the Beryli—even Sani and Kai and Alatha and Alana. All dead." Amadah moaned. "I once had a friend like your friend, a good friend, and even she died trying to save me. Your friend told me Kitisi was her name. And, of course, Kindra, if you can count her since she came back to us—but she isn't the same little Kindra I knew and loved. All of them are gone."

"My entire *clan* is gone, Amadah."

"Mine, too," Kilchi echoed.

"I always wondered why I was saved, why my friend spoke to me and warned me to leave Emraldi lands, but the other Emraldi weren't told what was coming for them. Why me? Why us? Then, I realized it was foolish to think such things and ask such questions. The answer to every why question is because, as Genesee used to say."

Amadah pushed off the wall and stormed to the sphere. "Fine. I'll stop being 'foolish.'"

"I'm just saying it isn't your fault they're dead, any more than it was my fault I collapsed."

"Oh, really? All my decisions led to where we are right now. If only I could go back, I would do so many things differently."

"If wishes made changes, we'd ne'er say goodbye. Genesee said that, too."

"What does that even mean?"

Aleshanee's heart was wrenching. Her friend was in pain, and everything she said seemed to make it worse. She reached out and caressed Amadah's back. "I'm only trying to help."

"Stop helping!" Amadah cried. She gasped out a sob and ground her fists in her eyes.

"Emotionality serves no purpose. Compose yourself," Chevei snapped.

375

"What's going on?" Enla asked, returning from her scouting expedition.

"Frayed are everyone's nerve endings, I fear." Misa sighed.

"We're hungry and exhausted and under a lot of pressure," Kilchi agreed.

"Come on, guys! We've been through worse things than this." Enla reached out her paws. "We've faced impossible odds and come through it."

Amadah closed her eyes, breathed out, and nodded.

Aleshanee gave a slight smile to Enla. She was right. This group had defied the impossible and survived. Why were they falling apart now? Realization dawned. "Dark ones!"

"What?"

"Dark ones must be here! That's why we're struggling so much."

"No, dear one. The dark ones are tending to their lord," Cla'ro said. "You struggle because you forget who you are."

"What have we forgotten?" Enla asked.

"Hope. Faith. Joy. Love. Peace. Remember?"

"We are not alone." Amadah closed her eyes. "I remember."

"We must stand together." Aleshanee smiled. "I remember, too."

Deep within the sphere a subtle glow blossomed. "Very well. Gather the sphere and be on your way once more. The road is difficult, and the cycle is drawing to a close, but stand firm." Aleshanee felt Cla'ro's gentle hand on her shoulder. "You are not alone."

CHAPTER FIFTY-TWO

The Chrysoli

Kola peeked his head around the huge double door of the great hall. The blinding light seemed to have withdrawn, along with the boiling heat. The air was still and heavy, and the heat was oppressive but not scalding, so he ventured down the steps and wandered across the compound, knocking on doors and calling out to the Chrysoli within that it was finally safe to come out. Here and there, a Chrysoli or two would meander onto the open area, but many remained indoors, fearing a return of the horrible heat.

He felt he needed to call a pride meeting, even though he had little hope and no answers to offer them. Still, the pride needed to know where they stood. Decisions had to be made.

He was startled by a pounding on the dome entrance. When he hesitated to answer, the pounding came again, rattling the shaky dome walls. A muffled voice cried, "Open for us!"

Were these the stragglers the Jacinthi told him were on the way? How had they survived the scorching heat? He hurried to open the door and found a filthy, blackened Angeni standing on the other side. Behind her, scores of muddied Turqosi, some bedraggled Chalcedi, and a few Jacinthi stood in straight lines like warriors prepared for battle. Were they still seeking to conquer the Chrysoli, or did they come with another agenda? It didn't matter, Kola realized. His pride was ill-equipped to fight anyone, no matter how ragged the attackers were. "What do you want?"

"I have come to say you no longer need to fear Skia Skotos. The Jacinthi and I are leading these Turqosi and Chalcedi back to my mountain, where we have food and water and safety—everything we need to survive. You and your kind are invited to come with us if you desire."

"Your numbers are depleted. Jasperi accompanied you but now I see none. What happened to the rest of your group?"

Angeni lowered her eyes. "I fear they did not survive the terrible heat."

Kola's eyes narrowed. "Why the sudden change in attitude? Not too long ago, you were threatening to destroy us."

"I apologize for my earlier behavior. Skia Skotos promised to fulfill my prophecy of all creatures living in unity on the high mountain, and I was willing to follow his lead and example to reach my goal. Now I see my error. The prophecy cannot be fulfilled by force or through fear. Hear the words from the ancient texts."

A weak and disheveled Kacina shuffled forward, unfolded some pages, and in a croaking voice read, "Send me your light and lead me; bring me to your high mountain, to the place where you dwell. I will go to the altar of my delight."

"Do you see? I am the one. I will lead every creature to the high mountain, and we will live for our own pleasure. Whatever we want, we will have. My prophecy will be fulfilled at the altar of delight."

Was this the answer Kola needed? Water, food, anything they wanted or needed given freely—still, he was unsettled. "What's the catch?"

"There is no catch. This was the promise given to me from the first—all creatures of all species living together in harmony and unity on the high mountain. You may ask the Jacinthi. They will tell you I spoke to them of this prophecy before the light fell from the sky and the horrible disasters befell us. I had them collect and store food ahead of any trouble." Angeni chuckled. "They thought I had lost my senses. They do not believe so now."

"And you're saying you're willing to share this food and water with us. Nothing demanded of us?"

"Of course not." Angeni offered an open-beaked smile, which looked strangely incongruous amid the caked mud streaking her face. "We would love for you to join us."

"What about the other group? Will they join us there?"

Angeni's smile faltered for a beat, then she broadened her smile. "Of course, of course. All are welcome."

"I will need to pose your invitation to the pride."

"May we enter your compound and rest while you have your meeting? Some of our group suffered greatly during the terrible heat."

Kola paused. Letting them in meant he was accepting their veracity. Did he believe them? He wanted to, but the unsettled feeling wouldn't leave him. Kwania's voice came back to him. *"What kind of creature are you?"* Her accusation still stung. He was not going to be the kind of creature who left the injured outside, vulnerable and uncared for—not again. "You may enter and come to the medichi for treatment and rest."

"How kind. Thank you for your generosity. We accept."

Kola led the tattered group across the compound to the science building. The Chrysoli walking outside stopped and stared at the troupe dragging themselves along, many of them drawing back in fear when they recognized who was entering. "Go through there. One of the medichi will tend to you."

"Again, many thanks for your kindness."

Kola gestured for one of his attendants to sound the call for a pride meeting. The clanging bell brought all Chrysoli onto the open area in the center of the compound. Kola stood on the platform under the bell pole. "Chrysoli, I come before you to report on our status. I won't lie to you—our situation is dire. We currently have no food stores remaining, and no water. Our wells have run dry, and reports are the water beyond Chrysoli lands has dried up. So, retrieving water back to the compound is impossible. Growing food is impossible. Our options are limited."

"What are you going to do about it?"

"An opportunity has presented itself to us. The group once led by Skia Skotos has returned..."

"And you let them enter the compound!" one of the Chrysoli cried.

"I did but let me explain. Skia Skotos no longer leads the group. The Jacinthi, Angeni, now leads the group. She explained she has long believed all creatures would come to the Jacinthi mountain and live together in harmony and unity. She claims she followed Skia Skotos to fulfill that vision, but now she sees he wasn't trustworthy. So, she and the rest of his armies are walking now to the mountain. They invited us to go with them. Angeni claims they have food and water at the mountain, which they offer to share freely."

The Chrysoli murmured amongst themselves. Some voices sounded angry to Kola, others encouraged and hopeful, so he couldn't tell how the discussion was going.

"Do you believe this Jacinthi?" someone asked.

"I—I have no choice. I do believe this is our only hope of survival."

"But to leave our land..."

"I know. Believe me, when they first came to our doors, I turned them down cold. I refused to give up our inheritance and abandon our ancestors. But now—I'm afraid we have no other choice."

"We could go to the burial plains."

"We could. But that would mean the end of the Chrysoli species. Are you prepared to make the decision to bring our kind to an end? I am not."

"How will we survive the journey? It's so far, and in this heat with no water..."

Kola nodded. "It would be difficult. Some might not make it. But I have decided we must take the risk and go to the mountain with them. Gather what things you can carry on your backs. Take only necessities. We will leave as the sky light falls and travel in darkness, hoping it relieves the heat. Any questions?"

The Chrysoli dispersed, and Kola made his way back to the science building. He found Angeni, who had cleaned her feathers as best she could without water, and donned a plain, white shift in place of her heavy scarlet robes. "The Chrysoli will accompany you to the mountain. We are preparing to leave. Our plan is to leave at sky fall and travel in darkness. Is this acceptable?" Kola chafed at asking Angeni's opinion instead of ordering her to leave with them, but circumstances left him little choice but to cooperate with this group.

"I believe we will be ready to leave at sky fall. We rejoice at your decision to join us."

One side of Kola's mouth turned up. "Very well. We will meet at the dome entrance at sky fall."

Was he making the right decision? Starving to death didn't seem like an acceptable option, but Chrysoli existing under the rule of another species was also untenable. What would they face when they reached the high mountain? And what of Kwania and the other group who walked with the white beast and its rider? Would they welcome them or fight them? Kola knew in his heart he would never fight Kwania. She had always been true, while this Angeni had changed her face and her allegiances more than once. If it came down to choosing a side, he would lead his pride to join Kwania. He just hoped it wouldn't come to such a choice.

CHAPTER FIFTY-THREE

The Turqosi

Leenha gestured for her armies to establish two lines on either side of the Chrysoli pride as they marched across the plains and into the valley leading to the Jacinthi mountain. Angeni walked at the head of the pack, holding a flaming torch aloft so all could see her and follow. As they walked, Leenha contemplated Skia Skotos' endgame. At what point would he reveal his presence to the Chrysoli? How was he planning to deal with that fire-breathing beast and its powerful rider? If they could bring her down, the rest of the group would cave like a rotten koloochee fruit. But Leenha was having her doubts about Skia Skotos' ability to defeat this creature and its light rider. Their powers might exceed his own.

In case Skia Skotos was about to fall, Leenha needed a way to convincingly change sides at the right moment. She could make a deal behind his back if she got the opportunity. She decided she would need to find a way to make it happen, perhaps through Kola, the Chrysoli leader, who seemed none too happy to be acquiescing to Angeni. She remembered Kola had an in with the beast rider's group, a Jacinthi who used to be friends with Angeni. Was that Skia Skotos' plan? To convince the Jacinthi, Kwania, that her friend, Angeni, had returned? Would Kwania fall for it as Kola had?

Leenha didn't like to be in the dark. She was used to her own manipulations running things from behind the scenes, not following blindly behind someone else, not knowing what they were doing and hoping their tricks would work. She needed to find a way to get back in control.

She sidled up to Kola, who marched behind Angeni. "Worried?"

Kola shot her a sideways glance but didn't reply. So, he wasn't one to forget past slights. Still, if it came to it and it meant death or survival, she was sure he would answer her then.

Leenha waved Lise over. "Scout ahead. Report."

Lise nodded, slithered outside Angeni's circle of fire, and was gone.

The Chalcedi, Cholena, could be someone else she could manipulate. Cholena had been willing to work with her before. If she thought Leenha was opposing Skia Skotos, as she once did, maybe Cholena would ease Leenha and her armies into the fold.

To Leenha's dismay, Angeni/Skia Skotos kept stopping the march. Either she was wanting to rest the troops before battle, or she was synchronizing their arrival at the mountain with the rising of the sky light. Leenha would definitely want to arrive in darkness, perhaps even catch her enemy unawares, so she couldn't fathom this strategy. Or perhaps Skia Skotos had no strategy beyond trusting his magic. Leenha definitely needed a back-up plan.

They were on another rest when Lise scuttled up to Leenha. Her hand motions said their enemy had one guard before the mountain, but no sign of the rest of the group, including the beast and rider.

"Where hiding?"

Lise shrugged. She swiped her eyes, indicating she hadn't seen any sign of them, so Leenha sent her back to her place leading the left column.

How could they hide that massive beast? Was it some magic spell? Could the beast and its rider disappear and reappear at will, like it had appeared from the sky during the fight on the plains? Her cowl fluttered, and she felt her chest tighten.

Angeni stood, extinguished the torch, and waved the armies forward. As they resumed the march and drew within sight of the mountain, Leenha became convinced she was on the wrong side of this confrontation. Now she just had to figure out how to make the switch without getting herself killed.

Chapter Fifty-Four

The Chalcedi

Cholena perched on the branch of a dead tree protruding from the face of the mountain, standing guard over the cave mouth where her friends were resting. Blessedly, the blistering heat had lessened with the setting sky light, although it was still unnaturally hot. Kindred was tending those who suffered from the heat, including Kwania. Cholena had helped Seri carry their friend into the cave when she collapsed, but when Cholena came back out for guard duty, Kwania was still unconscious.

Sewati came out from the cave. "Rest."

Cholena nodded and slipped from her perch. "How is Kwania?"

"Awake."

"Is she well?"

Sewati shrugged. "All weak from heat. Bad cycle for weakness."

"You're right about that."

"Rest before sky light returns heat."

"I will." Cholena started to go to the entrance when she heard Sewati suck in air. "What is it?"

He pointed. "Look far."

"I can't see anything."

"Movement. Someone coming."

"Can you make out who it is?"

"Too dark."

"Hmmm. Maybe you should go inform Kindred."

Sewati scurried back into the cave, leaving Cholena squinting into the distant valley, trying to catch any sign of movement.

As the edge of the sky light crested the horizon, Kindred came out of the cave with Sewati and Kwania and stood looking across the valley. Sewati pointed. Despite the shimmering film in the air, Cholena thought she could make out a distant, shapeless mass moving slowly toward them.

Kindred's mouth set in a grim line. "So it begins."

CHAPTER FIFTY-FIVE

The Jasperi

Amadah peeked around the rock outcropping where she and her friends crouched around the sphere. "It looks like the Chrysoli are with Skia Skotos' Chalcedi and Turqosi." She looked at her friends. "There's a lot of them. We've got to hurry."

"Can we beat them to the mountain?" Aleshanee asked.

"I think so. Let's go." They lifted the sphere and picked their way through fallen rocks and scree, using the slough from the rockfall as cover. The going was slow—too slow for Amadah's liking—but they had to remain out of sight or risk an attack by the Chalcedi.

"I think I see Kindred. At the base of the mountain." Enla pointed toward a tiny shimmer of white against the dark backdrop of the mountain.

Amadah breathed a sigh. "They made it, then." She smiled.

"Yes, that's Kindred. Kwania and Cholena are with her. Oh, and your Topazi friend."

"Look, more are coming out to join them," Aleshanee said.

"Seeing my kind, and my Papa."

"I don't see Kindred's beast, though," Kilchi said.

"They have fewer numbers." Chevei sighed. "They cannot stand against the Jacinthi, Turqosi, Chalcedi, and Chrysoli."

"Yes, but they have Kindred!" Aleshanee always managed to look to the positive. Amadah wasn't so confident.

389

"We can't risk letting Kindred know where we are because Skia Skotos could spot us, too. We'll have to get closer to signal her." Amadah gestured ahead. "Kilchi, do you think we can make it over that rise without being seen and cut the corner to get closer to Kindred?"

Kilchi raised his head and followed where Amadah pointed. "It's a tough climb."

"We can't be spotted."

"If we stay on the back side of the rise, we should stay out of the direct line of sight of the armies. They'd have to be looking directly at us to see us."

"Let's risk it. What do you say?"

Everyone nodded their agreement, so the group angled toward Kindred and started the steep climb up the hill. The going was rough, as Kilchi said. The footing was poor, with loose gravel sliding under their feet with every step, and huge piles of boulders barring their way every few metrics. When they neared the crest, where the greatest risk of detection faced them, they were breathless and exhausted. Still, no one asked to rest. Their friends were in sight.

Amadah saw Kindred direct her meager band onto the valley floor. Unlike Skia Skotos' armies, who marched in lines, Kindred had her followers form in a semicircle. She stood in the center.

"Listen!" Aleshanee whispered. Wafting on the hot breeze, Amadah could hear faint voices raised in song. "They're singing."

Amadah looked at Aleshanee. "Like before." Aleshanee nodded, her eyes doleful. "I think Kindred is trying to buy us some beats to get to the mountain. She must know we're close."

Chevei cleared his throat. "The temperature is rising quickly. It would be prudent to hurry."

If they made it down the back side of the rise, they would be near the base of the mountain. So close. Gripping the sphere, they half-slid, half-fell down the slope, and as they neared the bottom, they jumped down and scrambled the last few metrics to the mountain's base.

"Now what?" Kilchi asked.

"Now, we find our way through tunnels to the top of the mountain."

"But which tunnel? Where do we go in?"

"I have no idea."

Then, they heard Na'ro singing:

> "Strengthen your feeble hands;
> Steady your knees that give way;
> Say to your desperate hearts,
> 'Be strong, do not fear.
> The Great Love is here."

Proclaimer took up the song:

> "With a word, blind eyes will open,
> Deaf ears will hear,
> The weak will run and not grow weary,
> The broken will walk and not faint,
> And those without voice shall shout for joy.
> Water will gush forth in the wilderness,
> Streams will flow in the desert,
> And you will find your way.
> It will be called the Way of Holiness
> And it will be for the ones who walk on it.
> The unclean may not walk on it,
> Nor the wicked or the fools.
> Only those redeemed by the Great Love
> May journey on the Way."

A'ro cried:

> "See, the Great Love is here!
> We will not keep silent
> Till her vindication shines like the dawn.
> No longer will you be deserted and desolate.
> Because the Forever delights in you,
> You will be called Beloved."

Then, Veritor's strong voice resounded:
> "Pass through, pass through the stone,
> Walk up, Walk up the Way;
> Remove the barrier stones
> And raise a banner for all creatures.
> You will enter with singing;
> Joy will be your crown.
> Your path will be made straight
> And the glory of the Forever will be revealed,
> For the Forever has spoken it."

Amadah's chest felt full and rich, as if she had drunk warm milk thickened with honey. She thought, if it was required, she could lift the sphere with one hand. "I know what to do. We walk straight toward Kindred and join her in song, and the Way she has already made for us will be revealed."

"Our friends will sing with us, and the song will shake the foundations of the mountain!" Aleshanee cried.

Chevei clicked his beak. "Skia Skotos will surely see us."

"I don't think that matters anymore. You heard the song—only those redeemed by the Great Love can journey on the Way."

"Joyful is my heart, filled with hope. Make it we will, and save all," Misa exclaimed.

"What are we waiting for? Let's go!" Kilchi loped toward the field, no longer fearful of being discovered.

Enla started singing. "Rejoice! Rejoice! The Great Love is here!"

Aleshanee joined in. "We will be glad and rejoice in you. We will sing your praises."

Amadah's voice rang out. "Our enemies claimed, 'We have defeated them.' They shouted, 'They are overcome!' But we trust in your unfailing Love and rejoice in your salvation. For you are good and your Love is forever within us."

Kilchi chimed in. "We will be glad and rejoice in the mighty victory you bring. Your strength is our shield."

"Abundant are the good things you have stored up for us; in the shelter of your presence we hide," Misa sang.

Even Chevei took a turn. "You saw our affliction and knew our anguish, and you answered us and delivered us from the enemy's hands. You are the rock of unfailing Love."

The whole group picked up Chevei's refrain as they marched openly across the valley. "You are the rock of unfailing Love. You are the rock of unfailing Love."

Amadah saw Angeni rise into the air. Sparks shot from her fingers, the ends of her wings, and her eyes, creating a whirl of blue-white fire encircling her. She spread her wings and bellowed something unintelligible, and the Turqosi spread out.

"Prepare the attack!" Angeni cried.

"Wait! I thought..." Amadah heard Kola shout.

In response to Angeni's command, the Turqosi marched forward and took protective positions in two columns before Angeni, and the Chalcedi took to the air over them.

Kindred strode forward. "I see you, Nameless One. You cannot hide from me!" A stream of brilliant light coursed from her lifted hand and hit Angeni in the chest, and the mask that used to be Angeni's face melted, revealing the hideous, deformed visage of Skia Skotos.

"No!" Kola roared. "Chrysoli, with me!" He bounded straight toward Kindred, with the Chrysoli pride on his heels. Amadah tensed. Was he attacking?

Amadah saw Nadie and Hanai followed the Chrysoli, flying low to avoid the circling Chalcedi. Where were the other Jacinthi? The Jasperi? She couldn't find them in the chaos.

Kwania ran to stand in front of Kindred, waving her arms. "Kola! Stop!"

"No! We join you!"

"Come." Kindred's voice was like a quiet stream.

Kwania met Kola with a warm embrace, and he and the Chrysoli joined the circle. Then, Nadie and Hanai landed, and Meda ran forward and clasped Nadie's hands. Their song grew louder, stronger.

"Surround them!" Angeni screeched.

The Turqosi flooded up to surround the circle of Kindred's followers, but Kindred made no move to stop them. Instead, she turned to Amadah. "Shout for joy. Bring forth the water from the stone."

Amadah had to pry her eyes off the scene unfolding in the valley. She couldn't afford to think about what was happening to her friends there—all that mattered was the sphere. She remembered Proclaimer's song and realized it was coming to pass. The eyes of the blind were opened and the deaf could hear—Kola and the Chrysoli and Nadie and Hanai finally saw Skia Skotos for who he was. Now, she had to trust her friends, much weaker and fewer in numbers, would be able to stand against the attacking force. What was next? The water in the wilderness! "Shout, everyone. Shout for joy at the top of your lungs!"

Enla and Kilchi threw their heads back and howled. Misa closed her eyes and cooed like the Saphiri sang underwater, and the sound vibrated off the mountain's face. Chevei hooted and cawed, while Aleshanee belted her song of praise. Feeling the well of emotion rising from her gut, Amadah opened her mouth. To her, it felt like the music came from somewhere else, as if the entire Whisperers' choir joined their voices to hers. Her song gushed out to combine with the cacophony, and the air reverberated with their symphony.

From high on the side of the mountain, an avalanche of stones rained down with a booming crash, then an effluence of water burst from the mountainside, creating a waterfall down the face of the mountain. "Everyone, go to the water! That's the Way."

"This way!" Luxor called, pointing her sword toward the waterfall. They ran to the mountain, splashing through refreshing pools of water that flowed out onto the valley. Just as Proclaimer predicted, they saw an opening to a tunnel behind the pounding water.

"The Way of Holiness!" Amadah cried. Without a moment's pause, Misa led them straight through the streaming waterfall and into the cave.

Chapter Fifty-Six

The Jacinthi

Kwania gripped Kola's paw as if she was keeping him from escaping back to Skia Skotos, but in reality, she was afraid of the Turqosi and Chalcedi surrounding them and needed his strength. So many of them. How could they possibly win? She saw Kindred turn, so she swung around and saw Amadah and Aleshanee and the others disappear into the new waterfall with the sphere. Kwania heard Kindred release a deep exhale.

"Make for the waterfall! Stop them!" Skia Skotos had obviously seen the sphere, but his command came too late.

Kindred raised her hands high. "You cannot follow them on this path. The Way is blocked to you."

"I will destroy you all, then nothing will stand between me and the oculus. I will be there before them and stop them from placing the sphere, and you will be powerless to stop me."

Kindred stared impassively at the ranting entity flying over the armies, with the face of Skia Skotos and the sarkikos of a defiled Jacinthi. "Do your best, beast of the darkness."

As Skia Skotos lifted his arms above him, collecting balls of sizzling sparks in his hands, Kwania heard a deafening roar from above and behind her. She turned, and there, rising from the mountaintop, was Kindred's white beast. It soared high over Skia Skotos, circled his armies, then landed next to Kindred. She whispered to the beast, and it

397

took to the air. Skia Skotos hurled the swirling projectiles slicing through the air toward Kindred, but the beast dove and deflected the bolts, which carved into the ground near Kwania's feet. Her skin prickled from their charged dance through the dirt.

Leenha directed the Turqosi to rush the waterfall. The white beast drew a sonorous inhale, then opened his mouth and blasted a wall of fire down on Skia Skotos' armies. The screams of the Turqosi as their skin burned was nauseating, and Kwania had to turn her eyes from the tableau to keep from vomiting. Another jet of flames from the white beast, and more Turqosi burned. Their high-pitched squeals cut through the air like Skia Skotos' sparks as they ran to and fro, flailing their arms, trying to escape the fires consuming them.

One stumbled blindly into the circle near Kwania. She recognized this Turqosi as their leader, the one who stood beside Skia Skotos at the Chrysoli dome entrance. Her burning cowl made a halo of fire around her bulging eyes. "Too late. Too late." The Turqosi collapsed in spasms beside Kwania. The stench was horrific. Kwania jerked her head away from the sight.

At a command from Skia Skotos, Chalcedi flyers rushed the white beast, attacking from all sides, but the beast whipped its horns through the air and cleaved their sarkikos in two. Its tail grasped a Chalcedi, crushing it like a constricting serpentus and flinging it to the ground, where it landed with a sickening thud. Slicing with its claws, the beast decapitated two more Chalcedi before the rest of them retreated, deaf to Skia Skotos' commands to keep attacking. But the retreat did little good, for the white beast pursued them, spurting fire until every Chalcedi was aflame.

Kola howled hysterically; his crazed eyes bugged out with fear. The fall of the beast's fierce wrath was ghastly to behold. Kwania could only gape in horror at the scene. Death was everywhere she looked.

Somewhere in the deep recesses of her mind, she realized Kindred was talking to her. She blinked and shook her head. "Wha...?"

"Take the others to the tunnel behind the waterfall. Hurry! Go now!"

Kwania shivered and tried to fluff out her feathers to awaken her senses, but her world was moving like it was stuck in sap oozing from a tree trunk, and she was no longer a part of herself. She stared at her hand as if she were outside her sarkikos watching someone else, then she looked blankly at Kindred.

"Go!" Kindred shouted to waken her from her shock.

Once Kwania started to move, she felt like she was back in her sarkikos again. "Follow me. Come, everyone. This way. Hurry!" She pulled Kola's paw, still clutched in her hand.

"Chrysoli, with me," he roared.

They raced across the valley toward the mountain, with the Topazi and the other slaves and the Chrysoli in tow. When they reached the waterfall, she stood to one side, Kola to the other, and guided their group one by one into the tunnel. Kola was the last to duck through the water, but Kwania remained before the waterfall, mesmerized by what she saw unfolding.

Skia Skotos was writhing in the air, spewing sparks in every direction in his anger. Blackened Chalcedi and Turqosi and Jacinthi dotted the valley. The white beast circled the scene, spewing occasional bursts of fire—Kwania imagined it was checking for living creatures—then landed beside Kindred.

"Beast of the darkness, Nameless One, come and face me. Your followers are destroyed, and the field is leveled. Now, this is between you and me."

As Kindred walked toward Skia Skotos, the white beast beat its massive wings to rise into the air, breathed in again, then blasted fire straight down into the ground. At first, nothing much happened, then Kwania gasped as the dirt became molten. The lava-like pool spread and deepened as the beast continued to pour fire into the ground.

"Come meet me on this hallowed ground, enemy of all that is good. Or will you flee, now that you do not have other creatures to hide behind?"

"Wretched child," Skia Skotos bellowed. "This cycle you will die!"

Kwania's eyes widened as, from the air around the dark lord, deformed, hideous looking creatures appeared. They were pitch black, so much so their thick, wrinkled skins had an almost bluish cast. Their eyes glowed red; their claws were warped like broken limbs, their wings stick-like and tattered along the edges. Were these the Dark Ones her friends had described? How was she seeing them?

In a blaze of light, other entities filled the air above Kindred. They were as bright white as the Dark Ones were black, and glorious to behold, although not delicate in their beauty—more resplendent than pretty, like the majestic beauty of the sky light from cycles past, before it became misshapen like the Dark Ones. The Light Ones numbered at least twenty, almost double the number of Skia Skotos' forces.

"This fight is between us, Phaini. Send your minions away."

"Ha!" Skia Skotos cackled. "And leave myself open to an overwhelming force with no defense? You must think me a fool."

"I do, in fact, but a pitiable one. Come down and face me. Let us have it over."

"Attack!" Skia Skotos screeched, and the Dark Ones dove onto the gleaming swords of Kindred's friends. The clash of swords rang across the valley, against the dissonant sounds of sizzling bolts crashing into shields and streams of light searing flesh. The frenzied ball of fighting entities caused Kwania to shrink back toward the waterfall. Still, Kindred walked forward and called. "Face me. Do you so fear someone you call a mere child?"

"I do not fear you, cursed child. I hate you!"

"Then face me and express your rage in its fullness. Allow it to consume you once and for all."

"And why should I fight you? You would only send your beast against me like you did my armies."

"My pantheralatus has another task, as you see. You only need face me, and me alone."

Without warning, Skia Skotos dove down, claws extended, and grabbed Kindred, lifting her up into the air. He separated his claws apart as if to rip her in half, but Kindred, still as calm as a winter lake, touched his limb. Skia Skotos howled in pain and dropped her.

Kwania gasped in an icy breath as Kindred fell, but Kindred came to a stop and hung in mid-air. How was it possible? She had no wings, and her beast was far behind her.

The fire in Kindred's palms spread, climbing up her sarkikos like a vine around a tree until she was engulfed in it. "I will not toy with you, beast of the darkness. The cycle of flames is upon you." Kindred flew forward like a shot and grappled Skia Skotos. He clutched Kindred to his chest, then tried to scramble back as her fire seared his leathery flesh. Kwania could smell the vile reek from across the valley. But Kindred wouldn't release him. The fire roasted him, and he screamed and shrieked while she wrestled him closer and closer to the pit of lava the white beast was creating.

Suddenly, Skia Skotos rose out of Angeni's sarkikos, leaving Angeni burning in Kindred's arms. Kindred cast the limp sarkikos that was Angeni to the ground, then rushed the fleeing Skia Skotos and wrapped her arm around his head. He howled in agony. "Relent," she commanded. "I offer you the chance to ask forgiveness before the Forever, to return with us to the First World as one reborn. What say you, beast of the darkness?"

"I would rather die than bow again before the Forever or stand below you upon your throne. I shall never again grovel or scrape."

Kindred folded his wings around his sarkikos and embraced him in her arms. "The Forever seeks only to love you. Will you allow it?"

"Ha! The Forever seeks power over me."

401

"The Forever has never forced you to do anything or asked anything of you beyond that you accept love and share this love with others. Is it so difficult a thing, to love?"

"I am above all creatures!" Skia Skotos cawed. "I am the dread God of darkness and shadow. All creatures should bow before ME."

"Your kingdom come." Kindred sighed. She flew over the growing lake of lava. "This is your kingdom, the realm of death. Enter now and take your throne."

With those final words, Kindred hurled Skia Skotos, screeching and writhing, into the glowing red magma. As he sank, the lava flowed into his mouth, cutting short his final howl. A column of fire shot into the air out of the lake as he disappeared.

The white beast puffed a white cloud from his nostrils, and the top of the molten lake darkened and hardened to stone. Skia Skotos was no more.

Chapter Fifty-Seven

The Jasperi

Amadah scraped her back against the curving stone wall as she pulled the sphere along the tunnel, which was just wide enough for the sphere but not for the sphere's carriers. Chevei, pressed against the roof of the tunnel, tried to hold the sphere aloft in his claws while fluttering his constricted wings. Kilchi and Enla hunched side-by-side beneath the sphere, carrying it on their backs, while Misa and Aleshanee pushed it from behind. The tight space, combined with dragging the sphere up the steep incline, made for a rough journey up the mountain. Navigating sharp turns, like the one they now faced, was extremely challenging.

"Any idea how much farther?" Kilchi grunted from beneath the sphere.

Amadah groaned as she squeezed the sphere around the curve. "I've noticed the temperature is rising, so that probably means we're close to the exit. Of course, we don't know if the exit is at the top where we need to be, or if we'll have more climbing to do."

"What do you think is happening in the valley?" Enla sounded nervous. Amadah understood—she was anxious about it, too.

"We would do better to remain focused on our task instead of worrying about Kindred," Chevei said. "She seems quite capable of taking care of herself."

"Still, we care about her," Aleshanee replied. "We can't help but be concerned for her well-being."

Amadah paused before the sphere. "Another curve ahead." The group moaned in unison.

"Come on, we made it this far. We can do this!" Enla said.

"If this is the Way of Holiness, I'd hate to see the Way of Hardship!" Kilchi said. Amadah chuckled. His humor was a welcome relief from the pressure she'd felt for so long.

Metric by metric, they crept along, shifting the sphere and their positions as needed to get around the obstacles the tunnel presented. "We've got to be close now. I'm burning up." Enla wiped her paw across her brow.

Misa cleared her throat. "Becoming concerned about what we will face."

Amadah paused again, her hands on her knees. "What do you mean?"

"Having this much heat already when yet underground, not a good sign is this."

"You think the awful heat from the last sky light rising has returned?"

"Likely it has."

A grim realization gripped the group— the worst of their struggles may not be over. Amadah believed facing Skia Skotos or getting around him would be the hardest part of the journey. In her mind, the high mountain was going to be a refuge for them, a cycle for celebration and rejoicing in their victory. Of course, she had no idea what would happen when they positioned the sphere on the Jacinthi altar, but all the difficulties they faced thus far pointed to a glorious result, if the dangers and losses were worth it.

Fala's face flashed across her mind's eye. She set her mouth. "Let's try to push a little harder. If it's getting hot up there, it's only going to get worse."

They hefted and pulled, pushed and rolled, hoisted and heaved, until Kilchi called for a stop. "Phew!" He was panting so hard his chest heaved like a bucking banask as he lowered the sphere from his back. "It's worse than a Carneli heat wave in here."

"I bet we could bake Emraldi cakes on these stones." Aleshanee's breaths were shallow and rasping.

"Mmmm. I'd love a piece of cake right now," Enla murmured.

Kilchi raised his lips above his fangs. "I'd settle for a bowl of water."

Chevei fluttered down and perched next to his friends. "The next stretch appears fairly straight, but it is a sharp incline all the way. How do we want to proceed?"

"Rolling?" Kilchi suggested.

"Risky." Amadah tilted her head, one brow raised. "If it rolls back on someone..."

"Squish." Enla slapped her paws together.

"So, back to lifting it?" Kilchi threw back his head and stared at the tunnel ceiling.

"I suppose." Amadah knew everyone was near the end of their endurance, because she felt as unfocused and irritable as they seemed. When she stood, a wave of dizziness caused the edges of her vision to darken. "Hey, we need to hurry. We're getting climb-weary."

"Last leg!" Enla exclaimed. "Let's get it over." She stood, wobbled a bit on her bowed legs, then bent over, only to topple face-first onto the stone floor.

"Enla!" Aleshanee ran to her side and felt her cheek. "She's so hot. All that fur—she needs some water." She reached into the pack slung over her shoulder and pulled out the last remaining drops of their living water. "Here, Enla, take this."

Amadah bit her lower lip and frowned. She hadn't counted on them using all the living water before they even reached the top of the mountain. Everyone was reeling, not just Enla, but they didn't have enough for everyone. She decided Enla and Kilchi needed to drink the remaining drops, since they were carrying the bulk of the weight. "Divide it with Kilchi. They're going to need it the most."

"I can make it," Kilchi protested.

"We can't afford for our two strongest backs to falter. Drink the water. It isn't much but it will help."

"Getting worse as we reach the exit is likely," Misa added.

Kilchi relented and drank a few precious drops of the living water. Enla sat up as he finished his sip. "Much better now."

Kilchi dropped the empty container. "That's the last of it."

Amadah's throat tightened. They needed to hurry. Not only was it a race against the sky light's exploding, it was a race against the end of their physical endurance in the rising heat. Would they make it? Amadah felt her hope waning. "Enla, do you have some encouragement for us?"

Enla smiled. "We're so close, I can feel it. I believe at the top of this rise we'll find our exit. Then, straight to the round chamber, place the sphere in the center under the oculus, and—well, whatever happens then." She put her shoulder against the right side of the sphere.

"You heard her! Almost there." Kilchi pressed against his side of the sphere. With a quick flap of his wings, Chevei landed atop the sphere and wrapped his talons on either side, lifting as Kilchi and Enla pushed it up and onto their backs.

The exhausted troupe labored up the steep rise. Amadah felt a sharp increase in the temperature with each metric they gained. As they reached the top of the rise, Amadah called out, "I think I see light ahead!"

"You were right, Enla." Aleshanee beamed.

"Not much farther."

The tunnel flattened out, but the heat escalated dramatically. Amadah's lungs burned, so much so she tried to keep her breaths shallow. She could hear the others wheezing and gasping. "Wait! Put the sphere down."

"Gladly." Kilchi groaned and stretched his back.

"We can roll it the rest of the way. But we need to think this through. Do you see how bright the entrance is? I know it'll look brighter because we've been walking so long in semi-darkness, with only Luxor's sword as our light, but even with that, it's much brighter than normal. What will we do if we get outside and can't see?"

"I can try to navigate by smell," Kilchi offered.

"But what smell are you following? Skia Skotos lived on this mountain last, and based on what Meda and Nikani told us, the odors he left behind will be most foul. How will we make it to the altar? We won't know where we are, and even if by some miracle we recognize where we exit, we'll still have to make our way to the right chamber, the one with the oculus in its ceiling."

"I know where the altar is. Angeni took me there." Aleshanee glanced at Enla. "You remember, Enla?"

"I do, but I don't know if I can find it blind."

"As long as we all keep our hands on the sphere, we won't lose each other, but we've got to be careful we don't roll the sphere straight off the mountain because we can't see where we're going. Any suggestions?"

In the silence that followed her question, Amadah thought she heard voices from down the tunnel. "Do you hear that?"

"Hearing talking." Misa cocked her ear toward the voices. "Worrying the Dark One's armies are following."

"No, they can't. Remember?" Aleshanee sang. "'The unclean may not walk on it, nor the wicked or the fools' They can't follow this path."

"Wondering then if Papa and the Saphiri are following."

Amadah broke into a grin. "Seri and Sewati! They can't touch the sphere, but if they're anything like Fala, they can navigate without using their eyes at all, and they will be fine in the worst heat. They can help us!"

"If that's who is coming," Kilchi added.

"Going back to see who it is." Misa slid gracefully down the steep incline and disappeared.

"Let's roll the sphere to the entrance while we wait. If Seri and Sewati can help us, I want to be ready to move." Amadah, along with Kilchi, Enla, and Chevei pushed the sphere near the mouth of the tunnel. The heat was oppressive at the entrance, and as Amadah feared, the bright light was painful to her eyes. What would they do if Seri or Sewati were not with the group they'd heard in the tunnel?

They heard more excited chatter approaching, then over the rise, Meda, Seri, and Sewati appeared.

"We heard you may need our help," Meda said. "I have walked many of the mountain's tunnels with Nikani, and I can readily find the chamber you seek."

"Topazi scout," Sewati said.

"Oh, thank you. We made it this far but didn't know how to deal with the blinding light. And if we felt our way along by trial and error in this heat, we'd never make it."

Meda grasped Amadah's hands. "I will accompany you. You may need my help finding where you need to go."

"Flyer not made for heat. Bad idea." Seri shook her head.

"I know the layout of the entire mountain, and I know where the oculus chamber is located."

"Topazi find. Wait here." Seri and Sewati slithered around the sphere, careful to heed Amadah's warning not to touch it, then disappeared into what looked to Amadah like an empty, gaping bleached-white hole.

Meda walked up to the sphere and touched it as if caressing the petals of a delicate flower. "Since I can touch the sphere, once they return with a path, I will act as the connection between the sphere and the Topazi."

Amadah's heart swelled again with hope. There was something about having friends who genuinely desired to help that made the burden seem much lighter, and the impossible task seem possible. But the wait drew out and her ebullient feeling passed.

"I should have gone with them." Meda started to walk out of the tunnel, but Amadah restrained her.

"No, they were right. Then we'd have three missing instead of two."

"Do you think they were overcome by the heat?" Enla asked tentatively.

"They are desert dwellers. They had—have—the best chance." Loss tugged at Amadah like quicksand sucking her down into a pit, and she had no vine or branch to catch herself and pull herself back up. The litany of her losses paraded once again through her mind like a funeral dirge: Nikani, Yiska, Sani, Alana, Kai, Alatha—now, her dear friend, Sonta, was missing. And Fala. Dear Fala, her bound mate. Who else would she have to lose? How much more weight could she bear without going under?

"Wait, I hear something!" Kilchi cried. Amadah heard it, too—the scrambling of claws against stone.

Seri popped her head into the tunnel's mouth. "Come."

Relief washed over Amadah in a cool wave. Quickly, Meda positioned herself in front of the sphere, one hand touching it and the other holding Seri's claw. The remainder of their group gathered behind and beside the sphere to steer and push it from the tunnel.

When they stopped from the tunnel into the searing light, the blast of hot wind took Amadah's breath. Her sarkikos was instantly on fire, as if Turqosi spit coated her skin, bubbling it into pus-filled blisters. How would they ever make it to the oculus chamber? "We must hurry."

With all the strength she could muster, she shoved the sphere. It was soon obvious Seri and Sewati had cleared their path because the sphere rolled easily enough, but Amadah feared the distance would be too great.

"I recognize where we are. We are near Catori's cave. He and I were here when the Chalcedi captured us." Chevei paused, and when he spoke again, his tone was grim. "The chamber we seek is across the mountain."

No one spoke again. It took too much effort.

Amadah felt more than heard a loud whomp beside her. She felt for Enla's fur, but the space where Enla stood was empty. Enla had fallen.

The pace of the sphere slowed with the loss of Enla's powerful legs. "We must keep going!" Aleshanee cried. She must've heard Enla fall and guessed what Amadah was thinking. In her head, Amadah knew Aleshanee was right, but her heart felt like a tree trunk being split by a spark from the sky. She gathered herself, dug her heels in the sparse dirt, and shoved the sphere forward.

A few beats later, Amadah heard a faint voice, seeming to come from a great distance behind her, but she couldn't make out the words. She wondered if the fuzziness of the voice was due to its distance or because she was losing her senses.

"Misa!" Kilchi called. "Here!"

After a few more beats, Amadah finally understood the words. "Bringing water." A sense of relief flooded in through the growing fog in her mind. Misa was bringing help.

Still, they pressed forward. Amadah thought Misa would come straightaway, but she was yet to catch up to them. Perhaps she had stopped to give water to Enla—maybe she even helped her back to the tunnel, which meant they would have to hold on. Just hold on. Hold on. These words became her anchor, her one coherent thought.

Aleshanee was the next to collapse. With a squeak and a sigh, she fell off the sphere, her tiny sarkikos barely making a sound as it toppled to the ground.

"Misa will come." Amadah wasn't sure if Kilchi was talking to Aleshanee or to the three still pushing the sphere.

"I—I do not know—if I—can make it," Meda's voice sounded to Amadah like she was hearing her through a conuci shell like the old game Jasperi children used to play. Amadah herself had played that game with Nikani when they were growing up, and later with Kindra - before everything happened. Amadah could see the waving, thick green

410

branches of her home. She could feel the splash of water droplets from the blowing leaves. She shivered and opened her mouth to catch some of the droplets in her mouth, but her tongue scraped against rough dirt. What was happening? Had she fallen from her tree? No, impossible. She never fell.

Something wet nudged her cheek and turned her head. Ahhh, there they were. The droplets from the tree fell into her parched mouth like balm. Then, she felt splashes over her head and neck. It must've started raining. She felt a tinge of disappointment. She loved playing in the rain, but Nikani wouldn't join her. He was too afraid of getting sick. Come to think of it, she felt a little feverish. The chill returned. Her whole sarkikos shook. Her skin was burning. Something wasn't right.

"Come, Amadah, take water." She opened her eyes to see Misa's face looming over her, cradling her head in her lap. How strange. She leaned up and drank from a heavy pouch dripping with cool water. Misa splashed some more water on her face and over her chest and arms. Then, she remembered. The sphere.

She pushed herself up, but her head started to swim, and she almost collapsed. Misa gave her the pouch. She took a long drink, returned the pouch to Misa, then struggled to her feet, propping herself against the sphere to keep herself upright. "We've got to move." Her voice echoed like it came from someplace far away.

"Meda and Chevei are still down," Kilchi reported. "We have no choice but to wait for them to recover."

Amadah's brain felt like she imagined scrambled eggs felt in the pan. Something in Kilchi's reasoning was wrong, but she couldn't put her finger on what. While Misa and Kilchi tended Meda and Chevei, she called for Seri and Sewati. "How much farther?"

Seri's replied, "More ahead than already done."

"We aren't even halfway there?"

"Not half."

A squeezing panic rose in Amadah's chest. "We'll never make it at this rate. Misa, can you and Kilchi manage to push?"

"I'm still good to go, and so is Misa right now, but..."

"We have to leave Meda and Chevei and push on."

"How far do you think we'd get with just the three of us pushing and no one connected to Seri to keep us on the path?"

"We have to try. Staying here guarantees failure."

"Hotter," Sewati observed. "Soon heat too much even for Topazi,"

"Seri calls. Follow voice."

"That's right, Seri can watch us and keep us on track."

"Needing aid are Chevei and Meda." Misa continued to splash water over the two Jacinthi.

"I am able to manage," Chevei murmured, struggling to sit upright.

"Leave them some water, but we need to go now if we have any hope of making it. Everything within me says this is our only chance—the sky light is ending and if we don't make it, we all die." Amadah pushed feebly against the sphere, but it didn't move. "Help me!"

Kilchi joined Amadah behind the sphere, then Misa, after a final check of her two patients, stepped next to Kilchi. Together, they shoved as hard as they could, but the sphere only rocked forward. "Harder!" Amadah lowered her shoulder and pushed with everything in her. The sphere started rolling.

"You are not alone." The whisper was like a gentle breeze, barely noticeable amid their grunting and the grinding of crystal against stone, but Amadah sensed it and remembered. As she drove the sphere ever forward, she murmured, "Help us. Please! We can't do this alone. Please help us."

"Here!" Seri called, and on they rolled.

When Amadah's vision began to blur and darken along the edges, she hefted Misa's pouch in one hand and drank deeply, then held the pouch over Kilchi, who opened his mouth to drink. Amadah then passed the pouch over Kilchi's head to Misa.

However, the reprieve was brief, and her vision soon crept in from the edges again. She became aware she was shaking like Fala on the Chalcedi mountain in the cold season. She had almost lost Fala there, on that very mountain in the snow. She could see his eyes glazing over, his tongue lolling, his head slumping to his chest. She realized her head was bobbing, too. Was she hot or cold? She couldn't tell.

"Here!"

"Fala?" Amadah was sure she'd heard him call. "Where are you?" In her mind, she spoke those words, but her mouth no longer worked right, no matter how hard she tried. She had to find him! He would die in this cold.

"Here!"

Fala was ahead. She tried to shove the obstacle between them out of her way, but it just kept rolling forward and she couldn't get around it. She realized she couldn't feel her feet, and she had to catch herself on the obstacle to keep from falling—she hated that thing, whatever it was. It was keeping her from saving Fala.

"We are here, Amadah. Do not give up. Keep going. We will help you."

"I have to get to Fala," Amadah tried to say, but her tongue was thick and stiff, and she couldn't form the words.

"I know. I understand. We will get you there."

"He'll die in this cold."

"We have him in our hands. Keep going. Hold on."

"Hold on. Hold on." She wanted to tell Fala she was coming, that help was on the way, but her sarkikos betrayed her. All she could do was keep going, like the voice said. Keep going. Hold on.

"Here!"

She followed the voice, Fala's voice leading her to him. She had to hold on. A wet pouch slapped against her face. She grabbed it without conscious thought and upended it into her mouth. Keep going. Hold on.

Kilchi moaned beside her. The obstacle seemed to get heavier, but she couldn't think about why. She had to keep going, keep pushing, get to Fala, hold on.

"Here!"

Fala sounded closer. Would she reach him before it was too late? She could not lose him. She needed him. They were bound. Forever. She kept pushing and pushing and pushing. She couldn't stop. She couldn't give up. She had to hold on. For Fala.

Her leaden feet betrayed her again, and she stumbled against the obstacle and fell. The obstacle rolled just beyond her reach. When she tried to get up, she found she couldn't without something to lean against. Her frustration and fear erupted from her in an explosive cry of anguish. "Fala!" Her vision greyed to black.

CHAPTER FIFTY-EIGHT

The Topazi

Seri grabbed Amadah under her arms and dragged her into the chamber with the round hole in the roof. The Carneli and the Saphiri had fallen along the way, but Seri knew all Amadah cared for was getting the ball to the chamber, so she focused on that task. She knew she and Sewati were not permitted to touch the ball—Amadah had made that very clear—so she made helping Amadah her priority. Sewati had gone to retrieve the water pouch from where Amadah had dropped it. Her normally green face was almost white except for the ugly red blisters raised on her flesh. To help her, Seri propped her feet up on some stones stacked against one curved wall.

Sewati slithered in with the pouch, and while Seri held Amadah's mouth open, Sewati poured the remaining water in, then Seri closed her mouth over the water to force her to swallow. Both of them stood over her and waved their tails, creating a breeze of sorts, but the air they were moving was too hot for the movement to help much.

Finally, Amadah's eyes fluttered open. "Wha...where am I?"

"Chamber." Seri offered Amadah a Topazi version of a smile, pointing to the oculus. "Here."

Amadah closed her eyes. "Thank you." She looked around the chamber, her eyes widening. "The sphere!"

"Outside," Sewati said.

"Where?"

"Not far."

415

"Where is Kilchi? Misa?"

Sewati shrugged. "Fainted."

Amadah groaned. "How can I move the sphere in here by myself? I can't move it alone."

"Moved it alone before," Seri pointed out.

"Did I?" Amadah remembered the whispers and offered a half-smile. "I guess I wasn't really alone."

Sewati shrugged again. "Hotter now."

"I have to get the sphere in here and..." She stopped, noticing the floor. "No, this isn't right. The ground is supposed to be dirt. There is supposed to be an indentation in the dirt beneath the oculus to hold the sphere—like a cradle for it. They covered the floor with wooden planks."

"Sewati moves."

"Break it. Break it into pieces."

Seri and Sewati set about clubbing the wooden flooring and ripping it with their large claws, while Amadah made her way back outside. "Wait!" Seri called. Amadah stopped just outside the doorway.

"Seri help. Amadah not see."

While Sewati continued his violent demolition, Seri led Amadah back to the sphere. She leaned into the sphere. At first attempt, it didn't budge, so she grunted and shoved, then screamed. "I can't do it!" She gave a final, intensive push, but the sphere still didn't move.

"I can't keep doing this. My heart will explode. I'm already feeling dizzy."

"Seri and Sewati help."

"You can't help. Touching the sphere will kill you."

"Sky light kill Amadah then Seri and Sewati. Die for something or die for nothing. Topazi choose die for something."

"No! No, I will do it. I have to."

"If Seri starts sphere, Amadah can roll. Like before."

"You don't understand. You'll die as soon as you touch it."

"Seri understands."

416

Another sacrifice. Another loss. Another name on her list. Amadah closed her eyes against the blazing light, but it made little difference for the light still burned through her lids. "Seri, I…"

"Put hands on sphere."

No choice. Seri lifted her hands to the sphere, then Amadah heard a roar, a swoosh of air, and a blood-curdling scream, and the sphere jerked forward. She leaned into the sphere, and as Seri predicted, Amadah was able to keep it rolling with the momentum Seri created.

The tone of the light through her lids changed, and Amadah knew she had reentered the chamber, but the sphere was slowing, and her strength was failing. It wasn't enough. They'd failed. She felt movement beside her.

"Close to center. One more push." Before Amadah could speak, she heard a howl of pain, and the sphere rolled away from her hands. She heard a thud, followed by a whoomp and a whoosh. Amadah collapsed to her knees as the most beautiful music she had ever heard echoed through the chamber. Indescribable peace flooded her being.

With the sound of a million whirlwinds, a torrent of flame engulfed her—a flash of intense pain, then nothingness.

CHAPTER FIFTY-NINE

The Whisperers

Veritor stood over the carcasses of the Dark Ones, his sword raised high in triumph. The other Bellator and the Metanoi lifted their swords toward Kindred and joined their voices in song.

"You are worthy to stand in the portal
And break the Tempor's seal.
Worthy is the Great Love,
Slain and risen,
To receive our praise and zeal."

Kindred mounted the white beast and swirled her massive, curved sword through the air with a flourish. "Let us return home to rejoin this world with the First World when the portal opens. And let us hope for a great harvest." The beast beat its massive wings and took to the sky.

With whoops of joy, the Whisperers followed, soaring through the Tempor to the First World, where they waited and watched and hoped to see the light of the sphere burst through.

The waiting was agonizing. The white beast paced beneath Kindred's tense vigilance. The sky light vomited more and more molten matter, and belched fire from deep within its core, growing ever closer to the Second World, until in a blinding flash, the sky light exploded, and the Whisperers saw the sky light's fire engulf the Second World.

419

Their hearts froze in their chests. Were they too late? Was it all over?

After what seemed an endless pause, the 'Ro appeared before them, their faces beaming. "She did it!" Cla'ro cried. "The sphere is in place. It is finished."

A brilliant beam broke through the thick veil surrounding the Second World and shot through the vacuum of space to strike near the place the Whisperers gathered. Kindred urged her beast into the air and rode the beam of light to the edge of the dark veil. The Whisperers followed behind Kindred, then spread far and wide across the globe.

Kindred pointed her sword through the beam into the veil and swung it in a wide arc, slashing the dark veil. Again, she drove the beast forward, ripping the veil as she circled the Second World. The Whisperers grabbed the edges of the torn veil and peeled it back as if taking the skin from a citrus, until they flung the Tempor into the emptiness of space, and it was no more.

"The cycle for the Rejoining is upon us!" Kindred spun her sword in the air, creating a vortex around the Second World. "Let us begin the harvest."

The Whisperers sang, "The Forever be praised," and watched as a variety of familiar scenes flashed within the vortex, images of the different creatures they had encountered as they labored to save the Second World from eternal destruction. Some of the Whisperers felt great joy, others hope and longing, but for Veritor and some of the others the scenes brought a terrible mourning. Their wards had chosen the darkness. What would they choose now?

Veritor understood the wards would experience tremendous confusion and disorientation. Nothing would seem as it had before. The movements of life would no longer be linear with a beginning and an end. Having touched their ending at the sky light's explosion, they would not expect life, much less a life without the limits of Tempor. Forbearance was required, but the joy of the harvest was so complete, he knew he would have more than enough patience to go around.

Kindred raised her sword once more. "The harvest begins!" With a twirl of her sword, Veritor saw his ward, Angeni, rise into the air and fly into the vortex. The image of Veritor lifting Angeni from her sarkikos and showing her the stragglers approaching the high mountain from all directions flashed in the swirling light. Other memories cycled before Angeni's eyes, memories of bowing before the darkness, memories of betrayal and great fear, friendship and love, until finally, Kindred settled Angeni on the rock overhang where she first had the vision of all creatures together on the high mountain, living in peace.

Angeni gazed upon the world, beautiful once more—the lush green of the Emraldi fields, the golden waves of the Chrysoli plains, the brilliant blues of the Saphiri ocean. "How?" She looked at Kindred, who sat beside her on the rock.

"The glory of the First World exceeds anything you see before you, Angeni. Your vision of all together as one, living in peace, is fulfilled upon the First World's high mountain. Will you come with me?"

A tear moistened Angeni's feathered cheek. "I cannot. I am unworthy. Look at all I have done."

"I see." Kindred reached up and touched Angeni's cheek. "Will you give me your tears and allow me to cleanse the stain?"

Angeni groaned, bending her head to her feet as if to contain the searing pain of regret and anguish of shame within her chest. Kindred held her shoulders. "Will you give me your pain?"

"I cannot." Angeni's moans turned into heaving, gasping wails.

"Angeni." Kindred gently turned Angeni's face to her own. "Allow me to love you. Will you accept my love and forgiveness?"

"Leave me!" Angeni stood, shoved Kindred back, and flung herself from the overhang and beyond the vortex. Kindred wept. Veritor's howls echoed in the vortex.

When Kindred's tears abated, she rose and raised her sword. "Now, the sphere bearers." With a twirl of her sword, she lifted Enla into the vortex and spun her back through unfolding memory to the beginning of her journey where she was squatting in the Onyxi cave, staring out at the vast unknown world with Yiska by her side. Elegosi appeared beside her. "Hello, dear one."

"Hello." Enla didn't seem surprised to see her friend. With no Tempor, all she had ever experienced or ever would experience was in her memory. But her eyes looked glazed, and her mouth slightly slack. Eternity was a lot to process, and Enla seemed overwhelmed.

"I am here to take you to the First World, if you would like to go."

Enla glanced at Yiska, who sat smiling by her side, then looked at Elegosi with raised brows.

"Yiska is here with you, and Yiska awaits you on the First World." Elegosi smiled and stretched out his hand. "Will you come?"

"Oh, yes." Enla's voice was hollow with awe. "I will come with you."

"Come, then." Elegosi took her hand and helped her stand. Together they flew from the cave toward the beam pulsing from the sphere.

Enla stared in wonder at the scene below her. "The world isn't destroyed."

"This world was, is, and always will be destroyed, Enla. What you see is the world still bound in Tempor." Elegosi reached the beam and allowed it to carry the two of them to the First World.

Another swirl of Kindred's sword brought Chevei into the vortex. For the Jacinthi, Kindred picked the memory where he chose her, in the cave of tests before they found the sphere. As Chevei stared, dumbfounded, at his scrawls on the walls and floor of the cave, Paxor joined him. He placed an arm around Chevei's shoulders. "I have come to lead you to the First World. Would you choose to come with me?"

Chevei slowly turned his head to look at the magnificent being standing over him. "I—I have never seen your kind before."

"You see, have seen, and will see our kind, Chevei. The First World awaits you."

"I do not understand."

"Do not try to grasp after the First World with knowledge. Live in the experience and embrace it with your whole heart."

Chevei closed his eyes, breathed deeply, and smiled. "I will go with you."

While Paxor brought Chevei to the beam of light, Kindred pulled Kilchi and Misa into the vortex.

"Let them rest in the waters where they first met and where they fell in love," Chariti whispered.

"Very well." And with a flick of her sword, Kindred sent Misa and Kilchi to lounge in the waters at the base of the Carneli cliff, sharing their different worlds with each other. Chariti plopped down beside Kilchi at edge of the water.

Kilchi grinned. "We did it, didn't we?"

"You did indeed. We can go now to the First World if you would like."

"Wanting to go together," Misa replied.

Chariti gave her a warm smile. "Yes, you have always chosen and will always choose to be together. Take my hand." The three of them flew to the beam and disappeared.

Kindred pointed her sword to the field of battle before the high mountain and raised Leenha into the vortex. Admonitor stood before her. "Great warrior, I come to offer you the chance you sought at the end, the chance to choose wisely. Will you choose to come with me to the First World?"

Leenha didn't hesitate. "Yesss."

"Be warned, warrior. On the First World, there is no power to be gained—no position to be won. All stand together as equals before the Forever. You must relinquish your thoughts of control before you may enter."

Leenha's brow creased. "Purpose?"

Admonitor smiled. "Our purpose is to love, to share joy, and to join with the Forever."

"Why?"

"For the sake of righteousness and holiness and truth. All that is good is found in these things, not in domination and control. Will you let go of your desires for these things?"

Leenha worked her mouth, as if she was trying to chew these ideas into something she understood. Finally, she looked up at Admonitor. "Lost."

"I know. Will you allow me to teach you?"

Now, Leenha considered before she answered. "Yesss."

With a whoosh of air, Admonitor gathered Leenha and traveled the vortex to the First World to begin her transformation.

At last, Kindred raised Amadah and Aleshanee into the vortex and brought them to rest before her.

"My two witnesses, well done. The sphere rests, and the worlds are rejoined. Do you desire to return along the light to the First World?"

"Yes! Oh, yes!" Aleshanee's smile beamed as bright as the sphere's light.

Spa'ro was by Aleshanee's side in an instant, clutching her in a fierce embrace. "My dear one, I love you so. Welcome home." Aleshanee giggled with delight as Spa'ro led her by the hand up the beam of light.

Amadah hesitated. "Kindred, I'm afraid."

"What do you fear, fierce warrior?"

"I—is Fala—will he be on the First World?"

"He waits for you there. In fact, you have always been with him, and he with you."

Amadah lowered her eyes. "I'm ashamed to tell you I don't remember much about the First World."

Kindred threw back her head and laughed. "My dear one, the First World has no shame, and no fear." She waved her hand and something like a window appeared. Through the opening, Amadah saw a glittering lake like crystal. Beyond the vast lake stood a white throne. It was iridescent like a pearl from the Saphiri sea, and while it was white, it shone with all the colors of a rainbow. Rising above the throne stood an indigo mountain crested with the purest white snow Amadah had ever seen.

The throne sat upon a golden altar, polished to a sheen so bright it was as if the throne had its own sky light. Twelve columns uplifted the altar, carved from the holy stones of the twelve species who originally inhabited the First World. The columns reflected the brilliant sky such that a riot of color danced across the surface of the crystalline lake. A single tear slid down Amadah's cheek. "It's so beautiful."

Kindred passed her hand over the opening. "Look again."

The scene opened on lines of tables stretched as far as she could see. Simple but elegant white cloths covered the tables, each decorated with tiny pearls and gems along the edges. The tables were weighted with mounds of food, much of the food rare delicacies. Piled around the tables sat creatures of all kinds. Laughter rang across the green fields. Hands were clasped in friendship and love.

Kindred smiled. "The Great Feast."

Amadah's sharp intake of breath whistled through her teeth. At the end of one table sat Fala, and next to him she recognized her own auburn hair lying across his chest, as she leaned into his embrace. She gaped at Kindred. "How is this possible?"

"What is has always been and will always be."

A flood of breathtaking images returned to her memory, and a stream of tears wet her face. "Kindred, I desire to go to the feast, more than anything."

A new light spiraled down the beam from the First World, and her friend, Kitisi, materialized beside Amadah. Amadah gasped in delight. "I thought you were dead!"

Kitisi laughed. "You will see. On the First World, there is no ending. Come, let us go together."

One by one, Kindred lifted the remnant of the Second World into the vortex, beginning with Seri and Sewati, to whom she gave special places of honor at the table for their sacrifice. To all, she offered the choice to journey the beam of light to the First World.

But Veritor's attention remained on Amadah. Veritor had no one to take to the First World, for his ward, Angeni, had chosen the darkness, and now only existed within hatred and fire. So, rather than stand aside like a Watcher, he followed Amadah and Kitisi along the beam to see the reunion of a love so powerful it gave Amadah the strength to continue when her own strength failed.

Kitisi set Amadah's feet on the rich, soft soil of the First World, and Veritor couldn't help but smile at her expression—all expectation and hope. Surrounded by the greatest beauty ever created, Amadah had one thought, one desire. "Kitisi, where is Fala?"

"Here."

Amadah turned to find her bound mate standing behind her, his eyes gleaming with the love of the Forever, his arms outstretched, his mouth wide with pure delight. Amadah melted into tears of joy and bounded into his arms. Through her laughter and tears, she choked out, "We are bound."

Fala buried his face in her hair, holding her so tight Veritor thought she might burst. "Forever."

About the Author

As an award-winning author, professor, and Christian counselor, I've spent my life helping people with various aspects of mental health, equipping clients, students, families, and yes—even nations in crisis—to tap into who God created them to be, understand how He has wired us as human beings, and discover that the Kingdom of God is within us—always.

My husband, David, and I enjoy working and writing together. Our passion is to help others explore and deepen their relationship with Jesus Christ, and our work and our writings are geared toward that goal.

Our children are grown with families of their own. Our son, Hayden, is a teacher, married to Natalie, a nurse. They have two children, Coen and Petra, our precious grandchildren. Our daughter, Lindsey, is a veterinarian, married to Kyle, an electrical engineer.

Our youngest son, Cody, passed away at the age of seventeen from a degenerative neurological disorder. His life stands as a beautiful reflection of what it means to live in the Kingdom of God within. You can read more about Cody's story at https://codylanefoundation.com.

Other Books by this Author

Fiction

The Interview
Sky Light Falls: Whisperers Book One
Sky Light Rises: Whisperers Book Two
This Hallowed Ground

Nonfiction

Wilderness Meditations
Strength in Adversity
Strength in Our Story
Seeking Treasures
Restored Christianity
Dwelling

Professional

Please Share the Door: I'm Freezing—Creating Oneness in Marriage
Trauma Narrative Treatment
Gold Stone

How to Connect
Websites— https://thedoctorslane.com
https://restoredchristianity.com
https://codylanefoundation.com
Facebook—https://facebook.com/dr.donna.e.lane
Twitter—@Doctordelane
Instagram—@doctordelane